a not so Prince Charming

CASTLETON UNIVERSITY

jennifer chipman

Copyright © 2024 by Jennifer Chipman

All rights reserved.

No part of this book may be reproduced in any form or by any electronic or mechanical means, including information storage and retrieval systems, without written permission from the author, except for the use of brief quotations in a book review.

Cover Art by @mellendraws

Inside Art by @flixia.art

❀ Created with Vellum

For the girls who always dreamed of being a Princess, and the ones still waiting for their Prince Charming.

And to the place that taught me that dreams come true, even if they're not how you originally expected them.

Playlist

A Dream Is A Wish Your Heart Makes - Lily James
Wildest Dreams - Taylor Swift
Dancing With A Stranger - Sam Smith, Normani
Dandelions - Ruth B.
Enchanted - Taylor Swift
Finally // beautiful stranger - Halsey
Bad Habits - Ed Sheeran
I know it won't work - Gracie Abrams
Don't Start Now - Dua Lipa
White Horse - Taylor Swift
Strangers - Kenya Grace
Foolish One - Taylor Swift
Hard to Sleep - Gracie Abrams
Forget Me - Lewis Capaldi
fOoL fOr YoU - ZAYN
If I Can't Have You - Shawn Mendes
Is There Someone Else? - The Weeknd
How You Get The Girl - Taylor Swift
There's Nothing Holdin' Me Back - Shawn Mendes
Late Night Talking - Harry Styles
I Wanna Be Yours - Arctic Monkeys

Strong - Sonna
Afterglow - Taylor Swift
Until I Found You - Stephen Sanchez
I Wish You Would - Taylor Swift
Starving - Hailee Steinfeld, Grey, Zedd
Nonsense - Sabrina Carpenter
Night Changes - One Direction
Today Was A Fairytale - Taylor Swift
Beautiful Soul - Jesse McCartney
Perfect - One Direction
Call It What You Want - Taylor Swift
Love Me Like You Do - Ellie Goulding
Glittery - Kacey Musgrave, Troy Sivan
She Is Love - Parachute
So This is Love - Ilene Woods
Love of My Life - Harry Styles
King Of My Heart - Taylor Swift
Now You Know - Hilary Duff
This Love - Taylor Swift
Welcome to New York - Taylor Swift
You Are In Love - Taylor Swift

Author's Note

While Ella & Cam are involved in (fictional) Greek Life Organizations, they may not be 100% accurate to real sororities and fraternities. I've taken some liberties for the sake of the plot, so please be aware you may find inconsistencies.
I hope you enjoy them all the same!

Content Warnings: discussions of grief/sibling loss (past), explicit sexual content, cursing and drinking.

And yet, through it all, Cinderella remained ever gentle and kind, for with each dawn she found new hope that someday, her dreams of happiness would come true.

CINDERELLA, 1950

CHAPTER 1

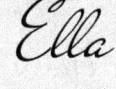

*O*nce Upon a Time... What a load of *bullshit*. My life wasn't a fairytale. I wasn't some princess just waiting to be swept off her feet by a prince, someone who needed to ride off on a white horse for my happy ending.

Of course, that might have also had something to do with the music currently blasting through the speakers. I stabbed the needle into the fabric in front of me, working it through the multiple layers.

"Ella!" my twin sister's voice called, fabric swishing as she opened the door to our shared room.

Biting my lip in concentration, I placed another stitch in my current dress project. Just a few more, and all the appliqués would be done. Tomorrow, I planned to start on the next one. But my portfolio was coming together, and I was so excited about it.

"You're not dressed yet?" She groaned, and I knew she was looking at my current attire—not at all ready for the events of the evening.

Ignoring her voice, I kept sewing.

"Ella. Come on." Her voice was right behind me, peering over my shoulder.

We'd shared a room for the last twenty years, and I couldn't imagine living apart from her. Even in our sorority house, we'd stayed living together.

Only right now, I wished I had a space of my own so that I could work in peace.

"Ro." Taking my foot off the presser foot, the machine stopped moving. I looked up at her, giving a slight roll to my eyes. "I'm almost done. Promise."

She sighed, but the sound was resigned, like she'd expected this from me.

"You can keep working tomorrow. Don't you want to go out with me?"

It was Halloween, and we'd both always loved the holiday. For so many years, we'd dressed in matching costumes, and then as different twin duos. One year, we'd been twin Lindsay Lohans from *The Parent Trap*. But it wasn't until I'd started seriously pursuing sewing that we'd branched out in our designs, coming up with unique ideas together.

She was already dressed in her Halloween costume, but make it *pink*—per usual. This year, she was a pink witch. "What do you think?" She did a spin for me, her curls bouncing from the movement.

"You look amazing." I'd made it for her, working on it from sketch to creation, but I hadn't seen the full outfit in action yet. Even during fittings, everything hadn't come together yet. But now, she'd finished her hair and makeup, all that was left to put on the pink and tulle witch hat sitting at the edge of her bed.

We'd practically been assigned our colors at birth. She was the pink twin, and I'd always been dressed in light blue. Not purple, for whatever reason, like so many sets of girl twins, but blue.

"Why aren't you wearing yours yet?" Ro—otherwise known

as Audrey Rose—collapsed onto her bed in a pile of tulle. "I said I was going to get ready."

Okay, *maybe* I'd gone a little overboard when I'd made her costume. It was hard not to when she'd smiled so much as I'd sewn all the layers together.

I winced a little. "What if I didn't go this year?" It was a thought that had been pinging in my head for weeks, but one I hadn't wanted to voice. Because I didn't want to disappoint my twin. Maybe I was just feeling a little jaded, too.

"But it's *Hallo-weekend*." Audrey pouted. "And we're *finally* twenty-one."

Halloween weekend was always huge on campus, but for once, I had no desire to go out and party. I had enough going on this year. Junior year was busy enough without going to big parties all the time.

Plus, as my sister liked to keep reminding me, we were newly twenty-one. We had celebrated our birthday a few weeks ago, and I didn't feel the need to party like that again any time soon.

"And what was the excuse for the *last* two years?" I said, raising an eyebrow, thinking about the last Halloween party I'd had to drag her home from.

"Fun costumes?" She wiggled up onto her elbows, looking at me over that puff of pink. "Come on. I heard the Delta Sigs are having a gigantic party." Her eyes grew wide. "Apparently, it's one to beat."

"Really?" It surprised me, since we'd been going to a different fraternity's parties for the last few years, ever since we'd rushed Pi Rho Sigma our freshman year. And now–I'd had my fill of it. I had no desire to get puked on by an eighteen-year-old frat boy who couldn't hold his liquor. Last year was bad enough. I scrunched up my nose at the thought.

But the Delta Sigma Iota chapter... We hardly interacted with them. I couldn't even tell you the President's name, or what he even looked like.

When I looked back up from my sewing machine, Audrey was pouting at me. "Come on, *please*. For me?"

She looked up at me with those pleading eyes, a face that was almost identical to my own. We shared the same blonde hair—though I usually wore mine up, while Audrey curled hers almost every day—and the same general stature, standing at five foot five. The major difference was our eyes—I'd inherited the crystal blue of our dad's, while hers were a brown that appeared almost violet, a color she'd gotten from our mom.

When it came down to it, I'd almost *always* cave for whatever she asked me to do. I was only thirty minutes older, and yet, she still had the little sister act down pat.

"Okay, okay!" I threw up my hands before moving to my closet.

The dress I'd designed was hanging up inside, waiting for me. Light blue—of course—and shimmery silk. It was some of the most beautiful fabric I'd ever seen. The smooth fabric practically slipped through my fingers when I ran my hands over it. When I'd found it at a fabric store, just enough yards for the dream dress I'd had in mind, I hadn't been able to resist. Even if the price tag was more than I normally liked to spend on fabric. With each cut, each stitch, I'd practically held my breath, only giving myself a moment to admire the garment once the whole thing had come together.

Our days of matching costumes were in the past, *however*, because, unlike Audrey, I wasn't dressed as a witch. My accessories were tucked into a drawer, hidden away in case I'd changed my mind. Because as much as I protested, I still loved dressing up. Still wanted to spend the night with my sister, and to see our friends.

"Yay!" She clapped her hands. "It'll be so fun, I promise."

I blew a strand that had escaped my blonde messy bun and into my bangs off of my forehead. "Want to do my hair?" If I was the crafty, seamstress sister, Audrey was the one with a talent for makeup and hair. At least one of us had inherited a proficiency in it.

"I thought you'd never ask," she answered, eyes sparkling with excitement as she grabbed her kit.

In another life, I thought she would make a phenomenal stylist, but ever since she was little, Ro had always known her end path. While she shined on stage, I preferred to hide in the background, working on sets and costume design for our school's theater department.

Even when she'd encouraged me to audition for musicals because of my voice, I'd never wanted the spotlight. I'd gladly stick to my spot behind the curtains.

Except... in the last year, I'd wondered if maybe I wanted *more*. Not being on stage–because knowing me, I'd trip and fall flat on my face (and I *had*, in the past), but I didn't really know *what* yet.

Wielding her makeup bag and a curling iron, Audrey sat me down at her desk as she went to town on transforming me. It was like this every time I let her do my makeup, like she was making me into the most spectacular version of myself. The shimmer she brushed over my eyelids made my blue eyes pop, and her perfect cat-eye never ceased to amaze me.

After brushing a coat of lip gloss onto my lips, the bobby pins came out, and my hair was styled into an elegant bun before I could even blink. She curled the front pieces and my bangs before tying a blue ribbon in my hair.

"What do you think?" Audrey asked, as we both looked at my reflection in the mirror.

"I swear, you're my Fairy Godmother," I laughed, touching my blushed cheeks. "Your transformations are like *magic*."

My sister gestured to her costume with a flourish and a wink. "Well, you made me *this*, so I guess you're mine as well."

"The perfect pair," I said, a grin on my face.

Truthfully, I couldn't be more grateful for her presence. When we'd both been applying to colleges, it had been obvious that we'd go together. The easiest decision I'd ever made. I was equally happy to have her as my best friend. Even if she was constantly dragging me to parties when I'd rather stay in my room with a new project and my favorite Taylor Swift album.

"Come on, go get dressed!" She laughed, poking at my shoulder. "It's getting late."

Rolling my eyes, I unzipped my Castleton University sweatshirt and wiggled out of my leggings, leaving them both in a pile on the floor.

"No one gets there when parties start, anyway," I grumbled, grabbing my dress and pulling it on over my hips. My bra had to go, because of the neckline of the dress, but I'd sewn cups into the bodice. "Zip me up?"

Audrey nodded, wordlessly cooperating.

Smoothing my hands out over the skirt, I stared in the mirror. I pulled the silver strappy heels out of my closet, shoving my feet into them. "Happy?"

"You used to dream about these parties, you know."

Ro had never stopped loving them, loving the attention and the socialization of fluttering about. Seeing all of her friends from other sororities and throughout campus.

I'd loved them too, once. Before. But she knew exactly why I'd no longer enjoyed them. I just shrugged. "Dreams change." *I'd* changed.

Now, I was more focused on my *dreams* for the future and how I was going to achieve them. Even if we were only juniors in college, graduation loomed like a giant reminder in my brain. There was so much left to do before then. An internship, a job. The rest of my dreams for the future... Those could wait. *Would* wait, if I had any say in the matter.

"Come on, not all guys are like that." Her voice was quiet. "You know it."

I sighed. I did. It was hard not to let one rotten apple ruin the bunch, but that was what I'd been doing for the last year. I wished I had her optimism, but seeing the guy you'd been going out with going down on another girl at a party really left a foul taste in your mouth.

But maybe what I really needed was to let loose. Hook up with someone in a meaningless fling and forget all about it by the next day.

"Finishing touch," Ro murmured, as she gently placed the tiara in my bun. "An outfit fit for a princess."

"Shall we?" I asked, linking my arm in hers. At least it couldn't be worse than last year.

Audrey's face lit up into a smile. And all of it—all of this—was worth it, seeing how happy she was. "Heck yeah. Let's go!"

She tugged me out of our room, down the stairs of the sorority house, and out into the darkness of the night.

The Delta Sigs' fraternity house was impossible to miss, with the thumping bass of the music audible even from a distance. I was glad that we didn't live on the same street as them, knowing that the party would likely go most of the night. It'd be impossible to sleep next to any of the fraternity houses when they threw a big party.

I groaned as she dragged me inside, knowing the chaos that awaited me.

We'd been dancing and talking to friends for the last few hours, and my social battery was about empty. My sister had abandoned me in the overcrowded living room about thirty minutes before, and I was just about to text her I was leaving when something distracted me—my eyes landed on a tall guy in the kitchen, with a slightly off-skew crown on his head.

Even from a distance, I could tell that he was tall, an easy-going smile on his face as he talked to some of the other guys surrounding him. He must have been in the fraternity, though I didn't recognize him specifically. And why would I, when we'd never spent time around their frat before?

Maybe it was better this way. He wouldn't know me either.

"Ella!" Audrey's loud voice shouted, rushing over to me as I pried my eyes away from the dark-haired guy in the kitchen.

"Did you see Sutton?" I shouted over the music, speaking of our dark-haired friend who was here with her baseball boyfriend. She'd originally rushed Pi Rho with us too, but had dropped because it wasn't really her thing.

"I did!" My sister grinned. "Her fishnets are *awesome*. I dig it."

Sutton's pale skin was perfectly accented by her bold, red lip, a look I always wished I could pull off but never quite thought it worked on me. Then again, without Ro, I would have been completely hopeless in that department, anyway.

"You'll never guess who's here at CU!" Audrey's shout interrupted my thoughts of makeup, and I blinked, trying to think through a list of people we both knew, but drawing up no realistic guesses.

"Um..." I said instead, fidgeting with the strap of my dress.

"Parker! Parker Maxwell!"

Oh. "The boy who lived next door to us when we were younger?" I glanced across the room at the brunette boy she'd just been talking to. I struggled to place his face. "Wasn't he like... your best friend until his family moved away?"

"Yes!" she gushed.

I vaguely remembered it. We used to play with all the kids in our neighborhood, and even if we were always best friends with each other, she *had* spent a lot of time with the boy next door.

"He must have been, what, twelve when they moved?" I asked, and Ro nodded. "And now he's going here?"

And of all the places to come tonight, that he was at the same party as us was crazy. It felt like more than a coincidence. If I believed in that kind of thing. And yet...

"You don't mind if I ditch you to catch up with him, right? Am I a terrible sister?" She winced. "I'm a terrible sister."

I shook my head. "No." A laugh escaped from my lips. "*Go.*" Audrey looked hesitant, but I waved her off. "Seriously, I'll be fine. Maybe I'll go hang out with Sutton." She'd been in the corner chatting with another one of her friends, but I'd only said it to reassure my twin, regardless.

Midnight, I read the screen on my phone, blinking at it. How was it already so late? I looked down at my heels. They matched my costume perfectly, and they were definitely an excellent decision—I loved how long they made my legs look, but my feet were hurting.

"I think I'm gonna go grab another drink."

And see if the hot guy I'd been sneaking glances at all night was still in there.

If fate was kind to me, maybe he would be.

CHAPTER 2
Cam

The sounds from the party were already blaring loud around me, dozens of bodies filling the bottom floor of the Delta Sigma house. We'd been planning this Halloween Party for weeks, and I wasn't surprised at all that it had gotten out of hand. All throughout the living room were student athletes, some that I knew well, as well as dozens of girls. Most of them were dressed in skimpy outfits, despite it being fifty-something degrees outside.

I was sure most of the houses on Fraternity Row were also hosting their own parties tonight, given it was Halloween Weekend on campus and no one wanted to waste that. It felt like *everyone* was here. Surveying the room again, I looked for my friends, ignoring the pounding bass emanating from the dance floor.

A fist met my shoulder, knocking me slightly off balance. "Hey, man!" He had to shout to be heard over the music.

I grinned, seeing Forest—currently devoid of his dark-haired girlfriend. "Where's Sutton?" I looked for her, but had no luck in the crowded room.

His eyes seemed to pan right to her. "She found a friend. They're over in the corner catching up." Following where he was pointing, I saw the two girls both sitting on the couch, deep in conversation.

Sutton was dressed in a cupid's costume, her little heart bow forgotten at her side, while Forest had an arrow glued to both sides of his shirt.

We moved towards the entryway, towards a quieter corner of the house.

"You're completely and absolutely *whipped*," I said, despite finding myself envious of their relationship. They'd been dating since Sophomore Year, though they'd met during orientation.

Forest was the pitcher of our school's baseball team, while Sutton was in pastry school. I always loved when the two came over and she brought us new desserts to try. Her apple turnovers made my mouth water just thinking about them.

"The love arrow, man." He gave me his best smirk. "You never know when it's going to come up and hit you." Even if I could hear the joking tone in his voice, I couldn't imagine it. Meeting someone freshman year of college and knowing that she was *it*, that she was the one I was going to be with for the rest of my life. Not because I didn't want that. But because it hadn't happened to me.

I rolled my eyes, scoffing, because it was incredibly cheesy. "Doubtful." Either way, I couldn't imagine it.

Sure, I'd dated a string of girls—ones who were all too excited when they found out about my parent's money. But none of them had lasted. Probably because of the former issue. I didn't need a girl trying to get into my pants just to secure her MRS degree, either.

Not to mention there was no time for complications when I was trying to get into one of the top law schools in the country. I'd be taking the LSATs this summer, and my rigorous study schedule was already planned. There was no room for failure, not with my entire future on the line in front of me. Not with my parents riding me to make sure I didn't fuck it all up.

"What, you don't want a pretty trophy wife to cart around

when you're a big hotshot lawyer?" A laugh sounded behind me.

I hated how much that sounded like my parents. Not that they said the *trophy wife* part out loud, but... They never let me forget they had *expectations* for me. Even though I was in my junior year of college, and that was the furthest thing from my mind. The joys of being their *only* son.

But as much as my parents might have had that expectation, my friends certainly knew I didn't feel like that.

I rolled my eyes as my dark-haired friend appeared in front of me. "Hey, Erikson. You made it."

James Erikson—though we usually just called him by his last name—was the quarterback of the football team. He'd donned a black leather jacket over a white t-shirt, brushing his long, black hair back like Danny Zuko from *Grease*.

"Wouldn't miss it." He grinned, his blue eyes sparkling mischievously. "What, exactly, are you supposed to be?" He looked my costume up as he brought a red cup up to his lips. How he'd snuck in and got a drink before I even saw him never failed to surprise me.

"Come on now." I looked down at my outfit, the blue ornate jacket and a gold sash that draped over my top. "I'm a *Prince*." The crown at the top of my head was supposed to prove that. A silly, last-minute costume, but it worked.

"Oh, is that what you are? Cameron Edwards, our very own campus royalty, dressed as a prince?" James laughed, and I punched his shoulder.

"Shut up," I muttered, rolling my eyes, rubbing at my knuckles. James was the tallest of our friends, an extra few inches on me, and a lot more bulk on him.

"Seems like someone stole *my* thing," Adam said, strolling up to join our now-group huddle. He hadn't even dressed in a costume, just donning a jacket over his button-up and dark denim jeans.

Forest chuckled. "Prince," he said in greeting.

The last member of our friend group—Adam Prince—finally joined us. He was the heir to the Prince Corporation, a star on campus of his own right. They were a mass manufacturer of goods, owning companies in practically every industry you could think of. He would inherit billions one day. I felt pressure from my parents, but I couldn't even imagine how it was for him.

"Good to have the gang back together," Erikson said, slapping Adam on the back.

I looked pointedly at him. "Why are you giving me slack for my outfit when he showed up like this?"

He chuckled. "You're too easy, man." Turning to the copper-haired addition to our group, he quirked an eyebrow. "Where *is* your costume, Adam?"

Adam rolled his eyes in response. "Fuck off. You know I hate this stupid holiday."

I'd met these fools our freshman year, when we were all housed in a quad together. If I was *campus royalty*, so were they. Our names were commonly heard around the halls, normally together, and we still spent as much time together as we could, even with all of our busy schedules. Between James and Forest both being on sports teams, and me serving as the current President for my fraternity—*Delta Sigma Iota*—it seemed like there was less time for us all to hang out anymore.

I was a legacy member, since my dad had also served as president during his time at our school. I'd always known I wanted to take up the mantle, but I'd never imagined how incredibly fulfilling it would be. It was only my first semester in office, but I already felt sad imagining leaving it. About saying goodbye to campus at the end of next year.

But I had my sights set on law school, trying to follow in my father's footsteps once again—wanting to make him proud.

"Anyone else need a beer?" I asked, looking back at the guys. The party had barely started, but I already knew I was absolutely too sober for whatever shit they'd pull me into tonight.

Forest shook his head. "I'm gonna go hang out with Sutton. I drove, so..." He was always the designated driver around his girl, anyway.

James waved us off, clearly having spotted whatever fling of the week he was currently seeing.

"I'm down," Adam agreed, following me into the kitchen.

"How's your semester going?" I asked, cracking open the tab on the beer can. "How's the new gig?"

My copper-haired friend gave a deep chuckle, taking a drink from his own can. "It's good. Surprisingly."

I raised an eyebrow. "Surprisingly? You're the ma—"

"Shhh," he said, looking around us as if checking that no one had heard me, his eyebrows drawing downward. "Don't blurt it out, man."

"Because it would ruin your *street cred*?"

He crossed his arms over his chest. "Exactly. It's not like I signed up for it."

I still hadn't gotten the full story out of him, but I imagined it wasn't something he readily wanted to admit to. Especially when it had ended up with him wearing a Chipmunk costume and running around at all our schools sports games.

That's us—the Castleton Chipmunks. Everyone liked to laugh, but I thought there were a lot of worse mascots out there. At least ours was an animal.

I glanced back at Forest and Sutton before looking at Adam. "Do you ever wish you had that?"

"Hm?" He looked and shook his head. "A girlfriend?" A snort. "No. I'm perfectly fine alone."

Shrugging, I rested my elbows on the countertop. "I don't know. Sometimes I think it sounds nice. Maybe I'm just tired of dating apps and hook-ups." Taking a swig of my beer, I looked back at my friend. "Maybe I just want what they have." Not love, just... companionship.

Adam sighed. "What do you expect? That you're going to look

up, and the crowd will part, and she's going to be standing there? The girl of your dreams? That shit doesn't happen, man. Not in real life." He shook his head. "That's a fairytale, not real life."

"I didn't..." Say that. I hadn't, had I?

My eyes drifted around the room, taking in the silence that had settled between us. There wasn't a specific person I was searching for, though I spotted many familiar faces and plenty of new ones, too.

A flash of blonde hair caught my eye, and I looked away, in a trance. *Who was she?* Our campus wasn't that huge, but it certainly was big enough that I didn't know everyone in this room.

I elbowed Adam in the ribs, getting an *oof* in response. "What was that for?" He groaned, rubbing at the spot.

"That girl," I murmured, unable to take my eyes off of her. "Do you know her?"

"Who—" He started, before following the tip of my finger.

Her blonde hair was tied up in an elegant bun, a small tiara decorating it.

Adam shook his head, the movement lighting up his strands of copper hair. "I've never seen her before. Not that I pay that much attention. She's not really my type, you know?"

I quirked an eyebrow, wondering what exactly his type *was*, if not a beautiful girl in blue, whose dress looked like it was sculpted perfectly to suit her curves. To hug every inch of her body, and yet—she looked every bit a princess.

"She's gorgeous," I said under my breath, forcing myself to look away.

"So go say hi." Adam quirked an eyebrow. "I'm sure she'll fall at your feet as soon as she hears you're the incomparable *Cameron Edwards*."

I made a face. "Don't say it like that."

"Alright." He shrugged. "I'm going to go find Erikson. See if he wants to play a round of beer pong."

Running a hand through my hair, I sighed. "I'll find you later?"

"Sure." Adam's lip curled up. "If you're not too busy."

I blinked, and he was gone, and the blonde's gaze had settled on me. Our eyes caught. Held. And something in her heated gaze almost... pulled me towards her. Drew me into her orbit. Like I was fucking enchanted, *entranced*. But I didn't want to look away. Didn't know if I could.

"Cameron!" One of my fraternity brother's voices called me, and I turned to answer him.

But when I turned back, the blonde was gone.

The next several hours were pure torture. Because I'd been trapped, doing one fucking thing after another and unable to find the blonde Princess.

Midnight. I groaned internally, knowing that even though it was the weekend, the local sound ordinances would mean I had to rein in this party soon. Turn down the music, and at a certain point—kick all the drunk college students out. It wasn't wild by any means, but there was no way I was risking our frat being disciplined because I was an irresponsible president.

Heading back to the kitchen, I looked for the guys—James was out on the back patio, a group of football guys and cheerleaders hanging around, the girls sitting on laps or arms of chairs—but I hadn't seen Adam in a while. Knowing the grumpy bastard, he'd probably slipped out before I could even notice. Forest and Sutton were holding each other on the dance floor, in their own sort of embrace—swaying slowly together, even though the music playing certainly wasn't slow.

I turned to say something to Jackson, one of my guys, but a blur of motion caught my eye, and I whirred—just in time to catch the falling girl.

It was *her*. I couldn't believe my luck. "Are you okay?"

She winced as I helped her stand up straight. "I'm sorry. These shoes are—" Her silver strappy heels made her legs look like a million bucks—and I couldn't help but picture what it would be like to have her legs wrapping around my waist, the only thing left on her body those hot-as-fuck shoes.

"I'm not."

The blonde's cheeks warmed as I openly perused her frame. "What?"

I leaned in close. Enough that I could feel her breath against my cheek. "I'm not sorry for catching you, Princess."

"Oh."

Bending at the waist, I bowed, kissing her hand. Sure, I was making a fool out of myself, but I couldn't find it in me to care.

"Thank you," she said, smoothing out her dress before looking up at me. Her bright blue eyes pinned to my face. "I should have worn more practical shoes. It's just that these matched perfectly."

I nodded, because I couldn't help but agree. "They really do." But it was more than that. Even in this room filled with dozens of girls, she stood out.

The blue dress she wore was elegant, understated—and despite the way my body heated from just looking at her—it wasn't *sexy* at all. The ripples of fabric hit at the knee, the neckline only giving the faintest hint of cleavage. And yet.

And *yet*.

"You look beautiful," I said, trailing a finger up her waist where I'd caught her. I hadn't been able to bring myself to move away, to stop touching her. Even though I knew I needed to.

"Not so bad yourself, Prince Charming," she smirked, looking me up and down, the unbidden heat apparent in her eyes. *She wanted me, too.*

But there was also... No glimmer of recognition. She didn't know me. And something about that was a relief. Because maybe I could be myself with her. Not have to expect the worst.

Could just lose myself in this. In tonight.

"We match," I said with a chuckle, finally bringing myself to step back.

She nodded. "That we do." The blonde looked nervous, absentmindedly fiddling with the hem of her dress, and I wanted to distract her. Wanted to get to know her.

It might not have been the start of a fairytale romance, but I wanted those plush, pink lips on mine. Wanted to watch her unravel in front of me. Underneath me.

"Do you want a drink?" I asked, stepping further into the kitchen towards my hidden alcohol stash. You couldn't be too careful in a house full of college students.

"Sure." Her eyes widened as I pulled out a bottle of vodka. "How'd you know that was there?"

I smirked. "I have my ways." Being President of this fraternity certainly helped. This was my house, after all.

Opening the fridge, I pulled out a bottle of lemonade before peeking over at her. "Do you have any flavor preferences?"

"What?" She looked up at me from where she'd been tapping her short nails on the countertop.

I held up two bottles. "I want to make sure you like whatever I'm giving you."

"Oh." She blushed and then pointed at one. "Raspberry, please."

We fell into silence as I mixed her up a drink before handing it to her. "Too strong?"

She took a sip before looking back at me. "No. It's good. Thank you." She curled up her nose. "I don't think I could drink another beer."

I laughed, pulling one out for myself. "It's not so bad once you get used to the taste."

Her eyes widened, comically. "That's a *thing?*" I thought she was being serious until she burst out laughing. "My mom says that all the time about wine. I still only like sweet whites, though."

"Mmm." I wasn't huge on wine myself, but I definitely could see where she was coming from. "How old are you? Sounds like I have an experienced drinker on my hands."

She giggled. "Not really. I just turned twenty-one last month."

Which meant I wasn't supplying liquor to a minor. That was good. Shit. Probably should have checked on that first.

"Me too. Newly twenty-one, I mean." I'd just celebrated my birthday before school started. "This summer."

"So... you're a junior too, then?" She traced the rim of her cup.

"Yeah," I agreed, watching her delicate hands, unable to stop myself from tracing the motion. "Can't believe we're already halfway through college."

The Princess—since we hadn't exchanged names, that's what I was calling her in my mind—propped her hip against the counter, leaning as she watched me. "What's your major?"

"Political Science, but I'm pre-law," I said, working my jaw. Thinking about my father's law firm and the spot that was waiting for me there. "What about you?" I asked, fixing my eyes on her face. On those gorgeous baby blues.

"Well..." She glanced away, nervously. "Don't laugh."

Laugh? Why the fuck would I laugh? Who'd belittled her dream, so that she felt like she had to give a warning about it? I raised an eyebrow, encouraging her to continue.

"I'm in the theater department. Majoring in Costume Design, specifically." Looking down, the blonde ran her hands over her dress again. "People like to tell me it's not an actual career, but..."

Tilting her chin up with my fingers, I forced her gaze to meet mine. "Who told you that?" My eyes focused on her lips as they parted in surprise. "I think that's cool as hell, Princess."

"Yeah?" Her face lit up. "I... made the dress I'm wearing, actually. And my sister's costume, too, but she's somewhere with an old friend—"

This time, it was my turn to lean back against the counter, and I made a little twirling motion in the air with my finger. She looked confused.

"Come on," I encouraged. "Show it off. Twirl for me." Prying the cup from her hands, I couldn't help but notice the small smile that curled on her lips.

Stepping back, she looked around before turning, and I couldn't decide what to focus on. The way her feet moved in those sexy silver heels, how the fabric rippled, catching the light and sparkling with every rotation, or the blush erupting over her cheeks.

"It's perfect." *You're* perfect, I thought, but didn't say it out loud. It was too much, especially considering I'd met her minutes ago.

Stepping in closer, her body was practically flush with mine as she took her cup back from my hands, her lips closing around the rim as she took a large sip.

"What's your name, Princess?" I asked, winding my finger through one of the blonde curls that framed her face.

She shook her head. "No names, Charming." Her eyes flashed with something, an emotion I couldn't quite read. "Let's just... enjoy tonight."

I grinned. That was something I was capable of. That's all I wanted.

"Do you want to go outside?"

CHAPTER 3

Outside? I blinked, wondering what I'd expected, before nodding and taking another sip of my lemonade. I liked how he was thoughtful enough to make me a drink. Even if it was basic—just vodka and raspberry lemonade. He didn't know that was my favorite flavor. My sister preferred strawberry, but I'd always been a ride or die raspberry girl.

I expected to just follow behind him, but he interlaced our fingers, the warmth from his grip instantly spreading throughout my system. Interweaving through the horde of bodies still in the frat house, the Prince pulled me onto the front porch, holding his beer out in front of him.

For all I knew, he did this with other girls all the time. It was an idea I had to swallow back, to stuff down. I didn't want to think about him—Charming, the nickname I'd given him feeling all too fitting—with anyone else. Not tonight. Swallowing back the bile in my throat, I watched as he led me to a set of chairs tucked into the corner of the porch.

There was something in his eyes as he'd watched me twirl for him in the kitchen, an unchecked lust that made me feel like I was someone entirely new. I'd never had anyone look at me like that before. Every time he called me Princess, his voice was practically a rasp against my skin.

"Cozy," I said as I settled into the large wicker chair, the chill of the evening air a welcome balm from the heat inside the party. I hadn't brought a coat, and my dress was essentially sleeveless, the sheer sleeves I'd sewn onto it giving me no protection from the wind.

He chuckled. "It's really nice in the summer."

I'd bet. We weren't too far from the beach, and much like the sorority houses a few streets down, it was only a short walk from both the ocean and our campus.

After finishing my drink, I set my cup on the side table before tucking my hands underneath my legs, not wanting to fidget even more.

"So, Princess. Tell me about yourself."

I cleared my throat, staring out into the night. "What do you want to know? I already told you I'm in Costume Design, and I have a twin sister who goes to CU too…" I trailed off. What else about my life was interesting?

"A twin, huh? What's her major?"

"Theater." I smiled, thinking about how Audrey came to life on the stage. "She wants to be on Broadway one day."

"And you?"

I looked up at him, our gazes locking. "I'd rather design the costumes for it." He nodded, taking another swig of his beer. "What about you? Any siblings?"

He shook his head. "No. Just me." He sounded almost… sad? Or maybe that was bitterness I was picking up? Either way, I found I wanted to chase that feeling away.

"Hey. At least there's no one to steal your stuff, right?" Sensing I'd found a sensitive subject, I focused on something else. "You said you're pre-law?"

"Yup. It'll be a few more grueling years of school before I'm able to join my father's firm." His hands toyed with the now empty-beer can, fiddling with the tab.

"That's your dream?" I was surprised to hear myself asking, but he also didn't exactly seem excited about the decision. "To join your family's practice?"

He gave a muttered agreement before pinning me with a look, instantly changing the subject. "Tell me something."

"What?" Was he drunk?

"Something you've never told anyone."

"Oh." I bit my lip. "I like to sing, but I have stage fright." I hadn't even told Audrey that. It was more than just not wanting to be in the spotlight. I practically froze whenever I had to give a speech, or present in front of the class.

And then there was my propensity for tripping on air. The two things did not mix.

He raised an eyebrow. "Really?"

I brushed one of my little curls behind my ear. "Yeah. I get all sweaty, and my skin gets all splotchy and red, and I want to die of embarrassment. Every time."

"I bet you sound as beautiful as you look," he murmured, pinning me with that dark gaze of his.

"Oh, I—" The warmth filled my face, like I'd summoned the splotches myself. "You're good at that, aren't you?"

"What?"

"Being *Charming*."

He laughed. "Maybe I'm just like this with you."

I wrinkled my nose. "I highly doubt that."

The silence settled between us as the night quieted. Even the sounds of the party inside dwindling to a dull murmur as people headed to their dorms and houses.

"Tell me something," I asked. "Something real."

Because I wanted this to be real. Wanted the heat in his eyes to mean something.

He looked up at the moon, high in the sky. "Sometimes I just want to say fuck it all and run away. Get on a plane, and go be someone else, somewhere else."

"Where would you go?"

He shrugged. "Anywhere. Somewhere." Charming shook his head. "I don't know."

"I think I'm afraid that my entire identity is so wrapped up in my twin that when we finally have to be apart, I won't know who I am anymore," I whispered. One last confession. Because we'd always done everything together, hadn't we? Theater, college, even joining the same sorority. I'd never even lived with anyone else.

"It's not."

I looked up, catching the intensity in his stare. "You don't even know me," I whispered, unable to drag my eyes away from his face.

"Maybe not." He stood up, holding out a hand. "But I'd like to."

Words failed me. Maybe it was the sight of this gorgeous, charming man standing in front of me—or how serious he looked.

"Do you want to dance?"

"Out here? With no music?" I looked around, because the porch seemed like the last place anyone would want to dance, and yet… It was perfect.

"Mhm." Pulling out his phone, he loaded a song and then hit play, the notes hitting my ear. "Besides," he murmured as I took his hand, pulling my body up to his, "this is much better than whatever they're playing inside, hm?"

Heat blossomed up my skin where he touched me as his other hand wrapped around my waist, and mine found his shoulder. God, he was tall. I'd thought that earlier, but he had to have been over six feet, and the way he was towering over me even with these heels made me shiver.

"Charming…"

He shook his head, shushing me with only a murmur. "Just let me have this, Princess. This moment."

I couldn't argue with that. Because even if there was a frat party going on inside, even if I'd just met this man… I felt comfortable here, in his arms. Everything else faded away, and then it was just us, moving in slow circles as his grip on my waist tightened.

The butterflies erupted in my stomach, and I had a hard time pushing them down. But I had to, if I was going to survive this night. This *wanting* that already threatened to burn me alive.

His eyes were focused on mine as we danced, and I didn't even hear the words of the familiar tune, because I couldn't look away.

Charming was handsome. But maybe that was an understatement. This close, being able to study his features, to inhale a scent that threatened to pull me under—it was too much.

Those brown eyes I couldn't keep my eyes off of all night dropped to my lips, and then back up, and I opened them to say something, anything, to not break the spell of this moment, the enchanted bubble we'd somehow created, but...

The music stopped, and he dropped his hands, stepping back.

I shivered, the chill of the night finally getting to me as his body heat faded away.

"Cold?" He asked, and when I nodded, he took off his coat, draping it around my shoulders.

"Thank you," I said, voice quiet against the dark of the night.

What time was it? I hadn't checked for what felt like hours. Not since Audrey had ditched me for Parker. Not since he had caught me.

I still couldn't believe my luck, that the man I'd been watching from afar all night had caught me when I'd slipped, my heel catching on the threshold, sending me directly into his arms. I wasn't sure what to call it, but it felt a lot like *fate*.

And maybe that was the line of thinking I couldn't afford. Not when it would take only steps to pull myself flush against his body. To tilt my head up, and press my lips against his.

I shouldn't, and yet... I wanted to. Wanted him.

Wanted to know what it would be like, just for one night. I

needed this. A night of fun. Of letting go. Maybe it wasn't the worst idea in the world.

Snuggling deeper into his coat, I inhaled his scent. He smelled like... Fuck, I didn't even know. But he smelled good. All spice and *man*, and it sent a bolt of lust through me.

"Maybe I should go," I whispered. *Ask me,* I thought. *Ask me to stay. Because I'm weak, and I can't say no. Not to you. Not when you're looking at me like that.*

"Maybe you should stay."

One foot moved, and then another.

And then I'd done it, my hands clutching his shirt, and all it would take was one press and every hard line of his body would merge with every curve of mine.

He rubbed his finger over my bottom lip. "Princess..."

"Yes?"

"Ask me to kiss you."

I tilted my head, looking up at him. Wondering how I could say no when he asked like that. Like there was nothing more he wanted, or needed, than to kiss me.

"Kiss me," I said, a soft breath against the wind. *Please.*

And then his lips were on mine, a soft press as his hands cupped my cheeks, and the nippy air didn't matter anymore. Not as I wound my arms around his neck, and that slow, searching kiss turned into something more.

The press of his lips turned hungry, and I gasped as he pushed his tongue into my mouth. Seeking, exploring, and each movement of his tongue against mine relaxed me further against him, until my hands were tugging on the ends of his dark hair, pulling him further down. Like if only I could get closer, could capture more of him, I could find this sensation I was chasing.

Needing, wanting to *feel.*

A small whimper left my lips as he pulled away, pressing his forehead against mine as he caught his breath.

"Do you want to come upstairs?" His voice was rough,

breathing unsteadily as he watched me. Like he couldn't get enough. Maybe the one who wasn't breathing properly was me.

I opened my mouth to say *No*—the proper thing to do—but what came out instead was, "Yes."

Yes, I *wanted*. Wanted him. Maybe even needed him. Needed more than the little touches, the lingering glances.

Why? I wouldn't normally say yes to this, but with him, something was different. He was kind. Caring. *Charming*. That nickname wasn't a lie.

The party was a low simmer as we reentered the house, silently slipping up the staircase with his hand clasped in mine. I was surprised when he didn't stop on the second floor, instead pulling me up a narrower set of stairs up to the third floor.

There weren't as many doors up here, and I wondered if this was reserved for the upperclassman, but that thought flickered away as soon as the door to his room was closed.

Charming spun me around, pinning me against the wood of the door with his body. His coat dropped to the floor, and I couldn't bring myself to care, because then his lips were on mine once again.

I barely had enough time to notice the queen-sized bed in the room before my eyes fluttered shut, and I lost myself in the kiss. Whatever we'd shared outside... It had been nothing like this.

He kissed like a man *starved*. I'd never had anyone kiss me like this before. He nipped at my bottom lip, and I opened for him.

"Princess," he groaned, pulling away to catch his breath. "You're killing me."

A smile curled over my lips. "What are you going to do about it, huh, *Charming*?" I toyed with the strap on my shoulder, letting it slide down.

He let out another guttural sound before his lips attached to my throat, sucking against my pulse, and my head hit the door as I moaned, *loud*.

But he didn't stop, letting go of that spot to kiss down my

shoulder, stopping at the top of my cleavage. I'd designed the thing myself, wanting it to be supportive but still a little conservative, and even if it wasn't sexy, I *felt* sexy.

My other strap joined the first and when I looked down at him, whatever I'd been about to say caught in my throat. The way he was looking at me...

"You're so beautiful," he whispered in a reverent breath, and for a moment, it felt like I couldn't breathe.

"Please." I didn't know what I was asking for, but I knew he'd give it to me.

His lips kissed the top of my breasts. Once, twice—and then he pulled me away from the door, spinning me around easily in his arms.

I shut my eyes, feeling the slide of the zipper as he dragged it down my back, exposing my bare skin. He hummed as he reached the bottom of the track. His fingers trailed up my spine, the touch intimate—soothing. It should have been relaxing, but I was on *fire*.

Moving my arms, I let the dress flutter to the floor, a pool of shimmery blue fabric staring back at me as it settled, and I knew what he could see now. The only things I still wore on my body were my panties and the silver stripy heels.

I wondered if I should feel more nervous, or shy, but I had no urge to cover up. Not when my nipples were already this hard, and I knew when he reached down, he'd find me absolutely soaked.

"Fuck." His hands fisted at his side. Like he wanted to touch, but couldn't bring himself to. "Look at you."

"You can touch me, you know," I said, biting my lip as I batted my eyes at him. Seductive temptress I was not, and yet...

He smirked, and I clicked my tongue as he stepped closer, tangling my fingers in the bottom of his shirt.

"This needs to come off," I said, pulling at the garment. The crown he'd been wearing clattered to the floor as he helped me pull off his shirt, revealing the lean, toned body I'd been dreaming about all night.

I ran my fingers over his abs as he directed his attention to my hair, pulling the tiara out before undoing my bun, letting the loose strands of my blonde hair fall down to my back and shoulders.

"Fucking perfect," he said, mostly to himself, as he stood back and surveyed me.

But I needed more. Needed those hands on me. Touching me. If his kiss had felt that good, I wanted to know what it would be like if he kissed me in other places.

Everywhere.

"Please," I begged, once again not knowing what I was asking for. Not caring. Then his hands were cupping my breasts, thumbs rubbing over my nipples, and nothing else mattered. "*More.*"

"Princess..." he groaned, resting his forehead against my collarbone.

"Charming." I gasped when his lips closed over my nipple, sucking deeply.

His tongue swirled over my tight bud, and—"Yes. Yes."

What was he doing to me? There was no way this man was real. Not as he sucked, licked, and lavished all his attention on my nipple.

Moving his attention to the other side, he repeated the process, and I let out a long moan.

He let go with a wet pop. "You liked that, huh?"

I nodded, breathless.

"That's just the beginning of what I have planned for you, Princess."

"Show me," I said, wanting all of it.

CHAPTER 4
Cam

Running my fingers through her hair, I couldn't help but marvel at how gorgeous she was.

Her peaked nipples begged for more attention, but I had so many things I wanted to do to the gorgeous blonde in front of me.

Lifting her up into my arms, I carried her over to the bed, depositing her softly against my comforter, watching those strands of golden silk spread out around her.

Fuck, she was beautiful. And in my bed. Which meant that for tonight, she was *mine*. Mine to taste. Mine to touch. Mine to fuck.

It took everything in me not to put my lips back on her tits, to lavish them until I had her writhing underneath me, but there was so much more I wanted to do to her.

Moving over her, I kissed her softly as her hands ran up the planes of my abdomen, exploring.

Her skin was smooth as I traced her skin with my lips and tongue, wanting to memorize the way she felt. Every curve, every piece of her deserved that.

She sucked in a sharp inhale of air as I pressed my fingers

over her slit, feeling the way the fabric was damp. "Are you this wet for me, Princess?"

Her only response was a moan as I slid the lace to the side, my touch light as I brushed over her entrance.

"I want these off," I said, tugging at the thin piece of lace that currently hugged her hips.

Those bright blue eyes focused on mine, and she gave a little nod, before I moved down her body, pressing my lips to her soft skin as I went. When I reached the waistband, I kissed her hip bone before snagging the fabric with my teeth, dragging them down her skin.

"Yes," she groaned as I drifted down her legs, torturing her with my unhurried pace, knowing exactly where she needed pressure and giving her none of it. "Please." She begged as I haphazardly tossed the scrap of lace behind me, not caring where it landed.

"What do you need, hm?"

Perching my body over top of hers, I chose one last moment of perusal down her body—the flush to her cheeks, the way her chest rose and fell with each quick breath—before I slipped off the edge of the bed, kneeling on the floor and pulling her body to the edge.

She gave a surprised sound as I positioned her just where I wanted her, giving me the perfect view of her as I parted her legs, exposing her pretty pink pussy.

"What are you doing?" She asked, though the words came out strangled as I took the moment to run my tongue over her entrance, taking a moment to circle her clit.

"Tasting you," I mused, using my fingers to spread her wider. "Now be a good girl and be still, Princess, hm?" I took another moment to kiss the inside of both her thighs before delving back in, doing just as I'd promised. Tasting her.

Lapping at her pussy, her flavor exploded on my tongue, and I practically moaned, dangerously close to coming in my own pants just from this. As it was, I was already impossibly hard in my slacks, unable to control my desire ever since I'd kissed her.

But she came first. I wanted to see her eyes blown wide with pleasure, and I wanted to be the one giving it to her.

I took my time, languid strokes that couldn't have possibly been enough, until she squirmed against my face, needing more friction. Humming, knowing the sound would go straight to her core, I moved my attention higher.

She bucked her hips as I moved to suck on her clit, alternating pressure as her body built higher and higher, and I slid a finger inside, a groan slipping from my lips as I felt how wet she was for me.

"Fuck," I muttered, pumping inside of her, knowing I was making an absolute mess but not caring. "Do you like that?"

"*Yes,*" she agreed. "Charming, please, I need—"

"I know what you need," I agreed, looking up at her from in between her legs as I slipped another finger inside of her, watching as she arched her back off the bed.

Fucking her with my fingers, I put my mouth back on her clit, and worked her higher and higher until I felt her clenching around me, little gasps escaping from her mouth.

Circling her clit with my tongue, I kept going. "That's it," I encouraged. "Come for me."

She did, and I kept working her through it, only pulling my fingers from her wet heat when she'd collapsed back against the bed, her cheeks an even lovelier shade of pink than when she'd blushed earlier, the color dusting her chest as well.

"Fuck, that was hot," I muttered, bringing my fingers to my mouth and sucking them clean. "So fucking good for me."

Leaning down, I kissed her roughly, wondering if she could still taste herself on my tongue. Our kiss quickly grew frantic, and I ground my erection against her, the layers of fabric the only thing keeping me from being inside of her. Fuck.

She cupped my erection, and I pulled back, searching her eyes. I wasn't sure what she saw on my face, but she nodded, and wordlessly, I peeled our bodies apart, standing while she looked up at me from my bed.

Her eyes grew wide as I shucked my pants and boxers off my body, leaving my erection standing in between us, hard and wanting.

Her hand reached out, tracing a vein up my cock, and I groaned. "If you touch me like that, this is going to be over before it's even started." Because her soft, small hand wrapped around me would be more than I could bear.

She giggled, breaking the tension between us. "Show me what you've got then, huh?"

"Can't keep the princess waiting," I agreed. Pulling a condom out of my nightstand drawer, I quickly rolled it on over my length, not wanting to wait another moment to be inside of her.

Climbing back on the bed, I positioned myself over top of her, caging her in with my body. I paused for a moment, holding myself back even as my tip pressed against her entrance. "Are you sure?"

There was no way I'd continue if she said no. If she didn't want this.

"Yes," she agreed. Her captivating face stared back into mine, and she looped her arms around my neck. "Fuck me, Charming."

That was all the permission I needed, and I thrust inside easily, given how wet she was from earlier. Being inside her was better than I'd imagined.

Her gasp filled the room as I filled *her*, and then her legs wrapped around my back, the straps from her heels digging into me. It was uncomfortable, but I didn't mind the hint of pain from those little buckles. Not when I had the mental picture of me fucking her in those heels still in my mind.

When I was fully sheathed inside of her, I stilled. "Fuck. You're... *perfect*."

"What?" Her cheeks were pink as she looked up at me.

"I need a moment," I said, squeezing my eyes closed.

Her hips rolled involuntarily, forcing me in deeper. "Charming," she groaned, and I couldn't hold back any longer, either.

Intertwining our fingers, I pulled out slowly, thrusting back in, though I wasn't able to keep up the unhurried pace for very long, and given the rapid pace of her breathing, I wasn't sure she could either. With every movement, her hips met mine, the two of us finding our rhythm easier than I'd ever imagined.

I groaned into her mouth as she kissed me again, our tongues mingling lazily as I plunged back inside of her, inhaling her sharp gasp of pleasure.

"You can—" she started, but I shook my head.

"I need you to come again."

"I-I can't."

"Yes, you can," I said, kissing her neck. "I've got you, Princess."

She cried out when I pressed my thumb hard against her clit, forcing her to grind against it with each shallow thrust inside of her, and I knew I was hitting just the right spot inside of her

"Right—right there," she trembled, throwing her head back as she came, her insides squeezing me tightly, and I didn't last long after that. I let go, spilling inside of her, filling the condom.

Our hands were still interlocked, her fingers woven around mine, as I kissed her softly before pulling out, moving to dispose of the condom and clean myself up.

"I'll be right back," I promised her, pressing a kiss to her forehead as I headed into my private bathroom.

Thank fuck I was President, because this was the only room in the house with an en-suite besides the one for our live-in advisor—aka our house dad's room. Right now, I definitely appreciated the lack of interruptions from my drunken brothers.

I wanted to keep my blonde princess all to myself for the night.

When I came back into the room, she'd wrapped my sheet

around her naked body, sitting up to watch me rummage around my room.

"Don't get all shy on me now," I said, brushing her hair from her shoulder to place a kiss against her bare skin.

"Should I leave?" She whispered.

"No. Stay." I didn't want her to go. Moving over to my drawers, I pulled out a pair of navy blue Castleton University sweats from my drawer, before pulling out one of my t-shirts and handing it to her.

"Mock Trial?" She asked, looking at the fabric in her hands.

I shrugged my shoulders, tying the string of the sweats waistband around my hips. "I figured it was soft, so…"

She nodded, running her fingers over it before pulling it over her head. "Thank you."

"I'm gonna run downstairs and grab us some water. Do you want anything?" I asked, ignoring the primal feeling I got from seeing her in my shirt. The possessive part of me that *liked* it.

A bigger part of me knew I shouldn't. Because she wasn't mine. Not after tonight. And I couldn't get attached to a girl whose name I didn't even know.

Not when this was a one-night thing.

Padding downstairs, I was relieved to find the house now quiet and empty, grateful I hadn't had to send everyone who didn't live here home, as distracted as I'd been by the girl in my bedroom.

"You're up late," said a voice as I entered the kitchen, and I startled, finding my fraternity brother, Jackson, sitting at the table.

"Yeah." I glanced at him as I grabbed two bottles of water out of the fridge. "What are *you* still doing up?"

"Homework." He shrugged, rifling his hands through his dark brown hair.

Tilting a water bottle towards him in response, I gave a nod. "Don't stay up too late." He might have only been a year younger than me, but I still felt a responsibility towards all the guys in the house. "Gotta sleep sometime, right?"

He snorted, looking at the second bottle of water in my hands. "I'm sure that's what you're doing too, huh?"

I gave him a grin, not deigning that with a response.

There was definitely no way we'd be getting much sleep tonight, but I didn't think she'd care much either. *One night.* I was going to savor it.

CHAPTER 5
Ella

Where were my shoes? I'd found my dress and underwear, practically thrown in opposite directions of the room, but my heels had somehow disappeared. I remembered wearing them last night, when we—

My cheeks warmed as I dressed.

No, Ella, I scolded myself. *Don't think about it. You have to get out of here.*

I wasn't sure why the urge to flee was so strong. All I knew was that I couldn't stay here. Even if we'd connected, it was just a one-time Halloween hookup. It didn't mean anything.

And I certainly wouldn't stay and wait for him to kick me out himself. No.

But thinking about it, staring at his muscular form under the sheets, that was a recipe for disaster. A repeat wasn't happening.

Even if I couldn't keep my eyes off of his bare shoulders, his muscles on clear display. He was surreal, a specimen that shouldn't be real. But he was. And I'd slept with him. Ran my fingers up his back, buried my fingers in his hair. Let him play with my body whatever way he wanted.

He was so handsome and charming, and it wasn't fair.

Not that he'd had to charm me into his bed—no. I'd done that willingly.

Especially when now I had to slip out in the wee hours of the morning, do the walk of shame back to the sorority house, and hope Audrey would keep her mouth shut when she saw my current disheveled state.

God, this was *embarrassing*.

She always told me not to sleep in my makeup, but I never listened to her. The glitter she'd brushed on my lids last night still dotted my lids, and there were black streaks from where I'd smeared my mascara and eyeliner. Plus, my hair was all tangled from Charming's hands. He'd loved running his fingers through my waves, and I wished I had a brush so that I could at least make myself look a little more presentable before running out of here.

Using my hands to brush through it—at the very least—I pulled it up into a bun, cursing the loss of my hair tie from last night.

And where the hell were my shoes? I'd been tiptoeing around the room for several minutes, but I still couldn't figure out where they'd ended up after he'd taken them off of me. I wasn't waking him up to ask, either.

The floorboard creaked under my weight as I moved towards his desk, and I froze, staring at his sleeping form. Holding my breath and my pose, I prayed for an easy escape. Charming turned over, but thankfully, didn't wake up. *Thank god.*

Letting myself have one last look at his body, appreciating his muscular back, I exhaled a short huff of breath before giving up. At least I only had to walk a few blocks to get home, anyway. Barefoot was better than being caught and having to face a potential rejection. *No, thank you.*

Giving up on my shoes, I flung open the door and fled into the morning, just as dawn streaked across the sky.

"Ro?" I whispered, turning the door handle for our shared room, hoping like hell that she wouldn't catch me doing the walk of shame and sneaking back into our room this early.

Unfortunately, while my luck *last* night had extended to multiple orgasms and the Prince who'd given them to me, clearly I was all out this morning. Audrey sat up, her pink sheets pooling on either side of her as she adjusted the sleep mask onto her hair—she insisted she couldn't sleep without it.

I swallowed roughly as her stare pinned me to the door.

"Where were you? You didn't text me to let me know you were okay or anything." Her eyes scanned over me, and she grimaced. I'd tried to wipe my face the best I could in the bathroom downstairs, but I was still in rough shape.

Holding up my phone, I made a sheepish expression. "It died, and I forgot to plug it in." It had been in my dress pocket all night, and I'd completely forgotten about our usual pact. We always told each other we were okay, so that the other person didn't worry all night.

Except, with Charming, I'd been so enraptured it hadn't even occurred to me.

"Did you have fun catching up with Parker?"

"Yes. Can you believe that after all these years, I found him again?"

I hummed in response, and Audrey's eyebrows rose on her forehead. Moving over to the closet, I pulled out a large sorority t-shirt and shedding my dress onto the floor. It wasn't as comfortable as Charming's t-shirt had been, though that had ended up on the floor during our second round, and I mourned its loss. I wish I could have kept it. He was right—it *was* soft. Damn, I wish I'd thought to ask what fabric softener he used.

"So we're just not going to talk about you?" she asked, like she was noticing how I'd spaced out.

"Nope." I flopped onto my bed, exhausted. I'd barely gotten a few hours of sleep before I'd snuck out of his room. As if he'd known the score, he made every second of last night count. I was sore in places I didn't even know I could be, but it was one hell of a night.

Closing my eyes, I wasn't surprised when I felt my bed move, Audrey settling on the bed beside me. It might have been a twin, but we were used to sharing such a small space. We always had been.

"Ella," she whispered, and I let out a small sigh. "Are you okay?"

That was what had me opening my eyes, looking into hers with concern.

"Yeah," I got out, though the word sounded more like a croak. "I'm fine."

"If you're sure…"

I was, wasn't I? It wasn't like I'd met the man of my dreams last night and then ran away from him. There was no reason I should feel this way about leaving a college hookup. He was a charming frat boy, and nothing more.

That was what I kept telling myself, at least. That it didn't matter.

Because it hadn't. It was just one night.

"Mmm." I shut my eyes, pretending that the face I saw when I closed them wasn't Charming's.

I'd let myself dream for the rest of the weekend—it was the one thing I'd always been great at. When I'd get an idea in my head, it stuck with me for days, even weeks. But that meant nothing.

So, much like my lost shoes, I bid a silent goodbye to my Prince Charming, hoping that fate was kind to me once again.

And that I wouldn't see him again.

If only fate could have been so kind.

CHAPTER 6
Cam

She'd left her shoes behind.

I couldn't believe how stupid I was, not exchanging names. Last night had been *amazing*, and I wanted to see her again. Just the few hours we'd spent together at the party, I'd been more interested in her than I had been in anyone in *months*. Years, even.

But she hadn't wanted to swap names. And like an idiot, under the guise of Halloween—and cause I thought it was really fucking adorable when she called me *Charming* in that sweet voice of hers—I agreed.

And despite everything, she'd left. I thought we'd had an enjoyable time together—a great time, even. Had I done something wrong? She'd been so enthusiastic last night, especially as I'd wrung pleasure out of her, and I'd liked how she was a little shy at first. Had I hurt her? I wouldn't be able to forgive myself if I had.

I wanted to know why. What I did that made her leave. I couldn't even ask her now. Hadn't even thought about asking for her number. Maybe because I'd just imagined she would be here when I woke up. Girls almost always overstayed their welcome, trying to get something out of me. But her?

She'd bolted.

Now I was fucked. How was I going to find her? I knew so little about her. Our school wasn't enormous, but big enough that I had no idea where to even start. All I knew about her was she was a blonde, and she was majoring in costume design.

Should I try waiting outside the drama building and see if she showed up? Maybe I'd see when the next performance was, even though I doubted she'd be in it. She told me she didn't like to sing in public, didn't she?

I wished I'd gotten to hear that idyllic voice of hers sing last night. It was filed among the many regrets, along with how I'd felt when I first woke up this morning, reaching over to the spot next to me in bed. I'd wanted to ask her for more. To see each other again. But it was cold. *Empty.*

The eyes I'd had kept shut had flown open. *Fuck.*

She'd run out on me.

There was one thing, though. My eye caught something tucked under the corner of my bed, forgotten. Those silvery sparkling heels I'd unbuckled, kissing off her legs.

She'd left me behind with nothing but the memories of last night and those damn shoes. The t-shirt I'd lent her was in a pile on the floor, and I picked it up, bringing it to my nose. It still had a faint trace of her scent, something sweet and floral that I couldn't quite identify.

"You're an idiot," I muttered to myself. "You don't even know her name." All I had was a pair of silver heels and a tiny morsel of information.

I collapsed back on the bed, throwing my arm over my eyes as the memories replayed through my brain.

And all I could feel was regret.

Re-assembling my burger, I sighed. *Hallo-weekend* was officially over, and Monday continued on like nothing had happened over the weekend. Nothing monumental.

Never mind the way I'd looked for her in every blonde I'd seen, but none of them were her. How did I find a girl just knowing her shoe size and her major? It wasn't like I could go down to the College of Arts and Sciences and demand a list of all the costume design majors, right?

No, that would be *insane*. I pinched the bridge of my nose.

"What's wrong with him?" James asked, sliding into our booth at the Commons next to Forest.

"The *love arrow*," he said with a shrug, taking a slurp of his soup. "I told him to be careful, but he didn't listen."

I rolled my eyes at the reference to the couple's costume he'd worn with Sutton. "I'm not—"

I wasn't in love. So what if I'd taken the beautiful blonde girl up to my bed that night?

Adam groaned, interrupting me before I could refute Forest's statement. "Can't a man enjoy his dinner in peace?" He'd already scarfed down one piece of pizza, and was starting on another. "I don't need to hear you talk about *love*." He made a face.

Forest gave me that look, like *one day he'll understand*.

"Clearly not," I muttered, taking a bite of my burger. Changing the subject, I turned to the other bench. "How's the season going, James?"

He looked up from his plate, grinning. "Fantastic. We're kicking ass and taking names. And the new kid on the team, Lucas, he's got skills. Dude's the new golden boy, I swear."

Forest nudged him in the side. "Someone had to take over your mantle eventually, Erikson."

"They never called me that." James shoved him back.

"Are you ready for the away game this week?" Adam asked our dark-haired friend as the rest of us chowed down on our food.

The two of them launched into a conversation about travel plans, and I scanned the seating area for the dining hall, just in case. Forest raised an eyebrow, and I shook my head.

Why had I told him *anything*?

"You're hopeless."

"She was just... different." I sighed. "I don't know how to explain it. I thought we had a connection." The conversation had flown so easily between us, and that wasn't something that came along with everyone.

"But she left?" He raised an eyebrow. "Even after all that?"

"Yeah. Didn't leave her number or anything. Just..."

"What?"

Her shoes.

I rubbed a hand over my face. "Nothing. It doesn't matter now. We had agreed that it was just one night. No names."

One night. One pair of shoes left on my bedroom floor. One girl I couldn't get out of my mind.

"Sure." Forest shrugged. "But it doesn't have to be."

"What? Did you not hear me? I don't even know her first name. The only thing I know about her is that she's in the theater department."

And what she sounded like as she came.

A noise that kept playing in my ear every night, and I couldn't get out of my head. Or her face as I slid into her.

"So, go find her."

My heart twinged, wondering what it would be like—being with *her*—but I shoved it down. There was no time for that line of thinking about my future. Right?

Besides, she'd left.

Fuck, I was a mess.

I sighed, because he made it sound so easy. Maybe in a movie, it would be. I'd turn the corner in the library and she'd be seated in a booth, the spot open like she'd left it for me. But this wasn't a movie, and our campus wasn't exactly tiny.

I didn't want to wait around on the off-chance I ran into her, but what else was I going to do? Ask everyone who'd been at the Halloween party if they'd seen a beautiful blonde dressed as a princess with legs for days? With those silver heels that had been hot as fuck when she'd wrapped her legs around my waist, forcing me deeper inside of her?

No.

Go find her.

How was I going to accomplish that? I didn't know, but I knew I was going to try. My parents hadn't raised me to give up easily.

I was determined to find my Princess and wouldn't rest until I did.

Even if I had to try that pair of shoes on every girl at this school.

CHAPTER 7
Ella

Looking up at our sorority house, I couldn't help the smile that spread over my face.

They'd built it off campus years ago, needing more space as the organization grew—but even then, we could house less than half of our girls in the house. Freshman didn't live in while they were going through the recruitment process, instead most choosing to move in their sophomore year. Between the sleeping porch and the other bedrooms, it was full of more estrogen than should be legally acceptable. And yet, the large, three-story building held so many wonderful memories for me.

My favorite part was the bright pop of color—our official color was pink, and they'd painted the house to match. It was a bubble gum color, with white trim, but in the last decade, one of the executive boards had spruced up the outside, adding pink rose bushes out front. The letters that adorned the front of the house were a familiar sight, one I'd looked at almost every day for the last few years.

Audrey and I had both moved in last year, and had been lucky enough to get one of the large shared bedrooms this year. It was practically home.

Unwinding the scarf from my neck, I hurried inside. After

my morning classes had finished, I'd gotten a text to come back to the house for a meeting, and since I was free until my late afternoon class, I hadn't minded.

Our house mom and sorority advisor sat in the study room, waiting for me.

"Hi, Ella," she said with a smile as I settled into the chair across from her, draping my powder blue pea coat across the back.

"Hey." I gave her a warm smile back. "What's up? Is everything okay?" We normally never met one-to-one unless there was something wrong that specifically pertained to my responsibilities, and from her text, I assumed this was urgent.

Ilene shook her head. "Not really. Lily... Well, she quit."

"What do you mean?" My jaw dropped. There was *no way* our sorority president had just up and quit. Not in the middle of the semester.

"She's moving home." She gave me a firm nod. "I hadn't seen it coming, but with her gone, I'll need someone to step into the role for the rest of the semester and this spring. I think you'd be a good choice." She gave me a warm smile. As if what she was suggesting wasn't absolutely insane.

"But I'm just..." *A wallflower.* I liked to blend in, not stand out. I did my best keeping my head down around campus. There was a reason I stuck to the background in the theater department, and why I'd run for this role on the executive board.

A dark eyebrow raised on her forehead. "My vice president."

"I'm not a figurehead." I finished the sentence I'd started before. "Behind the scenes stuff, sure. I'm good at that. Organizing, booking rooms, planning—I can do that. Leading the entire sorority?" I bit my lip. "I don't know if I'm the best person for the job."

"You are."

"Don't I need to be elected or something?"

Her pink lips curled up into a smirk. "Or *something*." Ilene never had a hair out of place, and she always looked impeccable.

I was especially envious of that right now, because I felt like a mess.

A groan slipped from my lips. "Why do I have a feeling I don't have a say in this?"

"There's only a month left of the semester, so having a special election at this point just seems like a waste of time for everyone. Getting candidates to apply, having an interview night, we just don't have time for any of it. But there's a special exemption in the bylaws that when the President steps down, the Vice President steps up."

You gotta be kidding me. "Of course there is." I winced, thinking of something else. "Who will take over my job?" There'd still be an empty seat on the executive board, after all. I couldn't exactly manage both jobs and still be a full-time student.

"Why don't you leave that to me?" Ilene gave me her best smile. "Just have courage. I have faith in you."

Before nodding, I took a deep breath. *I could do this.* The only person standing in my way was *me*, after all. I just needed to believe in myself. "Okay."

"There's one more thing." Her lips flattened into a thin line. "The Delta Sigs advisor reached out to me. He wanted to see if our chapters could partner up for the rest of the year."

"What?" I stared at her once again, wondering if my mouth was about to be permanently formed in a shocked expression. What did she mean, *partner up*? As in... work together?

With *his* fraternity?

Charming.

I didn't even know his actual name, but I'd been avoiding all mentions of their chapter—and their events—after my one-night-stand on Halloween. I didn't need to risk running into the man I'd slept with and then ditched the next morning again.

But of course, it was Charming's fraternity. Ilene shrugged. "He thinks it would be good for his guys. But I know. It was a shock to me too."

"But..." I protested, though I didn't have words to explain why I didn't want to be paired with them. Explaining my sexual hookups to the woman I looked up to certainly hadn't been included in my plans for the day, either.

"The school is looking closely into all the Greek life organizations. With all the hazing and incidents that have happened at fraternity parties the last few years, it's no wonder. So partnering with them is ultimately a good thing. It will help both of us provide a stellar image to the campus."

I almost groaned. When she put it like that, how could I argue?

"As the new president, I expect you to meet with their chapter president. His name is Cameron, and I have his number here for you. Extend the olive branch, Ella." She handed me a piece of paper with his contact information, as well as a binder that in big, block letters read CHAPTER PRESIDENT.

Ignoring the nervous feeling in my stomach, I folded my hands over my lap. "Anything else?"

"Oh, right? You can move into your new room any time you'd like, though if you'd like to wait until next semester, that's fine too."

"New room?" I blinked. *Leaving Audrey?* Even though I wasn't really leaving her—I'd only be a floor away, really—it still felt weird to think about.

"Well..." Her brow furrowed. "You want the president's room, right? It's the only other single in the house." Besides hers, since she lived here too. Our chapter was small enough that the chapter advisor also doubled as our house mom, which meant she pulled double duty often.

"Right." It would be crazy for me to turn it down, especially with all the space. And the privacy. But still.

"Then it's settled." She nodded her head, like she'd just mentally finished checking off a list. "That's all for now."

"Great." I gave her the biggest smile I could currently

manage—which was forced, but I'd tried—before grabbing my stuff and the binder so I could head up the stairs.

"Ella." She stopped me as I reached the door. "You're going to be great. I believe in you."

I was glad one person did. Giving her a nod, I headed upstairs, debating my current predicament.

President. Holy shit. *I* was going to be president. When I'd applied for the executive board last year, I'd picked this position for a reason. Audrey had become the Social Chair, planning fun events for our chapter, and I, well… I stayed in the background.

If I was being honest with myself, my apprehension came from working with Delta Sig. With the *not* knowing. I had a phone number practically spelling out my doom in front of me.

Why hadn't I gotten Charming's *name*? I rubbed a hand over my forehead, frustrated. There had been so many opportunities for me to ask, but even the next morning, I'd just slipped out without waking him.

Fuck my life. This is what I got for giving in to my instincts for one night. For chasing pleasure and fun, instead of focusing on the path ahead of me. The walk of shame was going to be nothing compared to the embarrassment of running into my Halloween hookup—because I had to stop thinking about him as Charming—again.

Collapsing on my bed, I typed out a new text to the number on the piece of paper.

ELLA

> Hi. It's Ella. The new President of Pi Rho Sig. I just wanted to know if you wanted to get together this weekend? Since we're apparently partnering up now…

Here goes nothing, I thought to myself.

Throwing a piece of popcorn in my mouth, I settled onto the couch in between Audrey and my sorority sister Suzie, who'd apparently stepped in to take my place as Vice President.

The girls had all gathered in the giant living room for a girl's night, complete with *too* many snacks and a showing of some of our favorite movies.

I figured some bonding time would be good, especially when I'd had to reveal the news to the chapter. Apparently, everyone agreed with Ilene's decision, even if I thought it was crazy. Me as President? They were out of their minds.

Audrey nudged me softly. "Everything okay? How are you feeling about all of this?"

My twin always knew when to check in on me. I leaned my head on her shoulder, appreciating the soft fabric of her cozy pink pajamas.

"It'll be fine," I whispered back, even though I lacked the same confidence in myself. "It's just a learning curve, right?"

"Did the president of Delta Sig get back to you?" Audrey asked, since I'd explained the whole situation earlier.

I nodded, munching on another piece of popcorn as my eyes focused on the TV screen.

"Oh, good. Just let me know if you need my help."

Squeezing her knee, I nodded. "I'm sure I will."

My fingers itched with the need to create, to distract myself by hiding myself in the sewing studio, to keep going till my back ached and I had a sense of accomplishment of a project done—but for tonight, I ignored it, bathing in the sense of togetherness with my chapter.

I could do this. Right?

First, I just had to get over my fears.

"Audrey," I murmured as the movie ended, poking at my sister's arm. "Can we talk?"

Her eyes flared with worry. "What is it? Are you okay?"

I nodded. "Nothing's wrong, I promise." Well, maybe that wasn't entirely true, but I was sticking with it. Pulling her into the quiet kitchen, I took a deep breath before blurting out, "*Ilenewantsmetomove.*"

"What?" Her eyes widened. Thank *God* Audrey always knew what I was saying, even when I talked a mile a minute. "Move? Where?"

I grimaced. "Well, since Lily moved out, her room is empty."

"Oh." Any worry faded away, replaced by sadness. "That makes sense. Having the big, single room."

"I don't have to." The offer slipped from my lips before I could stop it.

"You know I love living with you, Ell, but you don't have to give up the President's room so you can keep sharing with me."

"I know, but…" I blinked. Why was I trying to fight with her over this? "Are you sure? We've never not shared a room before."

We'd always been attached at the hip, as my mother liked to say. Wherever she was, I wasn't far behind. She was the bubbly, outgoing one who made friends and shined so bright, but I'd always been by her side, protecting her—and her fragile heart. Would she really be okay without me? My eyes were watery, and I tried to blink the tears away. Why was I so emotional about this?

"It's only upstairs," she whispered, pulling me into a hug. "Are *you* going to be okay?"

"Yes." I let myself relax into her comfortable embrace. "You know where to find me if you need me."

"Same goes for you, you know. I'm always here."

If we had twin telepathy, I liked to think we'd be sharing *I love you* into each other's minds, but since we didn't, we just squeezed each other tight.

"Okay." The words were strange, even coming from my mouth. "Guess I'm moving out."

Which left me with only one big dilemma floating around in my mind: *Charming.*

And what the hell I was going to do when I saw him again.

CHAPTER 8

Cam

My fingers drummed against the desk, but my eyes were focused on the clock that clicked above my professor's head. It had only been a few days, but I was already itching for the weekend. As soon as the bell rang—metaphorically, of course—I'd be free.

Fifteen minutes.

It had already been over a week since Halloween, but I hadn't given up on looking for the blonde. And when I found her, I wouldn't let her go.

At least, that was what I kept telling myself. I just needed to see her again. To verify if what we had was real.

Good enough that I could barely focus on my Political Analysis class, because I couldn't stop thinking about her. Stupid. I needed to get my head on straight. I knew exactly what my father would say if he knew the thoughts in my head.

"That's all for today," my professor's voice rang out through the room, reminding me exactly where I was, and I flopped my notebook closed and pulled my phone out of my pocket.

Even if I'd been daydreaming, I at least gave my professors the courtesy of having my phone on do not disturb in class.

A text from an unknown number had come through, and I slid it open to read the full message.

> **UNKNOWN NUMBER**
> Hi. It's Ella. The new President of Pi Rho Sig. I just wanted to know if you wanted to get together in the next few days? Since we're apparently partnering up now...

My fingers fumbled over the keyboard. My advisor had told me about our frat's changes, along with Pi Rho getting a new president earlier this morning. The meeting we were having later tonight was also a result of it. Apparently, their old one had up and quit the entire sorority, even though no one knew why.

Begrudgingly, I'd agreed with the partnership, because he wasn't wrong. Our image wasn't impeccable or flawless, like I needed it to be for my grad school applications. Working closely with a sorority with a squeaky clean reputation like them seemed like a good idea for all of us involved.

Plus, we'd never really partnered with any of the girls before, and maybe it would be nice to have a little less testosterone around.

> **CAM**
> Hi, Ella. I'm done with classes for the week, so I'm free anytime. What works best for you?

Three dots blinked on the screen, showing that she was typing, and I waited for a response as I walked out of class, keeping my eyes peeled for a certain blonde, like I expected her to appear in front of me after thinking about her in class.

"Cam!" a loud voice called out behind me, and I turned to see Forest hurrying to catch up with me, his backpack haphazardly slung over one shoulder.

He pushed his damp brunette hair back off his forehead, giving me a lazy smile. "How's it going?"

I shrugged, looking over at the theater building. "Not bad.

Can't believe there's only a month left in the semester." There were only two weeks until Thanksgiving break, and I was wholly unprepared to go home.

He slung an arm around my shoulder. "Still looking for your mystery girl?"

"Forest." Pushing his arm off of me, I held back my groan. "Don't make me regret telling you that."

But as much as he was teasing me, I'd needed to tell someone. And more than the other guys, I felt like they wouldn't understand. They'd see it as just a hookup, nothing more. But that didn't account for how I'd *felt*, even just talking with her. I'd had zero expectations, and as much as I'd loved every bit of attention I'd given her body, I would have been content just spending another hour or two outside on that porch.

A lopsided grin formed over his face. "How easily they fall."

Just then, my phone buzzed again.

> Tomorrow, 10am? We can meet at the coffee shop on campus if you want.

I quickly added her name to my contacts so I wouldn't forget, and then typed out my reply.

> Sounds good. See you then. Anything I need to bring?

Just yourself.

And maybe your calendar.

Cheeky, but it made me smile. I liked it. Slipping my phone back into my jacket pocket, I looked up at Forest, who had a strange expression on his face.

"What?"

"Who ya textin'?"

"No one," I grumbled. "Just a sorority girl."

"Oh, a girl, huh?"

"It's not like that." The words spilled quickly, like I couldn't even hold them in. "She's the new president for Pi Rho. Our advisors are forcing us to work together and plan joint events." I sighed. "I'm not interested in anyone right now. You know that." Just the Princess, but that was more of an obsession than anything.

"Sure." He patted me on the back. "Keep telling yourself that."

I groaned. "Did you have something you actually wanted to talk about?"

"Oh, yeah. The guys and I were talking about planning a trip up to Vermont over winter break. Want to join?"

A few weeks with them versus spending the entire break with my parents? "Hell yeah, I'm in. Are you bringing Sutton?"

"Yeah. We were talking about staying at Adam's parents' house near the ski resort and she might bring some friends as well." Forest waggled his eyebrows. "Maybe you could get your mind off of mystery girl."

"Sure, sure." It was doubtful, but spending time on the mountain did sound like a good way to decompress after the crazy semester. At the very least, I'd try.

"How was practice?" I asked Forest, knowing he'd been working hard to keep up with his training schedule even during the off-season. He was hoping to get drafted after graduation, which was made even harder considering most guys would skip college altogether if they were good enough.

Forest's family wanted him to have a degree, something for him to fall back on, and I couldn't blame them. Plus, selfishly, I was grateful he was here.

"It was good," Forest said, scratching the back of his head. "I'm just..." He shrugged his shoulders. "I have so much riding on this. My future."

My head bobbed in a nod, a silent confirmation. "I get it." I knew what that was like.

The LSATs were a looming date in the future, but if I didn't do well, my hopes of getting into an excellent law school were out the window. Which meant all my plans, everything they were riding on… it could fall apart in an instant. But I couldn't let it.

Just like I knew that getting picked for the draft was Forest's biggest priority now.

Rolling my shoulders back, I patted him on the shoulder. "I'll see you later?"

He nodded, and after telling me he'd send me the information for the trip this weekend, we said our goodbyes, and I headed back to the fraternity house.

A chorus of groans filled the room.

"What do you mean, we have to go to all their events, *too*?" That was Peter.

Richard, our fraternity advisor, was leaning against a table in the big communal space, scratching his dark beard as all the guys freaked out. The whole fraternity was here for our weekly meeting, and considering they'd just found out about the arrangement, I understood their concern.

My Vice President, Stellan, sat at my side, and the other executive board members who helped me keep this place from running into the ground were all also gathered around, watching intently. I knew this mattered more for us than the rest of them—we were the ones who would be impacted by it the most.

The rest of the brothers would just have to show up and put on their best faces.

"Look, I know it's a lot to put on your plates." He shot a glare at Peter for interrupting. "But if you have a class conflict, you're excused. And the Pi Rho girls have the same expectations being put on them." Richard had graduated from Castleton four years ago, so he was barely in his late twenties, and I knew he definitely still remembered everything from when he'd been a student—and a member—here.

I nodded from his side, glad I'd already set up a meeting with their president. Ella. "I'm meeting with their Chapter President tomorrow, and we're going to work on some joint social events as well. So don't complain *too* much. At least the girls will put up with us," I joked. "Is everything ready for the event on Sunday?" I'd invite them, since that was Richard's plan. Go to each other's events, add a few bonding events—things that would have the university see us in a good light.

No parties. He'd been very clear that we should tone it down. No wild parties that would end in anyone's suspensions, no noise ordinances violated.

Squeaky clean, he'd made me promise. No getting *involved* with them. To that, I'd winced. Richard knew how college boys were—and so did I. This was my fraternity, after all. Our parties normally involved multiple people disappearing into other rooms, and not always ones with *beds* in them.

Turning my attention back to our philanthropy chair, Derek, I listened as he went over all the last-minute details and coordination.

"Sounds great. Does anyone else have anything to add?" Richard asked, and the guys gave a chorus of nos. "Try not to get into too much trouble this weekend," he offered.

"Easier said than done," I muttered as the rest of the guys filed out of the room.

Richard turned, pinning me with a look. "You got this, Cam?"

"Yep." Absolutely. Probably. "I'm sure it'll be fine."

"Go easy on her. She's probably overwhelmed. She didn't have time to prepare for the role like you did."

Sometimes it felt like I'd prepared my whole life for this. To go to Castleton, be in Delta Sigma, become president, go to law school, join the family firm... my whole life had been prepared for me.

I avoided making a face. "Right. Do you know anything about her?"

He shook his head. "Just that Ilene said she's quiet, but that she thinks she'll do a good job. I think she was the Vice President."

"Huh." That made sense, considering it was November and it would be hard to integrate someone new into the executive board this far into the year. "I'll do my best."

"I know you will." His lips curved into a warm smile, and he patted my shoulder. "Proud of you, Cam. You're really doing a great job this year."

"Thanks." It was crazy, but sometimes he felt more like an older brother to me than just an advisor.

I headed to my room to study, my meeting with Ella tomorrow at the forefront of my mind.

CHAPTER 9
Ella

Ten a.m. the next day came by quickly, and before I knew it, I was sitting in the coffee shop on campus, my notebook and favorite pen in front of me, about to have what was, technically, my first meeting as president of Pi Rho.

I'd worn my favorite cozy white sweater with a pair of dark jeans today—the temperatures in November dropped quickly, furthered by the costal winds that rolled in. My hair was twisted up into a powder blue claw clip to keep it off my neck, leaving just my bangs out in the front.

"Ella, your order is ready!" The barista called at the counter, and I slid out of my seat, grabbing my bagel and white chocolate mocha from the counter.

Setting my stuff down, I went to settle back into my seat, when a deep voice sounded behind me.

"Ella?"

Why did that voice sound familiar? Racking my brain, I tried to place it, but when I turned around—

I knew the face staring back at me. The dark, combed hair. Those warm brown eyes. He towered over me—even more than he had on Halloween, since I wasn't wearing heels. *Charming.* My eyes widened.

"It's you," he murmured, a whisper so soft, I almost didn't catch it.

I swallowed roughly. I hadn't seen him since I'd left his bedroom before he woke up all those nights ago. Just how I wanted it. Because if I'd stayed there, if I'd woken up next to him—it was too much.

"I—" I opened my mouth, but no words came out as my brain tried to process the information. "Cameron?" I finally choked out.

He nodded, stepping closer towards me, so I had to look up at him to keep eye contact. "Hi."

"Hi." I whispered the word. He was here. Charming was Cameron. Cameron was *Charming*. Which meant...

Oh, God. I'd slept with the Delta Sigs *President*.

Cameron Edwards. How could I be so stupid to not know it was him? I'd heard the rumors, and I hated the idea that I was just another girl he'd slept with. Maybe it was just a regular thing for him. The thought made me cringe.

I couldn't bring myself to imagine him being with anyone else. The mere thought of it filled me with unease. Not after what we shared. But I wouldn't screw this up for the sorority because I was lusting after him, either.

"You know," he said, those lips that had kissed all over my body brushing against my ear. "I still have your shoes, Princess."

My cheeks flushed. He—He'd kept my shoes? What did that mean?

"Do you want to sit?" I blurted out, gesturing to the table. Desperately needing a way out of this topic. "I already ordered."

He nodded, plopping into the chair in front of me.

My eyes tracked his every movement, including the way he dragged his hand over his face, running his fingers through his perfectly styled hair. "You know, I've been looking everywhere for you."

My eyes widened. *You have?* "Why?"

Did he... want to hook up again? Because I couldn't do that. I wasn't that kind of girl. Part of me could barely believe I'd slept with him in the first place. One-night stands weren't like me. And yet, that night had been different.

Cameron shot me a look. "What do you mean, *why?*" His voice was rough. "That night was..." Perfect.

He'd been so charming. But maybe it was all just an act.

"A one time thing." I kept my voice calm, even though I felt anything but. "We said that." Along with not sharing our names, which seemed smart at the time and now it just felt dumb. "It was just to... scratch an itch."

What would it have changed if I had known who he was? Everything.

But a voice in my mind whispered, *nothing.* Even if I wouldn't take it back, if I didn't regret it.

"Right." He frowned.

Picking up my bagel, I spread a thick layer of cream cheese on it, avoiding his gaze.

I was trying to figure out how *Charming,* the man I'd spent the night with, was sitting in front of me. How, of all the guys in his fraternity, *he* was the one I was meeting with. The *president* I'd been paired up with.

"Coffee for Cameron," the barista interrupted my thoughts, and the man in front of me got up to get his own drink.

It gave me a moment to compose myself. To remember why we were there. I took a bite of my bagel, practically scarfing it down instead of saying anything.

Plopping down in his chair once again, he took the lid off his coffee—black.

Tucking my hair behind my ear, I flipped my notebook open, avoiding his face. "I brought our event schedule for the rest of the year. So we can try to work in a few joint events, and your guys can come to whatever isn't a sister event."

"That sounds good."

I eyed the space in front of him. "Don't you have anything to write everything down with?"

Cameron tapped his index finger on his temple. "I got it all up here, Princess."

"Don't ask me to bail you out when you miss something." I resisted rolling my eyes.

He gave me a sexy smirk, which I *definitely* shouldn't find attractive. It soured my mood. "I won't."

I scowled. "Okay. What do you have going on this month that we should go to?"

Crossing his arms over his chest, his lips kept that tilted smile. "We're having our philanthropic event tomorrow."

I wrote it down in my notebook. "Time?"

"Eleven to three."

"Attire?"

"Something you can get dirty."

I spluttered, coffee coming out of my mouth. "What?"

He chuckled. "It's a pumpkin smash." He looked me up and down, his gaze settling on my cashmere sweater. "So don't wear something that you wouldn't want to get pumpkin guts on."

"A… what?" I probably sounded like a broken record.

"You pay a dollar to smash a pumpkin." Cameron rested his head on his hands. "It'll be fun."

I nodded, even though I failed to understand why anyone would find smashing pumpkins to be enjoyable.

"We're having it on the academic quad." The big grassy area was in the middle of campus and had a lot of foot traffic, so I supposed it made sense.

"Okay. We'll be there."

That grin that threatened to do bad things to my insides lit up his face again. "Can't wait to see you smash a pumpkin, Princess."

I rolled my eyes, standing up from the table to throw my trash away. "I'm not your princess. Stop calling me that."

Cameron's face transformed, something that almost looked like hurt spreading across his features. But it couldn't be.

"Ella," he whispered, tilting my chin up so I'd meet his gaze.

I looked away. "I can't do this. Please. We just have to..." *Focus on sorority and fraternity stuff. Keep things platonic.* Avoid this, because we couldn't. I shook my head. "We can't."

There and gone in a flash, another smirk crossed over his face. "Okay then. May the best chapter win."

"Win?" I raised an eyebrow, trying to figure out how we'd gone from a one-night stand to... this. Whatever this was. "What are we competing for now?"

"To see who's the best."

"And what's the prize if you win?"

He stared straight at me, unblinking, not saying a word, but the idea was clear. *You.*

Swallowing, I tried not to let him see how much he was getting to me.

"See you tomorrow," I said, grabbing the rest of my stuff. "I gotta... I have to go."

"Ella!" He called after me, but I didn't turn around.

Apparently, the only thing I was good at anymore was *running.*

"Audrey?" I peeked into our shared room, finding it dark. I'd been too exhausted after the events of the previous day to even think about moving my stuff to my new room.

My bed was calling my name, but I couldn't afford to sleep. Not yet.

It had been a long day, starting with my meeting with Cameron. I still couldn't believe *he* was Charming. The man who I'd spent the entire night talking to, sharing some of my deepest secrets.

And now, I would have to work with him for the rest of the semester?

I groaned. "What sort of a cruel twist of fate is this, anyway?"

Sure, he *was* charming, and handsome, and the way he'd treated me—touched me—hadn't seemed fake, but it wasn't real, either.

"*This* is why I don't do hookups," I said to the silence, glad no one was around to listen to me mutter to myself. Either I got attached, or they did, and the one time I'd had the *perfect* night... The universe put him back in my path.

My sewing machine beckoned me, the project for class that I hadn't finished yet draped across my desk. My professor for my design class asked me this week if I could create some of the main costumes for the spring musical, and I'd been all too eager to agree. They were doing a play on fairytales, and I knew Audrey was already losing her shit over it.

But try as I might, I was staring at a blank page, my thoughts too occupied with Cameron Edwards to focus on anything else.

And how I was a coward who kept running away from him.

CHAPTER 10
Cam

Surveying the crowded quad, full of pumpkins and college students laughing wildly as they swing at the orange gourds, I couldn't help but crack a smile. This event was absolutely ridiculous—in every way—but it was also *fun*.

A crowd of girls came to stand at the edge of the field, wearing jeans and pink *Pi Rho Sigma* sweatshirts. I grinned as I caught sight of Ella, who was looking across the grass curiously. She'd pulled her hair into a bun, though it wasn't as fancy as the one from Halloween, but I recognized her instantly.

Handing my current job off to one of my guys, I made my way over to her.

"Hi." All her girls were at the check-in table, paying for swings. "You made it." I grinned. Seeing her here was more than I could have asked for.

"I said I'd be here." Ella gave me a curt nod, though she avoided my gaze.

"Want me to show you how it's done?" I asked, picking up a hammer. "First swing's on me." Hoisting it up so it rested on my shoulder, I gave her my best flirty smile.

She batted her eyelashes. "Oh yes, *Prince Charming*, because I couldn't possibly figure out how to do it myself."

"Exactly." I smirked, enjoying her quip. The reminder of that night. "Took the words right out of my mouth." I knew she was being sarcastic, but I couldn't help but dish it back.

At least she was here, and talking to me. That was enough for now, wasn't it? Even if I wanted more. Had craved more.

"Cameron." She narrowed her eyes as I crowded closer to her, but I couldn't stop.

"Ella."

She gestured between us. "This isn't happening."

Why not? I wanted to ask. Wanted to know why she pulled back—ran away. But a part of me knew, too how close she was to shutting me out, pushing me away. And we had to work together. So as much as I wanted to know, I couldn't ruin everything.

"But we're just having fun, right?"

"Oh, is *that* what we're doing?" Ella scowled at me. "I bet you say that to all of your girls."

I frowned. Didn't she know there were no other girls? There hadn't been, since that night. "What do you mean?"

She shrugged. "You're just trying to get me alone again."

Taking her hand in mine, I pulled her to an empty part of the lawn.

"Ella, what do I need to do to reassure you?" I let the mallet hit the ground and rested my hands on top of it.

Her blue eyes were so captivating, even as she looked at me with concern. I stepped closer, hearing her breathe hitch from our proximity. "Don't think for one second that there's anyone I want but you."

She blinked, her lips opening as she stared up at me. My eyes trailed down to her pink lips, remembering what it felt like to have them against mine.

But I needed to step back. Remember why we were here. What this was all about.

"We're here for our chapters, right?" I offered her. "So we're going to spend time together as Presidents. That's it."

"Okay," she agreed, her voice subdued. "Should we smash some pumpkins now?"

"Yes," I agreed.

Even though I didn't need to touch her, I couldn't help it. I certainly didn't need to wrap my arms around hers, or to move her hands onto the mallet and then put mine over the top. But I did.

Because I was weak for this girl, and it was all I'd been aching for ever since she left my room.

"Charming," she whispered, like she realized where we were all of the sudden. "What are we doing?"

"Isn't it obvious?" I murmured, raising both our hands up and swinging the mallet back. "We're having fun."

Guiding both of our hands down, I relished how our bodies fit together—just like I had that night.

I didn't look over at the sea of pink and blue that had mixed, but I was sure they were watching us. But if my guys saw me with my hands all over her, maybe it would give them a sign to keep their hands off of her.

When the hammer hit the soft pumpkin, it smashed into it, and I was surprised at the little shriek of laughter that emitted from Ella's lips. So she *wasn't* as unaffected as she appeared. A big grin lit her face, and her eyes brightened.

We stayed like that for a moment longer than was probably acceptable, just staring at each other. Fuck, I liked it. Being wrapped around her like this. I wondered what other things I could show her, just as an excuse to hold her.

Fuck, she was beautiful. A little tendril escaped her bun, resting against her cheek, and I held myself back from brushing it back behind her ear.

"What do you think?" I asked her, stepping back. I needed the space, before I did something stupid like kiss her again. If yesterday was any indication, she didn't want me, and I needed to remember that. It was enough just to spend time with her like this, wasn't it?

Her eyes brightened. "Can I do that again?"

I pretended to think about it before I bowed playfully. "This one's all yours."

She paused. "But I need to pay for it, right? I know this is your philanthropic event... I couldn't possibly..."

"Relax, Princess." I winked. "I got it. You can get the next one."

"Oh." She blushed as I walked over to my treasurer, handing him a five dollar bill. The rest of the sorority girls had spread out into little clumps throughout the field. Though we offered just one swing for a dollar, a lot of them had donated five.

"You didn't have to do that," she murmured as I stood back at her side.

"Maybe I just wanted to watch you smash the shit out of this pumpkin."

She looked thoughtfully at the pumpkin, and then back up at me. "Will you tell me about it? Your philanthropy?"

I nodded. Each Greek life organization on campus had their own, raising funds for a different cause, and we were no exception. Swallowing roughly, I focused on the pumpkin instead of her face. "We support the Children's Cancer Hospital. It helps with research and care, especially for those who can't afford it. I..." Shaking my head, I took the hammer from her hands. Ella had been watching me, not speaking. I couldn't explain my personal connection to the hospital. It was too personal, too raw.

When I'd come to Castleton, I'd known I wanted to join the Delta Sigma Iota chapter, just like my dad, but when I'd found out what cause they supported, I hadn't even considered the rest.

"It means a lot to you." She whispered, watching as I took a swing. Another few pieces went flying off.

"Yes." That was an understatement.

She took the mallet back, biting her lip in concentration as she swung back, before releasing her fury on the pumpkin. Ella let her swings fly—once, twice, three times—until the pumpkin was practically mashed on the ground, only small pieces left remaining.

"Whoops." The sly smile that split her face was dazzling. "Guess I didn't know my own strength."

She went back over to the table, handing another five dollar bill over before coming back and standing next to me.

"Ready for round two?" She pointed at another pumpkin, and I smirked.

It was like she knew I couldn't talk about it more, and was going to distract me the only way she knew how.

"Bring it on, Princess."

"Ella!" I huffed out, hurrying to catch up with her.

"What?" She spun, pinning me with that beautiful glare of hers, almost tripping in the process. Sensing her agitation, I did my best not to reach out my hands to catch her.

Even though I'd just been touching her earlier and was dying to do it again.

My hands ran through my hair as I gave her my best frown. "Were you really going to leave without saying goodbye?"

She looked off to the side. "You looked busy, so…"

After we'd smashed a few pumpkins together, trading taunts and retorts, Jackson had called me over, needing help, and then I'd been surrounded by my fraternity brothers and unable to escape to get back to her. Stellan had needed something, and when I'd finally gotten free, she'd been leaving.

"It looks like your girls had fun."

Ella wiped her hands on her jeans, still looking anywhere but at me. "They did. Thank you. I was skeptical, but…"

"You should really learn to trust me, huh?" I gave her another cocky grin. I couldn't help it.

She rolled her eyes, but then her face grew serious. "I'll admit, I *was* wrong about today."

"Does that mean I win?"

"Hardly." Ella's lips curved up in a taunting smile. "You said the best chapter would win, right? I don't think that can be determined by just one event."

I nodded, wanting to see where she was going with this.

"There's four weeks left of the semester. Which means... at least two joint events per week. Whoever has the most wins—for the event they planned—at the end of the semester wins."

We hadn't even agreed on the rest of the calendar for said joint events yet—mostly because she'd ran away from me again yesterday afternoon before we could finish syncing up—but I liked my odds. Mostly because either way, I was the one winning.

My prize was spending time with Ella.

I leaned in closer, my lips only inches from her ear. "And what do you get if you win?" I repeated her question from yesterday. She opened her mouth, but I shook my head. "Take your time. You gotta pick something *really* good, after all."

"And if you win?" she breathed, her voice sounding like pure sex.

"You let me give you another orgasm." The words slipped out before I could think better of it. Because I wanted more. Wanted her back in my bed. Wanted her to not run away this time.

Her cheeks were pink, her breath shallow as I pulled away. I could see the hesitation in her eyes, and fuck—I hated that.

I wanted to reassure her of my intentions. That there were no other girls. That I'd only seen her. But I needed to go slow, and earn her trust. Start small.

"Do you want to get dinner?"

Ella froze. "I... What?" Her blue eyes were wide, like the question had shocked her, the lingering embarrassment from my statement fading away. "Like a date? No."

I winced, pointing at the Castleton Commons, our biggest dining hall on campus. "Not a date. But maybe we could talk about upcoming events, and maybe plan a few of our own? Because if I'm gonna win this, I need to be prepared."

"Oh." The worry fled out of her, and she nodded. "I guess that makes sense." Ella worried her lip in between her teeth.

"So... Yes?"

She nodded. "Yeah. Okay. I can do that. Let me just tell Ro—" She glanced around the field, before seeming to spot whoever she was looking for. "Be right back."

Ella ran over to another blonde, and I realized quickly the resemblance between them. Her twin sister. They stood at the same height, and shared the same shade of blonde hair—even if her sister wore hers down, with bangs across her forehead—but even from the back, I knew exactly which one of them was mine.

Not yours, my brain reminded me. Sure, we'd slept together once. And we were partnered together for now. But that didn't mean she was mine. She'd made it obvious that it wouldn't happen again.

Did she regret it? I swallowed roughly.

There was no mistaking the way she was affected by me—or the way I was affected by her. She was, simply put, stuck in my head. When I closed my eyes, she was all I saw. It had never been like this for me before. I'd never wanted to chase after a girl. But with Ella...

She jogged back over, waving goodbye to the sorority sisters who were taking their leave now that our event was over.

"You're not going to introduce us?" I murmured into her ear, watching her sister and the gaggle of pink head out.

"Oh. I didn't..." Ella shook her head. "Next time."

I grinned. "Okay." I liked that there was a next time. Even if it was forced upon us, it felt like a promise.

The brothers were in charge of cleanup—that was the only way the University had agreed to allow us to host the event on the quad—but I'd thankfully delegated that responsibility. If they helped set up, or go get the pumpkins from the patch who'd sold us their sad, slightly soft pumpkins, they didn't have to clean up.

It seemed only fair that way. Plus, we just had to pick up the larger pieces and the vines—the rest would help fertilize the grass.

"Ready?" She said, giving me a conniving grin.

"After you, Princess."

CHAPTER 11
Ella

You let me give you another orgasm.

There'd been no mistaking the promise in his voice as he'd said the words, the pure lust dripping out of them. And if our night together had been any sign, he got off on giving, and I knew it was just as much for *him* as it was for me.

The worst part was I wanted it, too. There was no mistaking the way his words affected me, how his proximity made my body light up. If I wasn't careful, I'd be putty in his hands. But I couldn't. I wouldn't lose myself to pretty words and empty promises.

That was all he could give me, I tried to remind myself as I walked in front of him, all-too aware of his presence behind me.

Don't think for one second that there's anyone I want but you. Those words made me shiver. He wanted me, yes, but... was that enough?

We'd all worn our letters—our *PRS* crewnecks—today, though the November chill made me wish I had something more than the long-sleeved shirt I'd worn underneath. Luckily, the only casualty from today was the little ol' pumpkin splatter that had ended up on my Adidas sneakers, though at least it would wipe off.

The smell of food kept me going, and I didn't stop till I'd reached the door, though Cameron slid in before I could grab the handle and opened it for me.

Ever my Prince Charming, I thought with a smirk. This man was too chivalrous for his own good. How often did he use the same tricks to get girls into bed with him? The thought soured in my mouth, and my face fell.

"Ella?" He asked, only now realizing he'd been talking to me. "What do you want to eat?"

I shook the thoughts from my head. There was no need to think about who he was sleeping with, because I didn't want to know. "I'll probably just get pasta." I could get a salad, but the idea of a tasty bowl of fettuccine Alfredo was too much to pass up. Especially when the pasta station was one that rotated.

Cameron nodded, picking up a tray after he adjusted the neck of his collared jacket. He looked good—maybe *too* good, but ever the part of the fraternity president. His letters were adorned over his chest, the small logo embroidered on.

I ordered, surprised when he did the same, following behind me and taking my plate, balancing both on his tray before he headed over to the coke machine, filling up a cup for himself.

The commons was bustling with other students in a rush to eat, crowding around the grill to place orders. Even though it was the weekend, mealtimes were still busy here, especially considering most students lived on campus or right nearby. I didn't have a meal plan anymore, since the sorority house was off-campus, but even I still grabbed a bite here quite a bit since it was convenient.

And I liked that it was so easy to run into friends here—even if sometimes all I wanted was to hide in my own quiet bubble. I waved to my friend Gus who sat on the other side of my room. We had a lot of classes together, and he'd helped me a lot on coming up with ideas for designs. I wondered what he'd think about seeing us together, and then blushed at the thought.

Because we weren't *together*. Not like that.

He held out a cup for me as I looked back. "Want anything?"

"Oh. Um…" I pretended to look at the options, even though I always got the same thing. "Raspberry Fanta, please." Thank goodness for Coke Freestyle machines. I'd drink Orange Fanta when there was nothing else, but I definitely preferred the Raspberry. The blue Berry flavor was good too, but I didn't find that very often.

He chuckled to himself as he filled the cup, handing it to me and then making our way to the register, where he grabbed a brownie and a cookie. I raised an eyebrow, but he just gave me a small smile.

The girl read off our total, and Cameron handed her his card.

"Wait," I said, waving my hands. "You don't have to pay for me."

"It's fine," he insisted. "This was my idea, so I should pay."

I sighed, giving in too easily. "Fine."

Leading us to a booth in the empty corner of the restaurant, Cameron slid into one side, the tray with our food in front of us. Neither of us said a word, just digging into our pasta.

I sighed in happiness as the flavor burst onto my tongue. "I love this place," I almost moaned around my bite. So many college cafeterias had sub-par, flavorless food, but practically everything here was delicious. "So good," I said, shoveling another bite into my mouth.

When I looked up, he had an amused look on his face, watching me eat. I took a drink of my Fanta, trying to ignore the heat rising to my face. What was it with me and embarrassing myself around this guy?

When we'd finished eating, I slid my bowl to the side, pulling out my phone and setting it down in front of me. "Okay. So."

"So," he responded, doing the same with his food.

"Guess we should sync our calendars, huh?" Cameron quirked an eyebrow at my comment, and I fumbled with my next statement. "For the… sorority and fraternity events?"

"Right. That's what I thought you meant." He nodded, and I gave him a weird look. What else would I mean?

"Maybe we could plan a bonding event?" I bit my lip. "My sister's the social chair, so I'm sure she could come up with something with your guy—"

"Oh, no, Princess." He flashed his teeth in a grin that definitely wasn't going straight to my core. "If we're going to win, it has to be entirely planned by our group. No sharing."

I furrowed a brow. "That's not fair. Do you know how much *I* have going on this week?" I had sketches due for my final project in my design class, and another project to finish for my history of fashion class.

He shrugged, looking nonchalant. "That's our deal."

It only seemed fair that we each contributed one event, but I hated when he pulled the logic out on me. Reminding me that this was a competition. That he was the enemy, and I had to take him down.

"This week, we've already got a community service event planned, if your guys want to come to that."

"This service event… what are we talking here? Planting trees? Helping at the soup kitchen? Volunteering at the food bank?"

"Trees." I made a noise with my lips. "What are we, amateurs?" I leaned in really close, beckoning him in with my fingers. When our faces were close enough that I could have pressed my lips to his with one fluid moment, I whispered, "*Puppies.*"

He stared at me, dumbfounded. "Puppies? That's not fair. You'll totally win."

I crossed my arms over my chest, smug. "Guess you'll have to outdo me then. And it better not be some lame toga party."

Cameron's lips titled up in a smile of his own. "Be careful what you wish for."

"What *do* you guys have going on this week?"

"I'll text you the details," he said with a wink.

"What else do you guys have coming up? Our Fall Formal is in three weeks."

He rattled off the rest of his calendar from memory, proving to me what he said the other day—he, in fact, did not need to write it down.

Once we'd finished, everything penciled out, including a few question marks we'd have to fill in this week with the help from our own executive boards, Cameron set back, his arms resting across the top of the booth as he stared at me.

I didn't know how his gaze always felt like more. That he was seeing all of me, through me, but I had to look away from those deep brown eyes.

He was looking at me like he'd looked at me on the porch outside of the fraternity house.

"Ella." He whispered my name, and I looked away, not sure if I wanted to think about that moment again.

Was it real? Or were those whispered confessions just another way for me to let my walls down, so he could weasel his way in?

"Tell me something real," I said, echoing our conversation from that night. I'd meant to say something else, to brush him off, but at the moment, it was like no one else existed in the dining hall. It was just him and me, in our own little bubble.

"You look beautiful today," he said, reaching across the table to brush one of the short pieces of my hair back, his index finger running over my cheek with the motion.

"Cameron…"

"Call me Cam." The pleading tone in his voice was impossible to miss, as if me calling him his nickname would somehow change this thing between us. Maybe it would. Maybe that was why I'd been calling him by his full name all this time. "Please."

"Okay." I whispered, forcing my face to remain impassive. "Cam."

His entire demeanor changed from the one word, and it was *dangerous*. Dangerous how easy it would be to say yes to him. To ask him to kiss me again.

"I should go," I said instead, grabbing my plate to clear off the table. "See you in a few days, Charming."

The endearment slipped out, but the lazy smile that spread over his face made it worth it.

"Good night, Ella," he rasped, and I fled into the night, glad that he couldn't see the blush on my cheeks.

It was going to be an interesting few weeks, that was for sure.

Because I was in trouble. *Big trouble.*

Opening up Audrey's door, I snuck inside, ignoring how weird it was to be coming in here when I had my own room now.

My bed still sat empty, and I plopped down on it, letting myself have a moment to smile thinking about Cam's words and actions earlier. They were so opposite to my original assumptions of him, and I couldn't help but wonder how much else I had misjudged him.

Still, him telling me how beautiful I looked today hadn't left my mind since I'd left the dining hall.

"Ella."

"What?" I looked up, realizing she'd caught me thinking about Cam, and I felt my cheeks warm. At least she couldn't read my thoughts. We told each other everything, but for some reason, I didn't feel like sharing this.

"What's going on between you two?" Audrey asked, sitting at her desk while studying a script. "I saw how cozy you looked earlier." She raised her eyebrows suggestively.

"Nothing," I insisted. "He was just…" I frowned, trying to keep my focus entirely on the small embellishments I was currently sewing on by hand to my dress.

"*Ella.*"

Biting my lip, I looked up at her, needle and thread forgotten in my lap. "We slept together, okay?" Keeping this from her was too hard, and I needed someone to confide in.

"When? The other night?"

I shook my head. "No. Remember on Halloween, when I didn't come home?"

"Oh my *God*. You didn't tell me it was him!"

"I just found out who he was this weekend. We didn't exactly exchange names." My face was the color of a tomato, I was sure.

"If you didn't tell each other your names, what did you call each other?"

I looked away, mumbling under my breath, but when I looked back at her, her entire face was split in a grin.

"You're enjoying this *way* too much."

"Hell yeah I am."

"Well, if you *must* know…" I buried the lower half of my face in my sweatshirt, keeping just my eyes out. "Hecalledme-Princess." I said the words in a rush.

"What?"

"Princess. He… That's what he called me."

"Ella! Stop it. That's so cute."

"It's not like that." I rejected the idea. "We're not together. It was just a hookup. A one night thing."

She snorted. "That's not what it looked like today."

"I can't."

"Why not?"

"You know why." One heartbreak was enough. I didn't need another one to sidetrack my dreams—not again. "Besides, you've heard the rumors, haven't you?"

"Come on, El. You can't put too much stock in gossiping college students."

Maybe not. But I knew his type too well. I shrugged, stabbing my needle into my fabric, if only so I could ignore her all-knowing eyes.

"Are you telling me that if you went back and did it all over, knowing who he was… that you'd say no?"

No. That was part of the problem. I was drawn to him. To those warm brown eyes that kept catching me in their gaze.

He'd intrigued me that night, long before I'd known who he was. Charming had seemed... lonely. And I'd wanted to help make that go away. Hell, maybe I'd wanted it for myself, too.

It was a strange thing to be surrounded by people and still feel lonely. To feel like you're just floating through life, a little piece of you missing inside.

"Ella?"

"I don't know," I whispered, as close to the truth as I could give.

"Mmm. I think there's your answer, then."

She was probably right, as much as I hated it.

It was a few minutes of concentration before she spoke again, after I'd almost stabbed myself in the thumb too many times.

"Have you talked to Sutton lately?" Ro asked, starting to painting her toenails pink.

"I can barely keep up with everything, with classes and these events, let alone everyone else." Exhausted, I hung my head back. "I need a break."

"*Well,* she invited us to come up to Vermont with her and some friends for two weeks before Christmas."

"Oh?" That made me perk up. It sounded perfect. Not that I wanted to hit the slopes—knowing me, I'd fall on my face—but a week in a wintery paradise would help me relax.

"They're renting a big house up at a ski resort. I mentioned it to Mom, and she said it was okay with her."

"Are you sure?" I bit my lip. "I feel bad. We're not even going home for Thanksgiving this year." Between the formal and everything else we had going on, there just wasn't time.

"We'll still be home for Christmas and New Year's. Besides, I think it'll be fun."

I closed my eyes. It wasn't a tropical vacation spent on the beach, but I could make snow work too. Maybe *fun* was the distraction I needed.

Anything to stop thinking about Cameron Edwards and his damn eyes.

There were puppies everywhere, and everyone was *all* over it. We'd volunteered to help with a dog adoption event at a local park, and both fraternity brothers and my sorority sisters alike were fawning over the animals, sprinkling them with kisses and pets.

"This is awesome," Cameron admitted with a grin on his face as a basset-hound puppy licked his face. "How'd you know about this?"

"One of our alumni started it a few years back," I said, scratching behind the ears of a beagle who was currently sitting in my lap. "When she contacted me to see if we'd be willing to help with the event, I knew there was no way I could say no."

"You know, this gives me an idea."

"Hey! No piggy backing." I pointed a finger at him.

"No." He laughed. "I just think we should see if she'd be willing to bring some of the dogs by campus around dead week. Help with stress relief."

"Oh. That's actually..." A really good idea. I hated that he was right. "I think the chapters would love that."

One corner of Cameron's lip curled up, and he leaned in close. "That one's all mine, Princess."

Damn him. He was going to win if I didn't stay at the top of my game.

"I didn't need it anyway," I muttered, though I wasn't even sure how we were keeping count.

"Ella!" Audrey's voice made its way through the crowd, and when she spotted me, I could see the mischief written all over her face.

"Hi," I murmured to my sister.

Cam looked between us, and I wondered if he would say the same thing as everyone else. How we were identical—the major difference was our eyes. Or how people could only tell us apart based on the clothing we wore. It wasn't like our wardrobes were completely foolproof, though. I certainly wore colors other than light blue, and Audrey wasn't *always* in a shade of pink. Just most of the time.

"Cam, this is Audrey, my sister. Audrey, this is Cameron. My..." I trailed off. What was he to me? A friend? Barely. Something more? Hardly. "Delta Sig's President," I finally settled on.

Shuffling the puppy, he stuck his hand out, giving her a warm smile. "Hey there."

"It's nice to meet you, officially." Audrey took his hand, shaking it. "I feel like you're all Ella's been talking about the last few weeks."

Cameron smirked. "Oh, really?"

"Not true," I muttered under my breath, elbowing my twin in the ribs.

"Ow!" She shot me a glare.

"It's okay, Princess," he said, leaning in closer to me. "I like that you've been talking about me."

"Don't let it go to your head," I muttered back. "It's already big enough as it is."

"Not as big as my—"

I covered his mouth with my hand. "Nope."

Audrey laughed and gave us a little wave before heading over towards the adoption tent. "Have fun, you two!"

"So..." I looked down at him, still holding the puppy. It had settled down in Cam's lap, and he was scratching at its ears. "Have you ever had a dog?" It seemed so at home in his arms, so comfortable. Like it never wanted to leave. Maybe I knew why.

We'd practically always had one in my family, and it was one reason I loved this organization so much. They helped find homes for rescue dogs, all while giving back to the community.

"No. I always wanted one, though." His brown eyes were

suddenly far away, and I hated it. Like I'd uncovered a sore spot for him.

"Maybe someday," I offered, though that wasn't much.

"Yeah." His lips curled up into a warm smile as the puppy's eyes closed, falling asleep on him. "I hope so."

"I should probably get this little guy back," he said with a sigh, rising from the grass. "Wouldn't want him to miss out on finding a new home because I kept him all to myself."

"Probably true." I still hated disturbing the pup in my lap to do the same. "I wish I could take one home."

"Sorority house mascot?" Cam asked, standing up with the dog still snoozing in his arms.

"As if." I chuckled, imagining the can of worms that would open.

Shifting his sleeping puppy, he offered me a hand, helping me get up from the grass.

"Back to work, eh?"

"Yes, sir," I said, giving him a salute.

"Ella," he groaned.

With a wink, I skipped off towards the big playpen, knowing he was following behind me—with the knowledge of *exactly* what I was doing to him.

Maybe I was having just a little too much fun torturing him, but it was his fault. He'd started it.

I was just going to be the one to finish it.

CHAPTER 12
Cam

I'd been in a good mood since I'd spent the entire afternoon the previous day holding a puppy and sitting with Ella, and I didn't think anything could ruin that.

Except for one thing. My phone rang in my pocket, and I groaned at the caller ID.

"Dad?" I lifted the device to my ear. "It's not really a good time. I have class in a few minutes."

Forty-five, actually, but he didn't need to know that.

"That's okay, son. I just need a few minutes." I rolled my eyes, picturing my father at the desk in his firm where he spends most of his time. Even when I was growing up, there was a better chance he was at work than at home. "The firm just wanted to verify you're still interested in the internship this summer."

"Your firm," I say, as though that's not obvious. There might have been other partners, but his name was the one on the building. So—he wanted to check on me. To make sure I hadn't made other plans. Rubbing at my temples, I did my best to hold in my sigh. "Yes. Dad. I have the LSATs this summer, but other than that, I'll be there."

He made a humming sound. "Your mother is excited to see you soon for winter break."

"About that." I winced. Despite anything else, I loved my mom, and I hated to disappoint her. "The guys and I are going up to Vermont for a few weeks." Two, but I don't tell him that.

"Is that a good idea? Don't you have a lot of studying to do?"

"Dad…" I groaned. "I'll take my books up with me. I'm not going to slack off, I promise."

"I know you're not," he said with a grunt. "Because you're my son, and you always make me proud."

If that wasn't a loaded statement.

"I know," was the only thing that came out of my mouth. It's all I'd been trying to do since I was a kid. To make him proud. To get his attention.

I originally went into college pre-law because I wanted to join the firm, to carry on his legacy. But now, it was more than that. I genuinely loved what I was learning. What I was setting out to do.

And yet, I wasn't sure if his vision for my future and mine were the same anymore. If what I wanted was to move home and work underneath my father.

Maybe it was time to stop trying to make him proud, and to focus on making myself proud instead.

It was a start, at least.

After saying our goodbyes, I hung up the phone, shuffling towards class.

Wishing it wouldn't be another three days before I had a chance to see Ella again.

"Okay, *this* isn't fair," Ella bit out, looking around the movie theater we rented out for the evening, both the fraternity and sorority members excited to see the new superhero movie that just came out this week.

"You told me to plan it," I shrugged, settling into one of the two seats I'd saved for us. "Besides, how else was I going to compete against *puppies*?"

I'll admit, I'd been stumped at first, especially since she'd given me less than a week to figure something out for us *all* to do together.

Despite the short notice, we'd been able to pull this together fairly quickly, thanks to one of my fraternity brother's families owning the movie theater. Not just the local chain, but the entire corporation. Naturally, I choose not to share this information with the girl next to me.

The blonde who somehow always looked beautiful, even in a plain navy Castleton University crewneck and a pair of tight jeans.

"Just sit back and watch the movie, Princess." I wasn't opposed to finding other ways to shut her up if she didn't.

I could see her bite back a retort, and I hid my smile behind the bucket of popcorn.

The theater grew dark, and even the hush whispers of dozens of college students faded away as the opening sequence started.

Ella's knee brushed against mine, and I was surprised when she didn't move it, keeping that tiny connection between us. It felt like something new.

Maybe I could work with that.

"What do you think?" I whispered at one point, earning a glare from Ella, who quickly shushed me before I could say anything else.

I'd never had so much fun watching a movie before, but I supposed I'd never seen one with someone I'd really *liked* before, either. It was different with the guys. Watching her face, seeing her reactions—it was almost as good as the movie itself.

Plus, I had the perk of her body next to mine, and even when our fingers brushed over the popcorn bowl, or our elbows touched, she didn't pull away. Every time, it was like a little shock to my system.

I knew what she looked like, sounded like, *felt* like, and no matter how much she seemed to want to run away from it, there was no way I could forget any of it. And yet at this moment, when halfway through the movie, she looked over and gave me a warm smile? It was priceless.

I'd do anything to earn it again.

The night at the movies had been a win, and I was already planning the next one. Another way to make Ella smile, to see her come out of her shell.

All around me, the library was full of the sounds of students typing away on their computers, the occasional printing of papers, or the scratch of a chair against the floor. A brunette girl ran back and forth behind the desk, helping students out who needed to check out books or locate something.

And then, all of my senses narrowed, and everything faded away as I came across the girl I always wanted to see with papers spread all around her on the table, her face furrowed in concentration as she sketched on a piece of paper.

I looked over the table, eyeing the paper closest to me. It looked like an illustration from a fairytale book I read as a kid.

"What are you working on, Princess?" I ask quietly. Even if we weren't on the quiet floor of the library, I liked to respect people's study space.

"Oh!" she startled, clearly not having even seen me until I spoke. "Cameron. *Geez*. Don't just sneak up on a girl like that."

Sitting in the chair next to her, I let my backpack rest on the floor before I looked over her designs. "This looks really cool, Ella."

"Thank you." She dipped her head. "I'm designing some costumes for the spring musical."

"That's amazing. Are you going to be in it?"

"What?" Ella squeaked out. "*No.*" The words came out too fast, and she shook her head. "I don't perform."

"But you like to sing, right?" She'd told me that on our first night. A whispered confession in the starlight. It didn't have to mean anything, but I felt like it did.

I wondered what it would feel like if she trusted me enough to hear her voice.

"Yeah. But..." Her teeth dug into her lower lip. "I'm fine where I am. Besides, Ro's the lead."

"Really? That's awesome. And you're making her dress?"

"Yes!" Her blue eyes sparkled with excitement. "It's a musical based on a popular fairytale, and I feel like I have to do it justice."

"You will." I've only seen one of her projects, but I already knew it would be absolutely incredible.

She bobbed her head, looking down at the sketchpad and then back up to me. "Thank you."

"Anytime." I winked at her, dropping the piece of paper in my hand back onto her pile.

"I, uh... I think it's safe to say both of the events of this past week were a success."

Ella nodded. "I agree. Everyone seemed like they had fun." She cleared her throat. "I think we need another joint event for bonding, though. Get the groups together more," Ella said, biting the end of her pen. "We've got your service event next week, but..."

I hummed out a response, trying to think of something else to appease both of our advisors. The end of the semester was right around the corner, plus we had her sorority's ball all before dead week.

"I feel like this was a terrible idea," she groaned. "Planning everything at the last minute is the worst. I keep throwing things at Audrey, and she gives me that, *'really?'* look back."

It *was* true, although us planning things on top of our regular events we were supposed to attend *might* have had something to do with that. Parties didn't count, because the girls weren't allowed to host them in the sorority house, especially not with alcohol.

"I've got it." I grinned, unable to hold back my enthusiasm for an event I knew the guys would *love*. And Ella would *hate* it, which I would absolutely enjoy to no end.

She frowned. "Why are you grinning?" The pen came out of her mouth, and she pointed it at me. "I don't trust that look."

"Princess," I sighed. "When have I ever given you reason to doubt me?"

Those gorgeous blue eyes narrowed. "Cameron. I told you to stop calling me that."

"But I *like* it."

"What's your idea?"

"Laser tag."

Her eyes widened, and I wanted to know what she was thinking. Her expression quickly morphed into a frown. "What, guys against girls? No way."

I shook my head. "We'll divide everyone up. Intermix the teams. You want them to mingle, don't you? And then afterwards we'll feed everyone pizza." Ella just stared at me. "What? Everyone loves pizza." Even she couldn't disagree with that statement—it was a universal fact that college students loved pizza, especially *free* pizza.

"Fine. We'll do it your way."

"Of course we will. But... wait." I stopped her. "What was your idea?"

She shook her head, closing her notebook. "Nope."

"Ella." I frowned. "You can tell me." Reaching out, I placed my hand over hers. "I won't laugh."

"I was just going to suggest something stupid, anyway," she grumbled. "Like bowling or an ice cream social."

Both things that were easy to organize and could host a hoard of people. They had merits. "Those aren't dumb."

She rolled her eyes. "Yeah, but they're no laser tag either."

"You just don't like it when I'm right, do you?" I huffed in amusement.

"*Nope.*" She said the word with a little pop before shoving her papers and sketchbook back in her folder, and then into the backpack. "I should go."

"You're coming tonight, right?" I asked, hoping she'd say yes. It was crazy how I'd blinked, and the semester was already almost over. "To the party?"

And somehow, it felt like she was going to slip away from me. Sure, we still had things planned—and the formal—but after that, I wouldn't see her for over a month.

We'd be on winter break, and I'd be hours away from her in Vermont while she went home.

And it felt like the longer things went on, the more she pulled away from me.

"I don't know…"

"Ella," I rasped out, unable to help myself. "Please come. For me?"

She looked up at me, and I saw her work through the emotions on her face before she nodded. "Okay, fine. I'll be there."

I grinned. "Perfect."

I already couldn't wait.

"You have no chill," Stellan muttered as he caught me waiting by the door.

Maybe he was right, but I didn't care. I was just glad she'd agreed to come. The party was already in full swing in the background, but I didn't care.

Because she was *here*. Back in my house for the first time since Halloween.

"Hi, Princess," I say when her familiar blonde head of hair finally reached me, her sister at her side.

It was crazy, because despite being identical twins, they were so different. I'd thought it the first time, but the more time I spent with Ella, the more I knew I'd recognize her anywhere. And maybe that was just how deep she was under my skin that I felt like I had her entire being memorized, but she was the most gorgeous thing I'd ever seen.

"Hi." Her cheeks were pink, even the little tip of her nose—probably from the chilly walk over here in the November weather.

Either that, or my nickname flustered her. Maybe it made her think about that night we spent together. Which was possibly why I couldn't stop calling her it.

"Can I take your coat?" I offered, holding out my arm for the thick winter pea coat she was wearing with a scarf.

Ella looked down, as if realizing what she was wearing for the first time. "Oh. Sure." Pulling it off her body, she exposed a sexy little white wraparound dress that she'd worn with tights and a pair of wedged boots.

Audrey, in comparison, was wearing a tan sweater tucked into a pink skirt, and she leaned in to whisper something in Ella's ear before darting off into the crowd.

"Is that dress for me, Princess?" I murmured in her ear as I leaned in behind her.

"N-no."

"I think it is." I traced a finger up her spine, enjoying the feel of her bare skin under mine. It was as much as I dared to do. I wanted to pull her into my arms, to dance with her like we had on Halloween, to feel her lips under mine again—but I had to have patience.

I wanted her to want me the way I wanted her.

She shuddered at the motion. "Cam. We shouldn't." The fraternity house was teeming with both her sorority sisters and my fraternity brothers.

I sighed. "You're probably right."

"I always am," she insisted.

There's my stubborn girl, I thought, but instead of voicing it, I offered her my hand. "Want a drink?"

"Yes. Please."

I interlaced our fingers—not fucking caring what anyone thought—and headed towards the kitchen.

CHAPTER 13
Ella

For the second time this school year, I was standing in front of the Delta Sig house, a party waiting for me inside. Except this time, I also knew *who* was waiting for me on the other side, and it felt completely different.

"Audrey."

"Hm?" She turned to look at me, her cheeks slightly pink from the pre-gaming we'd done before coming.

"Don't let me make a mistake tonight."

"If you're asking me to make sure you end up in your room at the end of the night, Ell, I'm afraid I can't promise that."

Right. *My* room, because in the last week, I'd slowly moved all of my stuff. It was weird, separating all our clothes for the first time. We shared so many things—shoes, pants, hair accessories—and now, everything that had once been a pair was now all alone.

There was one perk, though: my new room also had a queen sized bed.

I was trying not to think too hard about the one in Cameron's room, the one I definitely would *not* find myself in tonight.

"I can't sleep with him again," I muttered under my breath. *Be strong, Ella. You can do this.*

It would be a disastrous mistake. One I couldn't take back.

"Ready?" she asked, her hand wrapped around the doorknob.

I nodded. "As I'll ever be."

Bringing the rim of the plastic cup to my lips, I let the sweet taste of raspberry lemonade and vodka explode on my tongue. He'd remembered. Of course he did.

I wasn't sure how I should feel about that. Maybe it had only been a few weeks, but it felt like he was constantly learning new things about me and tucking them away, like if only he could get a few more pieces, that he could assemble the puzzle that was *me*.

The worst part was he was right. I'd worn this damn dress for him, wanting him to pay attention to me. Wanting him to look at me like he was right now.

And *why*? I struggled to keep my composure around him. Maybe that was why I kept pushing him away. Why I kept insisting on this game between us. I needed to feel like I had some sort of upper ground, some foothold in this rivalry we'd created. Because if not, I'd have to admit the truth to myself, and that was not happening.

"Thank you," I said, though my voice wasn't as steady as I would have liked, and I hated how fast the alcohol seemed to affect my system.

That was the only explanation for how doe-eyed I currently felt.

"Of course, Ella."

God, I loved how he said my name. When he called me Princess, it was one thing, but *Ella*, in that deep, masculine voice of his... I wanted to melt.

I took another gulp of my drink, the smooth slide of the vodka down my throat distracting me from my thoughts.

He looked too good tonight. So good that I was forgetting why we'd been competing. Why I'd been determined to make him my rival. Why I couldn't fall back into his bed.

Friends with benefits could be fun, right?

He was wearing a dark gray henley and jeans, which should *not* have been delicious, but then I thought about how I'd explored his body, how he'd felt on top of me, and...

I shivered, but not from the cold.

"We should probably get back out there," I murmured, hands still wrapped around my cup so I couldn't reach for him.

"We should," he agreed.

Nodding, I looked up at him. At the way he was leaning over me, but his lips were just a few breaths away. If I leaned forward —just an inch...

But I didn't have to move because Cameron leaned in, his eyes holding mine. I wanted to get lost in them. To get lost in *him*. But I'd made a promise to myself. Not to fall back into his bed. Not to sleep with him again.

Those lips brushed against mine, and—

"We can't do this." I practically breathed the words into his mouth. He was that close.

"Why not?"

"Because we're *us*. There's too much at stake here to risk sleeping together again."

He hummed, the action going straight to my core. "But we're *us*." He said it like it was a completely different argument. "And we're good together. You know it too."

I shut my eyes. I might have wanted him, but that changed nothing. Didn't change the fact that he could have any girl he wanted. That he could have slept with a different girl every night since we'd met, and I wouldn't know the difference. But if that was all he wanted, I couldn't do it.

I'd realized that sex without feelings wasn't something I

could handle. If I slept with him again, I'd get attached. And I couldn't risk everything.

"I'm sorry," I said, slipping away from his body heat and back into the living room.

Audrey was sitting in the armchair, talking with one of Cam's guys. I was pretty sure he had introduced him to me last week—Jackson Richards.

Sitting on the arm of the chair next to my twin, I quickly gave Suzie and Peggy, who were sitting on the couch, a nod. They were all holding cards in their hand, and I realized through the laughter that they were playing Cards Against Humanity.

"Hey." I nudged my sister.

"Oh. Hi." Audrey looked at me with a question in her eyes. "Where's Cam?"

"He's..." I turned, looking back—and directly into his eyes.

"Right here," he said, coming to stand behind me. But he didn't move closer, didn't wrap his arms around me. None of the things I so desperately wanted, even if I couldn't allow myself to *need* them.

I shut my eyes, willing myself to be strong.

Another black card was chosen, everyone sitting around the table looking through to pick their best one.

"So, Audrey," Cam started, and I whipped my head around, eyes wide with concern. What could he possibly have to ask my sister?

Oh, God. He wouldn't ask her about *me*, would he? I might have told my twin, but I definitely hadn't told anyone else in my sorority that I'd hooked up with him. After all, I was trying to act professionally.

I didn't need any of them to think that the reason we were doing all of this was just because I wanted to hang out with my *boyfriend*. The idea tasted sour on my tongue. He wasn't my boyfriend, and he would never be.

"Ella told me you're doing a musical this spring." *Oh.* That wasn't what I'd expected.

My sister's entire body language changed, becoming more animated. "Yes! I'm so excited about it. Ella's making the costumes."

Cam's laugh was a deep, throaty chuckle. "I saw."

Audrey looked at me, one eyebrow raised, and then back at him as she put her card down. "I thought…"

"Oh." He shook his head. "No. I just saw her working on sketches at the library."

"They weren't very good." I hadn't even shown any of them to my twin yet. Most of what I'd drawn so far had ended up in the trashcan. They needed to be *perfect*, ethereal and woodsy and beautiful. "I'll figure it out."

"I know you will." The response came from Audrey, but it was Cam's face I focused on. The sincerity in them… I had to look away.

"You can always borrow my old fairytale books for inspiration," Peggy offered, picking up the stack of cards, and I perked up. "The illustrations are gorgeous."

"I'd love that." I'd found *some*, but I could fill a whole Pinterest board with ideas and still not have enough. Honestly, it was one of my favorite things, only matched when I stood in a room full of fabric samples and ran my fingers over the different textures.

The warmth from Cam's presence heated my back, and I could practically feel him there, even if he wasn't close enough to touch.

For the rest of the night, we chatted with the fraternity brothers and my sorority sisters gathered around the room. I tried to ignore his heated stare, taking a drink to ignore how much I wanted his lips on mine again, how every part of my body was screaming *yes* as my brain screamed *no*.

The weekend was over too quickly, and I tried to ignore the twinge of disappointment that nothing else had happened between Cam and I. I didn't want it to, and yet...

"Hey, Gus," I smiled, plopping into the chair next to him in our construction and draping class early Monday morning.

"Hi, Ella," Gus said, returning my smile as he tugged at his beanie. "How'd the party go?" He'd been meeting me after I'd run into Cam at the library, and I'd confided in him I didn't quite trust myself around him.

Something I hadn't even told my sister. She knew I'd slept with him, of course, and that a repeat was not in the cards, but... Maybe I'd just thought Gus would understand. He'd confessed his crush to me, after all.

"Fine." I flushed, ignoring the wave of dizziness that hit me suddenly. "I mean, it was good, it's just..." I rubbed at my temple.

"Are you okay?" He looked concerned. "You're not looking too good."

"I'm great," I said, though I wasn't quite feeling it. "Just tired."

He frowned. "Maybe you should go take a nap after class."

"I can't." A sigh escaped my lips. "I have class, and a million things to do." Plus, we had laser tag tonight. I'd be lucky if I even sat down to eat lunch today.

He just shook his head as our professor walked in to the classroom, and I fixed a smile on my face.

Everything was fine. I'd get through tonight, and then maybe the pounding in my head would subside.

Maybe I'd just take a nap first.

CHAPTER 14
Cam

I scanned the crowd, but there was one head of blonde hair completely absent from the crowd of sorority and fraternity kids who were excitedly chatting amongst themselves as we waited for the buses to take us to laser tag.

Like I'd promised, everyone was hyped up, and to my surprise, they didn't even complain about being paired up together. Some of my guys were excited as hell to play against each other. I didn't think it hurt that they also got the bonus of attempting to flirt with the Pi Rho girls.

But where was Ella?

I pulled out my phone, sending her a few texts in rapid succession.

CAM

Where are you?

We're leaving in 10 minutes.

If you don't text me back, I'm showing up at your door.

Are you okay?

ELLA

Don't come over. I sent Suzie to run the event in my place.

Just go. Have fun.

I frowned. It wasn't like her to not show up to an event. Especially not when she'd been so determined to prove me wrong throughout our little competition of hers. And maybe I was just a little worried.

Spotting her sister Audrey, I jogged over to her. "Hey. Is Ella okay?"

She looked concerned as well. "She said she didn't feel well, and she was going back to sleep."

"I'm going to go check on her," I said, the words slipping out before I could think better of them. I turned to look for my guys, spotting my Vice President, and handed him my clipboard. "You're in charge. Have fun!"

It was only a short walk back to the sorority houses, and the whole time, all I could think about was Ella. How bad was she to skip out on an event?

When I arrived at the sorority house, one girl was just leaving, and luckily let me slip in before the door closed.

My legs ate up the stairs up to her door, and when I finally reached her room, I practically banged on the door. I didn't hear any movement inside, so I knocked again. "Ella! I know you're in there."

Ella opened the door, skin pale, her eyes missing their usual sparkling pallor. "What?" She'd clearly been sleeping, her voice groggy as she looked at me. Her light blue sleep set looked damp with sweat, and I couldn't stop my frown as she shivered.

"Ella." I cupped her cheek, forcing her eyes to meet mine, and slid my other hand over her forehead. "Holy shit. You're burning up."

"I'm fine," she croaked, ignoring the obvious. "I-I just need some sleep."

"You're not fine. You're sick." I crossed my arms over my chest.

The stubborn girl formed her lips into a pout. "Just go without me. I'm going back to bed."

"Like hell I'm going and leaving you like this," I said, forcing myself inside her room. "Have you taken anything? Been drinking liquids?"

She shrugged, but said nothing else, just stared at me.

"I'm going to go get some stuff. You change out of these sweaty pajamas, alright?"

Ella looked down at herself, like she'd only just noticed what she was wearing. She nodded, toying with the ends of her ratty hair. "Maybe I should shower," she mumbled.

I nodded. "You do that, and I'll be right back, okay?" I made a mental checklist of things she'd need. It'd probably be easier for me to take care of her back at my place, since I had the room to myself, but I wanted her to feel comfortable.

After running into the small market on campus and grabbing a pack of Gatorade—blue raspberry flavored, since I knew that was her favorite—some soup, and other essentials she'd need, I swung back by my house and grabbed a few things from my room as well. Sweatpants, a t-shirt and sweatshirt, and my pillow. At the last minute, I grabbed an extra shirt, throwing it into the bag I'd carried just in case.

I'd grabbed her keycard on my way out to open the front door, letting myself in to her room without preamble.

She stood, still wrapped in her towel, looking a little less pale than she had a half hour ago. A hairbrush was in her hands as she brushed through her wet hair.

"How do you feel?" I asked, setting the bag of stuff down next to the bed.

"Like death," she admitted, sighing like the admission cost her. "It's probably the flu. My whole body hurts, and I have a headache, and it's like my body can't decide if I'm freezing cold or burning up."

"Okay." I nodded, taking the hairbrush from her.

"Hey." Ella reached for the brush back, but I shook my head.

"I got this." Working out the tangles, I let the damp strands settle against her back. When I finished, I set it down on the dresser.

Ella looked down at her towel, the color coming back to her cheeks as she blushed. "Um, I'll just..."

I turned around, facing the door as I listened to her rummage through her drawers. I didn't want to think about what she'd be putting on, nor her naked body. Now wasn't the time. Not when she was sick, and she needed someone to take care of her.

Clearing my throat, I said quietly, "I brought an extra shirt in there. In case you want it."

I hadn't forgotten the sight of her in my t-shirt that night, and maybe that was the reason I'd grabbed a second one out of my drawer. This one was a navy Delta Sigma shirt, but I'd picked it for the same reason I'd picked the first one.

"Mmm," she said, fabric rustling as she slipped it on over her body. "This is soft."

When I turned around, she stood, legs bare but everything covered by my shirt, too large for her slight frame. "It looks good on you," I said, the words catching in my throat.

She gave me a small smile. "You think?"

"Mhm."

"Well, then it's a good thing you're not getting it back." Ella wrapped her arms around herself. It was a good thing that even in her state, she still managed to joke around.

"Keep it," I agreed. It looked better on her, anyway.

I looked back at her bed. "Do you have clean sheets anywhere?"

Sitting on the edge of her desk, she nodded, directing me into the closet. Ella remained quiet as I stripped away her sheets, replacing them with new, clean ones. Once I finished, I began unpacking the rest of the things I'd brought.

I placed the bottle of Gatorade on her nightstand before

handing her the flu medicine I'd gotten at the store. "Take this," I instructed.

"Bossy," she whispered, but complied, drinking it down with the blue liquid.

With the flirty remark lingering in my thoughts, I retrieved my sweats from my bag in a hurry. "I'm gonna change into something more comfortable." I didn't exactly want to wear jeans as I took care of her. "Be right back."

Ella pulled back the clean sheets of her bed, and I nodded, glad that she was letting me take care of her. I'd let her sleep for a bit, and then I'd make her some soup later.

Heading down the hall to the singular male bathroom—there was one on each floor for guests—I swapped out my pants for the gray sweats and pulled on my sweatshirt.

Before I left, I pulled out my phone, typing out a text to my VP, Stellan. Even when I was disorganized, I knew I could always count on him to get things done.

CAM
Everything going okay?

STELLAN
Yeah, man. How's your girl?

CAM
She's got some sort of bug.

Just going to stay here with her in case she needs me.

Sorry to miss the event.

I held back the reply that she wasn't *my* girl, because I didn't want to deny it. That was what I wanted, even if she'd fought me at every single turn.

When I got back to her room, leaving my folded jeans on the floor, still holding the other bundle I'd brought back from the bathroom with me.

Climbing onto the bed, I settled in behind her, letting her rest her head against my chest. "Cameron—" she protested weakly. "I'll get you sick."

"Shh, baby. Just let me take care of you, okay?" I brushed the hair off her sweaty forehead, dabbing at her skin with the wet washcloth.

She nodded, snuggling into me further. "Okay." Her word was barely audible, but I heard it all the same.

"I'm sorry for making you miss it," she whispered.

"I'd rather be here." It was an admission I couldn't afford, but I'd said it, anyway.

"Mmm," she agreed sleepily, and I watched her eyes close as I traced my finger over her cheek.

Beautiful. Even like this, hair damp against her pillowcase, drowning in my shirt, skin flushed from fever, she was as beautiful as ever.

I placed a kiss on her forehead, wondering how I'd gotten so lucky as to find her.

Wondering how the hell I was going to keep her.

CHAPTER 15
Ella

There was a warm hand on my back, running a soothing motion over my spine, over and over. I couldn't remember the last time I'd been held like this. Maybe when I was a kid, and my mom had taken care of me? I snuggled in deeper, thankful for the soothing presence.

"*Ella,*" a warm voice called. A voice I wanted to burrow into. "Ella."

"Mmm." I buried my head into the warmth, inhaling a familiar, comforting scent. Spicy and delicious, and maybe a little like… *Charming.*

"Ella, baby. I need you to wake up and take some more medicine," the voice spoke again as a cool hand rested against my forehead. "We gotta get your fever down."

Groggily, I blinked my eyes open, finding my face buried in Cameron's chest. "What?"

He held out a hand with some pills before offering me a bottle of blue Gatorade. "Take these."

I nodded, gulping them down and chasing them with a swig of liquid, before his hand settled against my head again. The cool sensation almost made me moan, with how stark of contrast it had to my overheated body.

"What time is it?" I managed to get out, trying to focus even though my eyes hurt. We were supposed to leave for laser tag in the late afternoon after classes were over for the day, but looking out my window, it was dark outside.

It had started as a headache with some minor body aches until whatever I had hit me like a landslide.

Cam rubbed at my back, and I slumped against him. "*Sorryyouhaftatakecareofme*," I blurted out, slurring the words.

"It's fine." His voice was a rough chuckle. "Go back to sleep now."

"Okay." I sighed into his chest, letting my eyes flutter shut. "Why are you so cozy?" He had no business being the perfect pillow.

And I drifted back off into sleep.

The sun was shining through the window the next time I woke, and I groaned as I looked at my phone resting on my bedside table.

I'd missed my first class.

Pulling the covers back, I went to stand up, trying to ignore how weak my body felt.

"Oh, no you don't," came a voice slipping back in my door, carrying a tray of—

"Did you stay here all night?" My eyes grew wide.

Shit shit shit, I was so dead if Ilene found out. She didn't enforce a lot of rules, but we were *not* supposed to have boys stay over. If they were even in our rooms during the day, we had to keep our doors open.

He set the tray on my desk before coming over and forcing me back in bed.

"You're not going anywhere, missy."

I pouted. "Cam. I have to go to class. And you can't be here."

"You're still running a fever, so no, you most definitely can *not* go to class, Ella."

I rubbed a hand over my face. "You... stayed."

"Yes."

"And you took care of me."

"Yes." He said it so matter-of-factly, like he couldn't imagine doing anything else.

"Why?"

"*Why?*" His eyes bugged. "Jesus, Ella. Why do you think?"

I didn't know. Or maybe I just didn't want to think about it, because then I'd have to confront more uncomfortable truths.

"Here." He placed the tray on my lap. "Eat." I surveyed the food. Oatmeal, a bowl with pineapple, strawberries, and raspberries, and a little mandarin orange that had been peeled. Even all the little white stringy bits had been taken off. On the side was a mug of tea, a cold water bottle, and another little pack of flu medicine.

"How'd you do all of this?" Sure, we had some stuff in the kitchen, but...

He looked suddenly shy. "I asked Richard for Ilene's number."

"Your advisor?"

Cam nodded. "Yeah. She knows you're sick. And that I'm taking care of you."

"Oh."

She knew he was here.

He'd taken care of me, and he'd made sure my house mom knew, too. Never mind that we were breaking the rules.

I looked down at the oatmeal, my eyes swimming with emotion. Did he know what he was doing to my heart? I doubted it. "Thank you."

Spooning a mouthful of oatmeal in my mouth, I ate as Cam moved around my room, cleaning up.

"I would have emailed your professors that you couldn't make class today, too, except I don't know your password." I thought I detected a faint pink hue on his cheeks. "Or what classes you have."

"Is this your way of asking me for my class schedule?" I snorted, even though the action was a little painful. I really did ache *everywhere*. Ugh.

"I certainly wouldn't say *no* to it, Princess."

Rolling my eyes, I reached for my phone. "Not happening." Never mind the fact that the semester was almost over, anyway.

And that giving him my schedule felt way too much like being in a relationship, and we definitely weren't doing that.

"This is the absolute worst time to get sick," I groaned. "I have so much going on in classes this week."

"They'll understand." Cam came over, brushing my bangs off my clammy forehead.

"You should really go," I whispered. "I'll get you sick."

"Trying to get rid of me so soon?" He took the tablets off the tray, peeling off the back and waiting till I held out my hand to dump them in it. "I had the flu shot. I'll be fine. Besides, I hardly ever get sick."

"Spoken like a true man," I grumbled.

He cracked a smile. "I was beginning to think you'd forgot."

My face flushed as I took a deep inhale of the hot tea, spluttering it all over myself.

"Charming." I narrowed my eyes.

He grinned. "There's my Princess."

"I'm not *yours*."

He shrugged, handing me a napkin to clean up my chin and not saying another word as I finished the tray of food.

After I'd finished, he brandished my laptop, and after I'd sent out a few quick emails to my professors, I could already feel the exhaustion settling back into my bones.

Like the only thing my body wanted to do was *sleep*. "Don't you need to go to class?" I said with a yawn.

He waved me off. "Mine's not till later. It's fine."

Mmm. "Okay."

"Get some rest."

I closed my eyes, and when I'd almost fallen asleep once again, I swore I'd felt the press of his lips against my forehead.

Ella,

I'm sorry I couldn't be there when you woke up, but I had to get to class. There's soup for you to reheat in the fridge, and I left medicine and the thermometer by your bed. Make sure to keep drinking plenty of fluids and some vitamin C.

If you need anything, text me.

I mean it, Princess. Anything.

Cam

"Damn him for being so perfect." It wasn't fair. He was a Prince Charming in every sense of the word.

A knock sounded on my door, and I looked down. I was still wearing his t-shirt. Picking up one shoulder, I sniffed it, comforted by the faint smell of him that was left behind.

"Who is it?" I asked, and Audrey poked her head in.

"Are you feeling any better?"

I shook my head, a resounding *no*. "Don't come in here. I don't want you to catch it right before finals." Not when hers required her full range of motion and her *voice*.

"Ilene told me what happened."

"Oh?"

"I think she's a little smitten with your boy. I can't blame her."

"He's not *mine*," I groaned.

"Sure, sure." Audrey waved me off. "Keep telling yourself that."

"He risked a lot taking care of me," I murmured, knowing how many rules Ilene had allowed him to break. Curfew, no boys... And that didn't even include him giving up laser tag, even if he'd seemed fine with it. Or how he'd held me all night, even if I could definitely give him the same bug I had now.

"You never even let me take care of you like that," Ro complained.

"That's because I don't want you to get sick, too. Our bodies are identical. They do stupid things."

"Still. That doesn't stop you from taking care of me."

"Okay... Fair point." I winced. "It wasn't like I was given an option. I was too out of it last night to realize what Cam was doing, and by the time I wasn't just asleep all day, he'd already left."

I showed her the note.

"Ella."

"What?" I frowned.

"He might not be yours... But you're definitely *his*."

"That's not... No." I couldn't deny it fast enough.

"He *likes* you, Ella Grace. Admit it."

Not the *full name* drop. I rolled my eyes at my sister. "We're not even friends, not really. And we've basically been fighting all month. We're—"

"Is that what you call it? Fighting?" Audrey smirked. "I'd call it *flirting*."

"Ro. He's not interested in me like that. He's just..." I didn't know what he was. "Invested in this partnership going well." I swallowed roughly. Yup. That was it.

"Sure." She patted my knee through the sheets. "Keep telling yourself that."

"Audrey."

"Mm?"

Instead of looking at her, I wrapped my blanket around my shoulders and gazed out the window. "I'm scared." The words were a soft whisper.

"Of what?"

"Getting my heart broken." Again.

I didn't think I'd survive a second time. Not when I already liked him this much, even when I kept denying it.

"Oh, Ell." Audrey climbed onto the bed, wrapping her arms around my shoulders. "I don't think you have to be scared of him."

"Why not?"

"Because in the last few weeks that I've seen him talk to you, I've never seen him so much as look at another girl. Not one." She rubbed soothing circles over my back. "So… maybe let him in a little."

I blinked. I'd just assumed that he'd been sleeping around. If we'd hooked up the first night we'd met, what was stopping him from doing that with someone else? "But…"

She shushed me, putting a finger over my lips. "Do you want something for dinner? I'm on Ella duty tonight."

"I'm feeling better, I promise." I'd probably sweat out most of the bug, anyway. Whatever I had hit me like a train wreck, but thanks to Cam and his continued assurance that I took medicine and drank liquids, I already felt way more like a person than I had yesterday.

Which meant I probably needed to suck it up and be a human again.

And then find Cameron and thank him for taking care of me.

My cheeks flushed as I thought about the way he'd dropped everything. Called me *baby*.

Maybe I'd been wrong about a lot of things.

CHAPTER 16
Cam

"There's the winning quarterback!" I exclaimed, slapping James on the back. We'd won our home game this week, and the fraternity house was full of rowdy college kids, all celebrating.

My eyes were practically glued to the door, waiting for Ella to come in. It had been almost a week since I'd taken care of her with the flu. We'd texted since, but I hadn't seen her in person.

I didn't want to admit the fact that I missed her. But I did.

It was weird, because it had only been a few weeks that we'd been spending time together, but I couldn't help but look forward to every encounter. There was always something new, a moment between us, a memory that I'd store away for safekeeping. I couldn't help but feel like we were slowly chipping away at whatever walls she'd put up.

We were playing the game between us, but I also wanted her to know that this wasn't just a hookup for me. That there wasn't another motive behind me wanting to spend time with her. Sure, if spending time together ended up with my face between her thighs, I'd be the happiest fucking man alive, but that wasn't what I craved.

Her attention was the greatest reward she could give me.

"Hi, Cam," a redhead—Amelia, I was pretty sure her name was—batted her eyelashes at me. She wasn't from Ella's sorority, but I knew she was in one of them. I moved a few feet away, still staring at the door.

"Hello," I said, keeping my face blank, my tone devoid of all emotion as I waited for the blonde, whose presence always made me feel lighter, to walk in to the frat house.

Another body slid up to my other side—a dark-haired girl. Danica? I was pretty sure they were sisters, though I had no idea who was older, just that I'd seen them around before.

"You look lonely," she said, and I shook my head. Stepping off to the side again.

"I'm just waiting for someone."

"Maybe…" Amelia started. Her lips were dangerously close to my neck, and it felt slimy. I didn't want her near me—didn't like her proximity to me at all. I tried to step back, but the other sister cornered me as well. "We could keep you company while you wait."

Did they not hear a single word I'd said? "I'm good. Thanks."

"But—" Danica put her hand on my bicep, and I shrugged it off, pushing away from them.

"I said I'm good. I don't…" I grit my teeth, my eyes connecting with Ella's.

When had she gotten here? How much had she seen?

"Ella," I murmured, walking towards her, but she was faster, bolting out the back door. "Fuck." I growled the words to no one, heading outside.

When I caught up with her, I grabbed her wrist, pulling her around to face me. "It's not what it looked like."

She did her best to look unaffected, but I could see what was bubbling under the surface. "Cam, I… It's none of my business what you do. It's not like we're together."

"I'm not sleeping with anyone else, Ella." Grabbing her face, I held it in my hands. "I haven't. Not since Halloween."

"Okay," she breathed out, but she wasn't making eye contact

with me. It was like she was determined to look anywhere *but* at me.

"Ella. Look at me." My voice was rough. I needed her to understand. Needed her to know how much she fucking undid me. How I couldn't get her out of my thoughts.

When her eyes finally connected with mine, I couldn't stop myself.

This time, I didn't ask. This time, I kissed her.

"I'm not fucking sleeping with anyone else. I don't want to, either." Leaning in, I held her gaze as I pressed our foreheads together. "There's been no one but you." *Not since I'd laid eyes on her for the first time.*

Pressing my lips to hers, softer this time, I felt some of the anger melt away from her frame.

"I'm not mad at you," she finally gasped out, her hand curling into my sweatshirt.

"You're not?" I raised an eyebrow, because it seemed like she was.

"No. I'm mad at myself." Her cheeks flushed red. "For being *jealous*. And them, because they wouldn't leave you alone. They just—" She let out a huff of anger, which I found surprisingly adorable.

"Hey." I squeezed her hands. "It's okay."

"No. It's not." Ella huffed. "Cameron…"

I kissed her again, if for no other reason than to shut her up. Not because I liked the way it felt when her lips were on mine, or I thought I might die without it.

"Hi," I murmured when she finally looked me in the eye.

"Hi." Her forehead connected with my chest. "I don't know what's wrong with me."

A chuckle escaped from my lips. "*Nothing* is wrong with you. You're perfect." I meant it, too. "Are you feeling better?" I'd been concerned all week. Had she eaten enough? Taken her meds?

She nodded. "Yeah. Thank goodness. Not sure I could have spent one more minute cooped up in that room." Ella took a deep breath. "I never got to thank you. For taking care of me. Whatever you told Ilene…" Her shoulders sagged. "You saved me. I could have gotten seriously in trouble for you spending the night." The toe of her shoe dug into the grass, and I could tell she was trying to distract herself with the action.

"I just did what anyone would do."

"No." She shook her head. "You did more than that, and you know it. No one else would have…" Ella cleared her throat, finally looking at me again. "In any case, I owe you."

I can't hold myself back from brushing one strand of her hair back behind her ear. She had left it down today, and I was so obsessed with her hair that I couldn't help it. "You don't owe me."

"Hmm?"

"You. Don't. Owe. Me." I paused at each individual word. "I don't want a favor for taking care of you, Ella." My throat constricted at the thought, trying to choke out the words. "Not when I couldn't even think of leaving you like that." I'd always been a natural caregiver. Ever since I was little, I'd always wanted to take care of the people around me. The people I cared about. My little—I cut off the thought. It was too hard.

But this? It was more than just wanting to make sure she was okay. I needed it.

"I…" Her hand wrapped around my wrist, pulling me behind her, and I let her guide me into the house.

"What are we doing?"

She slammed the door shut and swiftly locked it behind her. "I don't *know*," she huffed out, turning on her heel to face me. I'd thought I'd tempered her anger, but suddenly it had flared up again. "Who won the bet?"

I shook my head. "Don't know. I stopped keeping count." I never really had been. "Why?"

When she spun around, all I could see was just in her eyes. Pure need.

"You promised me," she whispered, her voice rough.

Like I'd be able to forget that.

She didn't need to tell me twice.

Pinning her up against the bathroom door, I kissed her *hard*. My tongue swept into her mouth, demanding, *taking*. I kissed her like it was the last time I'd ever be able to, because I didn't know if this *would* ever happen again. So I was going to take my time and devour her properly. I lifted her hips, bringing our mouths to an even better angle.

Pulling away, I focused on her face. "What do you need, baby?" I hadn't been able to stop myself when the endearment slipped out before, and I certainly wouldn't stop now.

"I want you to fuck me," Ella groaned, "like you *mean* it." She wrapped her legs around my waist, her core grinding against me.

God, but I wanted to. If the painful bulge in my pants was any sign, I'd needed it, too. But this wasn't my bedroom, and I wasn't thinking clearly enough to drag her back in there.

"*Princess.*" I nipped at her neck. "I don't have anything on me."

While I'd love nothing more than to bury myself in her tight, wet heat, I couldn't risk that. I'd never gone without a condom before, and even if she was on birth control, there was always a chance.

"But I promised you an orgasm," I started, my lips splitting with a devilish smile, "so that's what you'll get."

"I didn't win, though," she breathed out as I lifted her onto the bathroom counter. Like she wasn't thinking clearly, either.

Because making her come was *my* prize, but suddenly, she made it sound like it was hers, too.

"This way, we both win." My eyes sparkled with mischief as I kneeled in front of her, pushing her panties to the side to thrust my tongue inside of her, groaning the minute her taste exploded on my tongue.

"Fuck," Ella groaned as I licked her, taking the time to reacquaint myself with her body. It had been almost a month since

Halloween, since we'd been together last, and yet this was what I'd been unable to get off of my mind. Her. Her taste. The feeling of my head being buried between her thighs.

It was everything I wanted. Everything I needed.

"I've missed this…" I groaned, pulling away to look up at her even as I remained between her thighs. "Tasting you on my tongue."

"Don't stop," she pleaded, her fingers twisting into my hair, guiding me back where she wanted.

I was happy to oblige—licking, sucking, even the scrape of my teeth against her clit, spurring her on.

Ella moaned, and the sound was music to my ears. "Yes," she cried. "Right there. *Yes.*"

"Come for me, Princess," I murmured. "I wanna feel you clenching around my tongue."

Pressing my thumb against her clit as I continued fucking her with my tongue, gentle strokes I knew had to be driving her insane from the way her breaths had shallowed out, those little gasps that were like gold fucking stars.

I was right—she was the ultimate prize.

"Cam, I-I'm so close—" was the only warning I got before her orgasm hit, the long moan drowning out everything else as her pussy fluttered around me. I licked up her release, only pulling my thumb away as her body loosened.

Standing up, her grip on my hair loosened, and I straightened her panties.

Ella scrambled for the button of my pants, trying to open it.

"No." I kissed her roughly, messily, letting her taste herself on my lips. "That was enough for me." I'd take care of myself later. For now, at least she'd given me this.

"But…" She frowned, her fingers running over my painful erection. "You don't want me to take care of you?" Cocking her head to the side, she observed me with curious eyes.

"This was about you." I brushed the hair off her forehead, her cheeks flushed from the release. "That was our deal, remember?"

"Right."

I held out a hand, and she hopped off the counter.

Fuck, as much as I wanted her mouth on me, to be inside of her, this was worth it. Because I was slowly gaining her trust, and that was *everything*.

Because little by little… I was winning over Ella Ashford, and every victory was sweeter than the last.

CHAPTER 17
Ella

"C*am*," I moaned, throwing my head back as he ravished me with that damn tongue.

"You're so fucking beautiful when I go down on you, Princess," he praised. "Such a good girl."

I wasn't sure if it was his words, or whatever he was doing with his mouth, but I came *hard*, the rush through my body stirring me.

My eyes opened. Fuck me. A dream. It was a dream.

I was dreaming about him now, too?

How did he get under my skin so easily? With one touch, one look, one *taste*, I was practically on fire.

It had been five days since our frantic bathroom hook-up at his frat party, and I'd done my best to avoid him. Next week was dead week, which meant that the only event we had left to get through together this semester was… The formal.

The formal that I still didn't have a date for. Not technically. I probably could have asked someone to go with me—anyone, really—but I hadn't.

Why hadn't I?

Oh, right. There was my problem. Cameron *Charming*

Edwards, who'd screwed up my brain and make me unable to think straight for the last month.

It was a miracle I'd even gotten my stitching right for my class projects, let alone focus on studying.

Such a good girl. I closed my eyes, but his voice was all I could hear.

But when he'd told me he didn't need more... it had stung. Because I wanted to go down on him, too, and he hadn't let me.

I'd never been especially confident about it, and because of that, I never did it with any of the guys I'd hooked up with.

But Cam was different. Special. I knew he'd take care of me, that he'd make sure I was comfortable even as he used me however he wanted.

And yet... My eyes stung. *This was about you. That was our deal, remember?*

I'd also basically begged him to fuck me, and even if he'd made me come on his tongue, he hadn't given me any more of him.

Shit. What was I *doing*? How was I letting myself get so caught up in a guy?

"I'm an idiot," I said with a groan, shoving my hands over my eyes as I collapsed back into my pillow.

It would be fine. He'd taken what he wanted from me, so now... all of it would be over, anyway, wouldn't it?

The fighting, the... flirting. The spending time together.

I should have felt relieved. Maybe this way I wouldn't feel like I was going to internally combust every time his thigh pressed against mine.

But I wasn't. The truth was, I didn't want to stop seeing him. Didn't want the semester to end, and Cam and I to stop being... what were we, anyway?

Friends? Or was it something more?

My mind kept drifting back to that first night, the way he'd looked at me, *touched* me. The way his eyes hadn't been able to stay off of me, even when we were just talking about mundane topics.

You want him, my body whispered to me. Or maybe that was my head? I didn't think it was my heart, but maybe she was a fickle beast, too.

I wanted.

Damn him.

That dream was still on my mind later when I went to get dinner, and saw him sitting alone with a plate of food in front of him. Quickly making up my mind, I changed directions, heading straight for him.

I slid in to the booth in front of Cameron as he raised an eyebrow. "I didn't know we were meeting tonight."

"We weren't. But I saw you sitting alone, and I thought I'd join you." I placed my tray down, finally taking a moment to look up at him.

At those eyes that had looked up at me in my dreams. I shivered, a full body movement that I was hoping I could blame on the fact that I wasn't wearing a jacket, even though it was plenty warm inside the commons.

He was smiling. "Hi, Princess. Did you miss me?"

"No," I denied, taking a bite of my food instead of answering truthfully.

"I think you did. I think that's why you sought me out."

Why had I thought this was a good idea? "I can leave," I muttered, getting ready to stand up.

His hand slid over mine, holding onto my wrist. "No. Don't go."

The way he was holding on felt like he was holding onto me like a lifeline.

I nodded. "Okay."

We ate in silence for a moment before the sound of sneakers squeaking on the tile floor caught my attention, and I looked up to find three men—three *tall, athletically built* men—standing in front of us.

"Did you get started without us?" One of them asked. He had dark hair, bright blue eyes, wide shoulders, and a cocky grin on his face.

The lankier one—a brunette wearing a CU Baseball shirt—looked over at me. "Oh. Shit. You've got company." Though he looked familiar, I couldn't quite place him.

"Um. Hi." I did my best not to gape at all of them staring down at me.

"Yes." Cameron glared at the rest of them. "Go away."

"Now, that's no way to treat your best friends." The first one grinned, offering me a hand. "Hi, I'm James."

"Erikson." Cam rolled his eyes. "Leave her alone."

The third one—with auburn hair—chose this moment to speak up. "Come on, scooch in. My soup's getting cold."

Of course, Cam and I ended up smack dab in the middle of the circular booth, our legs pressed up against each other and his friends on either side of us.

"Ella," he sighed, like he couldn't believe we'd ended up here. "These are, unfortunately, my best friends. James Erikson," he pointed at the one with black hair, darker than his own, "Forest Carter," the brunette—who I now realized I recognized as Sutton's boyfriend—"and Adam Prince." The slightly grumpy one with reddish hair. "Guys, this is Ella." He nodded at me.

"Hi." I gave a hesitant wave. "It's nice to meet you."

Taking another bite of my salad, I watched the four guys, seeing how comfortable they were with each other. They almost acted like brothers.

"So... what are you all majoring in?" I asked, figuring maybe I should get to know these guys that Cam was so close to. Not for any specific reason, and certainly not because I thought I'd be sticking around him, but if they were important to him, well...

James—the tallest of the bunch—gaped at me and then looked over at Cameron. "She doesn't know who we are?"

Cam shrugged. "Didn't know who I was, either."

I blinked. "What?"

"Do you not pay attention?" Adam frowned on the other side of me.

Clearly not. "Not sure what I was supposed to be paying attention to." I shrugged.

"This guy," Cam said with a laugh, pointing at James with his thumb, "is the star of the football team. Forest is on the baseball team, and Adam, well..." He cocked his head at his friend. "What do you do again?"

Adam grumbled. "You know damn well what I do."

I didn't feel like getting in the middle of their conversation, so I gave a mumbled, "Oh." Was I the only girl on campus who didn't know the four of them? I had paid little attention to boys in the last year. Not since that disaster of a party. I'd sworn off crushes, even. I didn't need a man to make me happy—I could do that myself.

Forest gave me a warm smile from my side. "Hi, Ella."

"Hi. It's been a while."

"Wait. You two know each other?" Cam blinked, his eyes full of surprise.

Forest nodded. "She's friends with Sutton. Get it together, Edwards."

"So you knew?" Cam said, the tone of his voice almost... upset? But that didn't make any sense.

"No. Not until later."

"Knew what?" I whispered to Forest.

Cam shook his head, but his friend just smiled. "Nothing."

I rolled my eyes. "Way to keep a girl in the dark." Spearing my dessert—a pumpkin pie—with my fork, I took another bite, trying to tune out the noise of four college guys surrounding me.

When I looked up, Cameron's eyes were on me, searching my face. It was like he needed to make sure I was okay. "What?" I murmured, putting my fork down. My plate was practically empty, and I was full, anyway.

"You're just..." He glanced over at the other three guys, who seemed deep in some conversation about sports that I knew I wouldn't understand, even if I'd tried. "Quiet."

"So?"

"You're not usually quiet. Not around me."

"Oh." Maybe that was true. He got all of my fight, all the sass in my body—but in truth, I was an introvert. Socializing with people I didn't know took a lot of energy out of me. It had never been like that with him, though—I'd never felt like talking to him was an effort. It had always just been comfortable. "I'm just..."

Quiet around new people, because I never knew what to say to them. But how did I explain that to Cameron? He was so charming, outgoing and well-spoken. So he wouldn't understand why I was like this. Definitely not.

Cam bumped his shoulder into mine. "You ready for your fall formal, Princess?"

I realized quickly what he was doing. Trying to distract me. "I think so." We'd rented out the University's large ballroom space for it, and even though there were a ton of things that would have to be done day-of, once we could start setting up, I was as ready as I could be. "I'm... really excited." The formal was practically my *baby*, and even when I'd been vice president, I'd had a hand in planning it from the beginning.

Everything was going to be perfect, from the theme to the decorations.

"And then the semester will be over, and..." We'd stop seeing each other every week. I frowned at the thought. Why did I not like the idea of not seeing him regularly? I frowned.

"Are you going to miss me, Ella?" He asked, wiggling his eyebrows, repeating his earlier question.

"No." But the statement came out too quickly, and I could tell he knew I was just denying it.

Maybe I was.

A little.

Not that I was going to tell him that.

Sparkling lights were hanging on the ceiling, and the rest of the room was currently being decked out like a glittering, winter wonderland.

"We're here," came a familiar voice at my back as I guided the decorations into place.

Spinning around, I found Cam and a hoard of fraternity boys behind him.

"What are you doing here?" I asked, my eyebrow raising as I stepped back.

"Thought you could use some help." He shrugged. "Figured we could do the heavy lifting."

"Oh." My cheeks warmed.

He was here to help. Not because he had to be. I certainly hadn't asked. But maybe because he… wanted to be?

I tilted my head as I considered the thought—and then brushed it away. This was no time to be thinking about things like that. Not when our relationship—friendship, or whatever this was—had an expiration date. And hookups or not, I couldn't do this kind of thing without getting attached.

But maybe that was the truth. I was already attached. I liked him. I *liked* Cameron Edwards, despite every reason I shouldn't.

"Thank you."

"Of course." He nodded to the guys, who dispersed, each finding a girl currently putting up decorations and helping to take over.

My hands on my hips, I watched as my girls instructed his guys, and the flow of teamwork was almost overwhelming. It was almost like everyone was in… sync. After the last few weeks, of everyone spending time together, bonding, even serving the community together... It was like one family.

When I looked up at Cam, I couldn't help the pride that rushed through my body.

"Need help with anything else?" The words were whispered in my ear. It was *intimate,* and the shiver that ran down my spine was anything but appropriate for our current location.

"I don't think so," I said, watching the guys secure more decorations to the walls as the girls directed them from below. Dang, they were good. And I hadn't even needed to lift a finger.

"Ella?" Peggy's voice called, and I turned, finding her and Suzie holding boxes of t-shirts. "Where do you want the merch? Do we have a table?"

"Oh." I looked around the room. "Maybe in that corner?" I pointed, biting my lip as I considered the ideal flow of the room. We'd set up the DJ in front of the dance floor, and the photo booth was off to the side, but I forgot to mark off where the t-shirts and merch would go on today's floor-plan.

Our philanthropy was important, and considering a portion of our t-shirts would go towards that, as well as funds for running the sorority, they needed to be somewhere visible enough, yet not distracting from the flow or the event.

By the time I'd settled that fiasco, all the decor had been hung, and the tables that dotted the edges of the ballroom were fully decked out with their centerpieces. It felt like everywhere I turned, someone else had another problem that I had to fix, but when I stepped back, surveying the entire room, I knew it had all been worth it.

"It looks... incredible. Wow." I said the words to myself, but it wasn't long until I felt a warm presence at my back—and somehow, without looking, I knew exactly who I would find there.

"You're pretty good at this, Princess."

"What? Party planning?" I rolled my eyes.

He shook his head. "No. Leading."

Oh. My cheeks warmed under his gaze. "I mean, I just—"

"No. They listen to you. Because they trust you, and they believe in you. They *want* to follow you." He nudged my shoulder with his arm. "You can't fake that. It comes naturally."

Maybe he was right. I'd been overwhelmed that I wasn't doing enough, that I wasn't good enough to be president, but... I felt better now. I could do this. Maybe even *enjoyed* doing it. "Thank you." I dipped my head. *I've tried.*

"Of course."

"I have to go change," I said to Cam, ignoring the butterflies in my stomach.

"I'll see you tonight, Princess," he gave me a wink before disappearing through the door, probably going to do the same thing.

And the smile that split my face made me realize... I couldn't wait.

Not for the dance, but knowing I'd get to spend time with *him*.

CHAPTER 18
Cam

The girls really had outdone themselves, and we were just fucking lucky they'd let us come along.

I stood in line, tickets in hand.

Maybe I shouldn't have purchased two. Maybe I didn't *need* to. I certainly hadn't asked anyone to be my date. Didn't want anyone to be—anyone except for Ella.

The beautiful girl in the silver gown currently hurrying towards me. Fuck, but she was gorgeous. The most captivating girl in the room. Stunning, and sparkling, and there wasn't a thing in the world that could keep me from being by her side.

That was the truth, wasn't it? The reason I'd done everything I had this last month? Because I wanted her. I wanted… more.

"You didn't have to buy a ticket," is what she said when she finally reached me.

I shrugged. "Wanted to." It was the least I could do, wasn't it? Supporting her sorority? Getting all my guys to be here?

"Two?" she asked, her eyes filled with a hint of confusion. "Why do you have…"

Before I could let the hurt cloud over her face, I pushed the piece of paper into her hand. "The second one's for you, Princess."

"Oh. But…" She frowned. "You don't have a date?"

"No." I leaned in close enough for my lips to brush against her ear as her hands slid up onto the lapel of my suit. "Besides. There's only one girl I'd want to be my date." I pause for dramatic effect, dying to run my hands through her perfectly styled hair. "And that's the one in front of me right now."

"Cam." Her voice was quiet, like maybe she hadn't realized it yet.

"Be my date, Ella." Picking up her hand, I gave it a kiss. "Please."

She looked away for a beat before her eyes connected with mine. Those beautiful baby blues widened. Like whatever she found on my face, she'd deemed acceptable. "Okay."

I took a step back to look at her fully. "Princess, this is… Wow. You look…" A rough swallow. Gorgeous. Completely stunning. "Did you make this?" Reaching out, I rubbed the shimmery fabric between my fingers.

"Yes." Ella smiled, her entire face lighting up with the action. "Thank you."

Beautiful didn't even begin to describe it.

Reaching the front of the line, I handed my tickets to the sorority member collecting them, and then Ella slid her arm into mine.

"Hi, Ella," the girl at the table said to my date—because fuck yeah, she'd said yes.

"Cam, you know Suzie, right? She's the one who took over my position when I became president."

I nodded. I'd seen her around at the other events, and at the last party at the frat house, but I honestly had paid little attention to her. Any time Ella was around, it was like my gaze was locked on her. Like there was no one else I'd rather look at.

"Right. Hi." I gave a small smile to the mousy-brown-haired girl.

"Nice to see you again, Cameron."

I nodded, saying our goodbyes as we headed into the ballroom.

There was a photographer at the entrance, capturing photos of the couples walking in like it was a prom, and I looked at the girl on my arm. "Shall we?"

"You want to take a photo together?"

I hummed in response. "Well, you are my date, aren't you?"

"I think you're my date, especially if we're considering the fact that this is my event. You were just lucky enough to be invited."

There was no stopping the grin on my face. "Whatever you say, Princess. Either way, tonight, you're mine." I pulled her towards the photographer, leaning in to speak directly into her ear. "And I want a photo so I can look back at how fucking beautiful you are later."

Her cheeks turned an adorable shade of pink, somehow perfectly complimenting the lipstick she wore.

The photographer posed us, snapped a few photos, and then had us try a different pose.

"Happy now?" Ella said under her breath as we finished.

We walked towards the now-crowded dance floor, hundreds of college students dancing to whatever pop song was popular right now. I barely paid attention to any of it as Ella slipped her hand in mine.

"Yes." I flashed my teeth. "Very."

Not about the pictures, but because she was close enough, I could smell her perfume, those notes I'd decided were raspberry and peony and something else that was sweet, and all of it was so *her* I thought I'd never get sick of it.

"Well... What should we do next?"

"You tell me. It's your event." I looked down at her and watched as she bit her lip.

Ella was looking at all of it like she was seeing it for the first time, like she'd realized only just now that she could actually enjoy the event, and not just supervise to make sure everyone else was having a good time.

"They'll be fine," I whispered into her ear. "I think we can leave them alone to manage for a bit."

"I know. It's just…" She looked up at me through her lashes. "It's been a while since I did this."

I smirked, snaking an arm around her waist and squeezing her ass. "And what, exactly, my darling Princess, do you think this is?"

"Cam!" There was that pretty pink color again. "We're surrounded by people."

"So?"

"So…" She shook her head. "I just don't want anyone to get the wrong idea."

"If you think about it, it makes sense."

"What?"

"The two presidents spending the evening together. And it's not like they don't know we're not dating anyone." *Else*, my brain mentally filled in.

Because I sure as hell hadn't looked at another girl since this one had come tumbling into my life.

I was really fucking grateful for those shoes.

Our uninterrupted time together didn't last long—before we were surrounded by people. Girls congratulating Ella on the event, and my guys, who were all giving me thumbs up when they saw who was at my side.

"*Ellaaa*!" an excited girl practically screamed in my ear. "You look beautiful!"

"Thank you." The brunette girl pulled Ella in for a big hug. Her friend was a little tipsy, slightly slurring her words, but she seemed like she was having a good time, so I didn't comment.

"You made this?" the girl asked, touching Ella's dress, just like I had earlier. Like it was impossible to not reach out and feel that shimmering, splendid fabric that hugged her curves just right.

Ella's face lit up. "I did. I wasn't sure if I was going to have it done in time, but…" She raised her shoulders. "Miracles happen, I guess."

Like that miracle wasn't her and how fucking talented she was. It constantly blew me away.

Her sorority sister gave her a slight pout. "When are you making me one?"

I cocked my head, looking at the girl whose blue lace dress cut off at the knees. I was pretty sure I remembered her, but I couldn't place her name. Something that started with a W— "Wendy, right?"

Her eyes turned to me, as if she hadn't even realized I was here.

"*Ohmygod*," the girl slurred her words together, so they all came out at once. "You're here with him? *Cameron Edwards?*" It was like the wheels in her brain were turning, placing us together. "But he's—"

This statement was addressed to Ella, but I was the one who responded, wrapping my arm around her waist and tucking her body into mine. "Yes. I'm her date."

Ella's lip slightly tilted up as she processed my statement.

"I don't know when I'll have time," she addressed her friend. "There's already a lot of projects on my plate between classes, working on my portfolio, and doing the costumes for the spring musical."

Her designs for the musical had been on my mind, but I didn't want to pry. Especially not if she was stressed out, because I knew how one comment could pile on when you were already worried about something.

"Oh, that's too bad." The girl pouted, and I shook my head. I knew it was right on the tip of Ella's tongue to say *yes*, to promise something else, because I didn't think she knew how to say no.

"Sorry to cut this short," I addressed the brunette before steering my date away. "But Ella and I were just heading towards the refreshments."

"Oh. No worries." She waved goodbye, darting back into the crowd to a red-headed fraternity member that I recognized—Peter.

Huh. Good for them. I gave him a wave before we continued on our mission.

"Do you know everyone?" Ella groaned as we walked away.

I chuckled. "No. I just tried to remember your sorority sister's names. Seemed like the least I could do." The thought of why else she might think that soured in my stomach.

She hummed in response as we slid up to the bar, ordering two drinks. I was grateful for the glass, as it gave me something to do—sipping at my drink instead of confessing all my thoughts to her.

"Will you let me watch?" I finally asked.

"Hm?"

"Can I watch you sew sometime?" I cleared my throat. *Was that weird?*

She made a face. "It's not that exciting, you know. And I end up sticking needles into my finger an embarrassing amount of times."

I shrugged. "Don't mind." I didn't care if it was the most boring thing in the world—I wanted to watch her work. Wanted to memorize every face she made, to watch her work if only so I could get into her head.

"Okay."

"Yeah? You'll let me watch you?"

"Stop saying it like that," she mumbled. "You're making it sound dirty."

I laughed, an inaudible sound I couldn't control. Dipping my head low, I brought my lips to her ear. "Only if you want it to be,

Princess. Don't forget how much I enjoy making you come." I liked how much taller than her I was, standing at six foot two, even when she wore her heels.

Ella spluttered, practically spitting out her drink before glaring at me. "Cameron!" She teetered on them slightly, like I'd made her off balance, and I shot out a hand to steady her.

Handing her a napkin, she quickly dabbed at her chin before poking me in the arm. "Enough of that. Let's just have an enjoyable night."

"Who said we weren't?" I was having a great time.

For what must have been the dozenth time since we'd got here this evening, I looked around the room at the crowd. Everyone was laughing, smiling, dancing—and an awful lot of grinding that I wasn't sure belonged on a dance floor, even at college. Still, it was obvious how much all the members were enjoying themselves.

"I have to say, Princess, I'm glad we're not competing anymore."

She blinked. "What? Why not?"

"Because there's no way I could have beaten this. You did... amazing."

"Well, I had help. There's a whole committee." She looked away, almost... shy?

Like this wasn't an extremely successful, large-scale event she'd put on. That she was *running*, leading, even if she didn't want to phrase it like that. Ella deserved the praise for making sure everything came together. And like it or not, I was giving that to her.

"You're incredible."

"What?" Her breath caught.

"I don't think people tell you that enough, and I think that's a damn shame, Princess. You're constantly surprising me."

She gave a small laugh. "And that's a good thing?"

"Yes." I leaned in closer. "Definitely."

Ella stared out at the dance floor as her free hand ran over her hip, playing with the fabric as it settled onto her thighs. There was a wistful expression on her face, and I wasn't one to leave her longing.

The tempo changed to a slow song, and I held out my hand to her. "Care for a dance, Princess?"

"Cam..." Her voice was quiet, her eyes wide as she looked up at me.

"Come on. We missed out on the music for the first time. This time, we should do it right."

I knew she was thinking the same thing I was when she looked over at me, her breathing growing deeper. About the first night, and how good we'd been together.

"Let's dance," she agreed, taking my hand in hers.

"Thought you'd never ask," I said, giving her a wink before twirling her off to the dance floor—her hand in mine, the other on my shoulder as I curled mine around her waist.

Keeping her body close to mine like I'd wanted to all night.

Knowing that no matter what happened, I didn't want this to end. I didn't want to stop seeing Ella Ashford.

Which meant I needed to figure out a way to make her *mine*.

CHAPTER 19
Ella

A hand wrapped around my wrist, tugging me through the curtains.

"What the—"

"Shh, Princess," Cam's voice soothed. "It's just me."

"Charming!" I slapped his shoulder for good measure. "You scared me."

He smirked, pulling me in closer to his body. "Seemed like the only way I could get your attention. Everyone needed you."

"And did you?"

"What?"

"Need me?" I fluttered my eyelashes. Like the conversation we'd had only days ago wasn't playing in my mind on a loop.

"Fuck." Laughing, Cam tugged my body into his. "Always, Princess." He looked around for a moment, like he was deciding if the coast was clear, and then dipped his head, capturing my lips with his. It was everything I'd wanted. Everything I *needed*.

I melted into his arms, into the kiss, like we weren't in the middle of the hallway, both of our organizations on the other side of a thin piece of fabric.

Fuck, I couldn't get enough of him when he kissed me like this. Everything else just melted away, and it was just him and me and the way he was coaxing my mouth open. His hands slipped in my hair, and it was *everything*—

"Cam," I warned, as his grip dug into my hip—though his hand was desperately close to my thigh slit. Where I wanted it, needed it. And yet... "We can't."

Not here. Not where anyone could find us as I let him have his *charming* way with me.

"You say that, but..." His fingers dragged up the bare skin of my arms as his breath ghosted over my neck. "If I touch you, you're going to be wet for me, aren't you?"

His eyes flared with liquid lust.

I whimpered, because he *would*. How could I deny it? I had been—all night.

"*Ella*," he groaned.

"Not here," I whispered, holding onto his arms, like I needed him to stay standing. Maybe I did. And wasn't that the craziest part of all of this? How he knew just how to affect me? I hated how one touch, one word, hell, even one *look*, and I was melting for him.

"Come on." He pulled me towards a supply closet, barely big enough for the both of us to fit inside of it.

"Better?" Cam asked, and I could almost feel the smirk on his face rather than see it.

"Shut up and kiss me," I muttered, and my lips were back on his before he could say anything else.

I was all too aware of his presence, even in the dark closet, the cracks of light only giving us the faintest of illuminations.

His lips moved down to my neck, kissing and sucking, though never long enough to leave a mark, as if he knew I wouldn't want to be discovered, knew that this thing between us was still secret, and I didn't know how to feel about that.

Because on the one hand, I didn't want anyone to find out. And yet... I wanted him to mark me. Wanted the proof that I was *his*. Wanted to claim him in front of everyone, consequences be damned.

Pulling my dress up, his hand danced along my inner thigh before finding what he was looking for. And I knew he'd be proved right, but I didn't care, as long as he touched me, as long as—

"You're not wearing any panties?" He groaned, his fingers brushing over my core as I held back a moan.

I shook my head. "Didn't want them to show. The fabric—" It hugged my hips, and panty seams were not exactly my style.

"Are you trying to kill me?" Those lips found mine again, but he didn't give me what I wanted. But I wasn't above begging as I shifted my hips, desperate for friction. "Dripping wet for me, huh, Princess?"

"*Yes*," I agreed as he dipped a finger inside of me. I spread my legs further apart for him, resting my weight against the shelf so that I wouldn't fall. Trying to kill him? He was killing *me*. "Please."

"What do you want?"

"*More*," I begged, squirming in his hold.

"You're gonna be quiet for me, aren't you? My good girl."

I nodded, because I wanted to be his good girl.

One of his hands wrapped over my mouth as he added another finger, slowly plunging them in and out of my wet entrance.

"Fuck, look how good you're taking my fingers," he muttered almost mindlessly as he crooked his fingers inside of me. "I wish I could put my mouth on that pretty cunt of yours, baby."

I whimpered. I wanted that too. But I couldn't tell him as much, given that his hand was keeping me from letting out a ridiculously loud moan.

"I need you in my bed next time. Fuck."

Yes. Yes, a bed would be good. Much better than a stuffy closet.

Cam pressed the heel of his palm against my clit, and it only took a few more strokes with the added pressure before I was coming, and I bit down on his hand to stop from screaming his name.

I slumped against him as relief spread throughout my whole body.

"Feeling better?" He chuckled.

I nodded against the fabric of his jacket, wordless.

It wasn't enough, though. It would never be enough with him, not when I knew what it felt like when he filled me, so completely, reaching places in my body that no one had before, that even in all of my self-discovery I'd never even found.

Pulling his fingers out of me, the lewd wet sounds somehow louder in the small space. He brought those fingers up to my mouth, rubbing them over my lips.

"Taste yourself," Cam breathed, his eyes focused on my face as he slid those two fingers inside, letting me suck off my release from his skin.

God, that shouldn't have been so hot. It was erotic and ridiculous, tasting myself on his skin, as he watched me with a reverent breath.

It was that thought that had me moving as soon as he pulled his hand away. Before he could seal his lips against mine once more, I pulled away.

"I want you," I said, scrambling to unzip his dress pants. It had been so long since I'd had him inside of me, and that was a damn shame. Why hadn't I spent the last month doing this? Why hadn't I spent every night in his bed?

"Ella." His voice was rough, commanding. "Stop."

"Why?" I whined, a squirming, needy mess. The proof of that was all over his fingers, and I needed more.

He shook his head. "We can't." Even with the dark lighting, I thought I could make out a look of disappointment on his face. "I don't... have anything."

Right, condoms. How did we keep ending up in these situations? I knew it wasn't smart, that what I was offering to him was irresponsible and incredibly risky, but I didn't care.

"I'm on birth control."

Cameron's eyes connected with mine, and I watched as his gaze dropped to my lips, then back up.

At that moment, I wanted him to kiss me. Practically *needed* it.

My eyes fluttered shut, and I waited for the soft press of his lips on mine—but it didn't come.

I was a second away from begging when he spoke. "Ella." My name was barely a murmur as his hand moved to cup my jaw. He tilted up my chin, forcing our gazes together even in that dark closet. "As much as I want to be inside of you bare, and fuck, I do... We shouldn't."

"Oh." I stepped back, rejection stinging at my eyes. *Why was I so stupid?* He wanted me, but not like that.

Cam's face had morphed into a strange expression—one I thought looked a lot like longing, though I didn't know quite how to place it at the time—when I reopened them.

"What?" I frowned. "You're the one who just rejected me."

"Do you regret it?" His swallow was rough. "Me."

"No." I shook my head. It had been incredible. How could I regret the way his body could make mine practically *sing*? "How could I?" I always wanted him. Leaning up on my toes, I pressed a soft kiss to the corner of his mouth as if in demonstration. "I told you I want you." My hand pressed against the bulge of his slacks, finding the outline of his erection. Despite his body's response, he was pushing me away. I didn't know why.

Then a thought occurred to me. "Do you not... want me?" Maybe that was worse. He'd been chasing after me, sure, but... I thought I might die of mortification if he said that he regretted *me*.

"No." He winced. "I mean, *yes*, I do, I just... I want..." He struggled with his words. "More."

"What? More sex?" I struggled not to make a pained face, but it was hard. Maybe I *was* right, and that was all he'd wanted from me all along. Sex—good sex, great sex, even—but I was just a body to warm his bed. The blood drained from my face.

Pulling away, I was suddenly aware of just how cold it was outside when his body heat left mine.

"No." He caught my wrist before I could grab the doorknob, holding me in place.

I almost growled in frustration. "What are you saying, Cameron?"

"I like you, Ella. I want *you*. All of you. And until you're ready to admit that you want me, too..."

"But I *do* want you."

"Not like that. Not the way I want you."

I frowned. "Cameron. You're not making any sense." Sex, I could deal with. Sex made *sense*.

But what he was asking me for now... I bit my lip, unable to take my eyes off of his face even in the dim closet. Us, together in bed, we made sense. Everything else was the part that I didn't know how to deal with.

The flirty, charming mask fell away, and the man I'd gotten to know was all that was left underneath.

"I don't just want a hookup, Ella. I want *all* of you. Your mind." He tapped my forehead. "Your heart." He ran the same finger down to my chest, circling the spot where my heart must have been beating a million miles per minute. "And your body, too, yes. But not just someone to fuck. And if that's all this is to you..." He trailed off, not finishing the thought.

"Is that what you think?" I grimaced. "That I've just been using you for your body?" That stung. And it was even worse, because I'd just been thinking that of *him*. I winced.

"I don't know what to think. That's the problem."

"Cameron..."

He tilted my chin up to bring our eyes together. "I'm willing to fight for you. But I need to know that you want to fight for me, too. So until you are..." He shook his head. "We shouldn't do this anymore."

I blinked. "Are you telling me you're withholding sex until I tell you I *like* you?" Crossing my arms over my chest, I pouted at him. "That seems like a terrible punishment."

"If anyone's being punished, it's me, Princess. Because I'm always going to make you come."

My cheeks were hot as he lowered my leg back down to the floor, helping me straighten my dress.

He placed a kiss on my forehead before sliding out the door, only stopping at the last minute to make eye contact with me.

"You know where to find me when you decide what you want, baby." Cam looked serious. "I just hope that's me."

I didn't come out for a few minutes, not until my breathing had returned to normal and my cheeks stopped being on fire, and all I could think about were his words.

I want you.

But what did I want?

"Where were you?" Audrey murmured, looking behind me as if she expected someone to be right behind me.

"Bathroom," I murmured, because it was better than the truth. *Getting an orgasm* seemed like the wrong thing to say here.

"Did you lose Cam?" She asked, looking around.

"No." I mean, I had, but not in the way she was thinking.

Since he left me in the closet, I hadn't caught a glimpse of him. I didn't know if he'd left, or if he was simply avoiding me, but I didn't like the fact that he might have left without even saying goodbye.

After all we'd been through together in the last month, I think I deserved a little more than that.

A deep sigh ripped from my lungs, and Audrey glanced over at me. "You okay?"

"I will be." Once I figured out what I wanted.

But first... I had to get through the rest of this semester.

I was scared if I told him the truth—that I'd wanted him, always, ever since that first night, that I'd get attached. And when something happened, and we inevitably fell apart, I'd be the one picking up the pieces of my shattered heart.

Something I couldn't deal with again.

Straightening my shoulders, I headed back to the dance floor, in search of a *strong* glass of punch.

He wanted me, and as much as I hated to admit it to myself, I wanted him too.

CHAPTER 20
Ella

Unfurling my arms, I yawned as I looked at the car packed with our belongings. Fall semester was over, finals were finished, and we were ready to go.

Audrey had volunteered to take the first shift driving up to Vermont, but I wasn't complaining. It wasn't super far, but seven hours was a long time to drive straight through.

"Are you sure you two will be okay?" My mom asked on the phone, calling to check in on us after we'd said goodbye to Ilene and the sorority house for break.

"Yes, Mom," I said, huffing out a little breath of annoyance even though I really loved her. "We'll be fine. And we'll be home before Christmas."

"Okay. Just… call me later? The roads can get icy this time of year."

"We will, Mom," I murmured, looking over at Ro. "Love you." We said our goodbyes, and then I hung up.

"She's just worried about us, you know."

I sighed. "I do."

How could I *not* know? Maybe she was a little overbearing sometimes, but it was how she showed her love. And I loved her for always making sure we were okay. Even if sometimes I wasn't okay, and I didn't know how to lie to her about it.

"Ready to go?" Audrey asked, adjusting her sweater cuffs. It was always weird to see my twin in anything other than a dress. Even in the middle of winter, she'd just pull on fleece-lined tights with her dresses or skirts, so it was jarring when I saw her in jeans. Except...

"Wait." I frowned. "Are those *my* jeans?" I was pretty sure she didn't even own a pair. Especially not that specific pair.

"Um... maybe?" She tugged at the neck of her sweater that was adorned with a stripe of white lace on the bottom.

"I would have said yes if you'd asked," I grumbled. "We're not even living in the same room anymore! When did you sneak in and take them?"

She laughed. "I have my ways. Come on, let's hit the road before it gets too late. Do you want coffee?" Audrey asked as she climbed into the driver's seat.

"Yes. Definitely." It was *desperately* needed. I was just glad that finals were over and so were all other activities until spring semester started. "I cannot wait for this break."

From classes. From the sorority, and all of the responsibilities that came with being president. And most of all, from Charming, and the confusing myriad of emotions that came with him.

Especially considering the way he'd texted me every day since the formal, but he'd never pressured me into making a decision. Just sent me little notes to tell me he was thinking about me.

Maybe that was what had me second guessing everything. Because he didn't fit into any of my pre-conceived notions, and I knew it. So why was it fair that I was holding them against him?

All Cam had ever done was show me that he liked me, that he cared. And what had I done? Pushed him away—ran away? It wasn't fair to him, and I knew it.

Something I planned on telling him as soon as winter break was over.

Because it wasn't a conversation I wanted to have over the phone.

Audrey pulled off onto the highway, and once our coffee was in hand—iced, since it it didn't matter what the temperature was outside, I was a cold coffee girl—I finally relaxed into my seat.

A few hours later, we stopped for gas and food, which was absolutely necessary considering it was the afternoon and the only thing we'd had so far today was coffee.

"Want to take the next shift?" Audrey asked, holding out the keys as we approached the car, bags of snacks and drinks in hand. The tank was filled, and so were our stomachs, which meant that it was time to get back on the road.

"You just don't want to drive in the snow," I muttered as I accepted them, heading around to the driver's side.

She gave me a guilty smile even as she settled into the passenger seat.

After I'd gotten back onto the road, checking the GPS and our ETA so Audrey could update Sutton, we fell back into our usual comfortable conversations. We talked about our favorite designers, our favorite books, and the classes we were looking forward to next semester. The thing about going to the same college as your sibling was sometimes you got to take classes together—I always loved being able to work on assignments or study together—and sometimes you took the same professor that they did before.

It was nice having that to bond over and to give each other tips on.

Our other biggest topic of conversation? The trip. We'd never gone on a vacation before without our parents, which was strange.

"What are you looking forward to?" Audrey asked, glancing

over at me. "It's been forever since we've gone skiing." It really had. Our mom had broken her tibia when we were younger, and my family had gone from skiing every season to hardly at all.

"Sutton said there's a hot tub, right?" Nothing sounded better to me right now than relaxing my sore muscles, especially after being on the road for so long. "Also, definitely looking forward to her desserts." My mouth practically watered at the thought.

She was in pastry school and I would happily eat whatever she'd made. Especially if she whipped up one of her famous apple turnovers. *Yum.*

Ro joined me with a slight moan. "Yes. Fingers crossed."

The rest of our drive was filled with random conversations, singing Taylor Swift at the top of our lungs, and a comfortable silence that could only exist in a car with your best friend. When you didn't need to say anything at all to feel perfectly at home.

"Turn right here," my sister instructed as I pulled off the snowy road, onto the smaller, one lane road that would bring us to the house they'd rented.

"Are you sad Parker couldn't come?" I asked, the thought suddenly occurring to me.

She'd been spending more time with him ever since they'd run into each other at the Halloween party, and it wasn't often that she went without mentioning his name. Parker this, Parker that. He'd transferred to Castleton to play on our lacrosse team, something that Audrey had also mentioned to me—about a dozen times.

She fidgeted with the fabric of her sweater instead of looking over at me as I drove down the narrow road. "No. I mean, it would have been weird, right?"

"Weird." I blinked at her. "Why?"

"Because... he doesn't know everyone. I wouldn't have wanted him to be uncomfortable."

I raised an eyebrow. "Audrey. He's a student athlete. I don't feel like it would be that crazy, considering..." I trailed off, groaning as a thought occurred to me.

Sutton's boyfriend was Forest. Forest's best friends were... "Oh my god. *No.*"

What were the odds?

The house came into view, and I quickly threw the car into park, my eyes landing on the porch. Hitting my head onto the steering wheel, I cursed internally.

"Huh?" Audrey asked, poking her head up as she followed my line of vision. "What's—Oh."

"*He's* here." Logically, I should have been able to piece this together myself. "Charming." Cam and Forest were friends, and Sutton had said her boyfriend's friends were coming. Still, I hadn't thought about the fact that I'd somehow agreed to spend winter break *together.* "I'm so stupid. Sutton's boyfriend is Forest. Cam's best friend."

Audrey winced. "Maybe it won't be so bad? I thought things were good between you?"

Good, as in the orgasms he gave me, *yes.* Good, as in the way I was feeling about him? I was still conflicted, fighting the emotions raging through me.

Shrugging my shoulders, I turned to face her. "They were. They *are.* Sort of. I don't know." I released a deep exhale. "Everything's been weird lately."

"Weird... how?" Ro just raised an eyebrow. "Weirder than you two trying to outdo each other at events? Because Ella, that was..."

"Ugh. I know." My cheeks heated, thinking about our weird not-quite rivalry. Maybe it just boiled down to our sexual tension. "It's more than that."

More than hooking up on Halloween or how he would make me come without ever expecting any reciprocation. What was with that? It would have been so much easier to dislike him if he'd have let me return the favor. But he wouldn't even let me touch him.

And the worst part of all of it—I wanted to say *yes*.

Even if I wasn't supposed to like him, or want him, or any of the things that were currently running through my brain. And I certainly wasn't supposed to want more from him.

But that was exactly what he'd asked me for.

More.

I thought I'd have all of winter break to process my feelings—without him being around me twenty-four/seven. That I could prepare myself for what I'd say when I saw him again in January.

So much for *that*.

"What is?" Audrey asked, bringing me back to the conversation.

I gripped the steering wheel tighter, like we weren't currently whisper-shouting in a parked car.

"*Everything!*" Where did I even begin?

"You like him."

"Ugh. Yes." I rubbed my forehead with my pointer finger, because I couldn't deny that.

"And that's the problem."

I snorted. "*Clearly*."

"Ella."

"Yeah?"

"We should probably get out of the car." Audrey tilted her head towards the porch. "Everyone's staring at us."

"Oh. Right." She was right—the guys were all standing on the porch, staring at the car, besides Sutton, who was waving excitedly at us.

I swallowed roughly, then gave her a pointed stare. "Not a word of this. To anyone."

"Who would I tell?" She shrugged. "Your *boyfriend?*"

"Audrey Rose!" I gasped. "You wouldn't dare."

Her eyes twinkled. "You didn't deny it."

God, he looked good, with a dark gray henley on and a pair of jeans, normal and yet mouthwatering all at once. The worst part was knowing what he looked like underneath those clothes,

"Ells."

I was too busy staring at Charming to hear what she'd said. "What?"

"That he's your boyfriend. You didn't deny it."

Oh. I guess I hadn't.

"Well, he's not." I crossed my arms over my chest. "Now help me unload the car, please."

Opening my door, I wrapped my arms around myself before finding my coat in the backseat and pulling it on. Better, but it was still chilly outside, and my boots crunched the snow on the ground as I went around to the back of the car.

"I got it," came the voice that I loved, the one that had whispered countless filthy things in my ear.

"Hi, Cam." How was it possible that just his presence had my heart stuttering in my chest?

My eyes connected with his, and it was impossible to miss the way his gaze drifted down to my lips and then back up.

Like he wanted to kiss me.

Right here, in front of all our friends.

God, were we doing this? Was I really going to say yes? To... *more*?

"Hi, Princess."

"Hey." I cleared my throat. "Guess we should get inside, huh?"

He only hummed in response as Forest grabbed Audrey's duffel and the other guys grabbed the rest of the bags from the car.

Locking it behind us, I walked the few steps up the porch to the gorgeous house—I didn't want to know how we could all afford this, because it also looked giant.

"Audrey! Ella!" Sutton's nose was pink and her hands were shoved into the pockets of her red flannel as we joined her on the deck. Her excitement was obvious as she wrapped us both up in a hug. "I'm so excited that you're here!" Her voice grew low as she whispered, "Thanks for keeping me company. Four guys is *way* too many."

Cam chuckled behind us. "Imagine living in a frat house."

"Not sure the football house is much better," James cracked as he opened the door, and Forest rolled his eyes behind them as they all walked inside.

"Don't stay out too long." Forest kissed Sutton's forehead before joining them.

"It really is cold out here," Audrey agreed, rubbing her hands together. We hadn't really piled the layers on since we'd been driving, but I was regretting not grabbing a scarf or something.

Sutton laughed. "Agreed. The house is already nice and toasty. The guys got a fire going and everything."

"Ooh." That sounded nice. Wasting no time, we shuffled in behind them.

"When did you guys get in?" I asked Sutton as we headed towards the living room.

"Only about an hour or so before you. Forest and I drove up together since we're going to spend Christmas with his parents, and then the rest of the guys came up together."

"That must be nice," Audrey said with a lovesick smile. "Having someone to spend Christmas with."

"Yeah." Sutton sighed. "I'm really lucky."

I wondered what that was like. To have someone to go through life with. To love.

Because I'd always had Audrey, but it wasn't the same. And even past boyfriends, men whose names I didn't even want to remember, I hadn't loved them like that.

Like they were it.

But *what if?* The thought danced around my brain, like an annoying fly I couldn't quite swat away. But it took root; grew bigger and bigger. Like a pumpkin growing on the vine, I couldn't stop it. *What if I had someone like that?*

I stopped myself before I thought about the next question.

The one that I thought might be the undoing of me. I could admit that I liked him to myself, but any more than that... *No.*

"Yeah," I finally mused. "You really are."

Audrey had abandoned her coat and boots, and was warming herself by the fire when the guys came back into the room, plopping down on various couches and chairs.

"Your stuff is in the room at the end of the hall," Forest offered. "Figured you two would want to share."

"Sure."

"Sutton and Forest are in the master, and the rest of us have our own rooms," James added, like that was an important tidbit. That the rest of them would sleep *alone*.

I looked over at Cam and caught him staring at me, his gaze so focused and intense that I couldn't look away. It was like he was asking with his eyes. If I wanted to share his bed, all I had to do was ask.

It was simple, really. I just had to tell him what I wanted. *Him.*

"Big house," I mused, wondering where they'd found a five-bedroom house that hadn't cost an arm and a leg to rent during this time of year.

Adam made a sound with his throat, but said nothing.

Yawning, I stretched my arms. "I think I'm gonna go freshen up, and then maybe take a nap. It was a long drive up here."

I was tired—but also; I wanted a moment to compose myself. That was what I told myself as I found the bedroom Audrey and I would share, and slipped my coat off, hanging it on the rack before turning to my suitcase to unpack.

Or maybe that was just the excuse.

Especially when someone else slipped in the door a few moments later.

CHAPTER 21
Cam

She was *here*. Spending winter break with me.

After the formal, everything had been so busy between studying during dead week and finals that I didn't even have a chance to see her. Texting her stupid little things that reminded me of her was all I could do to not feel like she was slipping away from me.

So this felt a little bit like fate, us being together for break. Even if it wasn't planned, it was everything I could have asked for.

I thought back to when Forest had first proposed the idea, a chance to distract myself from the beautiful blonde girl I couldn't get out of my mind.

My Halloween hook-up. The thought made me snort. If only I'd known exactly how much time I'd spend with her after that.

Still, I'd never imagined she'd be here. Even though I'd wanted to invite her, especially after the formal, I hadn't. It felt like too much, and she hadn't even said that she wanted to be with me.

So the idea had sat inside of me like a lead weight, pulling me down and down.

And despite all that, it was like fate had intervened, bringing me the girl in a sparkling carriage—never mind that it wasn't pulled by horses—she was here.

"You didn't tell me the friends that Sutton were bringing were Ella and her sister," I whispered to Forest as we walked into the house, carrying their bags in for them. It was the least we could all do. I was a big fan of chivalry, and if I couldn't carry my girl's bags in for her, what was the point of all the hours I spent in the gym?

He gave me a guilty look. "It never came up."

I shook my head. "Beginning to think you just have a selective memory when it comes to Ella."

We headed towards the room we'd picked for Ella and Audrey. Even though if I'd have had my way, she would have been sleeping in my bed.

It was my biggest regret after the formal. That I'd stopped it before things could go further. That I hadn't taken her back to my place afterwards. That I'd only had her in a bed once. That I'd never gotten to wake up next to her.

But I couldn't push too hard, because I had the feeling I would lose her entirely if I did.

"Or maybe you're the one who never asked," Forest muttered as we set the bags down.

I sighed. "Maybe not." Why would I have thought to?

"Either way, she's here," he said, patting me on the shoulder. "And now you have the chance to really woo her."

"Woo her?" I raised an eyebrow.

My friend chuckled. "Yeah, man. Buy her flowers and shit. Girls love that. Make her dinner. Take her on an *actual* date. Not that weird sorority and fraternity competition you were doing. *Woo her.* Show her how you feel."

"That's... actually a great idea."

I'd spent the semester flirting, even agreeing to her silly competition just to spend time with her, but I hadn't really shown her I was serious about her.

Not yet.

"And that's why he's the one with a girlfriend," James said, another one of Audrey and Ella's bags joining the ones we'd carried.

"Hey, we don't *want* girlfriends," Adam mused as he entered last. "I don't want to do all that crap. And neither do you, Erikson." He elbowed our baseball-playing friend.

Forest's sigh echoed through the room as we walked back into the hallway. "One day, Adam, you're going to eat your words, and I cannot wait to be there to see you totally stumble when you actually have someone you *like*."

"Unlikely."

It was my turn to laugh. Because I'd been the same sorry piece of shit at the beginning of this year, hadn't I? Not wanting to get attached to anyone. Having one-night stands or drunken hookups at the frat house. And yet one night, one conversation with Ella had been enough for me to forget all of that.

She'd captured my attention. Captivated me. And all I wanted was *more*. More time with her. More moments alone.

"How much you wanna bet she's not going to spend even one night in here?" Adam murmured to James. "Just look at him. He looks like he's one second away from barging in and sweeping her off her feet like some caveman."

"I can hear you, assholes."

He might have been right, but I still wouldn't give him the satisfaction of agreeing with him.

Rolling my eyes, I headed back to the living room.

Back to Ella.

My feet had practically moved on their own as Ella went to the bedroom. She was like a magnet, and there was only one purpose in my mind. *To be near her.*

"You're here." I hadn't been able to stop the words from slipping out.

I leaned against the door frame, staring at the back of her head as I held myself back from reaching out to touch her. To confirm that she was real and not a figment of my imagination.

To stop myself from running my fingers through the hair I loved so much. Or burying my nose into her neck to inhale her scent that always calmed me.

"Cameron." She looked up at me, her eyes filled with a myriad of emotions I didn't know how to translate. "I didn't know…"

"It's not like we talked about our break, Ella." I bumped the door with my hip, shutting it behind me as I entered the room.

"I didn't mean to intrude on your trip." Her voice was quiet.

Did she think I didn't want her here?

"Intrude? Fuck that. I'm happy you're here."

"You are? But…"

"I told you I wanted more, Ella. In what world would that mean I didn't want to see you?" I shoved my hands in my jeans pockets to stop myself from cupping her cheek.

"Mmm, well… good." She stepped forward, her hands finding my chest, smoothing up towards my pecs.

"*Good*?" I repeated, breathless. What did that mean?

Was she saying yes?

Ella leaned up, pressing a soft kiss to the corner of my lips. "Mhm." My hands wrapped around her hips as she repeated the motion to the other side.

"Hi," she said as she pulled away. "I'm happy to see you, too."

This time, I kissed her. Just a gentle press, but I couldn't stop smiling through it.

"Do you still want to… you know… clean up?" I raised my eyebrows suggestively.

"Cam!" she laughed as she smacked me on the shoulder. "We're not going to do that *now*, when everyone's outside."

"So… later, then?" I smirked, kissing her again.

"Maybe."

Smacking her ass, I gave her a flirty smile.

"I'll be waiting," I said. "Come find me when you're done."

Because I wanted to hear her answer, and I hoped it would be the yes that I'd been waiting for. The sparkle in her eye gave me hope that it was.

Half an hour later, Ella rejoined us in the living room, hair damp from a quick shower, and dressed in an oversized sweater and leggings.

The rest of us were scattered about the living room, Forest and Adam playing the newest FIFA game on the TV as the rest of us chatted.

Sutton and Audrey were curled up under a blanket on the armchair, clearly gossiping over boys.

My girl sat down on the arm of the couch next to me—not quite close enough that we were touching, but close enough so I could smell the sweet raspberry and floral scent of her.

"So, what's the plan for today?" Ella asked, her voice sounding calm and collected. Nothing like it had before in her room.

The guys shrugged. "Figured we'd settle in, maybe go to the grocery store later," Sutton remarked. "And then if you want to go skiing, we can get ski passes and rentals tomorrow?"

I was only half listening as Sutton explained, as I drew circles on the fabric of the couch next to Ella's knee.

I only started listening again when I realized James was talking to my girl.

"Is Ella short for anything?" James asked, flashing her a flirty smile. "Daniella, or Isabella, or…"

I held myself back from growling at my best friend. Maybe it was possessive of me, but I didn't want him flirting with her.

"No. My Mom just liked it." She fidgeted with her sweater.

"Any nicknames?" He asked, and her eyes met mine.

She held my gaze even as she answered, "No."

My lips curled up into a smile. *That's my girl.*

Because I called her Princess, and I knew for a fact that Audrey had her own nicknames, but I liked the idea that those were reserved for us.

Out of the corner of my eye, I watched Ella's fingers dance on the back of the chair next to my shoulder.

In response, I brushed my hand against her knee.

Shit, we were doing it, weren't we? Acting like we couldn't keep our hands off of each other. When had it started? When she'd been sick? Ella might have wanted to deny it, but we both knew the truth. That there was something more here than physical attraction.

Sutton loudly cleared her throat, pulling Forest up off the couch, who only weakly protested about the game. "We're gonna head to the store and get stuff for dinner. Anyone else want to come?"

Adam looked up. "I'll come. I don't mind cooking if you want to do dessert."

My friend beamed. "I think I can work with that." She grabbed the keys. "Who wants to drive?"

Forest took them, wrapping his hands around hers. "I got it."

Ella shook her head, looking out the window. "I might go explore."

"I'll come with you," I said without a second thought. If she wanted to go walk around outside, like hell, I was going to let her go alone.

James declined Sutton's offer, and the happy couple left, hand in hand, as Adam trailed behind them.

Audrey had pulled out a book and was curled up in the armchair, a blanket over her lap. I had half a mind to warn James away from Ella's twin, but it didn't appear I needed to, because he hadn't made a single flirty remark towards her.

Huh. Was he just doing it to Ella to mess with me?

"Okay. I'm gonna go grab my coat and boots," she murmured in response, heading into her room.

I did the same, both of us meeting in the front room. Ella had pulled on a white beanie with a giant pompom on top over her blonde locks, and the light blue down jacket she'd pulled on brought out her eyes.

"Beautiful," I whispered, running a finger over her cheekbone before she pulled away, clearing her throat. Like I needed the reminder of who else was in the house and might hear us.

Like I cared.

I didn't mind if they all knew that we were together.

But that required us to actually *be* together.

I opened the door for her, following her out into the winter wonderland. Up here in the mountains, everything was covered in a thick blanket of snow, and there was nothing quite like it.

Ella slipped her hand into mine, and I stuck both of our hands in my pocket.

"So." Ella finally said, a few minutes into our stroll. I liked this—wandering with no purpose. The neighborhood was full of large houses, just like the one we were staying in, and many had strung up lights for Christmas.

"So."

"About what happened at the dance."

I'd expected this—known it was coming—and suddenly, I wasn't afraid of what her answer might be anymore. Not with her hand interlaced in mine, and not with her presence close enough to provide a balm to my soul.

I could have flirted. Could have dropped the *'When I made you come on my fingers in a closet?'* line, with a smirk on my face. But I didn't do any of that. Instead I said, "Yeah?" With my heart practically in my throat.

"Do you still want that? All those things you said?" She

turned to look at me fully, her bright blue eyes practically pinning me in place.

I like you, Ella. I want you. All of you. My words echoed in my mind.

Yes, I still meant them. How could I not? How could I not want her? Not when she'd eclipsed my world in a blanket of light blue, glitter and raspberry, and all I wanted was *more*.

"Yes."

"So we're doing this?"

"Are you saying you like me, Princess?"

Her cheeks were already pink from the cold, her nose an adorable shade of red, but they deepened as she blushed. "Maybe."

I laced our other hands together. Bent my forehead down to rest against hers.

"Tell me you want this. Us. That it's not just about sex."

I want all of you. Your mind. Your heart. Your body. All of those words I'd said.

"It's not just about sex," she confirmed, her gaze suddenly more focused on our hands between us than me. "You make me feel comfortable. I like spending time with you. I…" Ella shook her head, watching as I ran my thumb over her knuckles. "I want this. I want us. I want *you*."

"Thank fuck," I breathed, dropping our hands so I could tilt up her chin—bringing those beautiful eyes back to mine.

"Cameron?" Her voice was breathy, needy.

"Yes, baby?"

"Kiss me."

"I thought you'd never ask."

And then her lips were on mine—or maybe mine were on hers, because I didn't know who'd moved first—and the rest of the world melted away, lost in a flurry of snow as we lost ourselves in that first kiss.

Not our first, but the first of many promised.

The first that felt like it really meant *something*.

CHAPTER 22
Ella

I want this. I want us. I want you.

I hadn't imagined letting the words slip so early, but it was like his proximity melted away all of my defenses, and I couldn't imagine not giving him the same promise he'd made me.

And after two weeks, I was rewarded with *this*.

The most magical kiss. The snow fell around us, little snowflakes that landed in my hair and on Cam's eyelashes, and when we pulled away, a little out of breath, I couldn't help but giggle.

Cameron pulled me into him, tucking my body under his arm. I wasn't complaining, because his body heat instantly warmed me, even with the chill of the winter day.

"This is nice," he hummed.

"Mhm," I agreed, glad I'd come on this walk. "Sorry it took me so long to realize what I wanted."

His eyes were full of desire as he looked back at me, but he shook his head. "You never have to apologize for deciding what you want."

His sincerity flooded through me, and I couldn't help the little shiver that ran through me.

"How did you guys find this place, anyway?"

"Oh." Cam looked almost... shy? "Adam's parents own the place. They let us use it for break."

"They didn't want to spend time with their son?" I grimaced.

He scratched the back of his head. "I'm not sure they ever really have. They're so busy running their company that sometimes it feels like they forget he even exists."

"Oh. That's sad."

"Mhm." He was quiet, and I wanted to know what he was thinking, but I didn't want to pry too much, either.

Maybe because this thing between us was still so new. We'd shared things before, but never such personal things about our lives. Our parents. It seemed like he had experience with that himself.

Further down the path—at some point, we really would need to head back to the house, especially as it got colder—I spotted a tall girl with icy blonde hair arguing with a brunette.

"I wonder what's going on with those two," I wondered out loud.

And then the recognition hit me. The icy blonde was *Elise Andersen*—one of the best figure skaters on our campus. Her dad was the coach of our hockey team, so it made sense. It was like the ice was in their blood.

The man at my side smirked. "That looks familiar."

I stopped, staring up at him. "What?"

He just kissed the side of my head, ignoring my question. What did he see that I didn't?

"I'm just glad you stopped fighting with me. Fighting this." He pulled me in tighter.

"*Cam.*" We hadn't even defined what this was yet, or put any labels on what we were doing together. Sure, we'd spent last semester flirting and fighting, but... Were we *dating* now?

"Come on." He tugged on my hand before sticking it back in his pocket. "Let's leave those two love-birds to work their shit out."

"Should we go back?" I asked, taking in the snow as it came down harder, the temperature dropping. Cam wasn't even wearing a hat.

"A little longer," he said, squeezing my hand. "I want to savor this."

"Okay," I said back, a whisper on the breeze, butterflies tumbling in my stomach.

We kept walking for a while until we came upon a frozen lake, the bench at its banks mostly clear of snow. Cameron plopped down first, and then patted his lap.

"Ah…" I placed my hands over my cheeks, aware of my body's natural response to him.

"Come here, Princess." His hands wrapped around my waist, and he tugged me down, settling me on top of him.

"Hi," I whispered as he brushed a loose hair back behind my ear, his finger brushing under my beanie.

"Hi." He kissed my forehead.

"What are we doing?" I asked, because while this place was pretty, it was getting colder outside, the snow falling down harder.

"I don't want to go back yet. To share you with anyone." He brushed his nose against mine.

"You don't have to hold me like some sort of possessive boyfriend," I whispered to him a few minutes later when he hadn't moved from his current spot. He rubbed his thumb over the back of my hand, the motion somehow simultaneously soothing me and lighting me on fire.

"But what if I want to?"

"Hm?" I looked up at him, and his eyes were dark.

"What if I *want* to act like a possessive boyfriend?"

I swallowed roughly.

The thought lingered in my head, desire burning hot inside of me. It was a sensation that didn't fade, even when we got back to the house, cold and damp, to the smell of cooking food.

I hadn't been kidding when I'd said I was excited for the hot tub. Even if the walk to the steaming water was cold, given it was twenty-something degrees up here on the mountain. Thank goodness the patio was covered, otherwise everything out here would be covered in the same dusting of snow as the winter wonderland that surrounded us.

After dinner—Adam had made a French dish that practically melted in your mouth, and Sutton's chocolate lava cakes were to die for—I'd told Audrey I wanted to relax before sneaking outside. I needed a moment to shut my brain off—necessary, for an introvert stuck in a house full of extroverts and athletes.

Shedding the plush robe I'd worn out here onto a chair, I dipped my toes into the warm water, a small moan escaping from my lips as I slid my body in. Heaven.

Leaning my head back, I rested my head on the cold stone edge, staring up at the stars. They were so much brighter here, nestled against the mountains, and I couldn't help but close my eyes, humming a familiar tune.

"Enjoying yourself, Princess?" came the voice I couldn't get out of my head, and I cracked my eyes open, seeing Cam sitting on the edge next to me, wearing swim trunks and a sweatshirt.

"*Ohmygod.*" My hand flew to my heart. "You scared me."

Maybe I should have been more aware of my small bikini top, the way it revealed everything. My hardened nipples showed through the thin fabric, and I knew his gaze had honed in on it.

The difference in temperatures outside was doing something to my brain. That was the most logical conclusion.

He smirked, whipping the sweatshirt off and revealing the muscled chest I hadn't gotten to see enough.

Cam was right—it was a shame that we'd only been in a bed once. I wanted to trace those abs with my tongue, to memorize the map of his body with my hands, feel his weight on top of me. Because I couldn't get enough.

"Don't look at me like that," he murmured, sliding into the water on the other side of the tub. There was enough room for everyone in the house to fit, and yet, the space felt smaller just with Cam's addition.

"Like what?" I asked, all too aware of the way my body was drawn to him. How I wanted to move through the water and climb onto his lap. To run my fingers through his hair as he put his mouth on me.

"Like you want me to touch you."

"And what if I do?"

"All you need to do is ask, Ella. You know the words to say. What I want to hear."

I did, but... "Here?"

His eyes were dark, pupils dilated as he moved through the water, coming closer to me. One hand gripped the edge on either side of me, caging me in.

"What do you want, Ella?"

You. "Everything."

He reached around my neck, undoing the top of my swimsuit, letting the fabric fall between us.

"I don't—" I protested, looking back towards the windows of the well-lit house.

"No one's going to come out here," he promised. "They're all watching a movie."

Besides, his body was blocking most of mine, anyway. Chances are, they wouldn't see anything. And maybe the idea of getting caught turned me on more than I'd like to admit.

I couldn't stop thinking about the way he'd made me come in that closet, how hot it had been. I wanted that again.

Being pinned in place by him, his powerful arms keeping me in place, that broad chest fully on display in front of me... I ran my tongue over my lips as I stared up at him, all-too aware of my nipples now on full display.

For him, always for him.

Only for him. I'd never let anyone else do this sort of wicked, depraved things to me before. But I liked it. I didn't feel like the quiet, shy good girl when his lips were all over my body. When he whispered those filthy words into my ear.

"Do you want this?" He asked, bending down so his lips ghosted over mine.

"Yes." I arched my back, bringing my chest closer to him. "Please."

"I like you begging," he murmured, but he made no move to touch me or kiss me. Not even as I moved to reach for him. "But I like it when you scream my name even more."

I liked the sound of that. In a flash, he'd straightened, grabbing me by my hips and lifting me to rest on top of the spa.

"Charming," I groaned as he pushed my knees apart.

He positioned my legs so they would rest on the top of his shoulders before delving between my thighs. "I could spend forever tasting you, and I don't think it would be enough," he muttered, before dipping his head down and lapping at my clit.

I moaned at the sensation, the cold stone at my back a stark contrast to the heat running through my body, remnants from being inside the hot tub.

He flicked his tongue at my entrance, licking and sucking and driving me wild as he flattened his tongue before repeating it all over again. Grabbing at his hair with my hands, I dug my fingers into his scalp, like I was trying to hold him there, to force him in deeper.

Looking down, all I could see was the top of his head—those dark strands I'd buried my fingers into, and his eyes looking up at me as he ate me out like his life depended on it.

Fuck, why was that so hot?

I cried out when he sucked my clit into his mouth, the delicious pressure causing me to orgasm faster than I ever had before.

Cam stood up between my thighs, wiping his mouth with the

back of his hand. "That was what I wanted to do to you at the formal," he said with a smirk as I sat up, still trying to catch my breath.

I slid back into the water, letting out a long moan when the heated water caressed my sensitive flesh.

Cam sat on the bench in the water before pulling me on top of him, letting my legs straddle his lap. I was all-too aware of how the only thing separating our cores was the thin fabric of our swimsuits, but there was no hiding his erection as I rocked against him.

A small gasp escaped my lips as he nipped at my neck. His hands wrapped around my waist as I moved my hips again, desperate for relief, for the press of his body against mine.

Kissing a line down my throat, he sucked the sensitive skin there for a moment before moving down my collarbone, licking and biting at my skin as he went.

"Cam," I groaned, already wanting more.

"I love the way you say my name," he said, voice rough. His tongue circled my nipple before sucking it into his mouth. "Love these pretty pink nipples, too," he said, lavishing them both with attention as his thumbs dug into my skin. He flattened his tongue as it dragged over my nipple before nipping it. "I've been thinking about them all the time, Princess."

I threw my head back, losing myself in the sensation, even as I squirmed against his hold, desperate for more.

"What do you want, needy girl?" He asked, silencing me once more with the flick of his tongue against my neck. "Tell me what you need, so that I can give it to you."

"I need you," I said, repeating my words from earlier. "Inside me."

His eyes were dark, pupils fully dilated as he bobbed his head. Burying his face in the crook of my neck, he inhaled—as if he was trying to commit my smell to memory, to absorb it into my system.

I slid my hand down his swim trunks, wrapping my hand around his long, thick cock.

"Ella," he groaned as I pushed the fabric down, allowing him to spring free under the water.

I pumped his length with my hand, moving up and down in long, tight strokes. I wanted to taste him like he'd done for me, but given the reality of our situation, thought I'd better save that for another time.

Cam's head hit the side of the pool as I continued like that, perched on his thighs, his hard erection at attention between us.

Too long. It had been too long. Why hadn't we been doing this all semester?

Why had I ever left his bed?

I wiggled on his lap, eager to put him inside of me, when his hand clasped over the top of mine.

"Ella." This time, his voice had a tone of warning, and it was like a shock to my system.

What was I doing? Oh, God. This wasn't like me. I wasn't normally this… brazen, *bold*. He brought it out of me, turned me into some sort of sexual creature that I didn't even know.

I liked it, and yet, even then, I knew how bad of an idea it was to let him thrust inside of me here. With no protection, and… The haze of lust cleared from my eyes.

"I believe you promised me a bed next time," I said into his ear, a seductive tone that I barely even recognized as my voice.

He groaned as his core brushed against mine once more before I climbed off of him, not even bothering to retie my swimsuit.

Bending down to retrieve my robe, I gave him a wink before heading back into the house, all too aware of the way my hips swayed as I walked back into the house. I was burning alive with heat, so much so that the cold nip of the air barely affected me.

"Good night, Charming," I said, one last sway of my ass as I opened the door. "Sweet dreams."

I'd meant to go back to my room. Had fully intended to shower the chlorine off of my body, and slide into the bed I'd be sharing with Audrey.

But then, why was I in Cameron's room? On his bed?

He'd wrapped his hand around my wrist before I could enter the house. Had picked me up into his arms, my front pressed against his and my legs around his waist, before I could even blink.

Had carried me into his room, deposited me on the bed, which was probably the most comfortable one I'd ever laid on, and now stood, staring over the top of me. My robe was parted, letting my nipples peak out, and I knew all it would take was for him to remove my swim bottoms before he could slide inside of me.

"That's better," he murmured, his gaze seeming to linger on every element of my body, every aspect of my frame. "Fucking beautiful."

He shed his swimsuit bottoms. I swallowed roughly as he padded over to the bed, his cock already half-erect between his thighs.

The sight wasn't new, and yet it still affected me like it had the first time—knowing how much bigger he was, how much he would stretch my body.

Reverently, he pulled the robe apart, kissing me softly as he reached around my back, untying the second string of my bikini top. But he didn't stop there, didn't put his mouth back on my body, just kept moving down, down, down—till he reached where the little bikini bottoms hugged my thighs. He kissed my hip bone before pulling down each side, helping me lift my hips to remove the wet material from my body.

And then, robe shed and swimsuit forgotten, I was naked

and wet underneath him, my hair spilling out across the sheets as I looked up at him.

He was so unmistakably handsome, it was almost unfair. His jawline was perfectly structured, and his face—that damn face—made me want things I'd forgotten to dream about.

Something *more*.

Reaching up, I ran my hands over his face, like I needed the connection to know this was real, and not another dream.

"Say you're mine," he whispered as I held his face in between my hands.

"I'm yours." Whatever that meant, I knew in my heart that it was true.

"You're sure?" Cam asked, looking suddenly so unsure of himself for a man who had his tongue buried inside of me less than twenty minutes ago.

"Yes," I agreed, wrapping my arms around his neck. Kissing him tenderly.

Pushing at his chest, I flipped us over so that he was the one underneath *me*. Taking what I wanted. Taking what we both needed.

"There's condoms in the nightstand drawer," Cam said, and I nodded, grabbing one out and tearing the foil package open. He let me stay in control as I rolled it down his length, too eager to stop.

Finally, he was sheathed, and he watched me as I settled my body over top of his, those warm brown eyes trailing my body like he was capturing every detail.

Straddling his thighs, I guided him inside of me, moaning at the fullness. It had been so long since I'd felt this full, and it was magnificent.

"You feel so good," I gasped as I worked myself down his cock, inch by glorious inch. It was only when I was fully seated on him, my knees coming to either side of his chest, that I let go. "So deep," I cried out, having a hard time holding back my voice.

My palms were flat on his chest as I rode him, both of us finding our rhythm, seeking our mutual pleasure.

Cam rocked his hips up into me as he gripped my hips, helping me ride him.

"Such a good girl," he praised, making my body light up. "Taking all of my cock. Riding me so well."

"*Yes,*" I moaned, rocking back and forth to grind my clit down on him. He brought my hand to my entrance, parting my fingers so they would slide around his cock. "Feel how good you take me," he instructed, and I could feel it every time he surged inside of me, as I moved up and down on his cock.

"*Fuck.*" I squirmed, grinding and writhed on him, not able to get enough.

My eyes shut as I threw my head back, moving faster, chasing my climax as I bounced on him, sliding up and down on his length, each shallow thrust he provided causing me to see stars.

"I want you to come for me," Cam said, stroking my insides with each movement.

He hit *that* spot inside of me, and I let go with a moan, feeling my insides clench around him.

"Fuck," he muttered, taking over as he pumped inside of me, his hands helping my hips move even as I rode out the waves of my climax. "I'm gonna—"

"*Yesssss,*" I cried, needing him to find release with me.

He came with my name on his tongue, like it was a prayer, a benediction.

"Ella," he whispered as I slumped against his chest, my body well-spent. "I think you're gonna kill me."

"Sorry," I giggled. "Do you think anyone heard us?"

Cameron rubbed my nose with his thumb. "Hopefully, the movie was loud enough to drown us out." If not, I would be completely mortified. My twin was out there, for crying out loud.

He got up, disposing of the condom in the trash and cleaning himself up before climbing back into bed with me.

"We should probably be more careful next time." I traced circles over his pecs, enjoying the feeling of his naked skin against mine.

Cam's hand tangled in my hair, and he pulled my head towards his, bringing our lips together.

"What was that for?" I asked when he pulled away.

"For choosing me," he murmured, that same hand running down my spine.

I didn't say anything else, just laid my head in the crook of his shoulder, enjoying the feeling of his arms wrapping around my body, letting the warmth soothe me to sleep.

"Ella?"

My eyes had closed, only moments from falling asleep when he'd spoken the words, but I let my eyes flutter open. He was staring down at me, one arm still wrapped around me, and his gaze filled with so much care.

"Mhm?" I murmured, cuddling against his chest.

"Promise me you'll be here when I wake up?" His voice was low, quiet, but somehow it filled the entire room.

Sliding my hand up his chest, I let it rest over his beating heart. "I promise, Charming."

He kissed my forehead, and we fell asleep just like that, all wrapped up in each other.

CHAPTER 23
Cam

Our first full day in Vermont was spent on the mountain, though Ella had stayed in the lodge, her design sketchbook and a varying amount of swatches in hand.

I'd never slept as well as I did last night, with Ella curled up next to me. And waking up in the morning, with the first thing I saw being that beautiful head of blonde hair, sleeping on my chest like a pillow... I was so gone for this girl.

I didn't know what I would have done if she'd said no. If she had decided she didn't want me, us.

But I was the luckiest guy in the world, and I knew it.

Because I got to kiss her good morning, and now I got to stare at her work, erasing and sketching the same drawing for what felt like the fifteenth time in the last ten minutes.

"Don't you want to ski?" she finally asked, looking up at me as I drank from my mug of hot chocolate.

"Nah." I'd gone down a few runs, and now I was perfectly content watching her work.

"But... You bought a pass." She squished up her nose, making a face.

I shrugged. "There're more days." Plus, I'd rather spend time with her.

"Okay." She shrugged, going back to her sketchpad.

"What are you working on?" I asked, watching as she erased part of her drawing once again. "Is that a design for Audrey's play?"

"Oh, no." Ella looked bashful as she looked up at me. "I'm just working on something for my portfolio. The designs for the play are just about done, though. Next step is sending them to my professor. Do you want to see?"

I nodded, coming around behind her as she flipped backwards in her sketchbook.

"This one's for Audrey's character. It's a fairytale, so she's the princess." It was a dress with a full skirt that hit mid-calf, decorated in little tiny flowers that she'd drawn as well as shaded in.

"You did this?" I asked, though I wasn't shocked at how talented she was. I'd seen her designs before, and I knew she had a gift. "This is amazing, Ella. Wow."

"Thank you." She flipped to the next page, showing me the design for the lead male character, a prince. The jacket was structured, with slightly poofy sleeves, drawing in elements from historical designs and whimsical fantasy.

She showed me the other designs, which were all just as stunning, though the one she'd drawn for her sister was my favorite. "What about you?" I asked when she finished. "Is there one that you'd wear?"

"Oh, no. I'm not performing." She looked at me like I'd grown a second head. "I'd fall flat on my face. You've seen me practically trip on air, right?"

I hummed in response, turning my attention back to the book in my lap.

"What?" She scowled. "It's Audrey's thing, not mine."

But it could be yours. If she wanted. I'd caught her singing to herself on multiple occasions—she was *good*. Better than good.

"I'm happy where I am," she whispered. But it felt more like she was telling herself that, instead of me.

"Okay. As long as you're happy, that's all that matters," I said, leaning over and kissing her forehead.

Settling back in my chair, I picked up my book, but half of my attention was on Ella, who'd flipped back to her current design, humming as she returned to her earlier process.

I lost track of time with us like that, catching eyes every few minutes, the blush on her cheeks deepening every time it happened. Our knees would brush under the table, and she would shy away before we touched again a few moments later.

It felt oddly intimate, even if we were just sitting at the table lost in our own activities.

"There's the happy couple!" James's voice was loud in the lodge, the rest of our friends following behind. Sutton was holding Forest's hand, the two of them sharing their own secret smiles.

"Oh, but we're not..." Ella started, looking over at me.

I raised an eyebrow. I'd wanted to give her time before I sprang a label on her, but maybe we needed to have that conversation sooner rather than later.

After last night, I knew I wouldn't be able to give her up. It felt like something fundamental had changed between us, and I didn't want to look at it too closely.

Because it was too soon to assign any other emotions to this. I liked her—a lot—but that didn't mean there were any other L words currently applicable to our relationship.

I shook my head, refocusing. "We're not *what*, Ella?"

"Um." She shook her head. Looked over at her sister. Shrugged.

Sutton plopped down on the bench next to Ella, and our table was quickly full of a bunch of them, everyone shedding their wet snow gear next to them to dry.

Everyone devolved into conversation, and our peaceful silence was gone.

James elbowed me in the ribs. "How's it going in here, Cam?"

"Good." I held up my book. They didn't need to know I'd barely read a word.

Adam looked at the cover for a moment before addressing me. "That one was good. Read it last year."

It was good. The parts I'd been able to pay attention to, at least. When I hadn't been staring at the girl across the table.

I nudged her knee with mine. *Outside?* I mouthed, wanting to have more time alone with her.

Ella nodded.

"We're gonna take a walk," I said to the table, grabbing my coat and pulling it on before helping Ella into hers. She spun around to face me, moving to zip her coat, but I stopped her before she could.

"Let me," I offered, pulling the zipper and making sure none got caught in her hair.

"I *can* zip my own coat, you know, Charming. I'm not incapable."

"Never said you were." I resisted kissing her in front of all our friends.

Not yet, anyway. Not when she still had doubts about what we were. What this was.

We walked outside of the lodge. The sun was shining high in the sky, making the snow seem to sparkle.

"Wow. It's bright out here," Ella murmured, covering her eyes with one hand.

Grabbing her free hand, I interlaced our fingers, pulling her off to the side of the lodge, out of sight of any other resort guests.

"Come here," I said, pulling her into my arms. Even with a giant puffy coat on, I enjoyed holding her like this.

"Cam," she said as I tucked us into an alcove. "What are we doing?"

"Talking," I said, my lips curling up in a smile.

She rolled her eyes. "You know what I mean."

"Do I?"

Shuffling us closer to the side of the building, I pressed her against the wall. Caged her in with my arms.

"What are *we* doing, Cameron?" She looked at the ground between us instead of into my eyes. Fuck that.

I wanted those gorgeous baby blues on me.

"I wanted to kiss you."

Her lips parted as she brought her gaze to mine.

"Didn't think you wanted me to do it in front of all our friends."

She shook her head.

"What do you want?" I asked her, rubbing my nose against hers.

Leaning in, I pressed a soft kiss to the side of her mouth. Then the other.

I hovered over her lips, wanting her to tell me she wanted this, too. Us.

"You said you wanted everything," Ella whispered.

"I did. I *do*." I really wanted to kiss her.

"And... we're sleeping together." Her cheeks turned pink, as if she was remembering last night.

"We are." I raised an eyebrow.

"And we're... friends?" Fuck, was that what she thought? Even after I'd told her what I wanted. Was that why she'd been holding back?

I shook my head, leaning our foreheads together as I kept myself propped up on the wall. "We're way past friends, baby." I pressed my lips against hers, gently.

"So... I'm your girlfriend?"

"Fuck yeah." One corner of my mouth tilted up. "I thought that was implied."

She leaned up, kissing me this time. "That's good."

"Oh, it is?" I grinned.

"Mhm. Because I really wanted to call you my boyfriend."

Her face split into a blinding smile—even brighter than the snow—as she wrapped her arms around my neck.

I lifted her up, bringing our lips level, and we let our mouths do the rest of the talking, tongues tangling in a kiss that wasn't at all gentle or sweet.

Tasting, licking, sucking—our lips were a frenzy, like we couldn't get enough of each other.

Ella moaned into my mouth as she tangled her fingers into the hair at the nape of my neck, and we finally pulled away, breathing deeply.

Tugging a blonde strand of hair out of her bun, I curled a finger around it. "I can't wait to take this down later," I murmured, loving the way it shone like spun gold in the sunlight.

"You like my hair?"

"I fucking love your hair, Princess."

"Mmm." She kissed me again, and I pressed my erection into her core, inhaling her gasp as she rocked her hips against me.

I groaned at the tightness in my pants. "I'm gonna need a few minutes before we go back inside, baby."

Ella giggled, and the sound was the best sound I had ever heard.

Her cheeks might have been permanently pink, but it was worth it.

So, *so* worth it, when we re-entered the lodge, still holding hands, and I tugged her into my side, grinning at the group. We had shed our coats as soon as we'd come back inside, feeling overheated for more than one reason.

"Hi," Ella breathed out, squeezing my hand.

"The lovebirds are back," Forest crooned, earning a smack in the shoulder from Sutton, who just glared at him.

"Yup," I said, moving back to the table. I didn't even try to deny it.

The group had moved around while we were gone, and I tugged Ella over to an empty spot, sitting down before tugging her into my lap.

"So…" Audrey started, looking between me and her twin.

"We're together," Ella said, wiggling on my lap to get more comfortable.

Everyone cheered, like they'd been rooting for us all along, and I took their momentary distraction to lean my head closer to Ella.

"Careful, Princess," I whispered in her ear as she pressed her ass into my cock. My ever-growing arousal that I'd had months to get used to around her, but I couldn't help it. One look at her and it was like that very first night all over again. One whiff of her scent and all I wanted to do was to get my hands on her.

She looked at me, rolling her eyes slightly, but I didn't miss how she scooted back further, grinding onto me just slightly.

"You'll pay for that later," I promised.

"I'm counting on it," she murmured back.

"Guess it's just you and me now, man," Adam said to James, clapping him on the shoulder. "We're gonna have to get used to both of them ditching us for their girlfriends."

Audrey let out a dreamy sigh, and I raised an eyebrow at Ella, who gave me a look that promised *later*. Whatever was going on with her sister, I couldn't imagine it was easy to watch your sister fall for someone when you were alone.

Shit. Falling for each other.

Is that what we were doing?

Somehow, I knew the words rang true. I'd never let myself think them before, but I was.

I was falling for Ella.

CHAPTER 24
Ella

There was no stopping my yawn. After a long day of skiing and spending time with everyone, I was absolutely exhausted. Not to mention, Cam had kept me up for half the night, using his tongue and fingers in ways I had only imagined before this.

"I'm gonna go to bed," I said, addressing the group. Cam kissed me on the cheek as I got up off his lap, and told me he'd be in soon.

Honestly, that wasn't even the weirdest part of this entire trip.

Audrey had looked at me funny this morning, when I'd stumbled out of Cam's room wearing one of his t-shirts, but she had said nothing, only gave me a small smile.

"I know," I'd groaned, grabbing my clothes and going to shower. "Don't start with me."

"I didn't say anything!" she yelled after me, her lip twitching with a smirk.

But I'd pulled on my thermal leggings and long-sleeved t-shirt before pulling on my thick, cozy sweater and a pair of jeans, figuring if I was going up to the slopes with the rest of them, I might as well be warm.

Though I hadn't been in the mood for skiing.

What I hadn't expected was for Cam to spend most of his day with *me*. I'd figured I would have time to be alone with my thoughts, to process everything that had happened the night before, but it turned out that silence with him was exactly what I'd needed. Every so often, I'd stop working on my sketch, and look up, finding him engrossed in some science-fiction novel, and then he'd look up too, catch my eye, and smile.

I couldn't help as my cheeks warmed, thinking about it now as I brushed my hair.

"What are you wearing?" Cam's voice startled me from my current thoughts, and I looked up to find him leaning against the door frame.

"Oh." I blushed, looking down at the shirt I'd pulled on. It was the one he'd given me when I was sick, and he'd come over to take care of me. "Sorry. You probably want it back…" I didn't particularly want to give it up. Even if it no longer smelled like him, I liked sleeping in it. Probably too much. I wouldn't admit how often I did it.

His eyes flared. "No. Keep it." Stalking towards me, he wrapped his arms around my middle, buried his nose in my hair. "I like you in my clothes, Princess."

Spinning me around, he lifted me onto the counter and placed a hand on either side of my legs. "But you know what I like even better?"

"What?" My breath caught in my throat.

He kissed my neck. "You in *nothing*."

I hummed in response as he whipped the t-shirt off my body, his eyes taking the time to track over every inch of my body. Including how I wasn't wearing any panties.

"I told you I'd punish you for earlier," he said, kissing down my chest. "Where should I start?"

I knew exactly where I wanted him, but he avoided all of those areas, content to torture me slowly.

Licking, sucking, kissing my neck, collarbone, chest, until

finally his hands cupped my breasts, those thumbs rubbing over my nipples in slow strokes. Finally, he put his mouth to the tortured buds,

"Cameron," I whined, practically writhing on the countertop. "Please."

"Are you going to be a good girl for me?" He asked. "Let me bury my tongue in your sweet pussy, Princess. I wanna taste you on my lips when I make you come for me."

Oh, God. He was going to kill me. If not with his tongue, then with those filthy words. "Yes," I agreed, nodding my head wildly.

Pulling me to the edge of the counter, Cam kneeled in front of it, bringing his head level with my entrance.

The first swipe of his tongue against my clit was relief, but the second was pure bliss. And when he fluttered it, driving me wild? It didn't take me long before I was panting, crying out, clenching around his tongue as he massaged my clit with his thumb.

Cam licked his lips as he stood back up, a wicked grin on his face. "I'll never get tired of eating you out."

I wrapped my legs around his back, bringing his body closer to mine as I used my hands to explore his chest. Tracing his abs with my fingers, wishing my tongue was in their place instead.

I wasted no time at all unbuttoning his pants, hastily shoving his boxers down with them so I could get my hands on his cock.

Wrapping my hand around the base, I tugged, enjoying the groan that spluttered from his lips in response.

"Now, I want to taste *you*," I said, tracing his tip as I swiped the drop of liquid off of it.

Finally prying my eyes off of *him*, I looked up, finding his warm brown eyes gazing at me with heat—intensity. Desire.

"Thank fuck that this room has a private bathroom," he muttered, picking me up off the counter and carrying me to the bed. Audrey's room—the one I was supposed to be sleeping in—as well as Adam and James's all shared one.

My shirt—his shirt—lay forgotten on the floor.

Cam sat me on the bed, quickly discarding his pants and shirt before coming back to me, his fingers tangling in my hair as he pulled me in for a kiss.

When we pulled apart, I reached for his cock between us, my fingers curling around his hardened shaft.

"Let me put my mouth on you," I begged. While he was always going down on me, I wanted to return the favor.

I leaned down, running my hand up his length before taking the tip into my mouth, closing my lips around it.

"Fuck," he groaned as I flicked my tongue around the rim, taking my time to worship him like he always did me.

As I ran my tongue down his shaft, I massaged his balls, enjoying the way Cam was coming apart at my touch.

Reaching down with my other hand, I rubbed at my clit as I sucked more of his length into my mouth, taking just enough of him in that I didn't gag.

My saliva dripped out of the corner of my mouth as I took him in deeper, flattening my tongue so I could slide him in and out.

"Look at you," he praised. "Taking my cock so well."

I whimpered as he hit the back of my throat, slipping a finger inside to combat the emptiness I felt.

Pulling back, I sucked on his tip again, intending to continue, but before I could, he pulled me off.

He reached down, pulling my fingers out of me and groaning as he replaced them with his own. "You're so fucking wet. Did you that turn you on, huh? Sucking me off like a good girl?"

I nodded eagerly, but he must have noticed my expression, because he said, "I don't want to come down your throat." His voice was rough, like it was taking everything in him to hold back.

"Where do you want to come instead?" I fluttered my eyelashes.

He growled, pushing me down onto my back. "Inside of you."

"So do it." Opening my legs so he could settle between my thighs, I guided him towards my entrance.

Cameron swallowed, his eyes growing wide as he looked at the spot where the two of us were connected. So close. If he just pushed, I'd have him inside of me.

"Are you sure?" His tip pressed against me, and I wiggled, wanting him inside of me *now*.

I nodded. "I'm clean. And I haven't been with anyone else in a long time, if you want to…" Plus, I was on birth control, a fact he already knew.

"Me too." He kissed my knuckles. "It's been a year. At least." Cam groaned. "And I got tested before the semester started, so…"

"I want you inside of me," I said, reveling in the stretch as he pushed in. The thought of being with him with no barriers was a temptation I had never felt with my previous flings or boyfriends. I was willing to take the risk with him, wanting to experience him fully.

"*Fuck.*" He let out a guttural sound as he slid inside, inch by glorious inch. "You feel so good." His eyes flew shut as he stilled, like he was trying not to move too fast.

Trying to make this last.

"Move." I begged, squirming as my body adjusted to his size. He was so big that I didn't think I'd ever get used to it. "I need you to move."

"*Ella.*"

He thrust himself fully inside of me, burying to the hilt.

Every inch of me was impossibly full, and I rested my hand over my stomach, like I could feel him deep inside of me if I pressed down, and then I did, and—

"You're so deep," I moaned. "Feels so good." My eyes fluttered shut from the pressure as he rocked his hips, pumping into me in a steady rhythm.

How was it possible that it just kept getting better? Sex with Cameron was like nothing I'd ever experienced before. Maybe it was the way he was a generous, giving lover—making sure I'd always come first. He was attentive, thorough, and knew just how to touch me to light up every inch of my body.

Pleasure rolled over me in waves, and I couldn't make it stop. Didn't *want* it to stop.

And when Cam interlocked our fingers, bringing us to climax at near the same time, I thought I might live in the moment forever.

No matter what happened next, I didn't want to let him go.

After we'd cleaned up, Cam's t-shirt once again covering my body, we were back in bed, cuddling.

I'd never pegged this man as one before this weekend, but he was a grade-A cuddler. Adding it to the list of things I hadn't expected from him, I quickly settled on the realization that it was growing more rapidly by the day. He was nothing like I expected. Maybe that was why I'd said yes to him in the first place.

"Will you come with me?" He asked against my hair, running his fingers through the strands.

"What?" I flicked my eyes up to his.

"Skiing. Tomorrow. Will you go? Please?"

"I don't know... It's been a long time." It wasn't like I didn't like it, but I was apprehensive about going up again. People always said it was like riding a bike, but... I wasn't exactly the most graceful on my feet. And after my mom's accident, I was more than apprehensive about it. Physical activity and me didn't really get along. The treadmill at the gym was dangerous enough.

"I'll hold your hand the whole time," he promised.

"Why?" I couldn't hold back my blush.

"Because I want to. Because I don't want to be apart from you." Cam snuggled into me, burying his nose in my hair. "Because I want to hold your hand as we ride up the chairlift and to see your face light up as we fly down the mountain."

"Okay." I couldn't deny him anything, after all.

And maybe I should have said something, should have slowed us down. This was all moving so fast, wasn't it? We'd gone from hooking up to spending every minute together in a flash. And yet, I didn't want to stop it.

So… I didn't. I just snuggled deeper into his arms, falling into sleep the same way I was falling into him.

"Are you sure about this?" I asked, staring down the mountain. I'd rented skis and equipment in the morning, and after going down the kiddie hill—several times—I'd finally felt confident in going down one of the beginner slopes.

As Cam had promised, he held my hand the entire ride up the chairlift, and though we weren't actually holding hands now—mostly because of the poles I had a death grip on—he *had* stuck by my side.

"Everything will be fine," he promised. "I'm not going to abandon you."

It didn't feel like he was talking about skiing.

"Okay." I nodded, staring down the mountain.

He helped secure the goggles to my face before nodding at me. "Ready?"

Confirming my skis were clicked in properly, I took a deep breath, staring down the hill to the lodge below.

"Ready," I confirmed, pushing off with my poles.

The wind whipped around me as we made our way down the hill, gliding in large, swooping motions over the snow.

Other skiers flew right by us, but I didn't mind.

The adrenaline rush brought a smile to my face, even as I felt the nip of the cold at my cheeks. It was like we were flying down the mountain, and I let out a giggle as we soared.

"Have fun?" Cam asked at the bottom as I shoved the goggles up my eyes.

"Wanna go again?" I asked, feeling appropriately breathless.

He laughed. "Yes. Glad you're enjoying yourself."

I nodded enthusiastically, trying to take a step towards him, but between the skis and everything, I practically tripped on the air, stumbling into Cam's open arms.

"Thanks for catching me," I mumbled, wanting to bury my face in his coat in embarrassment.

"Always." He tilted up my chin to bring our eyes together. "I'll always catch you, Ella."

I shivered, but it wasn't from the cold.

"Come on," he murmured, looking back at the lodge. "Let's go warm you up."

I protested I wasn't cold, but then I thought of something better. My lips curled up in a sly smile. "What if I have other ideas on how to... warm up?" Wiggling my eyebrows, I hoped he picked up on what I was suggesting.

"I think I'd love to hear those ideas," he said, bringing us practically nose to nose.

"It involves you..." I drew circles on his jacket, fumbling with the top of his zipper. "And me..." He nodded, hanging on every word. "And the shower."

"Fuck it." He helped me out of my skis before tossing me over his shoulder. "Let's go."

I laughed, feeling a warm glow flow through me.

And I let it settle all the way back to the house, wishing this moment never had to end.

Wishing we could live in this moment forever.

Wishing nothing ever had to change.

The days flew by in a blur, much faster than I would have liked.

Cam and I skied together, we watched movies cuddled together on the couch, and I'd spent every night in his bed. Wearing his shirt.

He'd made me come more times than I can count, sometimes on his tongue, occasionally with his fingers, but it just kept getting *better*. Especially when he thrust inside of me, making me see stars faster than should have been humanly possible.

"I don't want this to end," I murmured, wrapped in his arms as we woke up on the second-to-last day. Our limbs were tangled together, like we needed to be touching in every conceivable way.

"I know." He kissed the crown of my head.

"Come home with me," I breathed, not sure why the offer felt right, but it *did*. All I knew was that I didn't want to say goodbye to *this*. Not when everything was so good, and felt so right.

"Ella." He sighed, brushing a strand of hair back and tucking it behind my ear. "You know I want to."

I frowned. "Then *do*. Come."

"I can't."

"I know." But I still sighed, wishing that it wasn't the reality of our situation.

"It'll only be two weeks," he promised. "Then we'll be back at CU, and you can see me every day."

"Every day? Being a little assumptive, aren't we, Charming?"

Cam nuzzled his nose into my neck. "Yes. Because I don't want to let you go."

I hummed into his hold. "So… What should we do today?" I asked, running my fingers through his soft, dark brown strands. "I saw there's a sledding park nearby." I'd had my fill of skiing, but I could be persuaded to slide down snow on an inner tube for the day.

"Yeah?" He grinned.

"Wanna share an inner tube, boyfriend?" I gave him a little wink.

"I like that."

"What?"

"That's the first time you've called me your boyfriend."

"Oh." Was it? I guess I hadn't realized how good it would feel. "Well, you are."

Satisfaction pursed his mouth as he lifted me onto his lap.

And then he showed me just *how* much he enjoyed it when I said the words, making me repeat them over and over as he used his fingers and tongue.

I soaked in every moment, taking advantage of all the ones we had left.

Knowing pretty soon, we'd have to say goodbye.

CHAPTER 25
Ella

"You know you're going to have to let go of me at some point, right, Princess?" Cam murmured into my ear as I wrapped my arms tighter around his neck.

"Just let me have this," I mumbled, knowing I needed to say goodbye. Knowing that the cars were loaded, and our peaceful winter break vacation was over.

I hadn't known just how much I needed this. How much I needed *him*. How easy it would be.

"You'll text, right?"

He smoothed over the back of my head. "Every day."

"Mmm. Good." I finally pulled away, stretching up on my tiptoes and kissing him softly before lowering my body back to the ground.

If I did any more, I knew we wouldn't make it in the cars, and everyone was waiting for us.

"Two weeks," he promised. "Once you're back on campus, text me, alright?"

I nodded, knowing I'd be counting down to that day.

Cam's hands cupped my face. "No going and meeting anyone else while you're at home, Ella. Remember, you're mine." Without another word, he bent down and kissed me deeply, slipping his tongue over my bottom lip until I opened for him. The tongue that had memorized my body explored my mouth like we had hours instead of only moments left together.

Breathless. He'd stolen all the air from my body, from my lungs.

"Cam."

He chuckled, resting his forehead against mine. "Go, Ella. Or I'll sweep you back into that bedroom and show you just how much I don't want to leave you."

I looked back at the car, Audrey sitting in the front seat with the ignition already running.

"You could still come home with me," I mumbled, even though I knew it was a moot point.

Besides, it was too soon, wasn't it? Bringing home your boyfriend of less than a month for Christmas?

Maybe.

Still, I hated it.

"Bye, Princess." He kissed my forehead and then gave me a little smack on the ass. "Be a good girl now, hm?"

The heat stole into my face as I watched him walk away, waiting until his car door closed before I turned around, marching myself back to our car without looking back.

Okay, I took one last little sneak peek, catching his wink through the car window, and then I slid inside the warm car.

"Don't say anything," I warned Audrey, cupping my cheeks with my hands as if I could hide my blush.

She just laughed. "I wasn't gonna."

"Let's go home."

Looking around our home, I was surprised to find how much I missed the ski trip. Being surrounded with laughter, all our friends. Even if I'd spent every moment possible with Cam, we'd still spent the evenings playing card and board games with our friends, seeing who would do the most ridiculous things during truth or dare, watching movies, and enjoying the peaceful snowfall of the mountains. Adam and Sutton had cooked for us, not letting us in the kitchen because they wanted to show off their skills—and because they didn't trust the rest of us. Fine by me.

But most of all, I missed how easy it had been up there.

ELLA

I miss you.

I wish you could have come home with me.

CAM

I miss you too, Princess.

How's your Christmas?

Fine.

I frowned. Just *fine?* I hated that for him. I wanted him to be having a better time with his family.

"You texting Cam?" Audrey asked, glancing over at my phone.

"Yeah." I tried to hide my face in my shirt.

"You really like him, don't you?"

I nodded. There was no point in denying it—I really, really did.

I really wished he had taken me up on my offer and come home with me. After all, Christmas at the Ashford house had always been a joyous occasion. Even when we were growing up, our parents had done their best to spoil us, and above all, we were loved. The fireplace was on, and we cuddled up under blankets, watching Christmas cartoons until the early hours of the morning, when our parents finally made us go to bed.

We always complained, but they'd told us that Santa wouldn't show up unless we fell asleep, so we'd curled up under our comforters, in the bedroom we'd shared, giggling until sleep finally took us.

This Christmas wasn't much different. Audrey and I were still cuddled up on the couch, sharing a massive blanket, yawning as we watched our favorite cartoons from childhood. There were no longer any presents from Santa wrapped under the tree when we woke up, but all we really needed was family.

But it felt like I'd left my heart behind in Vermont. I knew Cam's relationship with his parents wasn't great, and I hated to think of him being miserable over the holidays.

> ELLA
> Just fine?

> CAM
> Eh. Dad's working. Mom is, well... Mom.

> Oh. Sorry to hear that.

> It's okay. How's your family?

"So, who's this boy?" My mom asked as she sat down on the chair next to us, a bowl of freshly popped popcorn on her lap. I gave her a weird look, but she just laughed. "Ells, you've been buried in that phone all night. I know you've been texting someone. Is it the same guy as you were talking to this semester?"

"It's... He's no one." I said, burying my hand in the bowl of popcorn and throwing a few pieces into my mouth to avoid her gaze.

"He's not *no one*," Audrey interjected, and I stared daggers at my twin, who was clearly all-too eager to throw me under the bus. "He's the president of the frat that Ella's been working with."

My twin senses were clearly *not* working. I shoved at her with my foot. I didn't need her spilling my newfound relationship to my parents before I'd even had the chance to tell them I had a boyfriend.

"Really?" My mom raised an eyebrow. It wasn't like she didn't have experience with fraternity boys—she'd been in a sorority in her day. Though hers had looked a lot different from how PRS did now.

"It's not like that," I protested, though I didn't really know what it *was* like. "He's really sweet." My voice was low, hardly a murmur.

And although I'd invited him home with me for Christmas, to spend these last weeks before classes started back up with me, I wondered how my parents would have reacted if I *had* brought him home.

Would they like him? Why was it so important to me they *did*?

"As long as he makes you happy," my mother said. "That's all that matters, sweetie."

Audrey reached over, squeezing my ankle as I nodded.

Looking down at my phone, I realized I'd never responded to his last text.

ELLA

Good. We're just camped out on the couch watching old Christmas movies.

CAM

What's on? I'll join in.

You're gonna... watch the same movie?

Yeah.

Why?

Is that weird?

No. I like it.

I quickly sent him our next movie choice: my favorite, *Rudolph*, since this one was almost over.

He texted me throughout the whole thing, sending me his

thoughts, and I'd never imagined that watching a movie together long distance could be this much *fun*.

One more week, I thought to myself, closing my eyes as I tucked myself into bed that night. Once I got through New Year's, we'd be back at CU, and maybe I'd stop feeling like my heart was on my sleeve.

New Year's Eve. A night of champagne, confetti poppers, and those god-awful noisemakers which I really could have done without.

But another year was here. I wrapped my arm around my waist, looking out at the party spread throughout the club building. I didn't really feel like celebrating much—not when Cam wasn't here.

Our family normally went to the same party at our country club every year for the occasion. Growing up, we'd been surrounded by other kids our age, but now, surrounded by dozens of other college kids drinking and dancing and laughing, I moved to the outside patio, staring out over the grounds.

It was chilly, but not enough to go back inside in search of my jacket. Not yet, at least.

"What's a pretty girl like you doing out here all alone?" A familiar voice said behind me, and a surge of adrenaline burst through my veins.

I turned, finding the dark-haired man I'd grown so fond of over the last few months standing there, wearing a delicious suit, looking at me like I'd hung the moon in the sky. *He was here.*

"Cam!" I shrieked, jumping into his arms. "What are you doing here?"

"It's almost midnight."

"So?"

"So... tradition dictates that you owe me a kiss." He tapped his finger against his cheek. "They say whoever you kiss at midnight, you'll spend the rest of the year with. So obviously, I couldn't let you kiss someone else."

I rolled my eyes. "Like I would have kissed anyone else."

"I couldn't take the chance," he breathed, cupping my cheek with his hand. I nuzzled into it, relaxing into his hold.

But he didn't kiss me. Not yet. It wasn't midnight, I supposed. Still, I wanted him to kiss me now, the greedy little thing that I was. It had been almost two weeks since he'd touched me, and my body was starved for him.

Cam set me back onto my feet, stepping back to drag his eyes down every inch of my body. "I like this," he said, plucking at the strap of my glitzy party dress.

I shivered as he traced the same finger over my collarbone and then down my shoulder.

"Are you cold?"

"No," I murmured, feeling flushed with heat, despite the cool air kissing my skin.

He ran his fingers through my hair, toying with the ends. "You wore it down."

I'd loosely curled it, wanting to feel pretty for tonight, even though I played with my hair way too much when I left it down.

Nodding, I bit my lip. "I was going to FaceTime you later, and I know you like it like this, so…" I looked away, hoping I could hide the embarrassment that always found its way to my cheeks around him.

"You were going to call me?" He asked, a puzzled expression on his face.

"Well, yeah. It's New Year's Eve, and you're my boyfriend, so…" I quirked an eyebrow. "Who else would I call?"

Cam's face formed into a pout, and I rubbed my thumb over the lines. "What?"

"You haven't." He cleared his throat. "Called me, I mean."

"I didn't…" *I didn't know you'd wanted me to call*, is what I almost said. I hadn't expected him to react like this. "Did you want me to?"

Because I'd wanted to. I just hadn't wanted to seem clingy.

He curled his arms around my waist, tugging our bodies until they were flush together, and rested his head in between my breasts. "Of course I wanted you to," he said, not raising his head. "I missed you."

"But we were texting every day, and you didn't say anything, so…"

"Because I was trying so fucking hard, Ella. Not to ask you what you were wearing. Not to see if you were in my shirt. If you had put those little fingers inside your pretty pink cunt, pretending they were mine." He gave a groan of exacerbation. "I was trying to control myself."

"Oh." If I hadn't been blushing before, I definitely was now. "I would have shown you," I said, barely audible. If it wasn't for how close we were standing, he wouldn't have heard me.

"Ella," he groaned. "Princess. Are you trying to kill me?"

I looked down at his slacks, the outline of his erection showing.

Did you? I wanted to ask, but I thought I knew the answer.

"How'd you know I was here, anyway?" I raised an eyebrow.

He grinned. "Audrey."

"Oh." The heat ran to my face. "What'd she say?" I would kill her if I found out she'd told Cam I was lonely and missing him. Even if I was.

"Nothing." He kissed my forehead. "Told her I needed to see my girl. She told me where to find you."

"Mmm." I gripped his lapel tighter, holding our bodies together as his grip tightened on my waist. "Cam?"

"Yeah?"

"You still haven't kissed me, you know."

He laughed. "Impatient, hm?" He glanced down at his watch. "There's still five minutes until midnight, Princess."

I leaned back against the railing, taking the time to stare at his face. That sculpted jaw, those cheekbones—and those eyelashes which should definitely be illegal, because it was unfair that his were so pretty while I had to apply layers of mascara onto mine.

"Ella."

"Hmm?" I was still staring at his face. Wondering how I could get him to kiss me *now*, not in five minutes. Or four. Whatever we were down to.

He laughed, lowering his mouth so they were only inches apart, ghosting his lips over mine. "It's not midnight yet."

"Tease." I huffed, pushing off of him and walking towards the bridge that crossed the river of the property.

Staring down at the water, I focused on the moon's reflection, only looking up when I noticed Cam's form joining me.

Cam draped his jacket over my shoulders as I shivered, staring out over the bridge over the large pond.

"It's beautiful," I murmured, even though I felt like I could see my breath. But the world was quiet, still—*gorgeous*, under the moonlight and in a slight layer of frost.

"Yeah," he agreed, and then I felt a finger running over my cheek. When I looked up at him, his gaze was squarely focused on me, not our surroundings. "Very beautiful."

"What time is it?" I breathed, knowing we were too far away from the party to hear the countdown.

Not caring one bit, because there was nowhere I wanted to be but here.

Cam chuckled as he looked down at his watch before pulling me close.

"Happy New Year, Ella," he murmured, kissing me softly.

The kiss I'd waited all night for. Maybe even my whole life for.

I curled my fingers into his hair, tugging his mouth back down to mine. "Happy New Year, Cameron."

With any luck, this next year would be my best yet.

CHAPTER 26
Cam

Driving down here was worth it. Of fucking course it was.

But seeing her face light up as she saw me, realized I was there, and ran into my arms... that was fucking priceless.

Even if I had to leave soon to get back home, it was worth every minute I'd spent in the car.

For that New Year's Kiss alone, I'd do it all over again. We'd curled up on a bench near the cute little bridge after we'd finally parted from each other, lips swollen and breaths ragged.

A river ran through the property, giving us the perfect backdrop of water running and crickets chirping in the quiet of the night—only disturbed by the occasional firework still being set off nearby. The lawn behind us was perfectly manicured, and if the rest of the details hadn't indicated the country club's status, the golf course visible in the background would have.

But in this moment, I was just appreciating my girl, sitting with me, because nothing else mattered. Christmas with my parents had been quiet and uncaring, but her texts had gotten me through.

Ella's legs were folded over mine and her hands rested in my lap like we were greedy for each other's touch.

She was still wearing my suit jacket around her shoulders, over that sparkling fucking dress that felt like it belonged at a nightclub, not some country club new year's party.

If there was any sign of how irrational I was with this girl, it was how much I enjoyed seeing her wrapped up in my jacket. How big it was on her.

How much I liked holding her, just like this. I ran my thumb over her knuckles, feeling a shiver run through her body.

"I should go," I murmured, sliding my hand over her hair. "I have to drive home."

Ella looked up at me, her lips pulling down into a frown. "Stay," she insisted. "The roads aren't safe."

"But your parents…" I couldn't hide my grimace.

"Won't care that their daughter is in a stable, safe relationship and would probably love to meet the guy their daughter has been talking about for months." Her eyes widened like she'd said too much. "Forget that I said that."

"Nope." I chuckled, curling my fingers under her chin. "I'm afraid that's not possible, Princess. Come on, you can just tell me you liked me."

"Cam!" Ella's cheeks flushed. "We're dating. It shouldn't be a secret."

"Mmm. Maybe I just like hearing it. That you liked me."

Her fingers fiddled with the open buttons of my shirt. "Well…" she trailed off, making me work for it. "Maybe a little." Her voice dropped another octave, like she was shy—unsure. "Just stay, okay?"

A seductive smile tugged across my lips. I kissed her neck before standing up, offering her a hand. "Should we go back inside, then?"

Ella nodded. "I'm sure Audrey's wondering where I am."

I chuckled. Her twin had seen me head outside earlier, so I

doubted she wondered that at all. She knew exactly what we were up to.

"No funny business," she said, poking at me in the chest before interlacing our hands. "Ready to go meet my parents?"

Nodding, I swallowed roughly as I kissed her knuckles.

Was I really doing this?

Apparently, the answer to that was yes.

"Don't be nervous," Ella whispered to me as we stood on the front porch of her house. They lived in a big house in a nice neighborhood, but it was nothing like mine.

I wondered what she would think if I brought her to my childhood home. Though home might have been an understatement. I'd practically grown up in a mansion. Though none of it was mine, not really. It was all family money, the family business —what I would one day take over and inherit, sure, but none of that was based on my skills or merit.

I hated that.

"I'm not nervous," I lied as she squeezed my hand. Because of all the people in the world I wanted to impress, to make a good impression on, it was Ella's parents.

She opened up the door, tugging me behind her.

"Mom?" she called out, weaving into the living room. The entire house was still decorated for Christmas, the tree in the living room still lit up despite the late hour. "Dad?"

"Ells?" Her mother padded into the room with a robe wrapped around her. "Are you guys just getting home?"

"Well..." Ella looked at me as her mom entered the room, and then back at her. "Audrey said she was going to stay for a little longer."

Before we'd left the party, we'd caught up with her twin, and after they'd talked for a moment, the twins sharing a hug, Audrey promised to text when she was on her way home.

"Oh. Hi." Ella's dad joined the room too, wearing a pair of plaid flannel pajama bottoms and an Ashford Carpentry t-shirt. I made a mental note of it, since Ella and I had never discussed what her parents did before. He slid in next to his wife, wrapping an arm around her shoulders.

"This is Cam. He drove down to surprise me," Ella said, not one hint of fear in her words.

I squeezed her hand this time, wanting her to know I was here.

"Cameron Edwards," I offered, throat dry.

"Leah Ashford," Ella's mom said, introducing herself to me, "and this is my husband, Stephen."

Ella's dad stuck out his hand for me to shake, eyeing me skeptically. I couldn't blame him, not when I was with one of his two precious daughters.

"It's a pleasure to meet you both," I said, wincing slightly at the grip of his hand. "I was going to drive home tonight, but it's late, and Ella didn't want me on the roads…"

"Nonsense. Of course you should stay here," her mom interjected. "There are a lot of drunk drivers out tonight. Dear, want to go get the guest room ready?"

Ella shook her head. "He can just stay in my room. With me." She wrapped her hand tighter around mine, if that was possible.

I choked, my eyes wide. I'd never have expected her to be so bold. As if us being together wasn't obvious. My jacket still engulfing Ella's thin frame, her hand in mine.

Her mom's eyebrows furrowed. "Ella, can I talk to you in the other room?"

Ella sighed. "Sure, Mom." She dropped my hand, looking back at her dad. "Play nice." Her eyes flashed to mine, and she mouthed, *Sorry.*

I shook my head. It was *good* to see that they were worried about who their daughter was dating. She didn't understand, because she'd grown up with parents who loved her enough to *care*. When had I had that, besides them caring about me not messing up my future career?

Her dad stepped up, pinning me with a glare. "What exactly are your intentions with my daughter? Because if you're going to hurt her, or break her heart…"

"I care about her, sir. All I care about is making her happy." Breaking her heart would be like breaking my own. Not that I was ready to admit that out loud. "It's still new between us, but I plan on staying with her for as long as she'll let me." Swallowing roughly, I kept my eye contact with her dad. Hoping to show him how serious I was. But words didn't matter in the grand scheme of things, did they? It was actions that mattered.

"No funny business?" He asked, and I shook my head.

"I promise. She's it for me."

Stephen Ashford stared at me for a long moment before nodding his head, clearly finding whatever he'd been searching for in my face. "Keep her safe." He stuck his hand out again, but this time, the handshake felt almost welcoming.

"Always," I agreed.

Ella and her mom returned from the other room a moment later. I tried to catch her face—was she upset? What had they talked about? Was her mom really okay with this? A thousand questions were racing through my brain, but it all quieted as Ella gave a little smile, sliding back to my side.

I didn't know what to expect from her mom, but she came over and squeezed my shoulder before standing back with her husband. A little *welcome to the family*, it almost felt like. Maybe that was too good to be true—too soon, but I wanted it. Wanted these people to become my family one day.

"Everything good?" she murmured, wrapping her arms around my waist.

"Mhm," I said in response, taking a moment to inhale her scent.

"We're going to bed," Ella's mom announced, guiding her husband back into the bedroom.

"Good night!" Ella yelled back, wrapping her hand back in mine and dragging me up the stairs behind her.

"So, this is your childhood bedroom, huh?" I couldn't help but look around. "It's cute." The walls were painted her favorite shade of light blue, and they'd been decorated with paintings of princesses and other memorabilia from her childhood. Dolls sat on top of her bookcase, filled with titles I recognized reading when I was younger, too.

Ella's cheeks were pink, and I pulled her in close, my hands palming her ass as I placed a kiss on her nose.

"Hi."

"Hi," she murmured back, her hands tangled in my shirt.

"I can still go sleep downstairs if you'd rather, baby. We're not doing anything tonight."

"We're... not?"

I laughed, shaking my head. "In your parents' house? I think your dad would kill me to know I defiled his daughter under his roof."

"Oh." Her cheeks were pink. "But you're still gonna sleep in my bed, right?"

I kissed her softly. "That depends."

"On..." She let my jacket fall down her shoulders.

My eyes looked over at her drawers. "What are you wearing to bed, Princess?"

She smiled, kissing me back before rummaging through and pulling out my t-shirt. "This?"

I smirked. "Good girl."

"Will you unzip me?" she asked, spinning around and brushing her hair off her back.

Placing a kiss on her bare shoulder, I slowly tugged down the zipper, exposing the bare skin of her back. When it hit the bottom of the track, Ella shrugged the straps off, leaving me with a view of her creamy, soft skin as the dress slipped to the floor.

"Fuck," I groaned as she turned to me, pressing her hardened nipples against my shirt. She'd only worn a tiny pair of lace panties under that dress, nothing more. "You're not playing fair."

Ella batted her eyelashes. "What do you mean, Charming?" She pulled my shirt over her head, covering those tits I loved. "I'm just getting ready for bed."

She gave me a wink before whirling out of her room, leaving me to tear off my shirt and pants while she was in the bathroom.

Left in just my boxers, I slid under her covers, claiming my side of the bed. I scrolled on my phone as I waited for her, yawning since it was already pretty late.

She came back from the bathroom, face now clear of any makeup.

"So, we're just gonna… sleep?" Ella raised an eyebrow at me as she pulled back the covers to get into bed.

"Yes."

"Nothing else?" She slid her body in next to me, nestling her ass into my crotch.

"Ella," I warned as she shimmied her body till we were a snug fit.

"What?" she asked, trying to sound innocent. "I'm just trying to get comfortable."

I stiffened, my cock already growing hard in response. How was it possible it had only been two weeks and I needed her this badly?

"We shouldn't," I said against her ear as my fingers danced over the hem of *my* shirt against her thighs, knowing what I'd find underneath.

"Please," she begged. "I need you." Ella's hand clasped over mine, and she guided me to her entrance, pressing my fingers against her wet pussy.

No panties. *Fuck.*

"Ella," I groaned.

"I can be quiet," she promised. "They don't need to know. *Please.*" She twisted her head, kissing me as I pressed my fingers deep inside of her, inhaling her little breathy noises.

"You want me to fuck this sweet little pussy, baby? Even though your parents are downstairs?"

"Yes," she agreed, grinding her ass against my dick. If I'd been half hard before, it was fully at attention now,

"Needy little thing," I said, kissing her neck as I hiked my t-shirt up to her ribs, cupping one of her breasts as I continued fucking her with my fingers. "You like that?"

"*Yes.*"

Teasing her nipple with my fingers, I crooked my fingers inside of her as she whined. "What do you need?"

"You to fuck me." Ella writhed underneath me. "Make me come, please."

"How do you want it?" I nipped at her ear. "Use your words, Princess."

"Your cock," she whined, sliding her hand backward to cup my erection. "I need your cock inside of me."

"You're gonna be the death of me," I muttered as she pushed my boxers down.

Grasping her thigh, I lifted her leg, sliding inside her from behind. Ella gasped as I sheathed myself fully inside of her.

Squeezing my eyes shut, I groaned, trying to hold myself back. "So damn good. You always feel so fucking good."

Moving in slow, shallow strokes, there were no words as we came together, moving in tandem without thought. Ella gave a soft cry as she came, and I followed quickly behind her, burying my face in her neck to keep from chanting her name.

Later, after we'd cleaned up, we curled back up together in her bed, warm and sated. Ella's head rested against my biceps and I had my arms around her—because I couldn't seem to let her go. Even if it was late, I watched her eyelids droop, fighting sleep myself because I didn't want the morning to come yet.

"What's your middle name?" She murmured, tracing a line over my abs.

"What?" I laughed.

"I just realized I didn't know it. Feels like I should, y'know. Considering where we are."

"It's Arthur." Grabbing her hand, I kissed each one of her fingers. "Cameron Arthur Edwards."

"Really?" She quirked an eyebrow.

I laughed. "My dad really liked Camelot and the legends of King Arthur and his knights when he was younger. Mom disagreed with it for a first name, but…"

"Mmm." She cuddled into my side.

"What's yours?"

"Grace."

"Ella Grace," I murmured. "Pretty. I like it." Ella Grace Edwards had a nice ring to it.

Not that it was something I should think about right now, but I couldn't help it. Not when we were curled up in bed together, warm and cozy, and she had her head resting on my chest. Not when she felt like mine.

"Do you have to leave tomorrow?" Ella asked, tilting up her head to bring her eyes to mine.

"Come back with me?" My voice was rough as I asked. "I know it's a few days early, but…"

"Usually Audrey and I drive back together, but…" she sighed, snuggling into my embrace. "I don't want to say goodbye."

A hum escaped my lips as a response. "I know." It would only be a few days, but I'd rather drive back to campus with my girl in my car, to soak up every minute we could alone before everyone else came back to the fraternity house. "Still… What do you think?"

She pretended to think about it for a moment and then said, "Okay."

"Okay, you'll come?"

"Yeah." Her lips curled up in a smile, and she kissed my cheek. "I'd go anywhere with you, Charming."

Her words warmed my heart, and I was going to wrap them up and keep them—the best present I could have ever asked for.

Happy New Year, indeed.

CHAPTER 27
Ella

My mom's words bounced around my head. Before we'd left, she pulled me aside, telling me how *charming* she thought Cameron was. We'd stayed an extra day, and Cam had done all of our family things with us—including helping my mom do the dishes after breakfast, and playing board games with us after lunch.

It had been the perfect day, and if my parents thought I was making the wrong choice, they hadn't vocalized it. And even though we'd been on our best behavior, Cam had made sure I knew he was there all day—a little touch here and there, asking me if I needed anything (as if we weren't in my house), and a kiss to the forehead whenever he left the room.

I was still trying to figure out what I'd done to deserve him.

With my suitcases securely in the back of Cam's car, a wave of uneasiness washed over me as we headed back to Castleton.

His hand was on my thigh, the car's audio system down low.

We'd been listening to a mix of his favorite artists in the car, and Michael Bublé's Christmas album was currently playing at my insistence. Namely that I wasn't ready for the holiday season to be over yet. I hummed along to the song playing, trying to distract myself from the feeling in my gut.

"You nervous?" he asked me, not taking his eyes off the road.

I looked up from my phone, focusing on his side profile instead. I'd been on Pinterest, making a board for a new project I'd gotten into my head. "For the semester? No." Not really. That wasn't the thing I was worried about.

We'd spent the last month in a bubble, where it was just him and me, and nothing else mattered. We were in a good place. But now, we'd be back on campus, with classes and organizations to run. Why did it feel like we'd be desperately clinging to each other despite not having enough time to actually *be* together?

That was what had my stomach in knots. That this thing—this good thing—could be over before it ever really began.

He squeezed my knee. "Talk to me, baby."

"It's nothing." I turned to look out the window, letting the thoughts swirl around in my head. "I just…"

How did I verbalize my greatest fears out loud? That I'd get attached, and just when I'd let myself love him, he'd leave? Because I knew how easy it would be to love him. How close I was to the feeling, already.

Maybe that was crazy. Maybe all of this was.

But it still didn't make me fear it any less.

He hummed in response, changing the subject. "I'm thinking pizza for dinner. What do you want?"

"Yeah. Pizza's good."

He kissed my knuckles. "Okay."

Luckily, Cam didn't say anything else—maybe he recognized I needed space. Whatever the reason, I was grateful, turning up the volume on the music, words from the Christmas song immediately flooding the car.

When we pulled up to the fraternity house, I swallowed roughly. "Are you sure about this?"

"What?" He frowned. "You staying with me for a few days? No one else is back yet. It'll be fine."

"No." I shook my head. Forced out the word. "Us."

"Am I sure about us?" He snorted. "Baby, I've never been

more sure." He leaned over, kissing my cheek. "Do you think I would have chased you for the last two months if I wasn't sure about you? That I like you? That I want *you*?"

I bit my lip. "No." It wasn't that, anyway. It was… everything else. "Everything just felt so much easier when it was just us. When we were just Ella and Cam. Not presidents, or anything else, just… us." Winter break seemed like a dream now. Sure, our friends were there, but we'd been in a bubble. Suddenly, it felt like that was bursting. My eyes filled with tears.

"Come 'ere," he said, opening his arms and pulling me onto his lap. "We're gonna be okay, baby. And no matter what, it's always going to be us."

"Promise?"

His lips brushed my forehead. "Promise."

That was all I needed.

I'd spent the last few days before everyone moved back in at the frat house, sleeping in Cam's bed and debating how many shirts I could steal without him noticing.

How were they so damn soft? I scowled, just thinking about it as I stood in the sorority kitchen, making breakfast. I'd slept in my bed last night, and it had been a stark contrast to how warm and cozy it was to curl up in bed with him.

"Damn Charming," I muttered to myself. Damn him for making it so hard to sleep without him. It wasn't like we could easily spend the night together now that the semester had started—I could get in major trouble if he was caught in my room after curfew, especially since I was supposed to set the example—and I was pretty sure my sorority sisters would notice if I started spending every night in someone else's bed.

I was so absorbed in that thought that I didn't even notice my house mom coming downstairs.

"Happy first day of classes," Ilene said, catching me before I headed out the door.

I paused. "Thanks," I murmured, giving her a small smile as I shoved a bite of bagel into my mouth.

"How's everything been? We haven't talked much lately."

"Good."

She drummed her fingers on the table.

Shit, I was going to be late for my first class if I didn't wrap this up quickly.

"What's up?" I asked her, slinging my book bag onto the table.

"We should talk."

I winced. "About?"

"Ella." She sighed. "I know you're involved with the Chapter President of Delta Sig. Cameron Edwards."

As if I hadn't seen this coming. I exhaled roughly. "Yeah. We're seeing each other." That was an understatement, but I didn't think she needed to know how many nights I'd spent in his bed in the last month.

More than I'd spent alone.

"I know I overlooked him staying here when you were sick last semester, Ella, but the house rules are rules. Even for the Chapter President."

As if that reminder didn't sting. "I'm aware." It wasn't like I'd been trying to sneak around with him. I didn't want to break the rules.

"You should put a stop to this before it gets too serious," she said, crossing her arms over her chest. "Guys like him are all the same."

I frowned. "You don't even know him." Not like I did.

And maybe the part of it I didn't want to admit—not to her, or to myself, was that it already was that serious.

If the butterflies that never seemed to go away were any indication, I was already in too deep.

I'd let him meet my parents, for goodness' sake. And I'd

never introduced my parents to any of the guys I'd been seeing before.

"Ilene." I rubbed at my forehead. "He's not going to hurt me." No matter what else I believed, I knew that. He cared about me. The way he was so tender and caring with me, like he was protecting my heart?

He'd chased after me. He'd spent months proving how much he wanted me. That couldn't all be a lie. Not when he'd told me he'd wanted more. More than just sex. I believed him.

"I have to get to class," I muttered, grabbing my bag and swinging it over my shoulder.

"Ella." Her voice stopped me, and when I looked back, her expression was almost... sad? Disappointed? Whatever it was, I hated it. "Just remember the rules."

I gave her a brief nod before hustling out the door and heading towards campus, needing the crisp walk to clear my head.

To keep that creeping doubt out of my thoughts.

Thankfully, I hadn't been late to my first class of the day, and I'd survived my schedule, barely fitting a quick lunch in the middle of my classes.

My last class of the day had been a last-minute addition to my semester, and I left feeling way better about it than I'd ever expected to.

Vocal lessons weren't something I'd ever really considered taking, but when spot had opened up in the beginner vocal class this semester, I hadn't been able to say no. I'd gotten lucky, and despite what I'd told Cam—I really loved singing. Maybe I didn't want to perform or be on stage, but I wanted to *sing*.

I'd gotten lucky that there was a spot since someone had

dropped out, meaning a few days a week, I'd be here, in the music studio classrooms, with Professor James as my instructor.

A smile curled over my lips as I closed the door behind me. I'd always worried about not being good enough. But she'd given me pointers, and worked with me, and for the first time since I was a kid, I was genuinely excited about singing in front of someone else.

A redhead peeked her head around the corner as I hummed to myself.

"You're fantastic."

"Oh." I flushed, not realizing that I wasn't alone. "I didn't realize anyone was listening."

"No, I wasn't—I'm next," she explained, pointing at the door. "I promise I wasn't trying to eavesdrop..." Her freckles dotted her entire face, her sheepish expression somehow making them stand out more. "I'm Arielle Thomas. You can call me Ari, though."

"Ella Ashford," I offered with a warm smile. "It's nice to meet you. I don't think I've seen you around before."

Not that I knew everyone, but I definitely was familiar with most of the people in the Performing Arts department, given my Costume Design degree and the time I'd spent in the Theater building. Which was a *lot*, considering with my current project.

She looked down at her toes, suddenly shy. "I'm a freshman."

"Ah. I'm a junior." I remembered that year all too well. Trying to fit in, make new friends, all while navigating a completely unfamiliar landscape. "Sometimes the adjustment can be rough. What's your major?"

She shook her head. "I'm still undecided. I wanted to do music, but my dad..." Arielle trailed off, shrugging her shoulders. "He doesn't really approve of the arts as a career. I'm on the swim team, too, and he wants me to get serious with that, or to take over the family business, but..." The redhead was an open book, all of her emotions showing on her overly-expressive face.

"I totally get it." There was a wince that crossed my face as I recalled some comments I had received regarding my degree. "My parents didn't get it at first, either. I'm going into costume design."

"Really?" Her eyes lit up. "That's so cool."

I grinned. "Maybe I'll bring my sketchbook and show you sometime."

"I'd like that." Ari's mouth curled up in her first genuine smile. "Thank you."

"For what?"

She shook her head. "I haven't really made a lot of friends yet." She rubbed at her shoulder like it was bothering her. "My cousin goes here, too, but he's the only person I really have."

I laughed. "I only had my twin when I started."

"She goes here too?" Her eyes were wide. "All of my older sisters have already graduated."

"All of them? How many do you have?" I loved having a sister, but I couldn't imagine growing up in a house with anyone other than Audrey. It had always been just the two of us—and sure, we fought, and often, but we were also best friends.

"Seven, but my parents adopted some of us." She laughed. "It was never quiet, that's for sure."

"I can only imagine. Just my sister and I were a handful."

Ari pulled her phone out of her jacket pocket. "I don't know if this is weird, but… do you want to get dinner together sometime? I could really use more friends."

"Absolutely," I said, inputting my number into her phone and then texting myself so I could save hers into mine. "I should go, but it was nice to meet you."

She beamed. "I should get in there. I really enjoyed talking to you as well."

After waving goodbye, I headed back towards the sorority house, thinking about how excited I was about the semester. Instead of what awaited me. *Judgement.*

Because I believed in Cam, in what we had, but what if she

was right? *What if he was going to make me fall in love with him and then break my heart?* What if there was some part of me that had reacted that way because I'd had the same worries myself?

Maybe I should have told him how I was feeling, but I didn't. I held it all inside, dreading the day it would finally spill out.

CHAPTER 28
Cam

"It's good to be back," James said, stretching his arm over the back of the couch as the guys all assembled at the football house. We'd survived the first few days of classes, and clearly, we'd use any excuse to all hang out.

For once, it was just the four of us—Sutton had a project she was working on, a recipe she was trying to perfect, I was sure. Ella had an event with her sorority sisters, meaning I couldn't invite her to hang out even if I'd wanted to.

And damn, I wished she was here.

"Some winter break trip, huh?" Forest asked, nudging me in the shoulder as he fiddled with the controls on the remote.

"Yeah, there were definitely some... interesting twists and turns," James said, waggling his eyebrows at me.

I groaned. "Are we really doing this now?"

"You're the one who went and got yourself a girlfriend," Adam said with a grin. "We are at liberty to tease the shit out of you."

"Yeah," I said, unable to keep the smile off my face. "I did." I could have denied it, but I didn't want to. It was still new, but I already regretted saying goodbye to her yesterday. The last few days together after coming back to campus had been *everything*.

But she'd had to go back to the sorority house, and even if I wanted her in my bed every night, I knew that wasn't an option.

We both still had responsibilities.

And despite what I'd told my dad, I hadn't studied for the LSATs over break, too busy being wrapped up in Ella, which meant that I really needed to get serious about studying and getting into law school after graduation.

I rubbed my fingers over my forehead, trying to ignore the pressure that I felt building—the feeling in my gut was that everything was about to change.

"What?" Forest frowned. "Everything okay?"

"Yeah," I said, forcing my face back into a neutral expression. "Everything's fine." Or it would be. Eventually.

"Can't believe the two of you are off the market now," James laughed, slinging his arm around Adam's shoulder. "Guess that leaves you to be my wingman, Prince."

"Fuck off, Erikson." Adam shrugged off his arm. "I don't need any help."

"Sure. That's why you've been with so many girls this year."

Adam rolled his eyes. "Maybe I'm just over all of that." He cleared his throat. "I'm gonna go get another beer. Anyone want anything?"

I shook my head, still sipping the first one James had given me when we'd arrived. I didn't plan on drinking much, since I wanted to see Ella before I went to bed tonight—and that meant keeping a clear head. Especially if we wanted to drive anywhere. I'd take the privacy anywhere we could get it.

"How'd you deal with it?" I asked Forest, knowing he'd been dating Sutton since freshman year, when we'd all lived together. "Wanting to be around her all the time. Being apart."

"It gets easier. We had to find time for each other, but that's what a relationship is. Making time for each other, even when everything is crazy."

"I don't want to fuck this up," I admitted. "I'm crazy about her."

"We know," he laughed. "It was obvious. The way you followed her at the ski house like a little puppy? Fuck, man. You're worse than I was."

I winced, knowing he was right. I had followed Ella everywhere. It had been hard enough to keep my hands off of her, let alone let her out of my sight. "But it gets easier?"

Forest snorted. "Fuck no. I still want Sutton all the time." He ran his fingers through his hair. "She's just accepted the fact that I'm greedy, and I'll eat up every minute of time she gives me."

I knew the feeling. Like I'd do anything just to be in her presence. It had been that way since the beginning, when I saw her across the room. "So, what'd you do?"

"Be her Prince fucking Charming, man. That's all you can do."

I almost laughed.

He couldn't have known Ella's nickname for me. I didn't think she'd ever called me it in front of anyone else. And yet, the words rang true. If I wanted this to last, I had to prove to her how much I wanted her—no, cared about her.

Even if our schedules got too busy, that was one thing I could always do. *Put her first.*

"Dad?" I tightened my jacket around me, not wanting the frigid January air to seep into my bones. "What's up?"

I'd just gotten out of class, and I was headed towards the main cafeteria to meet Ella for lunch while we both had a break in our schedules. Despite her fears, we were going to make this work.

I wouldn't risk losing her, not when I wanted her more than I'd ever wanted anything else.

And especially not after all the progress we'd been making lately.

"What's up?" I could practically hear him frowning into the phone, the growl clear in his tone. "I haven't heard from you since New Year's Eve, and all I get is a *what's up?*"

I grimaced. "I told you I was driving back to school early to get a head start—"

"But you didn't, did you?"

"What?" I froze. I hadn't told my parents about Ella. Maybe I'd wanted to, and a part of me knew I should have, but I knew my dad would find some way to ruin it.

"You didn't go straight back. Don't even try to deny it."

I gripped the phone tighter in my hand. "Were you tracking me?" That was the only way he could have known that I'd gone to see Ella. That I'd stayed at her parents' house.

"Who is she, Cameron?"

"None of your business." I almost bit out *it doesn't matter*, but I knew that wasn't true. And that wasn't fair to her. Ella deserved better than getting caught up in my shitty relationship with my dad.

I knew he cared about me, about my future, but was that an excuse for how he'd ridden my ass for the last three years?

"Did you even study for the LSATs over break?"

I wanted to lie, but a part of me couldn't. "I'll be ready for them, Dad."

"Don't forget about the internship. We're counting on you, son."

"I know," I mumbled, before we said our goodbyes and hung up.

Hustling into the library to get out of the cold, I instantly perked up as I noticed Ella sitting on one of the little stools by the fireplace. She was facing away from me, her hair swept up into a loose knot on the top of her head, the elegant line of her neck peeking out underneath her turtleneck sweater.

Sneaking up behind her, I nuzzled my nose into her neck.

"Cam!" Ella jumped up, winding her arms around my middle.

"Hi." I leaned in close, inhaling her scent, letting it wash over me like a wave of calm.

Ella frowned, pulling away. "What's wrong?"

I shook my head, wrapping my arm around her shoulders as she grabbed her bag off the floor. "Nothing." I didn't want to explain my family dynamic to her. Because her parents were kind and caring and loved her, and sometimes I felt like mine could completely forget I existed and nothing would be different.

"You sure?" She reached up, running her fingers over the space between my eyebrows. "You look stressed.

I chuckled. "Just tired." And I didn't sleep as well without her in my bed. Not that I'd tell her that. I already knew how she felt about staying over at the fraternity house every night—and after her advisor's warning, I wasn't going to fuck it up by staying in her room. "How was your morning?"

I'd feel like shit if anything happened to her because of me. She deserved the best. If I threatened that, I would never forgive myself.

She lit up. "It was good. And I have my vocal class after lunch."

"I'm proud of you." I kissed her forehead before we moved apart, both of us grabbing food before we settled into a booth.

Ella slid in first, and I sat down next to her on the same side.

"Cam," she whispered, her cheeks turning pink. "Why are we sitting on the same side?"

"Because I want to."

"Everyone's gonna see. They'll know we're—"

"Together?" I asked, using my finger to angle her chin towards me. "That's kinda the point, Princess." Dropping a kiss to her nose, I straightened, going for the sandwich on my plate.

I wanted everyone on campus to know exactly whose she was.

Mine.

Just like I was hers.

Back to school at the fraternity house meant one thing and one thing only—a giant party with hundreds of college kids shoved everywhere, drinking and dancing as the music blared in the living room.

But I wasn't paying attention to any of them—my eyes were, as always, glued on the beautiful blonde girl in front of me, her hair half up in some sort of clip, a baggy blue knit sweater hiding her frame, and a pair of white skinny jeans I wanted to peel off her body later.

Even like this, she looked like a princess. She was like one of those girls who could effortlessly run a social media account solely dedicated to showcasing her outfits, amassing hundreds of thousands of followers because of her impeccable sense of style. Perfect. And she was *mine*.

"Hi," I smiled, stepping forward to tug on one of the loose strands of hair she'd left down. "Missed you."

She looked around, and after deciding that no one was watching us, stepped up onto her tiptoes and kissed me on the cheek. "Hi."

Before she could drop back down, I gave her a kiss of my own, angling her mouth towards mine as I slipped my tongue inside.

"Cam!" She blushed, pushing me away. "What was that for?"

"I'm making up for all the time I couldn't do that last semester," I said, grinning. "And to think, we could have been doing this for longer if you hadn't been so stubborn."

Ella rolled her eyes as she slid her hand around my stomach, surveying the surrounding party. "I missed you too," she grumbled.

Hardly anyone even paid attention to us as I guided her towards the kitchen.

"Do you want a drink?" I asked, grabbing a beer out of the

fridge and pulling out the lemonade I always made sure we kept stocked just for her.

"Sure."

After we both had drinks in our hands, I held out my free hand for her, pleased at the warmth that filled me when she accepted it. Heading back to the couches, I placed my cup on the end table before tugging her down into my lap.

I couldn't resist my need to touch her as I snaked an arm around her stomach. My conversation with my dad earlier was still grating in my mind, and what I really wanted right now was to lose myself in her.

But I could be patient. I wouldn't be a caveman and cart her up to my bedroom. Not yet.

"Cam," she whispered, squirming against me even as I kept her in place. "What gives?"

"You're mine, Princess." Placing a kiss at the base of her neck, I gripped her neck with my free hand. "I'm not going to let anyone else have you."

"I don't want anyone else," she whimpered. "Just you."

"Good." Our eyes locked as Ella spun around, straddling my thighs.

I slipped my hands into her back pockets, letting myself cup a feel of her ass. "You're perfect." I kissed her neck. "How did I get so lucky?"

She shook her head. "I think I'm the lucky one."

Bringing my lips over hers, I devoured her mouth. Putting every ounce of the words I couldn't say out loud into it. Wishing we had more time, because it was all I wanted. One more minute, hour, one more night.

It wasn't enough. It would never be enough. Not when all I wanted was her.

CHAPTER 29
Ella

"You don't have to hang out here, you know," I said from my bedroom as I re-threaded the needle on my sewing machine for the fifth time. I was sewing with slippery thread, but it was necessary to get the perfect finish on the bodice I was working on. "I'm sure this is boring."

I turned around to peer at Cam, who was currently lounging on my bed, a giant study book open in front of him. I'd never seen him study so much, but I knew he had the LSATs coming up and how much were riding on them.

Cam looked up from his book. "I like watching you," he offered as an explanation. "I like when you get that little crease in between your eyebrows as you focus. Sometimes you bite your lip as you feed the fabric through the machine."

I didn't know how to feel that he'd observed me so closely, but I didn't hate it. I could feel my cheeks warming, and I looked back at the machine so he wouldn't see me blush.

There was a part of me that hated how fast this semester seemed to go by, especially since it felt like every free second was allocated. If I wasn't working on a class assignment or sewing a new piece, then I was probably at a sorority function. The boys still showed up at our events when they could, too, which was the one silver lining of all of it—because at least I got to see Cam there. Still, I'd blinked, and it was already February.

We hadn't talked about the future much. What it would look like next year, or when we'd graduated. I didn't know if that was a good thing or a bad thing—because if it was going to end; I wanted to savor the time we had together, didn't I?

But the fact of the matter was that I didn't *want* it to end. But he hadn't talked about where he was applying to law school, and I hadn't mentioned about the places I'd planned on sending my portfolio.

I'd lined up an internship this summer with a local theater company back home, and I'd shadow their costume designer and help her create the costumes for their winter production, which meant that most likely, we'd be spending the summer apart.

I bit my lip, thinking about spending that much time apart. Would it create distance between us? I didn't want that. I was already so used to having him around all the time, and it was weird to think that we'd go back to minimal contact.

It wasn't even about the physical aspects—the sex, even though that was still *good*—it was that Cam understood me. I didn't have to explain what I was thinking, and most of the time, he already knew. If I wanted to spend a quiet night inside, he didn't pressure me about going out. When my social battery ran out with everyone else, he would just gather me into his arms and hold me in silence.

Above all, I liked how he noticed the little things.

"Ella." Cam's hands clasped on my shoulders, and I almost jumped. "Why are you so tense?"

"Just thinking," I murmured, relaxing into his hold as he started massaging my tight muscles. "That feels *so* good." A moan slipped out, and he chuckled behind me. I'd probably been overworking myself, sitting here for too long without a break, and I was just thinking about all the ways Cam and I could *take a break* when my door flew the rest of the way open.

Audrey barged inside, and I was very grateful that my boyfriend still had his pants on.

She let out a cross between a shriek and a groan, before it occurred to her that yes, there were other people than her in the room, mostly considering it wasn't actually *her* room.

"Oh. Hey, Cam," Audrey said, and he gave her a slight nod.

"Audrey. What's wrong?" I frowned at my twin as she started frantically pacing back and forth across my floor. I didn't need my twin intuition to tell me something was wrong as I watched her run her hands through her hair, tugging at the strands like she did when she was stressed. "What happened?"

"The other lead dropped out of the musical. He's on academic probation, so they won't let him perform. And if they don't find someone to replace him, I'm stuck with Duke," she finally said, blowing a stream of air up her face that moved her bangs.

Oh. Her ex. "Really?" I hadn't realized that. Maybe I was too caught up in my bubble with Cam. I let myself feel guilty for a moment before refocusing on my sister. "Is there no understudy?"

"There is, but since we've barely started running lines, he already volunteered to fill the role." Her eyes rolled so hard, I thought they might get stuck there. "Like I want to kiss him on stage." Her nose wrinkled, and she shook her head. "Anyway. I don't know what to do."

"Is there nothing that Dr. Woods can do?" She was the department chair for the theater department, and also the one in charge of both Audrey's class and the spring program itself.

"No. And Duke won't leave me alone. He keeps trying to get me to agree to get back together. I don't know what to do, and Parker—"

"Parker?" I asked, raising an eyebrow. She'd told me they'd gotten close again, and more than once I'd seen them eating dinner in the cafeteria, but I was pretty sure that was all that it was. *Friends.* Maybe I'd read it all wrong. "Are you guys...?"

"No." Her cheeks went pink. "Never mind. That doesn't matter."

"Well..." I frowned. The costume was already started, sewn to the original specs, so now having to change it would be a more work, but I could do it. Rubbing at my temples, I sighed. "I wish I could help more, but I don't have any suggestions." Guys were short enough in the drama department as it was without someone dropping out of the play.

She sighed, and I opened my arms, enveloping my twin in a hug. "Thank you. That's all I needed."

Cam had just silently listened to Audrey and me go back and forth. After she'd left, he'd come back over to my bed, climbing in next to me.

"Sorry," I murmured as he rubbed a hand over my back.

"For what?"

"Interrupting our time together. I know it's hard enough as it is."

"You never have to apologize to me, Ella. Not for spending time with your sister." He chuckled. "You two are really close, aren't you?"

I nodded. "She's my best friend." *Besides you.*

I'd never admitted that before, but I knew it was true. Somehow, somewhere along the way... Cameron Edwards had become the person I wanted to go to when I was sad. When I needed to vent. When I needed to say nothing at all, because my social battery was drained and all I wanted was to be held.

And somehow, I didn't mind. Not one bit.

The week passed quickly, and then it was Friday, and I was free for the weekend. I'd barely seen Cam since we'd been hanging out in my room—just a few minutes here and there, and I wondered if I could sneak in time with him tonight. Pulling out my phone, I opened our text conversation.

> **ELLA**
> Want to get dinner later?

> **CAM**
> Can't tonight.
>
> We're supposed to be doing some brotherly bonding event.

> It's okay. I should probably study, anyway.

> I'd rather be with you.
>
> And I'd rather you be sleeping in my bed.

> Well... We can't always get what we want.

> Can't we?

> We're both going to get in trouble if I'm in your bed every night, Charming.

> Midnight rendezvous later? I want to see you.

> Yes.

I blushed, thinking about what exactly that would entail, before heading off to my vocal class, already excited for tonight.

The Psi Rho girls had a tradition for our philanthropic event each year, one I was absolutely not going to break. That was why I was currently sitting at the kitchen table at the sorority house, tying a ribbon around the basket that I'd filled with *date* activities.

One I would present on a stage next weekend and then, as the guys so eloquently put it, *auction myself off*.

In the years past, I'd always tried to blend into the background—to not stand out. But this year, I was the Chapter President, meaning not only did I *start* the event before handing it off to our emcee, I was also the first one to be auctioned off.

No pressure like kicking off the event that would raise us thousands of dollars for charity.

Just in time for Valentine's Day.

Though this year, for the first time... I had someone. The thought sent butterflies through my body. Sure, we'd slept together, and been intimate more times than I could count, but somehow this felt the most... real.

Despite all the time we'd spent alone, we'd never been on an actual date.

I blushed just thinking about it. We hadn't exactly made plans for Valentine's Day, but the idea of going out together was... exciting.

My phone buzzed, and when I looked down, my face split into a grin. I still had a few hours before I could see him, but I liked he was checking in.

> **CAM**
> What are you doing?

> **ELLA**
> Working on my basket for the auction next weekend.

He FaceTimed me, which made me laugh, considering he was just down the road.

"I wanna see," he said, his hair slicked back with sweat like he'd just been at the gym. I got a peek at the top of his shirt—tight and sweaty—and I resisted fanning myself.

Be strong, I willed myself. I did not need to go over there and find out exactly how he'd taste if I ran my tongue over those tight abs, and—"Ella."

"What?" I said, snapping out of my trance.

He smirked. "You checking me out, Princess?"

"No," I denied, too quickly. Because I obviously *was*.

"I wanna see your basket, baby."

I fumbled with my phone so I could prop it on the table. "Right."

"What are you wearing?" His voice was rough as I slid back into my chair.

Looking down, I flushed. I'd just grabbed something comfy to wear as I worked on my project. It wasn't like I'd intentionally put his shirt on. It was one of his Debate team shirts, and his last name was large across my back. I'd been slowly stealing shirts from him, squirreling them away to sleep in.

He groaned. "You're killing me."

I ran my tongue over my lower lip as my eyes narrowed back on his torso. The sentiment was definitely shared. "Don't you have to go hang out with your brothers?"

"Not till later. Now, show me."

Flipping my screen, I let him see the picnic basket filled with a cozy blanket, s'mores supplies, and all the ingredients for the perfect night under the stars.

"Looks nice," Cam said. He looked so good, lifting his shirt to wipe the sweat off his face, that my skin flushed. *Oh boy.*

"Hold on." I scooped up my stuff, heading up to my bedroom, because I didn't want to be around anyone else anymore. Not when he looked like *that*, and my brain wasn't working right.

I dropped my stuff on my desk before plopping onto my bed. "You're going to bid on me, right?" I fluttered my eyelashes.

"Of course. You think I'm going to let someone else have my date? Heck no."

I blushed. "Your date, huh?"

"Mhm. My date. My girl. *Mine.*"

Biting my lip, I watched as Cam ran his fingers through his hair. I wanted to replace them with my own.

"Ella." His voice was a wordless command.

"Yeah?"

"If you don't stop eye-fucking me through this phone, I'm gonna come over there and do something about it."

"And what are you going to do?" I asked, my voice low.

"Tear that shirt off of you and remind you how good I can make you scream my name. Or…" He made a contemplative sound, and I felt it deep in my bones. "Take you from behind so I can see my name on your back as you come." His voice was pure sex, and I shivered.

"Cameron?"

"Yeah?"

"You promise?"

"I always keep my promises, baby."

I hummed in response. Suddenly all I wanted was his hands all over my body, him filling me in ways that only he could.

A thought occurred to me, and I gave him a little smirk.

ELLA

> I don't want to wait until midnight to see you, Charming.

So I'd let him have a few hours of fun with his guys, and then… I was going over, and I intended to have him deliver *exactly* what he'd promised.

"Ella." Cam's voice was hardly more than a rasp as he joined me at the front door. "What are you doing here?"

"You promised," I said, out of breath after running over.

He looked around the living room, at the guys all gathered

around the TV, and then he moved towards me, eyes full of possession.

I'd pulled a pair of leggings and boots on, plus a sweater and coat, and had hurried over to the frat house.

It was irrational, but I hadn't been able to stop. I fiddled with the buttons on my coat and the brown of his eyes swirled like liquid heat.

"Come on, Charming," I said, starting up the staircase and turning to look back at him, one hand on my hip.

His nostrils flared as he took one look at me, and then stormed towards me, not stopping even as he reached the stair I was standing on.

Nope. He just hauled me over his shoulder and kept going up to his room, not stopping until the door was locked behind us and I was pinned against the wall. His hardness pressed against my leggings and I couldn't hold back my moan.

His lips descended over mine as his hands fumbled with the buttons of my coat, groaning as he encountered my sweater. That tongue delved into my mouth, devouring every inch of me as I surrendered to him.

"What?" I gasped as his lips connected with my neck. "It's cold outside." I pushed my boots off my feet, letting them hit the ground one after the other.

He pulled me away from the door to help me shed the coat, pushing it off my shoulder and onto the ground, and then my sweater joined it, pulled over my head and exposing the shirt of his I'd left underneath.

"Damn, but I love you in my shirt, Princess."

I rocked against him, needing to be out of these damn leggings so I could have him inside of me *now*.

"Patience," he muttered as he carried me over to the bed.

"Need you," I begged, haphazardly digging at his shirt to remove it from his body.

"I know what you need." Cam tugged at my earlobe with his teeth, his low voice making the arousal pool between my legs.

He plopped me down on the bed and tugged my legs to the edge in one fell swoop, and then my leggings and underwear joined the rest of my clothes, leaving me in just his t-shirt.

"Cameron," I moaned as he dipped his head low, prying my legs apart before taking one languid lick. "*Please.*"

He looked up, a devilish grin on his face. "I told you I'd make you scream my name, didn't I, baby?"

And he made good on that promise, sucking and licking and tasting me until I came, my back arching off the bed as I fell apart. "So wet. So good for me."

After the aftershocks had settled, he pulled away, lips shining with the evidence of my release, and it sent shivers of satisfaction through me.

Cam quickly shed his clothes, absentmindedly flinging them behind him as his eyes never left mine.

"On your knees," he ordered, and I scrambled up onto the bed, eager to comply.

I felt him settle on the bed behind me, his fingers teasing my entrance before he lined himself up before pushing inside me, entering with no warning.

One of his hands gripped my hip, hard enough I wondered if he might leave a bruise—if he might want to—while the other wrapped around my ponytail, tugging my head back. I could feel him everywhere, and it was almost too much—and then he started moving, not holding back. Fucking me just like he'd promised, his last name in full view on my back.

"Fuck, I like my name on you." He leaned down, bringing my back flush to his front as he kissed behind my ear.

"Maybe you should give it to me," I said, not even aware of the words slipping from my lips. Later I'd find a reason to be embarrassed, but for now, I couldn't find it in me to care.

"Maybe I will," he agreed, thrusting into me roughly.

I gasped at the sensation, the combo of his possessive hold and how he was filling me driving me closer to the edge.

Somehow this position, this angle, felt better than ever, and I was so, so close—

"Charming," I cried. "I need—"

"I know," he murmured, coaxing my body closer. "I've got you. Let go."

My body thrummed with pleasure as he tugged on my ponytail again as he withdrew and then slammed inside of me, driving me higher and higher until the orgasm burst through me, and the only thing that kept me upright was the hold he had on my body.

"Feels so good," he groaned as my body spasmed around his length, and I could feel him hardening inside of me—my orgasm setting off his own. "You always feel so fucking good."

He came on a chorus of my name, repeated over and over like he couldn't quite believe I was real. Like he couldn't get enough.

After we'd cleaned up, we both settled back into his bed, enjoying the moment. Being in his arms, letting him hold me—somehow, it had become my favorite place. I never wanted to leave.

And yet.

"I should go," I whispered, curling into Charming's chest as he wrapped his hands around my waist.

"You should stay," he murmured back. "Sleep for a while."

"Mmm."

And because I couldn't deny him—this, us—I did, falling asleep in his arms.

Pushing off my worries and fears for another day.

CHAPTER 30
Cam

Ella stood on stage, wearing a pretty blue gingham printed dress that I knew brought out her eyes. Not that I could see them right now. Even from my view in the third row, the lights made it hard to make out any specific details. Nevertheless, she was stunning.

"How's your girl?" James asked, settling in beside me.

"She's amazing." She was introducing the event, the charity that her sorority supported, and it felt like every guy had given her their full attention. I scowled.

You're going to bid on me, right? Like she had reason to worry otherwise. There was no way I'd let anyone else have a shot with her.

In her arms was the basket she'd shown me, tied with an enormous bow on the side. *Mine.*

Her eyes met mine, and I couldn't stop the grin that split over my face.

She was presenting on the date that you'd win by bidding on her—but I hardly heard a word as I focused on her face, her presence calling to me like nothing ever had.

Fuck, but she was perfect. And *mine.* I kept repeating the

word, because it was the only thing that calmed down the possessive part of me that hated anyone else looking at her.

"For a lovely date with the Pi Rho President, Ella, the bidding will start at one hundred dollars!" came the man's voice over the speakers. "Do I hear one hundred?"

Whispers spread through the crowd, and a hand shot up.

I glared, because it *wasn't* my hand.

"One fifty!"

"Two hundred!"

"We've got two hundred! Don't forget, all proceeds are going to the Pi Rho Sigma philanthropy to support Survivors of Domestic Abuse. It's a fantastic cause! Do I hear two fifty?"

Fuck that. I wasn't letting anyone outbid me, and I had plenty of money—plus, it was for Ella.

"One thousand," I shouted, and the room quieted.

James chuckled beside me as I practically stared down the rest of the room, daring them to outbid me.

"Sold, to the gentleman in the third row."

Ella's eyes connected with mine, a look of surprise on her face. I grinned up at her, giving her a wink. She looked away, and I was sure that there was a faint pink hue on her cheeks. She gave a little wave before disappearing back behind the stage, blowing a kiss to me before the curtain closed.

"Well, we're definitely off to a good start!" The host continued, and another girl came onto the stage, but I tuned it out.

I looked over at James, who was wearing a big, dopey smile. "What?"

"I've never seen you like this."

"Like what?"

"Like you're *enchanted*." He waggled his eyebrows.

"I just... It's not like I'm in love with her," I grumbled out. But I froze. I wasn't, *was* I?

Except... why did I want to spend all of my time with her? I wanted to be there for her when she was sad, and celebrate with her when something good happened. I wanted... I wanted everything with her. And I had for a while.

If I was being honest, I'd been falling in love with her ever since that first night.

I shut my eyes, processing the thought. I *loved* her. I was *in love* with her.

Fuck. I hadn't even taken her out on a proper date yet. She deserved better. I'd never been in love before, and I was already messing this up. At least I'd fix that tonight. I'd been planning this date for weeks, and it was finally here.

"What's that look?" James asked, poking at my shoulder. His eyes widened. "You *do* love her, don't you?"

"Shut up." I shoved at him. I didn't want to admit it to anyone but Ella. The girl who was currently backstage, helping organize all of her sorority sisters.

The rest of the event passed in a blur of pink and sorority girls, but I wasn't paying attention to any of them. I was replaying the same thought in my mind. *Love.* Love. I *loved* Ella.

I'd already had plans for tonight, but should I tell her? Or was it too soon?

Suddenly, there she was, standing in front of me.

"Hi." Ella had pulled on a cardigan, her heavy winter coat draped over her arm, and her face bright—like she'd just been smiling and laughing with the other girls.

"Hey, Princess." I held open my arms for her, feeling whole as she walked into them.

"You didn't have to spend that much," Ella said, dropping her face into my chest.

"Except I did," I said, curling my hand around her. Besides, I had plenty of money. Even if I never worked a day in my life, I'd never want for anything, but I still wanted to build my own legacy. Make my own way in life, independent of my family's wealth or my father's business. I wanted to prove to myself that I was capable of *more*.

Feeling so much love bursting through my veins, and I

wanted to tell her, wanted her to know—but did she feel the same way?

Was this as serious for her as it was for me? We still had a year left in college, and we hadn't discussed our futures together. Not yet.

I didn't want to spook her. Needed to make sure she was on the same page as me before I asked her to stay with me.

"Well, thank you. We beat last year's record."

I brushed the bangs away from her face. "Of course you did." I dropped a kiss to her forehead.

"Want to get out of here?"

"Yeah?" She waggled her eyebrows. "Where are we going?"

I grinned. "On a date."

Thankfully, I'd planned tonight out already, because after my realization earlier, it mattered even more.

"Cam." Her eyes widened as I pulled up at the restaurant. "This place is expensive."

I shrugged. "You're worth it."

She blushed, her fingers fidgeting with the hem of that pretty blue dress.

Getting out of the car, I came around to open her door, offering her my hand to help her out.

"What are you doing?" She whispered.

"Come on," I offered. "Let me take my girl on the date she deserves. No more sneaking around. Just us."

Her hand in mine felt like an admonition, like an acceptance of everything I'd been offering. "Just us."

Guiding her inside the double doors, we were quickly shown back to our private table, lit with candlelight.

"You know, I'm pretty sure *you* were the one who won the

date. But this feels more like I won," Ella said after we'd sat down.

"Don't worry," I said, picking up her hand and kissing her knuckles. "I'll cash in on that one, too." I fully intended on it. That blanket and a cozy night under the stars sound exactly like what we both needed, especially with everything we had going on at this point in the semester. Midterms were quickly approaching, then spring break, and after that was the sorority's spring formal. The remaining weeks of the semester wouldn't get any less crazy, that was for sure.

Ella pulled out the menu, looking over the options. Her eyes widened as they met mine. "Are you sure this is okay?"

I chuckled, thinking about some of the previous girls I'd taken out, the ones who'd been all too happy to spend my family's money, who'd come after me because they'd known how many zeros came after my name. "Yes, baby. Get whatever you want."

She hid her face back behind the menu, finally settling on a seafood dish with pasta, and when the waiter came around, I also ordered a bottle of wine for both of us to share.

While we ate, we mostly talked about classes, the rest of the semester, and Ella's projects she was working on. I was endlessly fascinated with her ability to create something out of nothing, the way she could take a piece of material and turn it into a piece of art.

After we finished our meals, Ella ordered a chocolate raspberry tart for dessert, and I pulled the last surprise I had of the evening out of my pocket.

"Got something for you," I said, opening the velvet box and grabbing the chain.

"Oh. You didn't have to—"

Standing up, I moved behind her, brushing her hair back to put it on her.

"Happy Valentine's Day, Princess." I dropped the pendant

against her neck, moving her hair so I could clasp it around her neck.

"This is beautiful." She brushed her fingers over the charm before looking up at me. It wasn't much—while I could have afforded something more expensive, I hadn't wanted to move too fast. "I didn't get you anything, though." Her lips turned down into a frown. "I didn't realize we were doing gifts."

I shook my head. It wasn't about that. "It's a reminder," I admitted. "Of the first night we spent together." It was a little silver heel, the sapphire stone embedded in the front reminding me of her bright blue eyes. "And so you never forget your shoes again."

She giggled. "Thank goodness for those heels, huh?"

"I was determined to find you, you know. Even if I'd had to go around campus with only your shoes, I would have found you. Except I didn't have to, because you walked into that meeting and it was like my heart had come out of my chest. My dreams had come to life. I know it's only been three months that we've officially been dating, Ella, but I—"

"Do you want to move in together?" Ella blurted suddenly, interrupting my thought.

"What?" I froze.

I'd just been about to say those three words, hadn't I? *I love you. I'm* in *love with you.*

"Next year, I mean." She bit her lip. "It's just something I've been thinking about. After my term is over as president, and I don't have to live in the sorority house anymore..."

"What about your sister?" I didn't know why I wasn't just saying *yes.* Living with Ella? Fuck, yes, I wanted that. I loved her. I wanted her.

But something was holding me back. What was it? Fear? That she wouldn't feel the same way as me? That we'd move in together, and even if we loved each other, she'd still leave?

The worries swirled in my head, and I couldn't stop them,

even when Ella rested her hand over mine. "She'll be okay. Besides, I think she might have her own someone now."

"Oh?" I'd heard her and her sister talk about some lacrosse guy Audrey was friends with, but I hadn't really paid that close of attention. Apparently I should have.

Ella nodded. "Her and Parker, well… I think there's something there. Even if she's denying it." She poked at her dessert, quiet for a few moments. "You want to live with me, right?"

"Of course I do."

"Then…" She worried her lower lip between her teeth. "Yes?"

I interlaced our fingers and squeezed her hand. "You don't think it's too soon?"

"Well…" Her nose scrunched up. "By the time the semester's over, it'll be six months. Plus, the summer doesn't really count, right? We'll both be home, anyway. I'd rather live with you than with someone random."

"Don't know if I will." I cleared my throat. "Go home, that is."

She looked at me funny. "You don't have an internship lined up with your dad's firm?"

"I did. I mean, I *do*, it's just…" I ran my fingers through my hair. "Spent the last few months thinking a lot about the future. About what I want."

"Oh." She looked sullen, and I almost laughed. Did she think I'd changed my mind?

"Princess, look at me," I murmured, my lips curling up as she offered me those beautiful eyes. "About *our* future. Together."

"*Oh,*" she said again.

"Yeah." I nodded. "I want to be wherever you are. I want you at my side. Or me, at your side. Wherever that is. Okay? So if you want to move in together, I want nothing more. If you want to spend the summer together here, I'd be okay with that. If you want to go home, that's fine too."

"You could come with me, you know," she offered, her voice low. "My parents would be okay with that."

"Are you sure?" I didn't think they'd really be too happy about the idea of me spending the summer living in their daughter's room, but I'd do whatever I could to spend more time with her.

Her head bobbed in response. "Yes. What do you want?"

"Everything."

The same thing I always had.

After I paid the bill, we headed back down to get the car and head back to campus. It was the perfect night—even if I hadn't had the chance to confess yet. I didn't want to ruin the moment, as perfect as it was.

My phone buzzed as we slipped back into the car.

DAD
I'll be in town next week.

I made dinner reservations for Saturday night at 7. The usual place.

I expect you to be there.

CAM
Okay.

Bring the girl you've been seeing with you, too.

I want to meet her.

Ella looked over at me. "What is it?"

I shook my head. "Nothing." There was no saying no to my dad, as much as I didn't really want to go—and even more that I didn't want to drag Ella into my family drama.

Would she stay when she realized how messed up we were? When she learned how much I'd kept from her?

I loved her, but was that *enough*? Was it enough for her, or would she run away from me once again?

Either way, I should have told her when I'd had the chance.

CHAPTER 31
Ella

CAM
What are you doing?

ELLA
Sewing.

Think you can spare a moment or two for dinner?

For my boyfriend?

Yes.

I sent a little winky face before looking at my current project, deciding I'd more than earned a break. Besides, sometimes it felt like I'd hardly left my room lately except for class and sorority events. I grabbed my lanyard, heading out to meet him.

As the semester got busier, the times I got to see Cameron dwindled, too. We caught each other for lunch in the cafeteria, sometimes a quick dinner off campus, or for study dates in the library.

That was also the reason I'd started going to almost all of Delta Sig's parties—because it meant that I got to see my man. Which still was weird to say, even if I liked it. Calling him my boyfriend, seeing his eyes flare with the hint of possessiveness that I loved when I was wearing his clothes… All of it was new. And I couldn't complain.

My phone lit up again during my walk, and I glanced at it, expecting it to be another flirty text from Cam, but it was from my twin.

I felt bad for spending less time with her lately, but this semester had been insanely busy—for both of us. Luckily, I still got to see her at the sorority events, and in the theater department, but I missed the alone time, too. Back when we'd roomed together, it never felt like I was this far apart from my sister. Like we were moving in opposite directions.

I didn't know how to get back to that.

AUDREY
Parker's going to do it.

ELLA
Sorry, do what?

AUDREY
Be the lead in the musical. With me.

Do you think he'll fit in the costume?

ELLA
Oh.

I think so? I'd have to measure him to be sure, though.

I wasn't sure what surprised me more—Audrey's childhood best friend reappearing out of the blue last semester or the fact that he'd actually agreed to be in the musical with her. From what I remembered, he was pretty quiet, and I knew from Audrey that he played lacrosse, so I couldn't imagine how the time commitment was going to work, but if she was happy, then I was happy for her.

> **AUDREY**
> Okay. The costumes are all in the studio, right?

> **ELLA**
> Yup. I have a few finishing touches to put on before dress rehearsals start, but other than that, they're almost completely done.

It was amazing, having made almost all of it from scratch. Of course, I'd had help—other students working alongside me—but they were *my designs.*

I was proud of myself for the challenge, and how much it had paid off. Even if I was getting credit for this, it still was a massive undertaking and I was glad I'd done it. With that thought, I smiled, putting all other thoughts out of my mind and going to meet my guy.

I tripped, tumbling onto the ground.

"Fuck," I winced, rubbing the knee that I'd scraped on the pavement. "That hurt."

"Think you need some better shoes, Princess," came my favorite voice, and despite the embarrassment—because, hello, I'd just tripped in the middle of campus—I took his hand and wrapped my arms around his neck, happy to see him.

"What's wrong?" I frowned at the worry lines on Cam's forehead, the way he was focused on his phone when we were both supposed to be studying.

We'd grabbed dinner off campus before heading back to the frat house, me draped across his bed with my sketchbook while he sat at his desk, focusing on a law textbook.

"Oh. I..." He grimaced. "My dad's coming to campus this weekend. He wants to get dinner."

"That's a good thing, isn't it?" He hadn't told me much about his relationship with his parents, but I knew I'd be ecstatic if mine came for a visit. Instead, he just seemed sullen. I wondered if it had anything to do with his Christmas only being *fine*. Why he didn't plan to go home for the summer. I wanted to pry, but wanted him to share with me on his terms, too.

Cam bit his lip, his eyes finally meeting mine. "He wants me to bring you with me."

"Oh." I worried my lip into my mouth. "And you don't want me to?"

"No. I mean, *yes*, I want you to come." He winced. "It's complicated. My parents are... a lot."

I held his gaze, needing him to know I meant my next words. "I'm not going anywhere, Cameron."

He nodded, wordlessly closing his textbook before climbing on the bed next to me, scooping me up and pulling me into his arms. "Ella?"

"Mm?"

He kissed my forehead. "Thank you."

"It's nothing," I said, meaning it. I'd be there for him—whatever he needed.

"No." He rested his forehead against mine. "It's everything. You're everything."

"You're everything to me, too." I brushed his hair back, running my fingers through the dark strands that had gotten longer over the last two months. I loved it, and I wasn't complaining about his lack of a haircut.

"I want you to know me."

I laughed. "I do." After the last few months, I knew how he took his coffee—black, with just a splash of milk. I knew his favorite TV shows. How he liked to read science fiction novels, though he would stare at me instead of flipping a single page. I knew that he wanted a dog, and that I'd never felt like home could be a person until I'd met him.

"No. I want you to know everything."

"Okay," I said, voice soft. "Tell me."

He nestled his head against my neck, his arms tightening around me. "Do you remember at the dog adoption event? When we talked about the Children's Hospital?"

I nodded in response. "Yes."

"I..." he hesitated. "The reason it means so much to me is that I had a little brother."

Had. "Oh, Cam." I interlaced our hands, holding his tight. I could only imagine his pain, how much it would hurt if I'd lost Audrey. She was my other half—my best friend.

He looked away, eyes distant. I could tell just thinking about it was painful for him, and I didn't want to make him relive that.

"You don't have to tell me," I murmured, softly running my fingers through his hair, tenderly massaging his scalp.

"No." Cam shook his head, kissing my knuckles. "I want you to know. I want you to know *me*, Princess. The good, the bad... Everything."

I nodded, wordlessly encouraging him to go on.

"He was diagnosed with cancer when I was ten, and it was... fuck, Ella. I'd never wanted to take away someone's pain as badly as I did then. He was my little brother, after all. I was supposed to protect him. To take care of him. And..." Cam shook his head, blinking away the tears. "Chemo worked, for awhile. He was still sick, but the cancer was shrinking. He was getting better. Except, he didn't. Dec... he was only eight. He looked so little in that hospital bed, tubes in his body and I—

"My parents... they've tried their best. But it's been hard." His voice was rough, like it was painful just to say the words. "They don't really know what to do with me. I feel like they've been handling me with a pair of white gloves ever since then. Like if they lost me too..."

"Cam." I wrapped both arms around his neck, tugging him

in close. Practically holding him against my chest. Wishing I could take some of the pain away.

"That's why I want to take care of you." He shrugged, burying his nose my hair. "I don't want to lose you."

"You won't," I croaked out.

"No matter what he says to you—about us—I need you to know that." Cam titled up my chin to bring our lips together in a soft press of a kiss. "I'm in this for the long haul, okay?"

"Okay." Snuggling deeper into him, I squeezed my eyes shut, thinking about all the things we'd left unsaid. All the words we hadn't uttered.

Ones I was starting to feel were true, down in the depths of my soul.

We hadn't talked about it again, but Cam seemed a little lighter after telling me about his little brother. Like it was easier for him now. There was an ease in the way he touched me, kissed me, in how he started sharing more details about his life with me. How he'd grown up. What his mom was like. How he wished his parents hadn't shut down after they'd said goodbye.

Maybe his honesty was the reason I couldn't get enough of him. Or maybe it was something else. Something deeper than that. Words that I hadn't been able to say.

That first night together had unlocked something in me—or maybe it was just him—a hunger that kept coming back. Somehow, it was better each time, like our bodies had known each other better than we had the whole time.

That was the best excuse I had for our sneaking off into his bedroom in the middle of a party for some *alone time*. The reason I was currently readjusting my top, skewed after Cam had used his fingers and tongue to drive me wild.

"How do I look?" I asked him, using my fingers to fix my unruly hair.

He grinned. "Like mine."

I playfully shoved at him before opening the door, the party down below still blaring. Midterms were over, meaning *everyone* had something to celebrate.

Meanwhile, I was trying not to focus on meeting Cam's dad. He'd met my parents, so why was I so stressed about meeting his dad? It felt different. Before I'd left for the semester, my parents had given me their stamp of approval on my *boyfriend*. In some ways, he was my first serious relationship. Maybe that was why it mattered so much to me.

We headed down the stairs, fingers interlocked.

There was a group of people crowded around in the center of the room, a loud commotion drawing my attention away from the man at my side.

"What's going on over there?" I murmured, looking away from Cam and towards the source of the noise.

The girl looked *pissed*, and the guy in front of her was none other than Cam's friend. "You…" A feisty brunette scowled at Adam, the front of her *white* shirt soaked through with what I could only assume was beer. "You asshole!" She shouted the words at him.

I was pretty sure everyone in the vicinity was staring at them.

Cam winced. "Think I need to go break it up?"

I shook my head. "I think she's got it covered."

"Sorry, beautiful." Adam offered her a boyish grin. "Can I help you clean up?"

That only made the girl's face redder. "No!" She threw her hands up in the air before storming out the front door, murmuring something under her breath.

Adam caught my eye and shrugged. "It was an accident."

"Was it?"

"What, you don't believe me either?"

Cam grimaced. "Just take the L, dude. That girl probably hates you now."

A sigh escaped his lips as he looked toward the door—where she had escaped. "Yeah. Probably."

"Come on, big guy," Cam said, looping an arm around Adam's neck. "Let's go get you some water."

"I'm not even drunk," his friend muttered under his breath, but I also noticed he didn't put up a fight with Cam either.

"Who was that?" I whispered to Sutton, who stood beside me as the guys had filed out. Her dark black hair was tied up with a red ribbon that matched the red lipstick painted on her lips.

"I think her name's Izzy?" She said back in a hushed tone. "I've seen her around at the library. She works at the reception desk."

"At least she can't spit in his food."

"What?" She laughed.

"If she worked in food service," I explained, feeling bad about my joke. "She'd probably fuck with his food just to get back at him. At least at the library, he's relatively safe." To be fair, he had completely soaked her top, and every inch of her body was visible through the wet fabric.

If it had been me, I knew that Cam would have swooped in before anyone even had a chance to see the wet spot, let alone to feel such embarrassment from it. Perks of having an over-protective boyfriend, at least. Not that I had any complaints. I like his protective, possessive side, especially when it came out in the bedroom.

"It's not like he spends that much time in there anyway," Sutton said, rolling her eyes. "I swear, I hardly see him study."

Cam laughed, sliding into my side. "And you?"

He slipped a cup into my hands, and I sipped on it absentmindedly, tasting my favorite lemonade. "What?"

"If that had been us, last semester, would *you* have sabotaged my food?" I didn't realize he'd caught what I said.

I thought about it for a minute, but the realization that I wouldn't have was quick. "I had the chance, you know."

"Hm?"

"To fuck with you. We could have both messed up each other's events." I held his stare. "We didn't."

But I hadn't, because... I'd liked him back then, even when I'd insisted I wasn't interested in anything more with him. I'd liked him since the very first night. It had been hard not to, not when he looked at me like he genuinely cared about what I had to say from the first moment.

I'd only run away because I was scared, and the fact of the matter was... I wasn't anymore. Scared about meeting his Dad, maybe, but only because I wanted to impress him. Because I was serious when I'd asked Cam if he wanted to move in together next year. Because when we planned our futures, I wanted them to include each other.

He laughed. "You just wanted me to win."

"Did not." My cheeks flushed, thinking about what he'd wanted for winning. Maybe I had, a little.

"It's okay." Cam wrapped his arms around my stomach. "I think we both won in the end." He kissed my lips. "Because I still got the girl, didn't I?" His fingers trailed down dangerously close to my thighs as he moved his lips directly to my ear. "And you got the orgasms."

One mention of it and my body was already heating, the desire pooling low in my stomach. "Charming," I groaned as he pressed a kiss to my neck, fluttering his tongue against my pulse point. "We can't sneak off again."

"Who says?"

I pushed against his chest. "Everyone's here."

He kissed my cheek. "Go have fun with your friends, baby. You know where to find me when you want me." Cam winked, and I watched as his form retreated into the other room.

I caught the sight of Gus across the room and waved to him,

wondering who he was here with. We didn't have a class together this semester, so I hadn't gotten to see him much.

My twin came to stand at my side, nudging my shoulder as my eyes stayed glued on Cam, who was laughing and talking to Forest in the next room.

"You love him," Ro said, and my cheeks warmed.

"What?" We hadn't said anything about love. It was too soon, wasn't it?

"He's in love with you too, you know," Sutton said, who'd been standing there for the rest of my encounter with him.

"I don't—"

"Ella." A sigh. "I see the way he looks at you." Audrey gave me that *look*, the one that always seemed to say *I know you better than I know myself*. Which was probably true, considering we'd shared everything, always, ever since we'd shared a womb. And we might have no longer been roommates, but she could still read me easier than almost anyone.

Anyone, except for Cam.

If I wasn't blushing before, I definitely was now. "And how does he look at me?"

"Like you're the moon and he's been gazing at a starless sky his whole life. Like he needs your air so he can breathe. So…"

"Audrey." I tried to remember to breathe. "I get it. You don't have to be such a hopeless romantic."

She sighed. "Is that so bad?"

"No." My voice was quiet. No, it wasn't. I *liked* that she romanticized life. Maybe it was time for me to start romanticizing *mine*.

To accept that maybe, just maybe… the things that I'd been denying were okay.

That my feelings were real.

And maybe what I was feeling *was* love.

CHAPTER 32
Cam

The day I'd been dreading had finally arrived—though it didn't seem so bad right now, with my girl getting ready in my bathroom as I finished tying my tie.

"How do I look?" Ella said, fluttering her eyes as she smoothed down her light blue dress. It was undoubtedly her favorite color, and yet I didn't think I could get enough of how she looked in it. How it made her eyes shine.

She was absolutely stunning in whatever she wore—but it was the way she fucking *sparkled* that enhanced every bit of her beauty.

"Perfect," I said as I wrapped an arm around her hip. "Like I don't want to share you tonight." I kissed the top of her head.

"Cam," she said, blushing as she pushed me away. Her eyes darted to the floor. "I just want to make a good impression on your dad."

"How could anyone not like you?" *Love* her, if I was being honest. If he didn't like her, he'd be an idiot. "Just look at me. You've had me in the palm of your hand since that first night."

"Stop it."

"Stop what?" I asked innocently, pulling her against my body.

"Being so charming."

"Mmm. No can do, Princess. Afraid you're stuck with me." I leaned close, my lips against her ear. "Why are you acting all shy now, when I had my tongue buried in you an hour ago?"

She came over here to get ready, and something about seeing her girly shit all over my bathroom counter, her stuff in my space, had made me hard. *Fuck*, but I liked it. Next year, it would be our reality every day.

I couldn't wait.

Ella groaned as I kissed her neck. "We're never going to get out of here if you start that now."

"So?" I grinned, but I pulled away. Even though I'd rather be alone with her than with anyone else, I didn't want to piss off my dad.

And despite everything, I *wanted* him to like her, too. Wanted him to get to know the girl that I'd fallen so deeply in love with. The one who I wanted to spend the rest of my life with.

Standing up to my full height, I brushed a hand down her cheek.

"You're so handsome," Ella murmured as she straightened my tie. "It should be illegal how good you look in a suit."

I grinned. "I'll remember that later, baby."

Extending my hand toward her, I kissed her knuckles as she slid her palm against mine, letting that feeling of rightness flow through me—carrying it with me for the night's events.

"Ready?" I squeezed her hand as we looked up at the restaurant.

"When you met my dad, were you scared?"

I laughed. "Yes," I admitted, honestly. "You brought me home less than two weeks after we'd agreed to date. Ella, I was completely terrified."

"What if he doesn't like me?"

"It doesn't matter." And it didn't. "Because *I* like you." *Loved* her.

It wasn't the right time, but fuck, I wanted to tell her that. Wanted to reassure her that nothing bad was going to happen. Because she was worth that. Worth everything.

Heading into the restaurant, we were taken back to our table, my father already seated and waiting.

He cleared his throat, standing up to face us. "You're late."

My dad had a similar height and build to me—of course, I was my father's son—and the similarities were obvious. Same dark hair, though my dads was graying. Same nose, same slope to our cheekbones, the same jaw. The only thing I'd gotten from my mom was my eyes, her warm brown color I'd always loved. They were nothing like the cold, steely gray eyes of my dad.

"Hey to you too, Dad. This is my girlfriend, Ella." I squeezed her hand, not letting go of the grip I had on her.

If I was younger, he'd have punished me for that comment, but there wasn't much he could do to me anymore. Not when I was an adult, and perfectly capable of running my life.

He could threaten to take away my inheritance, but if he wanted me to take over his company one day, he couldn't have it both ways.

"Hi, Mr. Edwards," Ella said, sticking out her hand towards him, a beaming smile on my girl's face.

"Hello." He shook her hand. "Mitchell is fine."

My girl nodded awkwardly, like she couldn't fathom that, and we settled at the table with Ella and I on one side—our knees touching, like neither one of us wanted to separate—and my father on the other.

After the waitress had come by—taking our drink and appetizer orders—he zeroed in on Ella. My first mistake was thinking he'd focus on interrogating me, and not her.

"So, what are you majoring in, Ella?"

"Costume design, sir." She sipped at her water, and I rested my hand on her knee.

He hummed in response before launching into his next question. "And what do you plan on doing with that?"

"Dad," I said sternly, not liking his line of questioning. He hadn't even seen her work.

"It's okay," Ella murmured to me. Like she was used to it. I fucking hated that anyone had ever invalidated her career to her. Like it was a cop-out, an 'easy' degree. It wasn't easy, that was for sure, but I'd watched her design and sew, and her entire face came alive when she was working on a project.

"I'm actually working on lining up an internship with a theater company back home. I'll get to work in their costuming department over the summer. And hopefully after graduation, I'll be able to do it professionally. My plan is to work on Broadway."

"Hm." My dad's face didn't soften, even when he looked over at me. "And you? How's the internship search going for you, son?"

I didn't want to tell him I'd applied to several firms in New York City, planning on following Ella wherever she went after graduation. That I wasn't sure I wanted what he'd planned for me anymore. So instead, I settled on, "It's going fine."

"The firm is happy to have you, you know."

"I know." But was that what I wanted?

No. I knew it down to my soul, especially sitting at this table with him. I felt suffocated under the weight of his expectations.

Ella's hand slid in mine, and she squeezed it. I appreciated her touch—her silent reassurance.

"And studying?"

"Oh, Cam's practically got his nose buried in that book these days, Mr. Edwards. I practically have to pull him out so we can get dinner most of the time."

My father frowned, but it *was* true. Ella wasn't exaggerating. Any spare moment that I wasn't working on class assignments or studying for tests, I was studying for the LSATs. I couldn't wait till it was over, so at least I wouldn't have all the apprehension around it.

"I'm all registered to take them in June."

"That's good."

Ella frowned, cutting in. "Your son is doing an exceptional job, you know."

"What?" My dad stared at her.

"He's been working his ass off—pardon my language—all semester, serving as president of his fraternity, and still doing extremely well in all of his classes, but you can't so much as ask him how he's been?"

"Ella..." I said, my voice soft.

"No. It's not fair. You don't deserve to be treated like this." She pinched the bridge of her nose. "Cam told me about his little brother. I'm so sorry for your loss, but that doesn't justify how you've treated Cam for the last decade."

Telling her about Declan had felt good. Like someone else would help me carry on my little brother's memories. One day, I would tell her everything—how he loved Pokémon, and collecting rocks, and how his face would light up when I came home from school when he was still too young. But that could all wait.

We had time. Because I wasn't going to let her go.

He frowned. "You told her?"

"Yeah, Dad. I'm tired of dancing around the subject, acting like Declan didn't exist. I miss him too, you know. And I know Mom does, but maybe there are other ways we could have coped besides packing up all his belongings and pretending everything was okay. It wasn't." It never was.

He looked away. I knew it had hurt him too, losing one of his sons. But I was still here. After they'd lost Dec, they'd still had me—but instead of giving me attention, I'd been shuffled between nannies and then boarding schools until my high school graduation.

Luckily, our food was delivered at that moment, saving us from any further conversation.

Ella shivered as she picked at her pasta, and I looked over at her. "Cold?"

She shook her head. "I'm fine."

"Nonsense." I shrugged off my jacket, draping it around her shoulders. I ignored my dad's look and settled back in my chair. "Better?"

"Yes," she said, voice quiet. Subdued. "Thanks."

"Anything for my girl." I kissed the side of her forehead.

After we finished eating, my dad cleared his throat. I thought maybe he was going to apologize, but he just placed his napkin on the table. "Dessert?" He asked.

I shook my head, wanting to go. "I don't think so. We should get back. We have an early morning tomorrow." The sorority and fraternity had planned another joint-service event. It didn't start until the afternoon, but he didn't need to know that.

"It was nice to meet you," Ella said as we stood up, wrapping her arms around mine. I noticed she didn't offer a hand to my dad again. Good. He didn't deserve it.

My dad worked his jaw, and I narrowed my eyes. "What? Just spit it out."

"I think you're wasting your time."

Ella froze, still clutching onto me, and I gritted my teeth. "*What?*"

My dad crossed his arms over his chest. "You need to get serious, not have a distraction." He drew his attention away from me, looking over at Ella, who just looked... sad. "I don't think you're good enough for my son."

"Dad." My grip tightened on Ella's hand. "Don't talk to her like that. Don't talk to the woman I—" *Love.* Fuck. I knew exactly how I was going to finish that sentence.

"She just wants you for your money." My dad crossed his arms over his chest, addressing me.

"What?" Ella gasped. "How could you think that?"

"No, she doesn't." Because she had no idea how many zeros come after my name. I winced. *Because I didn't tell her.* "You don't even know her, Dad. You can't possibly know how hard she works, how fucking incredible she is. Ella doesn't need me to achieve her dreams. But you can be damn sure that I'm going to stand by her side, proud as hell as she does."

And I meant it. Ella didn't need me, but that didn't mean that I didn't need *her*. I'd follow her anywhere, if she let me. I'd fight her battles for her, not because she needed me to—but because I wanted to.

Ella turned to me, her voice low. "I should... I'm sorry. I should go." She tightened her arms over her chest, rubbing her arms even as my jacket remained draped around her shoulders.

"No." I narrowed my eyes at my dad. "Stay. He should go."

"Cam." Her voice was pained. "I just... I need a minute."

"Wait for me outside, please?" I pleaded with her, because if she ran away, it would break my heart.

She nodded, hurrying out the doors.

I turned back to my father. "What the hell, Dad? She's not a distraction. If anything, she's inspiring. Because I see how hard she works every day. So you don't get to talk to her like that. I love her, okay? I love her, and I plan on being with her for a long time. You can't have this both ways. You can't think I should marry someone to have on my arm when I'm a partner at your firm one day and also think that my girlfriend—who has her own dreams and ambitions—is a gold digger or out for my money just because she has a non-traditional career path. In it for the money?" I laughed bitterly. "She doesn't even know how much money I stand to inherit—with or without taking over your precious firm one day, Dad. So you can say whatever you want, but know that you're losing me in the process. Because I'd pick her over anything. She's my everything."

"Son..."

"I'm done." I put my hands up. "I'm done trying to make you happy. To do things to impress you. I'm sorry, but I can't do it anymore. I'm going to live for me. And if you can't handle that, then I'll walk away."

I shoved my hands into my pockets, not even bothering to spare him one last look before strolling out of the restaurant.

Knowing my girl was waiting for me outside.

And that I needed to make it all okay.

I caught her outside on the sidewalk, her eyes shining with unshed tears and her hands scrunched up in the arms of my coat. It was huge on her, engulfing her frame, but I couldn't focus on that right now.

My asshole of a father had made her cry, and I needed to put a stop to that right now. Needed to make her understand everything was going to be okay.

"Talk to me," I begged.

She sniffled, shaking her head as she wiped at her nose with my coat sleeve.

"You need to let me in, Ella," I said, crossing my arms.

"I have!" She furrowed her eyebrows at me. "Of course I have. I've let you into my life, into my body, into my h—"

"But not your *mind*." I frowned. "You don't tell me what you're thinking, how you're feeling. You shut me down, and you run away. And I can't—I need more." I could beg and plead all I wanted, but I wasn't a mind reader. If she didn't tell me what was wrong, I couldn't fix it, or even be there for her. "Tell me what you're thinking. Please."

She just shook her head. "I can't do this right now—"

"Ella." My voice strained as I stood next to her. "Please, Ella. Don't run. Not from me. You can run from everything else, but stop running away from me. Run *to* me."

"I wasn't running," she mumbled, not making eye contact with me. "I just... I needed a minute." Her hands came up to her face, those fists balled up inside my jacket sleeves. "What was he talking about? Your dad?" Her voice shook. *"Money?* I mean, I didn't exactly think you were poor, but…"

"Fuck. This isn't how I wanted you to find out." I rubbed a hand over my face. "Not tonight. Not when…" I'd wanted to tell her how I felt. But now it would feel cheap, not genuine.

"Cameron." She held out a hand, squeezing mine when I took it. Like it was me who needed the reassurance, not *her*. "It's okay. But I think I have a right to know. If you meant what you said earlier."

"I did. Every word. I never want to be without you, Princess. You're the best thing that's ever happened to me." I wiped a tear away from her eye, rubbing over her cheekbone. "You really never looked me up, huh?"

She made a face. "No. Should I have?"

"Baby. Do you know what they call James, Adam, Forest and I?"

"Um… Campus royalty?"

I chuckled. "Yeah. It's not because they're on sports teams, or popular. It's all because of who our parents are. My trust fund is… more money than I'd ever know what to do with." Running my fingers through her hair to center myself, I focused on the woman in front of me. The woman I loved. "What he said is true. If you stay with me… You'd never have to work a day in your life. And if you wanted it, you could do exactly what my mom did."

She scrunched up a nose. "So… be a trophy wife?"

"More or less. But I know that's not you. That's not what you want."

"No." Ella shook her head.

"And that's not what you're going to do, because you're *so* fucking talented, baby. The world deserves to see your designs. And I'm going to sit back and watch you shine. Wherever you go, I will be right there beside you."

"But..." she gnawed on her bottom lip. "If your parents don't approve..."

"They can get over it." I leaned in and planted a sweet kiss on her forehead, making her giggle. "I don't care. I'm choosing you. Us."

"But can't they take away your trust fund?"

"No. It's not conditional. That's not how my grandparents set it up. Sure, they could cut me out of *their* wills, but I don't need their money. It doesn't matter, because either way, they won't do that."

"How do you know?" She made a face. "Your dad..."

I wrapped my arm around her waist, bringing her body flush against mine. "Because my mom won't stay away from her daughter-in-law." I grinned.

"Cameron." Her cheeks blushed. "We're—"

"I'm not proposing. Not now." She deserved so much better than that. "But one day, I'm going to get down on one knee and ask you to be my wife. Okay, Princess? And if you want to move to New York City so you can design for a Broadway production after graduation, that's what we'll do."

"But what about law school?"

"Who said there wasn't a law school in New York?"

"Oh," she mumbled. "I guess I hadn't thought of that. That you'd be willing to go with me."

"I'll go wherever you are, baby. Now, anything else?" I asked, rubbing my hand down her back. "Any other objections we need to get out of our systems? Because I'm not running away, and I need to know if I need to reassure you about anything else."

She shook her head.

"No running?"

"No running," she confirmed. "Cameron, I..."

I placed a finger over her lips. "Not now. If you're going to say what I think you're going to say... Not here. Please." Because I *needed* to say it first. Because I'd been waiting, and I didn't want it to be tainted by my dad's negativity. I couldn't help the smile that split over my face. "I want to say it first."

"You really are my Prince Charming."

"Of course I am, baby. That's why you're *my* Princess."

"Take me home?" Her voice was breathless.

I gestured to the car. "Your carriage awaits, my lady."

CHAPTER 33
Ella

So this is love. I'd known it before, even as it crept up on me the last few months, but I felt it now, more than ever. After standing up for Cam. After watching Cam stand up for *me*. Though I hadn't been sure of what exactly to expect from Mitchell Edwards, Cam had warned me he was distant. It was obvious, the way he pushed Cam without even worrying about his wellbeing.

I didn't go a single day without my mom asking me how I was, or telling me she loved me. When was the last time he'd heard that? I needed him to know it. I loved him more than I'd ever thought possible, and the second we were out of his car, in his bedroom, I planned on telling him exactly that.

The ride passed in comfortable silence—Cam's hand resting on my knee, rubbing small circles on my skin. Like he was reassuring me he was there. That he wasn't going anywhere.

Wait for me, he'd asked. *Don't run. Not from me.*

Run to me.

Didn't he know that was all I'd ever wanted? To have someone to run to? I wasn't scared anymore. Not of him, not of falling in love. Months ago, I hadn't known that. Because I hadn't known him. I hadn't taken the time to get to know him before I made a snap judgment—that he was some fuck boy, a frat guy who would never be up for more—and I regretted that.

Because Cam had never been that. At least, not to me. Not with me. He was caring, and compassionate, and *soft*. He hid his emotions inside, hardly ever daring to let them out, but when he did—when he showed the truest sides of himself—it was beautiful.

And I wanted him. Wanted more than just sneaking around and hiding this. Wanted to scream to the world that he was *mine*. I wanted everything.

He parked in front of the fraternity house, looking over at me. "Do you want to go home?"

Back to the sorority house, when all I wanted was to feel close to him? No. I didn't want that. I'd thought he might pull away, but he wasn't doing that at all. All I felt was relief.

I shook my head. "No."

"Do you want to come upstairs?"

Interlacing my fingers with his, I brought them up to my mouth, kissing his knuckles. Giving him my truth—for now, for always. "Yes."

Cupping the back of my neck possessively, he brought our lips together, murmuring out, "I want you."

"Me too," I said, snagging his lower lip with my teeth and tugging on it slightly. "Take me to bed, Charming?"

Cam plopped down on the couch in his room, running his hands through his hair before loosening his tie. His eyes fluttered shut, his head resting against the top of the couch as I leaned against his desk, draping his jacket over his chair.

"Cameron?" He only hummed in response, not moving, and I

continued, "Are you okay?" I moved in front of him, rubbing the material of my skirts through my fingers nervously.

"I should be asking *you* that, Princess."

"Your dad…" I sighed. "I'm sorry."

"You never have to apologize, Ella. Not to me."

Gathering up my skirts, I sat on his lap, the rest of my dress flowing behind me as I straddled him.

"You don't deserve that. You know that, right? You deserve so much better."

Because he treated me like I was everything, like I was precious and wonderful and I needed him to know that he was my everything, too. That anyone who treated him less than that didn't deserve him. Didn't deserve to love him.

But he was right, too. When I got scared, I ran. And I was so tired of running. Of not telling him how I felt.

I opened my mouth to tell him that, but then he cupped my cheeks, and the emotions swirling in his eyes made me choke up.

"He was a great dad, once. Maybe he'll come to his senses one day. Maybe he'll see what I see. But I don't want to talk about him anymore."

"No?" I asked, unable to keep my eyes off of him. His gaze was filled with so much sincerity that he had me enraptured.

"Tell me something real," I whispered, my words echoing the same ones I'd spoken on that very first night. The night I'd been drawn to him, without knowing why. There had been an attraction, sure, but I never would have imagined it would lead us to here. To this—us.

"You're so beautiful," he said with a reverent breath.

Like he couldn't believe I was real. I rested my hands on his shoulders, keeping myself perched above him.

He brought our foreheads together, and I didn't miss how his body trembled underneath my touch. "I love you."

My eyes flooded, heightened emotions running through me. "You love me?" I repeated, not because I doubted him. I'd heard every word he'd said to his father. But because I needed him to say it again. Because the butterflies in my stomach were overflowing, threatening to take flight. Tears spilled from my eyes—happy ones—and Cam brushed them away before kissing each cheek.

"Ella," he murmured, swallowing roughly, tracing over my cheeks, my jaw, his thumb rubbing over my bottom lip. "You're all I think about. The only one that I want. I've been so out of my mind in love with you since I first laid eyes on you. Like my whole life, I was just waiting for *you*. And I know now that I'd follow you anywhere, go anywhere you asked me to be. As long as I have you by my side, that's all I need. Nothing matters to me but you. I want to keep you happy, and watch you chase your dreams. So yes, Ella Grace Ashford—I *love you*."

"But, your father's company—"

Cameron shrugged. "It'll still be there. In five, ten, fifteen years—it's my legacy, sure. *If* I choose to follow in his footsteps." He tugged me closer. "But I meant what I said, too. I want to watch you accomplish everything your heart desires." His lips pressed against my forehead. "And I know you're going to."

I opened my mouth, but he slid a finger over my lips. "You don't have to say it now. I just needed you to know how I feel. I've known it for a while, but I didn't want to say it. It was too soon, and then it wasn't the right time, but—"

"But I do," I said, my lips parting as the words spilled out. "I love you, Cameron Arthur Edwards. You charmed your way into my heart and you never left. How could I *not* love you?"

He stilled, and I could practically feel his heart beating faster in his chest.

"I was so scared, Cam. Scared to let myself fall in love with you, and then have you walk away. I watched it happen to Audrey, and it broke my heart. So I wasn't going to let it happen to me. I was going to run away instead of seeing where this went, because if I didn't love you, then I wouldn't *lose you*. But that wasn't fair, not to either of us. And I know sometimes I'm quiet, that I don't say what's on my mind, but I'm going to be better. Sometimes you just have to be patient with me. Sometimes I need to shut the world out, but I promise not to shut you out. Not ever."

He nuzzled my forehead as a few loose tears dripped from my eyes.

"You taught me what it was like to be loved. I might have thought I'd been in love before, but I know now that it wasn't true. I'm grateful for that first night. For leaving my shoes in your room. Because it was my link to you. Even when I was scared and running, some part of me knew that I'd left a piece of myself with you. And it was my heart, too, I think. I didn't realize it until later, after the winter break trip, that I was falling for you, but I was. I was just too stubborn to see it until later. You've shown me how good it is to be loved, and for that, I'm forever grateful. You're the fairytale I'd always dreamed of but never thought I'd get. The love I'd hoped for."

"Say it again," he begged.

"I love you," I breathed. Cam kissed my face. "I love you." My lips. "I love you." One admission for every kiss of his as he littered my skin with soft presses of his lips.

He smiled as our foreheads rested against each other's, our mouths hopelessly close. "I love you," he repeated. "So much."

Lifting me up into his arms, I wound my legs around his waist as he carried me to the bed. Silently, he unzipped my dress, and I pulled on his tie, loosening it from around his neck.

"Ella," he groaned, pushing the dress off my shoulders. Kissing the bare skin up to my neck.

"I know," I whispered, unbuttoning his shirt.

And then, we didn't need words. Clothes were shed, littering the floor, and our lips met—tongues intertwining. He hovered on top of me, interlacing our fingers as he held my gaze.

Pushed inside of me, inch by glorious inch, and he practically inhaled my gasps as he kept kissing me through it.

There was only us, and *this*—letting ourselves go, succumbing to pleasure, feeling him with every thrust inside of me. His grip tightened on my hands, the luxurious slide of his body against mine driving me higher and higher. It wasn't hard and fast, or rough, and somehow I didn't need any of that right now. Just the weight of his body on top of mine and the slow, sensuous way he built my body enough was enough to bring me right to the edge.

I was so close. Crying out words I couldn't even decipher. I trembled as he brought his hand to my clit, rubbing it with his thumb.

"Love you," he whispered in my ear, and my muscles contracted, tightening around his length.

"Cam," I cried, letting my orgasm wash over me.

Feeling *everything* as we came together, again and again—knowing in my heart I never wanted this to end.

"I love you," I murmured before my eyes shut, curled up on his chest.

Falling asleep on top of the man I loved. The man who loved *me*.

The morning sunlight trickled in through the blinds, and I was greeted with my favorite sight in the world. A beautiful head of thick, dark hair and a gorgeous pair of brown eyes that crinkled at the edges as I opened mine.

"Hi," Cam murmured, kissing the side of my head.

"Morning." I yawned, stretching my arms. "We fell asleep, didn't we?"

"Mhm."

"Shit." I rubbed at my eyes. "I meant to go back to the sorority house. Ilene is going to catch on soon." Thank god it was the weekend, and I didn't have class today.

He snorted, sitting up with the sheet pooled at his waist. "You sure she hasn't already?"

My cheeks warmed. "I mean... We've tried to be discreet. It's not like we're all over each other at events."

Cam brushed a piece of hair back behind my ear. "I'm pretty sure Richard knows, baby."

"What?" I blinked. "What do you mean?"

He hummed. "You think no one notices you leaving the house in the mornings?"

"Well..." I grimaced. "I just didn't think your *advisor* would."

Cam shrugged. "I'm sure if he knows, Ilene does too. It's not like they don't talk. They're the reason we ever got paired up, after all." *Huh.* He had a point.

I opened my mouth to say something, to refute his claim, but I couldn't deny that he was probably right.

A thought occurred to me—our conversation from the beginning of the semester. We'd had meetings weekly since then, but Cameron hadn't come up again. Naively, I thought maybe she'd just forgotten, or hadn't noticed. Plus, I'd been *really* careful about him not staying the night, and leaving when visiting hours ended. Despite that, had she noticed how many nights I hadn't spent in my bed? The mornings when I'd shown up in last night's clothes—or worse, Cam's sweats?

"Oh, God. She's gonna kill me," I groaned.

"Why?" Cam frowned. "We're not doing anything wrong. We're two adults in a committed relationship." He curled a finger around my ear.

I nestled my head against his chest. "She warned me away from you."

He chuckled. "So?"

"So..." I rolled my eyes. "I don't know. I just feel guilty, I guess. Lying." Rolling over onto my chest, I clutched his pillow to my chest.

"We only have a few months left. And then..." He grinned.

His smile was contagious.

"Happily ever after?" I asked, joking slightly.

I really could have never imagined how the last few months

had gone. Becoming President, meeting *Charming* again, falling in love with him—all of it felt like a fairytale.

"Of course," he agreed. "Did you expect anything less?"

He spun us over, pinning me down on his mattress. "Everything will be okay."

"How do you know that?"

Cam leaned down to kiss me. "Because I love you."

"Oh, good," I joked. "Guess I didn't dream that then."

"Definitely not." He nuzzled my neck, kissing down my throat before I wiggled underneath him.

"I should go," I whispered. "Before we get caught."

He sighed. "I know. Later?"

"Later." I kissed him back. It was a promise.

That I would never run away from him again.

CHAPTER 34

Cam

Telling Ella how I felt was *everything*, and I didn't feel nervous or stressed about the future anymore. Because as long as we were together, as long as I had her, I could make it through anything.

In the grand scheme of things, not much had changed between us since my dad's visit, but what had changed was how easy it was to communicate my feelings now. I'd known I loved her for a while, but being able to say it was freeing.

For full transparency with our advisors, we came clean about our relationship. They'd been worried that we would sleep together, and then *actually* ruin things between our fraternity and sorority, but luckily, their fears hadn't come true.

Of course, they hadn't known that we'd slept together on Halloween or that I'd been looking for Ella since she snuck out of my room. How could they have? And even I hadn't imagined that we would end up like this when she'd left her shoes in my room.

Ella and I weren't just a fling, or a one-night stand. We were in this for real. A decision that had become more and more cemented over the last two weeks.

My phone buzzed—my father texting me once again. He'd

touched base a few times, but it was all still too raw. I wanted to spend this time dreaming about the future, not haunted by the past.

Like how we'd started looking for apartments for next year. We'd also agreed to spend as many weekends as possible together this summer, which meant a lot of driving with both of our internships—I'd gotten one with a law firm here in town, and Ella was working with the theater company in her hometown. But I'd be happy to make the drive for her.

DAD

I hope you'll reconsider about the firm.

Your mom misses you.

CAM

I'm not ready to talk about this yet, Dad.

Ella's important to me. I love her. And the way you acted... I just need time.

I'll call mom later this week.

I'm sorry, you know.

That we weren't there for you when you needed it. That we got so caught up in losing Declan that we forgot about how important you were to us.

But you are, son.

I want to be better. To do better.

It wasn't enough, but it was a start. A start that we desperately needed if we were going to mend the fence between us. If they wanted to get to know their future daughter-in-law, my dad would be smart to remember it.

Thinking about her—knowing I'd get to see her at the end of every busy day—made all of my worries float away. They weren't gone, but I could save them for later. Tuck them inside of me, alongside the hurt that I'd carried all these years. Hurt I was finally able to start letting go of, slowly but surely.

ELLA
Are you ready?

CAM
To see you? Always

Ha ha. Funny.

For the formal.

You're still my date, right?

Always.

In case it wasn't obvious, I always want you to be my date.

From now until forever.

If you say things like that, I'm never going to be able to let you go.

That's the idea.

Do you need any help setting up?

Some of my fraternity guys had volunteered to help again—turns out, they enjoyed showing off their muscles for the girls—but I hadn't been able to make it down to the ballroom to help yet.

ELLA
No, everything's pretty much done. The caterer just got here, and the flowers have all been delivered, so now I just need to get ready myself.

CAM
Come over.

> We both know me coming over there will only lead to me getting undressed, Cameron.

>> The full name treatment. I like it.

> Charming.

>> I just want to see you. Please?

> You saw me last night.
>
> And when I left your bed this morning.

Like that mattered to me. I'd have attached her to my side with a pair of handcuffs if I could, wanting to spend every moment of the day with her—but since that wasn't possible, I'd settle for sneaking in peaks throughout the day like this.

She could get ready here if she wanted—I had a private bathroom, and I'd be content to watch her get ready.

CAM

>> Maybe I'd prefer it if you didn't leave my bed.
>>
>> Please?

ELLA

> Okay, okay. I just have to swing by my room first. Audrey said she'd do my hair and makeup, too.

>> I'll see you after?

> Yes.

I grinned, pulling the tux out of my closet. She was going to look good, and I wanted to look my best, too. Not just as Delta Sigma's president, but for her. Because I was *her* date, and I'd be the one on *her* arm—not the other way around.

A little over an hour later, she stood in my doorway, chest heaving like she'd run all the way over here.

The corner of my lip titled up. Running towards me, at last.

"Hi, Princess."

"Hey, Charming." Her tongue slid over her lower lip as she perused my attire, her eyes looking especially heavy-lidded suddenly.

"Don't look at me like that," I groaned.

"Like what?" She asked innocently, brushing past me to enter my bedroom.

"You know what," I muttered under my breath, but then I was really taking in all of her, and my tongue got tied in my mouth.

I swallowed roughly, my eyes trailing down her frame. "Ella, you look..." There weren't enough words in the dictionary to describe how beautiful she was. "Holy fuck."

"You think?" She sat on the edge of my bed, smoothing down the fabric. "It's an Ella Grace original, you know. I hear one day they'll be high in demand." Her shoes peeked out of her dress— a pair of sparkly Keds she wore regularly—as she swung them back and forth.

"I know so. Because I'll definitely have the most gorgeous girl at the whole formal at my side. But..." I gave her a smirk. "You're missing something."

She frowned, looking down at her dress. It was gorgeous—a shade of dark, midnight blue that made her eyes shine like the fucking night sky. Gorgeous was an understatement. "I am?"

Nodding, I pulled out her shoes from behind my back. Those silver, sparkling heels she'd left in my room that first night. I'd given them back to her before, but the last time she'd worn them over here, I'd stashed them in my closet on purpose.

"Cam!" she gasped, playfully swatting at my arm. "I was

looking for those." Standing up, Ella reached her hand out for the shoes, but I pulled them back.

I flicked my tongue against the roof of my mouth. "Princess, have you not learned by now?" I guided her to the chair, having her sit in it like a throne, as I kneeled down in front of her. "I'm always going to take care of you."

Placing a kiss on her ankle, I guided the right foot into the straps, buckling it around her ankle before moving to the other foot. I kissed that one too, repeating the process before putting both feet back on the ground.

"The perfect fit." I looked up at her, something warming at my chest at the fact that we were here, and she was *mine*.

"How do they feel?"

Ella wiggled her toes. "Perfect. Let's just hope I don't trip in them."

"Mmm. You're perfect," I said, standing up and offering her a hand, pulling her towards me. "Clumsy and all."

My girl rolled her eyes. "It's not my fault! The ground is just..." She looked up into my eyes, trailing off with her objection.

"Don't worry. I'm always going to catch you."

Her hair was down tonight, elegantly curled with little sparkles dotting her hair. Magic. Her sister had performed magic. That, plus Ella's dress... "So beautiful," I murmured, running a finger over a curl. *The most beautiful woman I'd ever seen.*

"Cameron..." Her breath caught in her throat as she fisted the lapels of my jacket, pulling our bodies closer together.

"I love you." I rested my forehead against hers. "Just in case you forgot."

She giggled. "How could I? You only tell me every day."

"Just reminding you of your place."

"And what's that?"

"Mine." I leaned in to kiss her soft, pink lips—but she put her hand over my mouth.

"Audrey will kill me if I mess up my makeup," she whispered, and I placed a kiss on her nose.

"I know. I'm not going to." The mere idea of facing her sister's wrath sent shivers down my spine. She was all sunshine and smiles—I was terrified to find out what she'd be like angry. "Not till later, anyway." I gave her a mischievous grin.

She tugged on my bowtie. "After," Ella agreed, kissing my cheek. "Don't forget your mask." She winked and then spun around before leaving me alone in my room.

"I'll be waiting."

A Moonlit Masquerade. The theme was fitting, somehow perfectly *Ella* while being elegant and yet understated. The decor wasn't gaudy or overbearing, but the ceiling twinkled like the night sky and the entire floor was full of sorority girls in formal dresses, dates on their arms, masks on everyone's faces.

Which meant *my* girl was somewhere in this room, wearing her own sparkling ballgown, waiting for me. Why we couldn't have been a normal couple who showed up together, I didn't know. Except that then the crowds parted, and standing in the middle of the ballroom, there she was.

I didn't know why the urge to wax poetics hit me right then, but she truly was the girl of my dreams. I was a sap, and I knew it. The guys might have made fun of me for it, but fuck them. They'd understand one day.

Moving through the crowds toward her, I held my breath until I reached her. The mask covered the top half of her face, leaving her dazzling baby blues on display.

"Ella." I murmured, bowing deeply. I was aware I probably looked like a fool, but at the moment, I didn't care. Let people talk.

"Hi," she whispered back.

I adjusted the black mask that sat on my face. "What do you think?"

"You clean up nice." She slid a hand onto my shoulder. "But I've always thought that."

Grinning, I tugged at one of her curls. "You like a man in a suit, baby?"

She hummed in response.

"I'll wear one every day if I get to see you like this."

Happy. Radiant. My everything.

"Can I have this dance?" I asked, holding out a hand.

"Yes," she breathed, placing her much smaller hand into the palm of mine.

Everything felt right when she slid her hand into mine. Everyone else melted away as we twirled and spun across the floor. It was just her and me, eyes locked in our own little bubble.

God, I was lucky to love her. To have her by my side. I would have been happy to be there all night, holding her in my arms, but after the slow song ended, a loud, upbeat track took its place.

Ella laughed. "Guess that's all for that."

"There will be more," I said, low and deep against her ear. "And if not, I'll go talk to that band."

She swatted at my chest. "Want to go take pictures?"

I dipped my face low to kiss her cheek. "Lead the way, baby."

Wrapping her hand with mine, I let her pull me across the floor, knowing that the words I'd spoken to her before were truer than ever. I'd go anywhere for her, do anything for her. And I was glad we'd have these memories to look back on in ten, fifteen years.

Because that was how much I loved her. Enough for a lifetime.

"What are you thinking about?" Ella whispered, wrapping her arms around my waist as I stared at our Photo Booth pictures. We'd taken the nice, professional poses too, but these were more fun.

I tucked her underneath my arm. "How I want to remember this night for a long time." There'd be other nights that would be special, and there was something about knowing this was just the beginning that made it even more *fun*.

"Me too," she agreed.

"Look who it is," I murmured, seeing Richard and Ilene—my fraternity's advisor chatting with her sorority advisor over by the snacks. "Should we say hi?"

Ella blushed. "I already talked to Ilene earlier when we were setting up." She eyed them and then looked back at me. "Besides, they look a little too… comfortable with each other. Not sure I want to interrupt that."

I couldn't help the laugh that burst from my lips. "Do you think…?" I trailed off, wondering if she had come to the same conclusion as me as Ilene's hand rested on Richard's forearm.

"That they're sleeping together?" Ella asked, and I nodded. "Well, I didn't before, but now I do." It made sense that they had something going on between them too—after all, who else makes their organizations work together to 'improve their images'.

I watched as he fed her a strawberry, which gave me another idea for tonight. Something I could definitely arrange before I stole her away from the night's festivities.

Because I wanted to worship my princess.

CHAPTER 35
Ella

The night had passed in a blur—and I didn't just mean because of the amount of dancing we'd done or the few drinks I'd had that had kept me just on the edge of *happy* and definitely not drunk. Audrey had found me, and we'd even danced together, Cam disappearing as we shook our asses to Taylor Swift.

"Hey, Gus," I said, giving my friend a small smile as I adjusted my dress, waiting for Cam to come back. "I didn't know you'd be here. Where's your date?" I cock my head, only slightly surprised when Jackson—one of Cam's brothers—slid up to his side.

He gave Jackson a quick look before they intertwined their fingers.

"Oh." I grinned. "That's awesome. I'm so happy for you."

Jack returned my smile. "Have you seen Cam lately?"

I shook my head. "He slipped off, but I'm not sure where he went."

They chatted with me for a few more moments before bidding me goodbye, slipping back onto the dance floor.

When Cam returned, it was with a white rose in his hand, his hair looking like he'd just swept his hand through it repeatedly. I wondered if he was nervous. Didn't he know he didn't need to be? He'd already gotten the girl. I wasn't going anywhere.

"Want to take a walk?" He asked, holding out his hand for mine once again and indicating with his head outside to the gardens. Even if it was still chilly outside, since it was only March, and the temperatures during the day had only just started to rise. I'd been dancing enough to build up a sheen of sweat on my skin, and the cold actually sounded nice.

So I slipped my hand into his, knowing that I was a sucker, and I couldn't say *no* to that face.

Humming, I let him lead me outside to the gardens, letting my eyes trace over the part of the campus I loved, complete with the clock tower in the middle. The bells rang every hour, and I'd always loved hearing them, and being here right now felt like our own special place.

Like time had slowed down, paused just for us.

Dropping his hand, I ran ahead, laughing joyfully as I moved off the path. Slipping my feet out of my heels, I slid my feet into the cool, damp grass.

Closing my eyes, I let the cool air drift over my skin. "You know what this reminds me of?" I asked him, not opening my eyes. "New Year's. Outside, at the country club... When you came to find me." It was a significant moment in our relationship, even if I'd ignored it then. He'd met my parents, came home with me, and then practically had never left my side since. It was when everything started to feel *real*. Like we could really do this—be together.

I'd been falling in love with him even then.

"It was the best New Year's I've ever had." Hands down, no New Year's kiss compared to that one.

"Ella," he murmured as I spun in a circle. Opening my eyes, I looked back at him. He'd scooped up my heels, holding them both by the back straps in his hand. "You're gonna lose them again."

"Nah." I shook my head. "Not when I have you to pick them up."

"So lucky." He made a sharp sound with his tongue, which did things to me. Made my stomach tumble, my skin heat.

I needed a distraction. Needed a reason to keep my hands off of him—at least until tonight was over, and we could sneak away. Stumbling, like the ever-clumsy person I was, I caught myself at the last minute. Turning around, I spun in a circle before looking at him. In front of us was a gazebo, and the river that ran out to the ocean was nearby, giving us the perfect backdrop for a moonlight dance.

"Shall we?" I asked, unable to wipe the smile from my face.

"There's no music," he murmured, stepping closer to me.

I grinned. "That never stopped us before."

My mind wandered, thinking of that first night. He'd pulled out his phone, and played some instrumental music as we swayed on the front porch of the fraternity house and somehow… it had been magical.

Cam dropped my shoes on the bench next to us before gathering me up in his arms.

"You're making me feel like such a sap anytime I'm around you," he confessed. "I just can't help myself."

"I think you always were," I teased, standing on my tiptoes—I was much shorter than him without my heels, only coming up to his shoulders. "Don't worry though, I like it. Now…" I trailed my fingers over his shoulders. "Kiss me," I begged, winding my arms around his neck.

"What about your makeup?" He said, a smug smile on his face. Jerk. If I didn't love him so much, I'd do something about it.

"Don't care," I muttered. "Dance is basically over, anyway. Please?"

"Who am I to deny you?" He said, leaning in and kissing me delicately, sweetly, before adjusting our position so his hand was on the small of my back and mine was in his.

Waltzing in the grass, surrounded by moonlit flowers and the sounds of a fountain nearby—this was everything.

"Should we call it a night?" He brushed the hair off my forehead as he looked down at me. I enjoyed appreciating him like this when I didn't have shoes on—how tall he really was. "Or do you want to go back inside and dance more?"

I shook my head. "Take me home, Charming."

The team was in charge of take-down, and I wanted to be selfish. Wanted to put myself first.

Taking my hand, he guided me out into the night, the only sounds you could hear the slow movement of water—and my giggles as we headed to his car.

"Your chariot awaits, Princess," he said, holding open my car door.

"Thank you," I murmured, taking his hand as he helped me in and then buckled my seatbelt.

His eyes connected with mine, and my face heated.

Did he know about my surprise for him? What I'd hidden underneath my gown? It was part of the reason I'd needed more time when he'd asked me to come over earlier.

He started driving, but I frowned when we passed the fraternity house. "Where are we going?"

Campus was behind us—and so was the sorority house. He wasn't taking us to an after party or something, was he?

I really hated that idea, not when the idea of being alone with him right now sounded so good.

"You'll see," he said, pulling onto the parkway and continuing to drive. It was late, and I'd been drinking—though I'd noticed Cam had only had one drink early in the night—and the movement of the car lulled me into a light sleep.

"Ella," Cam murmured, waking me up as he opened my car door.

I blinked, looking between him and—the hotel behind him? "What are we doing here?"

"Wanted to surprise you," Cam said, a wicked grin on his

face as he leaned down to speak directly into my ear. God, his voice was dripping with sex. "You can be as loud as you want tonight, Ella."

And *oh*, if I wasn't awake before, I was wide awake now. The heat that had flown through my body was back, desire pooling low in my stomach, wetness gathering between my thighs, and I didn't care about anything else if he was looking at me like that.

"What are we waiting for, then?" I asked, sliding my hand into his before walking into the hotel.

"What's all this?" I gasped, looking at the room. "You really didn't have to."

There were flower petals in a path to the bed, and sitting on the nightstand was an ice bucket with a bottle of champagne. A bowl of raspberries sat next to it—my favorite.

Cam slipped our room key onto the TV cabinet before grabbing the champagne and popping the cork. Pouring two glasses, he handed one to me—but not before popping a few raspberries into it.

"What's this for?" We both clinked our glasses, taking a sip.

"Us." He downed the rest of his glass before taking another raspberry between his fingers, popping it against my lips. "Open."

I opened for him, letting my tongue dart out, licking his fingers, gathering up the juices. When the flavor hit my tongue, I moaned, the sweet tang of the berry lighting up my taste buds. I took another drink, watching with eager eyes as Cam ran a tongue over his bottom lip.

Finishing my glass, I ate the two berries that were inside, moaning again at the taste—but this time, for his benefit, not mine. His eyes blazed, and he moved closer to me.

Popping a raspberry into his mouth, Cam kissed me, and I

tasted the champagne on his tongue, the berry swirling between ours as he devoured my mouth, kissing with abandon.

"Tastes good," he murmured, wiping his lower lip with his thumb. "Sweet. Just like you."

I blushed furiously.

He shucked his jacket on the chair, undoing the cufflinks at his wrists. I watched him loosen his bowtie before slinging it off, like he didn't care where it went. He slowly unbuttoned his shirt as he held my eyes, and my eyes drifted down to his slacks, catching his ever-hardening erection. My body heated as he slipped the shirt off his arms—fuck, those forearms that I loved, his shoulders that I'd buried my fingers into so many times I'd lost count.

Why had I ever resisted this man? Why had I ever run away from him, instead of *to* him?

I reached around my back, trying to undo the laces of my dress—I was trying to remember why I'd made it so hard to get into when Cam appeared behind me, his breath warm on my neck, and those ample, nimble fingers took over, loosening the ties effortlessly, and then the midnight blue fabric I loved so much was on the ground. And I didn't even care that it was probably getting wrinkled, that I was sure I'd lost a few of the crystals I'd spent a painstakingly long amount of time sewing on, because he was standing in front of me, taking in full view of me, standing there clad in only my bra and panties.

"Is this all for me?" Cam murmured, his eyes taking in the blue lace set that hugged my body. I'd picked it out because it made me look good—but more than that, because it made me feel good. I toyed with the little ribbon in between my breasts before running a finger over the curve of my cleavage.

"Yes." I fluttered my eyelashes. "Do you like it?"

"Fuck," he growled. "I love it."

He paced forward, approaching me, and I walked backwards onto my knees hit the edge of the bed. Sitting down, I crossed my legs, wiggling my toes in the shiny silver heels.

When I looked up, Cam's eyes had darkened, watching me with every movement as he towered over me. Every inch of his body was finely sculpted, and God, I loved looking at him. Like this—beautiful and powerful and commanding as I traced each ridge and muscle with my eyes—and he gave that right back to me. Pure, unfiltered desire shined through his eyes.

"Ella," he groaned as I extended my foot towards him, knowing every inch of my skin was on display as I perched on the end of the bed—and not caring. He'd already seen all of me. We'd laid our truths bare to each other.

And I loved him, I loved him, *I loved him.*

Slowly, he kissed up my leg as he unbuckled the shoe. Cam's hand slid up to my knee as he slowly removed it from my foot, watching me with lidded eyes. My breath hitched as he dropped to the floor with a loud thud, and then pressed a kiss to my ankle before moving to the next shoe, repeating the process.

I was so turned on, a writhing mess as he dropped the second heel on the ground, another thud that I didn't care about, because for once, this was just us. No one was around—we didn't have to worry about his fraternity, or my sorority, or our friends hearing. None of that mattered, not in this moment.

It was just him and me, alone in our own little world. Alone in the fairytale that we'd created.

Cam kissed up my leg, not caring that I was crying for him, begging for him. His mouth ran over my inner thigh, leaving a mark on each side like he was branding me as his. Didn't he know he'd always be mine?

"Cam," I whined. "Please. I need you."

"What do you need, baby?" He looked up from between my thighs, a wicked grin spreading over his face.

His knuckle ran over my slit over the lace panties, barely applying any pressure.

"My fingers?" He ran one over my entrance, his eyes focused on the wet spot that was growing there. "My tongue?" He leaned down, burying his face in the fabric and inhaling deeply before sucking it into his mouth. *Tasting me.* "My cock?" Cam cupped himself, as if I needed a demonstration of just what he was offering. And I wanted it so badly.

"Yes, yes, yes." I didn't care which, not as he hooked his fingers into the waistline of the lacy underwear and slid them down my legs. It was a slow torture. *"Please."*

Cam threw them behind him, and my eyes drifted shut, waiting for him to use his tongue, to press those thick fingers inside of me—something, anything—but instead, his weight moved off the bed.

"Cam?" I frowned, sitting up, my lace bustier still hugging my breasts. But he hadn't left—no. His eyes were still intent on me as he discarded his pants and briefs onto the floor, his cock bobbing up with what I was sure was a painful erection.

"Need to see you," he groaned, fisting his cock. Running his hand up and down his shaft. "Show me that beautiful body, baby. Show me what's mine."

Reaching behind me, I unhooked my bra before dropping it on the floor, cupping both of my tits with my hands as I ran a finger over my hardened nipples. Fuck, I was so turned on.

I spread my legs for him, letting him get a good look as he worked himself.

"Come here," I moaned, pinching my nipples. "I need you too bad."

"Fuck." He dropped all pretense, moving to the bed to cover my body with his. "I can't decide how I want you, Ell. On top, so I can see those gorgeous tits bounce as I fuck you? From behind, so I can bury my hands in your luscious ass?"

I moaned, liking all of those ideas.

"Everything," I begged.

That would always be my answer.

CHAPTER 36
Cam

Two months later...

My door opened, a blur of blonde appearing before Ella slumped onto the couch next to me, her eyes shutting as soon as her head met my shoulder. "Thank god it's over."

"How'd it go?" I asked, referring to her last final—a presentation for her design class.

"Good." My girl yawned, tucking her feet underneath her as she cuddled up to my side. The windows were open, letting the cool spring breeze flow in.

"You know what this means, right? I grinned. "We *officially* survived junior year."

"Thank goodness. I need a drink." She pondered for a moment, and then added, "and maybe a nap."

Laughing, I smoothed a hand over her hair. "I can make at least one of those happen."

Probably the nap first—I was exhausted too.

Now that finals had finished for us, that meant we were surrounded by houses of college kids packing up, eager to head home for the summer. There was stuff to do, sure—packing up my bedroom, helping make sure everyone was checked out of their rooms, cleansing the house before it closed for the summer—but right now, I was content here with my girl.

"What's on your forehead?" I asked, reaching over and rubbing at the spot with my thumb. It was a piece of chunky glitter, probably from one of the many pieces she'd finished this week. Maybe from her final presentation today.

I wiped it off, and she grimaced. "You should see my floor. Not sure there's any amount of vacuuming that's going to get all that glitter out."

"Not yours for much longer." I kissed her forehead.

"I know." Hands in her lap, she fiddled with her thumbs. "It's weird to think about. Like saying goodbye."

Because we'd signed a lease yesterday. Our lease for our first apartment together. The keys were in my back pocket, and we were officially moving in together at the end of this week.

"Are you nervous?"

"To live with you? No." Ella burrowed deeper into my side. "I'm excited about that. But it still feels strange, you know? That Audrey won't be in the next room or down the hall. We've *always* lived together."

I curled my hand around her chin, tilting her head to bring our eyes together. "She'll be okay."

She sighed, but it was one of contentment, not worry. "I know she will." Besides, I was pretty sure, just like Ella, she had someone else to take care of her now.

"And so will we." I kissed her lips this time, my fingers brushing against her jaw as I ran my tongue over the seam of her lips.

"Of course we will." She sighed. "Have you heard anything else from your dad?"

"Not exactly." Because I'd been ignoring his calls, not wanting to talk to him. I was still mad about the way he'd acted when he met Ella, and I hadn't forgiven him for that. I needed time.

"Is he upset with you? About the internship?"

Shutting my eyes, I rested my head against her, the motion as she combed through my hair with her fingers soothing me. "No. Not about that."

She hummed in response.

"That feels good," I said, not wanting her to stop.

"I like your hair," she said. "Always have. It's so soft."

The feeling was mutual. I loved playing with Ella's hair as much as I loved messing it up. "So is yours."

A little giggle slipped from her lips, and I opened my eyes, leaning in close to her once gain.

"What do you think?" I murmured against her mouth. "Still want to take that nap?"

She only responded with a hum, before deepening the kiss. Her hand wrapped around my shirt collar. When we finally pulled apart, she was breathing roughly. With her head leaned on my chest, she whispered, "Should we go to the party tonight?"

"Do you *want* to go?" Sometimes living in a fraternity house, it felt like I'd had my fill of parties. Especially when they were almost every weekend, and I had Ella now. I was content just staying in and snuggling by her side.

Ella shrugged. "It's not my party."

"Mmm. Guess it's not mine anymore, either."

The transfer of power ceremony had already happened, which meant I was officially no longer the president of Delta Sig —just like Ella was no longer her sorority president. We'd still be involved next year, but not living in the houses, and not in leadership.

After how crazy the year had been, it was a welcome change. Time to breathe before we were thrust into the realities of post-graduate life. The so called "real world" that everyone dreaded.

My girl just rolled her eyes. "You know what I mean." A little sigh. "It's going to be surreal, isn't it? Saying goodbye to all of this? Maybe even a little bittersweet." Her eyes trailed around the room.

"Nah. This might have been our beginning, but it's not our happy ending."

Her lips curled up. "Oh? And we get one of those, do we?"

"Of course we do. Because you're my Princess, and I'm your Prince Charming." I pecked her forehead.

She furrowed her brow, pretending to look contemplative. "*Not* so."

"What?"

"My *Not So* Prince Charming." She grinned, switching positions to sit on me. "And I couldn't have asked for anything better. I wouldn't have it any other way."

"Just think..." I nipped at her ear, my hands moving to grasp her waist. "We could have been doing this for so much longer if you hadn't been so stubborn and kept running away from me."

Ella fiddled with the shoe necklace around her neck. I was thankful every day for that pair of heels, and for whatever force brought her to me. Fate, or destiny—even sheer luck. She'd stumbled into my life and I'd been determined to never let her go.

Ella. My Princess. The love of my life.

The girl I'd do anything for.

Moving her hair to the side, I kissed her bare shoulder.

"Cam," she scolded, like she wasn't the one who had straddled my lap. "We have things to do."

"Let me." I grinned. "We can do them later." I kissed at her neck. "Because I clearly need to remind my girlfriend how glad I am that I found her again, and just how well I'll take care of her."

"Mmm. Do you?" Her voice was low, dripping with lust.

"Yes." Another peck to her jaw. "But since you need reminding..."

She laughed, and we didn't leave the room for a long time—missing that night's end of the semester party entirely.

Not that either of us cared.

"There's the man himself!" James announced, his voice practically booming through the room of Adam's apartment. "Look who made it through his year as president."

Since he was the only one not living in a house with other students, it was our easy default throughout the year when we didn't want to disturb other students. Especially considering Forest and James lived in the baseball and football houses, respectively. Forest would be there for the summer, since they hadn't finished their season yet.

My friends had wanted to hang out one last time before we all went home for the summer, and I'd agreed, even if it meant I got less one-on-one time with Ella.

"*And* he got a pretty girl out of it," Adam said, slinging an arm around my shoulder.

Ella blushed at my side, and Sutton rolled her eyes, sipping on a drink.

"Yeah, yeah, assholes," I said, punching their shoulders, but I couldn't keep the splitting grin off of my face. Even with all of their teasing, they weren't wrong. It was in stark contrast to how I'd felt last Halloween—that I'd never find the person I was supposed to be with. Back then, I couldn't even conceive the idea that I'd fall in love with the girl I met at a Halloween party, let alone plan on being with her for the rest of our lives.

"Guess we can finally go on some double dates next year, huh?" Forest asked, a smirk on his face. Like he'd known exactly how this would all play out from the very beginning. "Now that you'll have more free time?"

"You say that like you're not finishing your last year in baseball before planning on heading out to the major leagues, Carter?"

Ella's face had lit up at the suggestion, and she turned to her friend. "Yeah! We should definitely do that."

"Is Audrey coming?" Sutton asked, nudging Ella's side.

"I think so. She's supposed to be bringing her boyfriend."

"So they're dating? For real this time?"

Ella shrugged. "I don't know. Audrey's been surprisingly tight-lipped about all of it."

"Ah."

I frowned. "What's happening?" Clearly, I was out of the loop.

My girl had dragged me along to see the school musical, happily pointing out in my ear which of the costumes she'd sewn or designed. Watching her see them come to life was incredible. And Parker—Ella and Audrey's childhood neighbor—had taken over the love interest role in the play to help her out. But last I'd heard... Well, I guess it didn't matter now.

Ella leaned in so she could whisper in my ear. "I'll catch you up later."

Audrey came in the door, her blonde hair so similar to Ella's curled in ringlets that went halfway down her back. I blinked, and I realized there was a quiet shadow at her side. The light brunette was none other than Parker. Transfer lacrosse star turned musical performer? It sounded like the plot of High School Musical to me, but maybe I was missing something.

The girls gathered in the kitchen, all giggling about something or other, so I took this opportunity to plop down on the couch next to the guys.

"You had a pretty exceptional year, too, huh, Erikson?" I asked him. CU might not have gone to the Championships this year, but they'd done well, making it into the Playoffs.

"Hell yeah. Bummed we didn't bring the championship trophy home, but we played our asses off this season."

"And how's the team looking for next year, *Captain*?" I raised an eyebrow, and he did his best not to smirk. Cocky bastard.

"It's great. Hopefully, our best yet. How's yours going, Carter?" He asked, nudging our friend. The baseball season was still going strong, which meant he'd be spending the next two months either on campus or traveling for games.

He looked over at Sutton, heaving a deep sigh.

"That bad?" Adam asked, raising an eyebrow as he sipped on his beer.

Forest shook his head. "It's not that. I've just been questioning if this is what I want anymore. Playing professionally after college, and all of that." He rubbed at his shoulder, not taking his eyes off his girlfriend.

"What would you do instead?" James asked, but Forest just shook his head.

"I don't know." He finally looked away from Sutton and back at us as he thrust his fingers into his brown locks. "I'll have my degree, but I haven't really stepped back from baseball to think about what I'd do after. It's just the thought of being on the road so much, hardly ever being home..." He shrugged. "It sounded great when I was sixteen, but lately I wonder if that's the life I want. Leaving her all the time."

I understood that, and I wasn't even considering a life on the road. But I'd watched my dad log countless hours of overtime at his law firm, leaving my mom to pick up the pieces, and even more so after they'd lost my brother. I silently vowed to myself never to do that to Ella. Because I wanted to be present, to share in our lives together.

"What about you?" I pried, nudging him. "How was your first year as the—" He punched me in the arm, hard, and I feigned innocence. "Still keeping it a secret, then?" I smirked. "Got it."

If he was so determined to keep this to himself, I wouldn't be the one to spoil it. Even though I didn't think he had anything to be ashamed of. Even if he *was* putting on a giant Chipmunk Costume.

A noise interrupted our conversation, and Parker came barreling through the door—*Audrey's* Parker. He looked around the room for a moment, giving us guys a nod before heading into the kitchen, pulling Ella's twin sister into his arms.

Dipping his head down, he kissed her—passionately, *hard*. Like he might die without it. Her arms wound around his neck, and then he was lifting her up into the air, his hands wrapped under her ass, keeping her supported as they made out in front of Adam's fridge.

They seemed to realize where they were, and he did his best to look sheepish. "Um, hi," he finally said, setting Audrey back down on her feet before turning to all of us. "I'm just gonna, uh, borrow my *girlfriend* now, if you all don't mind."

I was pretty sure we all sat there with the same open-jawed expression on our faces as he slipped his hand into hers, guiding her out the door.

Audrey was as pink as the clothes she always wore, trying to hide her embarrassment through her long locks of thick hair. Not that it mattered. We'd all seen it.

"Well, that was something," Ella remarked to me, sliding into my lap.

I grasped her chin with my fingers, doing the same. Planting a deep kiss on her lips, inhaling her taste and her sweet scent and everything I loved about her.

"Cam!" She did her best to look unaffected, though I was betting she wanted to bury her face in my shirt. "What was that for?"

"Thought it was only fair, since Parker was smacking on your sister."

She hit my chest, but not enough to hurt. "You don't have to kiss me in front of all of your friends," she whispered.

Forest chuckled at my side. "Pretty sure Sutton and I were worse freshman year. You should have heard these guys back then."

Adam wrinkled his nose. "I'm just saying, keep it in the bedroom."

"We all shared a room, dumbass." Forest lofted a pillow at Adam's head.

I missed those days—all four of us, in one quad room. It sounded crammed, but it really wasn't—since there were four of us, we had way more space than the typical dorm room. Plus, it had brought me my best friends. They were more than that, though. They were my brothers. The family I'd made.

And now, it included Ella, too.

Because I'd chosen her from that first day. From the very beginning.

Dropping my voice low, I brushed a hair back from her ear, glad she was sitting on my lap so I had easy access to her. "I love you," I murmured, feeling her shiver on my lap. "That's what it was for."

She dropped her head to my shoulder, giving a contented sigh. "Thank you."

"For what? Loving you? Not a hardship, believe me."

Ella laughed, her face lighting up, those brilliant blue eyes twinkling as she rested our foreheads together. "For everything."

"Always," I promised her.

And I meant it.

I'd love her—with everything I had, for the rest of all time.

Because I'd promised her a happy ending, and I was going to deliver on it.

One step at a time.

One pair of shoes at a time.

Epilogue

ELLA

"Congratulations to this year's graduating class of Castleton University!" The entire crowd cheered, and what seemed like thousands of hats were thrown up in the air at once before we all filed out of the stadium and outside to find our loved ones.

It felt like I blinked, and the day had finally arrived. Senior year came and went in a flash, and in some ways, it was the best year of my life. A lot of it was because I'd had Cam by my side, every step of the way.

We'd moved in to an apartment off campus together, and over the summer while I'd been doing my internship, as well as working on my portfolio—sewing designs in my new sewing room—he'd been studying for his LSATs and applying to law schools. He'd spent almost every weekend last summer at my house, and by the end, my parents adored him. Dad was taking him out golfing, and it made me happy to see them out together. Even if his parents didn't love him the way they should, at least my parents would.

Though they'd gotten better about his choices, too. Maybe

because he'd come clean to them about how much his little brother's loss had affected him, and they'd come to their senses. The first time I'd met his mom, she scooped me up into her arms, holding me tight. I'd expected an uptight woman, but that wasn't what I'd found at all. She'd cried, and told me how thankful she was that I was with her son.

It wasn't perfect, but what was? After all, I'd spent an entire month trying not to like Cam after we'd met, and look how that turned out.

Cam. His beautiful face—those angled cheekbones and sharp jaw I loved, the black hair I ran my fingers through every night and those chocolate brown eyes that I got lost in—appeared in front of me, looking as handsome as ever in his cap and gown. We both wore stoles with our fraternity and sororities' letters embroidered on them, even further proof that we'd made it.

Finish line crossed—we were done.

"We fucking did it, baby," he grinned, holding his diploma case at his side—and a large white bouquet that hadn't been there before. "Sorry, they aren't blue."

"Cam," I breathed as he placed the flowers in my arms and placed a kiss on the side of my cheek. "They're beautiful."

"I love you."

"You didn't have to buy me flowers."

He looked cheeky. "Yes, I did." Cam let his lips rest against my ear, and then he breathed, "Because I'm your boyfriend, Princess." A year and a half later, and that phrase still did things to me. In some ways, I still couldn't believe it. That I'd found him. That he turned out to be everything I'd ever wanted.

A chill ran down my spine at the possessive look in his eyes. "Thank you," I said, burying my nose in the pretty peonies.

"Ella!" The sound of my name being shouted startled me, and as I looked up, I saw a whirlwind of blonde curls and a pink dress—Audrey—running towards me, her face lit up with a bright smile.

"Ro!" I grinned, careful to shuffle my flowers, so they didn't get crushed, as I gave my twin a big hug.

"Hi, Audrey," Cam said, sticking out his hand in congratulations.

Audrey rolled her eyes, pulling him into a hug instead. "We're practically family now, Cameron. And in our family, we hug."

He looked at me, eyes full of emotion, and I knew exactly what he was thinking. But he needed to get used to it—because he was my family now. A decision made even more real by our bags packed in the back of his car, and the moving truck that held all the furniture we'd shared over the last year.

All of it was ready to drive up to New York City—our new home for the next few years.

"Thanks, Audrey," Cam said, hugging my sister back.

And then my parents were there, taking photos of Audrey and I, posed together, her in pink and me in blue just like we'd always been, showing off the caps that we'd decorated with flowers and sequins and glitter. Mine read *Keep on Dreaming*, and I'd bedazzled a high heel for the middle of it. It was fitting, especially considering I wore the necklace that Cam had given me, because a pair of shoes had, in fact, changed my life.

"Let's get one with your boyfriends!" my mom yelled, and Cam slid into my side, wrapping his arm around my waist. You couldn't have wiped the smile off my face.

I didn't even care that the new pair of heels I'd worn for the occasion were cutting into my feet, or how badly they hurt—because everyone I loved was by my side. My family—and the one I'd found here at CU.

Cam found his friends—*my* friends, now, and then there were ten of us crammed into one photo, because despite their objections to romance last year, even Adam and James had fallen in love, and then there was laughing, and hugging, and some tears were shed as we all prepared to say goodbye.

We still had tonight, at least, before we all went our separate ways. One last party, all of us and our friends crammed into Forest and Sutton's apartment nearby.

Distracted, I didn't notice Cam as he scooped me up into his arms, lifting me up off the ground and spinning us around. I laughed, unable to stop the giddy sound from escaping my lips.

My shoe fell off my foot, landing on the concrete, which only made me laugh harder.

"What am I going to do with you?" He asked, giving my ass a little smack as he sat me down. "I'm going to have to tie them onto you, aren't I?"

Bending down, he picked up my shoe, sliding it back onto my foot before standing back up. Even in my three-inch heels, he still towered over me, and I'd always loved that—how tall he was. How easily he could throw me over his shoulder or carry me in his arms.

Dipping his head down, he brushed his lips over mine.

A smile curling on my lips. "You're incorrigible."

Cam grinned. "I know. But can you blame me? My girlfriend is gorgeous, and she's *all* mine."

I wrapped my hands around his neck, placing a kiss on his nose. "No, I can't. Because my boyfriend is the most handsome man I've ever seen, and *he's* all *mine*."

He kissed me deeply, and I didn't care about all the graduates or the family and friends that surrounded us as our lips touched. As he parted my lips, letting our tongues meet, all I could think was, *I hope I'm at least half as happy as this, every single day.*

Because this was the beginning of our happily ever after.

And I intended to make it a good one.

CAM

Ella wrapped her hand around my wrist, pulling me into the bathroom.

"What are we doing in here?" I said into her ear, voice low and deep. We were at our college graduation party, celebrating with all our friends. Everyone here was now happily in a relationship, even my dumbass friends meeting girls they'd fallen head over heels for. I'd enjoyed teasing the hell out of them with Forest when they did.

But right now, my eyes were on my girl, who wore a silky blue slip dress and had a white headband, keeping her hair pushed back, all that lovely hair I loved hanging loose on her shoulders. I'd worn a suit for graduation, but my jacket was forgotten in my car, leaving me in just my white-button up with the sleeves rolled and cuffed, and a black tie.

She bit her lip, tugging on my tie. "Thought we might like a bit of privacy."

A devilish grin spread over my face. "You wanted to get me alone, hmm?"

Ella nodded, her tongue running over her bottom lip as she stared up at me. "We haven't been all day." We'd gotten dinner with both our sets of parents after graduation, and then afterwards we'd headed here to the party.

I leaned down, nipping at her ear. "They're going to wonder what we're doing in here if we take too long, Princess." Pushing down her straps, I bared her lacy bra to me before popping out her tit to circle my tongue around her nipple. Wanted to take my time worshipping each one, but then we'd really be caught.

She let out a small moan. "Let them." Her voice was husky. "I want you." She wrapped her arms around my neck as she kissed softly. "I want…"

"More?" I asked, my hands trailing down her spine, running over her smooth skin.

"*Everything.*" She echoed the words I'd said all those months ago. Her fingers tangled in the hair at the base of my neck, pulling my head down to meet her lips.

I lifted her up, setting her on the bathroom counter. "We have to be quick, Ell."

"I know." Her hands reached out, grabbing the edge of the tile as I pushed up her dress to her waist, tugging her panties to the side as I sunk a finger inside of her. "Hard and fast," she agreed.

"*Fuck*," I groaned. "So wet."

"Inside me," she begged. "Need you."

Not one to deny her, I unzipped my pants, freeing my hardening cock. Ella's eyes didn't leave my length as I fisted it, pumping it with my hand until I was ready, notching myself at her entrance before plunging inside.

Ella's hands grasped onto my shoulders, her nails digging in to my shirt, but I didn't even notice the pain as I sank into her wet heat, sheathing myself fully. I gripped her thighs—*hard*—and I wondered if my fingers would leave marks. Even though I hated knowing that I hurt her, that I bruised her perfect skin, I liked knowing she carried my mark.

Being inside of her still felt incredible, even after all this time. I'd wondered if the sex would ever stop being so mind-blowing—if I'd stop wanting her with the same fierceness, but so far, the answer was a resounding *no*. "You're perfect," I said, trying to hold back from making any noise as I fucked her hard on the counter, my cock wet with her arousal giving us the perfect slide in and out. I watched her stretch around me as she took me inside of her, the erotic sight somehow bringing me even closer to the edge.

Not wanting to come before she did, I brought my hand to her clit, rubbing it softly in circles, just the way she liked.

Someone knocked on the bathroom door, and I grunted. "Almost done!" Shit. There was no way we were getting out of here unsuspected.

"We know you're in there, asshole!" Adam yelled, and then

he sounded further away. "Can't believe they're fucking in my bathroom."

A female voice giggled. "You're just jealous you didn't think of it first."

He made a noncommittal noise, but I knew she was right. "Maybe."

I couldn't hear her response, not when Ella's pussy clenched around me. "I'm so close," Ella moaned, dropping her head against my chest.

"Come for me," I coaxed, not stopping my relentless pursuit, my hands holding her still to keep her from sliding against the mirror as I thrusted. When she let go, I followed close behind, spilling inside of her.

Our foreheads touched as I leaned in. "I love you," I murmured, kissing her softly as I rocked my hips against her, letting the aftershocks of our combined orgasm settle.

"Love you, too," she agreed, her eyes shining with tears. Hoping I hadn't hurt her, I wiped them away. "But we should probably go back out there," she whispered the words, looking at the door.

They could wait. There was another bathroom in this apartment, besides, if someone else needed one. "Mmm. With my cock still inside of you?" Our combined release trickled out around my length. And why did I like that so much?

"Cam." She buried her face in my shirt, hiding her embarrassment.

I pulled out, cleaning myself up before tucking myself back into my pants, and then lowered myself to my knees—putting myself right at the same level as her cunt, watching as my seed dripped out of her. Fuck. Using my fingers, I pushed it back inside before putting my mouth on her.

Ella let out a series of breathy noises as I licked her clean, before standing up and adjusting her top, placing a kiss on each breast before righting her straps.

"You're going to drip out of me all night," she murmured as I helped her off the counter, smoothing down her dress.

I grinned. "That's the idea." A primal part of me was extremely satisfied with that idea, especially knowing how it would make her squirm. Later, we'd go again, and I would take my time to kiss every inch of her body first.

She snorted in response, turning in the mirror to look at her appearance. "How do I look?" Her cheeks were flushed, but her hair was still perfect, and if you ignored the pink hue to her skin —and where we'd been, no one probably would have guessed I'd been fucking her in the bathroom.

Leaning down, I cupped her cheeks before bringing her lips to mine, kissing her once more—letting her taste us in my mouth. "Ready?"

She laughed. "For everything, with you."

"Good." I interlaced our hands and guided her back out to the party—and towards the next chapter in our lives together.

And if this was the beginning of our happily ever after, I liked to think that we'd gotten a pretty good start.

One month later...

"What do you think?" I asked, looking up at the brownstone as I slid my arm around Ella's waist. She'd left me in charge of finding us a place to live, since she'd spent most of her last months frantically finishing her final design presentation for her capstone class.

I'd taken one look at this place online and knew it was perfect. Ella hadn't gotten to see it yet, but I knew she would love it too once she gave it a chance.

"We can't afford this, Cameron," she groaned. "It's too much."

"I told you to let me take care of it." I squeezed her hip. "It's the least I can do."

"I'm not trying to live off of you—"

"You're not." I placed a soft kiss on her lips to shut her up. If anything, I was living off *her*, since I'd be going to law school full time for the next three years while she worked. "You couldn't."

Ella pouted. "Your parents are going to think I'm taking advantage."

"My mom loves you." I kissed her again to shut her up. "And Dad's coming around."

"Are you sure?"

"Yes." I laughed. Mom had fallen in love with her that very first time I'd brought Ella home. Sometimes, I thought she loved her more than me. Ella was the daughter she'd never had, and always wanted.

My dad, well… We were working on things. My decision to go to law school in New York wasn't exactly something he could disagree with, considering it was still one of the top ten schools in the nation.

But turning down the internship at his practice *was* something he'd disagreed with.

I hadn't cared. I'd made it crystal clear from the beginning—Ella was more important to me. And that he hadn't lost both his sons when Dec had passed. But I clarified that if he didn't change his tune, he *would* lose me. So I'd gotten an internship with a different firm without using my name or connections. I'd worked my ass off last summer, and it had felt… right.

Now I was going to do law school *my* way, too. And if I didn't end up at the family firm when I graduated, if Ella and I made our own home in a new town, I didn't think I'd mind so much. Because *she* was my family now.

James, Forest, Adam, and their girls were too, along with Ella's sister, and my life was full of love. Of laughter. I'd never been as happy as I was the last semester, surrounded by four other couples.

The guys ate their words, of course. But those were their stories to tell.

"Should we go inside?" I asked my girlfriend, the love of my life, as I pulled the key out of my pocket.

She was still pouting, trying not to look upset that she hadn't gotten her way, so I picked her up in my arms after I'd unlocked the door.

"What are you doing?" She laughed, that smile I loved finally bursting through.

"Isn't it obvious?" Quirking an eyebrow, I looked down at her. "I'm carrying you over the threshold."

"That's what newlyweds do, Charming. Not people moving into their first home together."

Technically, our first home together was the one we'd shared last year, but I wouldn't argue with semantics. Not when I wanted to do this. So I shrugged. "I'll carry you then, too. Whenever you need a reminder."

"Of what?"

"How much I adore you."

She hummed in response as I carried her through, depositing her onto the floor once we came into the entryway. One side boasted a living room, and the other a flight of stairs up to the second floor.

"What do you think, Princess?" I asked her. "What do you want to see first? Your new office, or your new tub?"

Her eyes sparkled. "There's a tub?"

"Mhm." I'd checked, and it could fit two people. Something I fully planned on taking advantage of tonight. We'd spent the last year in a cramped shower in our small university apartment, and I wanted the space to worship her right. "So, what do you think?"

"The bathtub," she agreed. "*Definitely* the bath."

Interlacing our fingers, we hustled up the stairs—practically taking two at a time, and I made good on my promise.

I showed her the new tub, and just how much I adored her. Loved her.

It was something I planned on doing every day for the rest of our lives together.

I'd never believed in fairytales, but somehow, they'd all come true, anyway.

Because I'd met my Princess one Halloween night, and every single moment since then, I'd been working my way towards this.

But it wasn't *The End*—it was just the beginning of our future together.

"I love you," she said, nuzzling her nose against mine.

"I love you more," I responded. "What do you want?"

"Everything," she breathed.

Always. I'd give it to her—forever.

Extended Epilogue

CAM

Three years later...

The lights came back on in the crowded room, an entire room of people cheering, but there was only one person I was here for.

Her.

The curtain came up, and the cast members took their bows, individually and then as a group, and the roar of the crowd didn't settle until the curtain was closed again.

I looked over at the blonde sitting at my side in an elegant gown, her hair pinned up in a bun that reminded me of the first time we'd met. The smile that lit up her face was so wide, her eyes red like she'd been crying off and on.

"They were incredible," Ella whispered at my side, even as everyone got up to exit the theater.

"*You* were incredible," I said back, placing a kiss on the side of her face. "I can't believe you designed all of those costumes." It was the opening night for the very first show she had the sole credit for —a musical, much like the one she'd worked on at Castleton.

"I had help," she murmured, a blush evident on her face.

"Take the compliment," I said into her ear, checking to make sure no one around us was listening in. "Or I'll punish you for it later, *wife*."

Her silver sparkly evening gown caught the lights as they came up, as well as the sparkling diamond that sat on her left ring finger, an ever-present reminder of the vows we'd made to each other. What I'd promised her four years ago, long before I'd ever purchased the ring.

"Cam!" she giggled as I kissed the side of her neck. "Not here."

"Mmmm. Where do you think, then?" I wiggled my eyebrows. "Want to see if the bathroom is free?"

She gave an exasperated sigh. "Cameron—"

"I know, I know." I was kidding… mostly. I stood up, giving her a hand. "Let's go congratulate your sister." Audrey had performed tonight, one of her first roles on broadway. How fitting that they'd both ended up here together.

Ella interlaced her fingers in mine, giving me a warm smile as I kissed her knuckles. "I'm so proud of you, you know," I mumbled against her hair. "You did it."

She still enjoyed being behind the scenes better than being on stage—which was fine with me, because I had her all to myself that way. Her and her beautiful voice, which she'd slowly gotten more comfortable sharing with me. Ella liked to blame it on being clumsy, but I was okay with that. As long as I got to catch her.

And fuck, listening to her sing for me… That was the biggest prize.

"I couldn't have done it without you."

"Nonsense." I slid my hand onto the small of her back as I guided her out of the theater. "You did *all* of this without my help." I gestured around us at the theater. She'd worked under some big names over the last few years and had been recognized as an up-and-coming talent on the broadway scene. The show was new, but she knew she couldn't turn down this job.

She shook her head. "No. I don't mean that. Just... in all the little ways. You being there for me? Holding my hand. Encouraging me. Loving me. You give me the strength, every day."

I kissed her cheek. "I love you too, baby."

Ella gave me a small smile, her eyes filled with longing—need—as we headed to the spot where we were meeting Audrey. Maybe she wasn't as unaffected as she wanted to seem.

Her sister stood, her fiancé standing at her side, a giant bouquet of pink roses in her arms and still wearing the dress she'd worn in the final number. She wasn't the lead role—not *yet*—she was living her dreams just like Ella was. And one day, I was sure she'd get there.

Just like I knew Ella would win a Tony Award for *Best Costume Design in a Musical* one day. She'd told me all about them—dragging me along to them this past summer, and I had absolute faith in her.

"You were spectacular!" Ella launched at her sister, enveloping her into a big hug as the girls both squealed.

"Thanks to your help! Look at what *you* made!" Audrey did a twirl, as if there hadn't been multiple fittings and dress rehearsals.

For them, none of that mattered. It never had. It was about being here, being together, and their bond that never wavered or lessened, no matter how much time had passed.

"We're pretty lucky," her fiancé mused at my side, and I had to agree.

"The luckiest."

After they'd excitedly babbled on for a few minutes, Ella came back over to me, her smile wide but her eyes drooping.

"Want to go home?" I murmured, cupping her cheek.

She nodded sleepily. "Please."

We had someone waiting for us to get back to, anyway.

I unlocked the front door with the keypad, letting Ella in first as a barking came from the other room. Our beagle puppy came into view, wagging his tail excitedly.

"Hi, boy."

He'd carried one of Ella's shoes in with him, a sight that made me smile. Those damn shoes.

"Bruno!" she scolded, taking the shoe from him when he dropped it.

"Maybe we should start locking him up when we leave," I offered, dropping to my knees to scratch his head.

She frowned. "But then he'd be sad." Ella joined me on the floor to give him love, her dress pooling on the floor as she stretched out her legs.

"What?" She raised an eyebrow at me, obviously catching me staring at her, but I couldn't keep my eyes off of her. Four years, and I didn't think I ever would.

"Are you happy?" I asked her, rubbing Bruno's belly. "Here? With this life?"

She made a face. "Of course. Why do you ask?"

I shrugged. "Just making sure." Lately, I'd just been feeling like something was missing. Like there was something more for our little family. "I want to fulfill all your dreams."

"You are," she reassured me, showing off her ring. "You always have."

I kissed her forehead. "Good." Standing up, I pulled the tie from my neck before offering her a hand up. "Should we go to bed?"

She fluttered her eyelashes. "Thought you'd never ask."

It was a long time before we fell asleep that night.

ELLA

My lips curled into a smile as I stared into the mirror, my hair pinned up to expose the long curve of my throat—just the way he liked. I slid my hand over my stomach.

We were celebrating Cameron's results from the bar exam tonight—he'd passed. Of course he had. He was too smart for his own good. But that was just one thing I loved about him.

It hadn't always been easy, adjusting to life in the city while he'd been going to school full time. There had been long nights of studying, of sewing, of seven thousand balled up pieces of paper with designs I'd rejected, but we'd done it all together. Every little fight, every achievement, every night spent wrapped up in each other's arms were ours *together*.

After his graduation this past spring, we'd gotten married over the summer in a gorgeous ceremony in the gardens at the New York Botanical Garden, and I'd never felt more like a princess—*his* Princess—than I had that day, dressed in an elegant white dress with a train that felt a mile long, and that didn't even include the veil that had been pinned into my hair.

And now... I had one more piece of good news to share with him tonight. Thank God the nausea had subsided long enough for me to get ready for dinner.

"Ella?" Cameron cracked our bedroom door open, letting in our puppy with him. Bruno immediately curled up into his bed at the corner of the room.

"Hey, Charming." I smiled as he padded towards me, wrapping his arms around my waist and pulling me into a hug.

"Hi, Princess."

I wrapped my arms around his neck as he kissed my cheek, and I sighed into his hold.

"Good day?" I asked as he buried his face in my neck.

He mumbled, "Better now."

"Are we still celebrating tonight?" I asked, running my fingers through the hair at the base of his neck.

"If you're up for it. I made reservations. Sutton said the chef came *highly* recommended."

"Oh?" I grinned. I couldn't help it. I was just too happy to keep it from him any longer. "Do you think they'll be okay with me eating for two?"

"Two?" Cam looked confused for a moment before his eyes grew wide. "Ella. Are you—"

I nodded, my eyes filling with tears as I grabbed the pregnancy test I'd taken earlier off the counter. "Surprise."

"You're pregnant." He dragged in a deep, shaky breath.

"I know it's fast, and maybe it's too soon, but..." I was pretty sure it had happened after the opening night for my show. It hadn't been long since I'd gone off birth control, so it was a surprise, but it wasn't an unwelcome one.

"No." He kissed me so tenderly my heart ached a little. "It's perfect. You're perfect." He slid a hand over my still-flat stomach. "*We're* perfect."

I gave him a secret smile. "It's still *really* early, so I don't want to tell anyone yet."

"Not even your sister?" Cam raised an eyebrow, knowing that Ro and I still talked every single day. Even if we'd both ended up in New York City, and saw each other often.

"I haven't even told her," I whispered. "I took the test this morning, after you'd left. I've been feeling nauseous lately, and I missed my period last week... But I wanted you to be the first to know."

"Fuck." His lips pressed against mine, more urgently this time, and I could tell it was taking all of his willpower not to throw me onto the bed, right then and there. "This is everything. All I wanted. You..." He looked down at my stomach reverently. "Them. Us. Our family." His voice got all choked up.

"Still want to go to dinner?" I ask innocently, fluttering my eyelashes at him.

"Not really." He laughed. "But now we have even more to celebrate."

"We *could* celebrate at home... or in our bed..." I gave him a little shimmy.

"I'll call the restaurant," he promised. "You... stay right where you are. I want to peel that dress off of you." He pointed at the bed.

"Yes, *husband*," I agreed, a rush of excitement flowing through me. I'd gladly do anything he asked me.

He groaned. "You're killing me, Ell."

I smiled, thinking of a baby that looked like him, his tiny nose. His beautiful brown eyes. Maybe she'd have my hair.

Either way, they'd be ours.

Cam wrapped his arms around me as he came back into the room, swaying us slowly back and forth, and I repeated his question from all those nights ago. "Are you happy?"

He chuckled into my hair. "Baby, you've made me the happiest man alive. I've got a good job, an amazing wife—who has the coolest job, thank you very much—and now we're having a baby. What else could I want?"

I hummed in response, turning around in his arms to rest my head against his chest.

"Tell me something," he whispered the words I'd uttered the night we met. All these years later, and we still used them often. "Something real."

"I love you," I said, sliding my hand over my stomach. "And I think I love them already."

"Me too," Cam agreed, nuzzling my forehead. "I love you so much."

Suddenly, I knew exactly what my first purchase would be.

A tiny pair of shoes.

After all, one pair of shoes changed my life.

And they lived Happily Ever After...
The End.

Want to learn more about Audrey and Parker and their fake-dating relationship? You can find their story in *Once Upon A Fake Date*, coming soon!

Acknowledgments

This book was inspired by my love of fairytales and the stories we grew up loving. If you know me, you know I grew up going to Disney and that I worked for the company for about five years, and that experience shaped my life in more ways than I can ever explain. I'll always be grateful for that.

To Gabbi: My person! What can I say except I love you, I miss you, and I appreciate you so much. Thank you for always supporting my writing and for being the hype girl I always need when I send you art or go on and on to you about my books.

To Katie W: You are so much more than a friend to me and I hope you know how much I love you! Without you encouraging my writing career, we wouldn't be here today, and I owe you so much.

To Katie D: Thank you for answering my never-ending stream of questions about college sports because I am clueless, and for letting me talk your ear off about my books whenever I want. I miss you every day and I am so thankful you're in my life.

To Olivia: I have no idea how we went four years without talking regularly, but I'm so glad to have you back in my life and for your constant trips to Florida. Thank you for your nonstop help with whatever I need—from ARC applications to candle making to spraying book edges. Ily babe.

To Arzum: My biggest hype girl!! You've been with me since day one and I'm forever grateful for our friendship. Thank you for all of the sunset photos, the reassuring words, and always always loving my characters and worlds. What would I do without you??

To Meg: The most darling, beautiful, wonderful, sweetest, funniest, prettiest friend ever. I have nothing to thank you for. I just think everyone should know how amazing you are. (She told me to write that.) Thank you for being my author buddy and our never-ending stupid text stream and ice cream jokes. Now stop reading this and go write your next book. 🔪

To my author friends (you know who you are): I don't know what I would do without you! Your reassuring words, sprinting together, the never-ending advice... I appreciate all of it so much. I'm so grateful for you!

To my ARC readers & my team: thank you for giving this book (and me) a chance. I hope you loved it, and fell in love with Ella & Cam like I have.

To my family, who have been the biggest supporters I could have asked for: thank you for recommending my books to everyone. I only get a little embarrassed when you tell people that they're "very spicy". Thank you for continuing to not read them.

To everyone else who's reading this now... Thank you. I couldn't do this without you, the readers!

Also by Jennifer Chipman

Best Friends Book Club

Academically Yours - Noelle & Matthew

Disrespectfully Yours - Angelina & Benjamin

Fearlessly Yours - Gabrielle & Hunter

Gracefully Yours - Charlotte & Daniel

Contractually Yours - Nicolas & Zofia (coming soon)

Castleton University

A Not-So Prince Charming - Ella & Cameron

Once Upon A Fake Date - Audrey & Parker (late 2024)

Witches of Pleasant Grove

Spookily Yours - Willow & Damien

Wickedly Yours - Luna & Zain (coming Fall 2024)

About the Author

Originally from the Portland area, Jennifer now lives in Orlando with her dog, Walter and cat, Max. She always has her nose in a book and loves going to the Disney Parks in her free time.

Website: www.jennchipman.com

- amazon.com/author/jenniferchipman
- goodreads.com/jennchipman
- instagram.com/jennchipmanauthor
- facebook.com/jennchipmanauthor
- x.com/jennchipman
- tiktok.com/@jennchipman
- pinterest.com/jennchipmanauthor

Printed in the USA
CPSIA information can be obtained
at www.ICGtesting.com
LVHW021223310124
770466LV00003B/343

9 781962 926058